Ascending

by

NICOLE PYLAND

Ascending

Royalty Series Book #1

Growing up fifth in line for the throne, Elizabeth never thought she would have to rule the small island nation of St. Rais. When a plot to take down the monarchy also takes her entire family from her, Elizabeth is thrust into the role of reluctant Queen. Not only did she lose most of her family, but she also lost the only love she'd ever known.

Palmer Honeycutt, a reporter for a popular New York City newspaper, was on vacation in a country nearly no one had heard of before. A deal she'd gotten at the relaxing resort and spa had been just what she'd needed. Little did she know that while she was trying to relax, the whole royal family would nearly be lost to tragedy, and a young Queen would present her a perfect story.

Both women approach their new relationship cautiously at first, but it doesn't take long for Palmer to start wishing the new Queen was someone she could spend more time with. Elizabeth also seems to have a lot of time for Palmer, which only confuses Palmer more.

After all Elizabeth has lost and what she's willing to give up for her country, is she also willing to risk it all to possibly find love again in an American reporter who's been there for her during the toughest part of her life?

To contact the author or for any additional information, visit: **https://nicolepyland.com**

BY THE AUTHOR

CHICAGO SERIES:

- Introduction – Fresh Start

- Book #1 – The Best Lines

- Book #2 – Just Tell Her

- Book #3 – Love Walked into The Lantern

- Series Finale – What Happened After

SAN FRANCISCO SERIES:

- Book #1 – Checking the Right Box

- Book #2 – Macon's Heart

- Book #3 – This Above All

- Series Finale – What Happened After

TAHOE SERIES:

- Book #1 – Keep Tahoe Blue

- Book #2 – Time of Day

- Book #3 – The Perfect View

- Book #4 – Begin Again

- Series Finale – What Happened After

BOSTON SERIES:

- Book #1 – Let Go

- Book #2 – The Right Fit

- Book #3 – All Good Plans

- Book #4 – Around the World

- Series Finale – What Happened After

SPORTS SERIES:

This series is related by a sports theme, not by characters.

- Book #1 – Always More

- Book #2 – A Shot at Gold

- Book #3 – The Unexpected Dream

- Book #4 – Finding a Keeper

CELEBRITIES SERIES:

- Book #1 – No After You

- Book #2 – All the Love Songs

- Book #3 – Midnight Tradition

- Book #4 – Path Forward

- Series Finale – What Happened After

HOLIDAY SERIES:

- Book #1 – The Writing on the Wall

- Book #2 – The Block Party

- Book #3 – The Fireworks

- Book #4 – The Sweet Escape

- Book #5 – The Misperception

- Book #6 – The Wait is Over

- Series Finale – What Happened After

ANTHOLOGY:

- The Meet Cute Café

FIRE UNIVERSE:

- The Fire
- The Disappeared

STAND-ALONE NOVELS:

- Reality Check
- The Show Must Go On
- Future Wife

YOUNG ADULT / NEW ADULT:

- The Moments
- Love Forged
- Pride Festival

EROTICA:

- Once a Month

CONTENTS

PROLOGUE

"VICTORIA, will you sit down already? We're landing soon," Elizabeth told her sister.

"Oh, my apologies. Are you the pilot now? No, you're my pain-in-the-ass, older sister." Victoria flopped into the empty luxury seat next to her. "Do you think Father will approve?"

"He hasn't met him yet."

"*You* have." Victoria turned her head toward Elizabeth as she buckled her seatbelt. "That's what this little mission was all about. Your opinion is important. If you sign off, Daddy will meet him next."

"You know you don't *actually* need his permission, right? That's just an old custom," Elizabeth replied.

"Please. It is *not* just an old custom; it's the law."

"That literally no one cares about anymore," Elizabeth added.

"Stop stalling and tell me what you think about David, Lizzy."

"You really love him, don't you?"

Victoria's eyes brightened as she said, "I do. I want to marry him. I know I'm only twenty-three, and Father said he wants me to wait a bit, but David and I have already been together for a year. Father hasn't even met him."

"He *is* pretty busy," Elizabeth reminded.

"He met both of our brothers' girlfriends by the time they'd been together for only three months."

"They're a little more important than us, though, aren't they? You know that," Elizabeth told her sister.

"Alex is a little *less* important now, isn't he?" Victoria

argued. "Martin has Edwina and Anthony, so Alex is off the hook," she added, speaking about her two brothers and the oldest, Martin's, two children.

"I suppose that's true," Elizabeth laughed.

The private secretary she and Victoria shared approached them with an ashen-white face and an expression that told Elizabeth the woman was either about to be ill from the slight turbulence of the aircraft or that something terrible had happened. Elizabeth hoped it was just the turbulence. Then again, she supposed, it could be both. The secretary stood over the two of them and attempted to gather herself.

"Your Royal Highness, Princess," she greeted both of them. "I am afraid I must inform you of something I am quite unprepared for."

"Rebecca, what's wrong?" Elizabeth asked, sitting up fully in her seat now.

"There was an incident." The woman swallowed hard.

"Incident?" Victoria asked, sounding confused.

Elizabeth placed a calming hand on top of her sister's hand on their shared armrest and stared up at Rebecca.

"There was an attack at the opening of the children's hospital. Your–"

"Attack?" Elizabeth cut her off.

"Your Royal Hi–"

"Rebecca," Victoria cut the woman off this time. "She's Lizzy. I'm Vicky. You've known us for five years. Just tell us," she prompted.

"I'm afraid your father is… The King is dead," Rebecca managed out finally, letting a tear escape her right eye. "Long live the Queen," she added.

But Elizabeth hadn't heard her. She'd only heard that her father, King Maxwell I, was dead. He was gone. Her father was dead? How was that even possible? He was fine.

"What?" Victoria asked, cupping her hand over her mouth now. "What? Wait." She lowered her hand. "You just said, 'Long live the *Queen*.'"

Elizabeth lowered her eyes to her lap. Her breath was coming in short gasps. Had she heard her sister correctly? She then looked back up at a still crying Rebecca, silently begging her to correct that statement because that meant something else had happened, too.

"Martin was there as well," Elizabeth realized.

"So was Alex," Victoria added, sounding as if she was about to cry.

"Your Majesty," Rebecca began this time. "I am so very sorry to have to report to you that both of your brothers were lost as well today."

"What?" Victoria's sobs began in earnest.

"The kids?" Elizabeth asked then. "Edwina would be Queen. She's—"

"Both of the children were by their mother's side," Rebecca replied, wiping her cheek. "Her Royal Highness Princess Lyla was also killed. Edwina and Anthony were taken to the hospital while we were in flight. His Highness Prince Anthony died in the ambulance from his wounds. Her Royal Highness Princess Edwina made it to the hospital but passed away shortly after. I am so sorry."

"Oh, my God," Victoria let out, clasping Elizabeth's hand tightly.

Elizabeth glanced over at her. Then, she remembered: Alexander, her brother, was married, too. Rebecca hadn't said anything about his wife, but she'd been there, too.

"Teagan?" she asked, referring to her brother's wife.

"The Duchess is…" Rebecca lowered her head.

"She's gone?" Elizabeth asked. "Teagan is gone, too?"

"Anyone else, Rebecca? You've just told us our entire family is dead. Is there anyone else you're forgetting? Did our third cousin, twice removed, also get murdered today? Do you have a list you have to check off or—"

"Vicky, stop," Elizabeth interrupted.

"I am sorry," Rebecca offered, adding, "Majesty, we are twenty minutes away from home. I'm afraid you'll need to change your clothes."

"What are you talking about?" Victoria lashed out at Rebecca again. "Her clothes? Our whole family is dead, and you're talking about clothing?"

"The black," Elizabeth answered. "The Queen wears black when the monarch dies. I have to wear black."

CHAPTER 1

LADIES in the royal family should sit with their knees and ankles together and only cross their legs at the ankle if needed. The tiara must be at a forty-five-degree angle when viewed from the side and must be worn during the bride's wedding day. They fold the napkin in half and use the inside part of the napkin when they need it to wipe their mouth. What else was there? The Queen should be the first one to start a conversation and, typically, with the person to her right. For the second course of the meal, the Queen will begin a conversation with the person seated on her left. Royal women were required to have their chins aligned to the ground, with hands on the side while walking. Was her chin aligned to the ground right now? Surely, that didn't matter on a day like today. She would be allowed this day, of all days, to look toward the ground.

Elizabeth hadn't been trained like the others. She'd had the lessons, of course – they'd all gotten those – but no one had expected her or required her to remember them because she'd only need *some* of them. She never should have needed lessons on being Queen of a country. It wasn't supposed to be like this. The bomb that had taken out her entire family, with the exception of herself and her sister, had been the first part of a two-part planned attack. The anti-monarchists had also planned to put a bomb on her plane in order to murder both Elizabeth and Victoria, rendering the country without a surviving heir that could actually sit on the throne. The second part of their plan had been foiled by a security guard at the small, private airport that hadn't let them get through.

There would be one funeral for all of them. It would be watched live by millions of people around the world. The people of St. Rais, a small island nation between Norway and Greenland, would line the streets of the capital city to mourn with her and her sister, now the heir to the throne should something happen to Elizabeth before she had children of her own. *Children*; she laughed internally as her dresser laid the pearl necklace against her skin. She hadn't planned on having any before. She was twenty-five years old, and she wanted to finish graduate school and earn her Ph. D. That was as far as she'd been able to plan her life because of her *circumstances.*

"Your Majesty, they're ready," Rebecca said, entering her bedroom.

"I'm not," Elizabeth replied.

"It's a private moment, Ma'am. It's yours alone."

"The only one I get before I have to share my grief with the entire world. Where's Victoria?"

"She's in the chapel, Ma'am," Rebecca replied. "She'll be along after you."

"Are we ever going to be allowed in the same room again?" Elizabeth asked as she stood and smoothed her dress down her legs.

"Of course, Ma'am."

"I've hardly been able to grieve with my sister since the plane landed."

"It's precautionary, Ma'am." Rebecca nodded.

"Stop this 'Ma'am' and 'Your Majesty' stuff, Rebecca."

"You are my Queen now, Ma'am."

"I know the custom. It's not necessary when we're in private. Please call me Lizzy."

"As you wish, Ma'am."

Elizabeth glared at her.

"*Lizzy,*" Rebecca acquiesced but seemed to not like how the name sounded coming out of her own mouth and nodded again. "Are you ready?"

"No, but I don't have a choice."

Elizabeth walked down the long, wide hall with its stained glass windows and ornamental fixtures with Viking influence mixed with a more traditional English one. As she passed the few palace staff members, they stopped and either bowed or curtsied to her. They'd done that before, when she'd been Her Royal Highness Princess Elizabeth Antonia Victoria Louise Hanover, but this time, it was different. Rebecca used to always walk beside her. Now that Elizabeth was Queen, though, Rebecca would always walk behind her, as would anyone else.

Elizabeth entered the room they'd set up just for her and Victoria, who would come in later to say her final goodbyes before the state funeral where they wouldn't be permitted to show emotion, as was the custom. Rebecca closed the door behind her, leaving Elizabeth alone in the room with seven urns. Her father was in the center of the room on a pedestal, like all the others, but sat back and a bit higher than the rest. To the world, he would be buried in a coffin as if his body hadn't been blown into pieces and in this urn was only what they could find.

Elizabeth knelt down in front of his urn as she'd knelt before him the day he'd bestowed her official Her Royal Highness title. She'd only been born Princess. Her Royal Highness was given to her upon her twenty-first birthday as the first daughter of the King. Upon her wedding day, he had planned to make her a Duchess as well, as was the St. Rais' custom. Now, she would never be a Duchess; she was the Queen. She'd give *all* the titles away if it meant she could have them all back.

She said her silent goodbye to her father since he wasn't a man who wanted his children to show much emotion when he was alive. Elizabeth figured he wouldn't want it displayed on his behalf now, either. Moving on to her brothers, Martin was first. Alexander came next. Then, Elizabeth said a quicker goodbye to Lyla, Martin's wife of the past seven years. She cried as she said goodbye to her niece, Edwina, who had been born Her Royal Highness because she was Martin's heir, and her nephew, little Anthony, a Prince; gone far too soon and only because they'd been born into this family. Her guilt at still being alive only intensified as she arrived at the urn of Teagan Gentry, who had been named Duchess upon marriage. Teagan had married Alexander only a year ago, and now she was gone forever. Elizabeth wiped at the tears in her eyes. She shouldn't be crying harder for Teagan than she had for her own father, brothers, sister-in-law, niece, and nephew, but she *was*, and she knew why.

She backed away then, and after a moment, gathered herself enough to leave the room before saying one last goodbye in private. When she exited the room, Rebecca was there. She escorted Elizabeth back to her suite of rooms to re-do her makeup. After that, it was time to sit in a bullet-proof town car, a separate one from Victoria's, and join the procession of caskets filled with urns.

***

"Majesty, are you sure it's not too soon?" Albert, the Prime Minister, asked.

"It's been two weeks," she replied, sitting down in the chair in her office.

She hadn't been able to enter her father's office; *her* office now.

"Yes, but the mourning period is one month, Ma'am."

Elizabeth didn't say anything.

"Very well." Albert sat down in the chair opposite her. "The bombs were planted under the small stage that had been set up for the ribbon-cutting ceremony. Altogether, there were fifteen lives lost outside of the royal family, including the hospital director, two members of the staff, your father's bodyguard, his personal secretary, and ten others."

"What are we doing for the others that were lost? They don't all get state funerals," Elizabeth replied, trying to remember to tuck her ankle appropriately.

"We've made arrangements for Victoria and your cousin Erik to make appearances."

"Appearances?"

"Yes, Ma'am."

"And?"

"Flower wreaths will be sent. We'll also compensate the members of your father's staff. Your private secretary has made the arrangements along with my staff."

"I'd like to pay my respects," Elizabeth said.

"Ma'am, we need you to make as few public appearances as possible right now, I'm afraid. The faction of anti-monarchists has only grown in recent years, and they're bringing their battle with traditionalists to our doorsteps."

"I knew there were problems. How did we not know things were this bad?"

"Things escalated quickly," Albert sighed. "We knew the approval rating for the monarchy was lower than ever, despite your father being a great King."

"People see the monarchy as rather useless; there's a Parliament and a Prime Minister." Elizabeth nodded.

"This country was founded with a monarchy three hundred years ago, and it will maintain the monarchy for years to come. You have my word, Ma'am."

"I'm not sure your word is enough, Mr. Jameson. Maybe we should abolish the monarchy altogether. Maybe this is the country telling us that's the right decision."

"Ma'am, did you see the streets lined with people?" Albert leaned forward in his chair, clasping his hands together. "They mourn with you, Your Majesty. They loved King Maxwell. They loved your mother, God rest her soul. They loved your brother and were ready for him to begin taking on more of a role in royal duties as heir. They've loved watching Edwina and Anthony grow up. They've celebrated with your family in all the successes, and they grieve with you and Princess Victoria over this and all of the tragedies."

"I thought losing our mother would be the hardest thing I'd ever go through," Elizabeth replied, referring to her mother's death two years prior due to a heart attack that no one had been prepared for.

"You have been through more than anyone should have to bear, Your Majesty, but this country wants its monarchy. A small faction of people disagrees, yes, and some of them are now locked away behind bars, at Her Majesty's pleasure. We will find the rest and lock them away as well."

"I pray you do."

"In the meantime, Ma'am, we must discuss your coronation and the next steps regarding your security."

"I expected that," she replied.

"Firstly, we must determine your name."

"I can't keep Elizabeth?"

"You know of our history with Britain, Ma'am. They've had two Queen Elizabeth's."

"Right," she replied. "I'm named after the first one."

"You are. But you are also named after other strong, important women; Elizabeth Antonia Victoria Louise Hanover."

"I am a Hanover. I'm a descendent of Queen Victoria herself. It doesn't get much more British than that." She allowed herself a smile. "And Albert is pretty British, too."

"It is. I was named after Queen Victoria's husband." The Prime Minister smiled as well.

"Why are *you* going over this with me? Shouldn't Rebecca be taking me through this? Surely, you have more pressing things to do, Mister Prime Minister."

"Ma'am, Rebecca will remain on as the Princess's private secretary, but you must now choose your own. In the absence of him or her, I told Rebecca I would help you get through this part of the process."

"Can't I keep Rebecca?"

"If you'd like, you can promote her, Ma'am. Victoria will then need to choose someone for her own staff."

"I'll discuss it with my sister first." Elizabeth nodded.

"Very well. Back to your name, Ma'am."

She stared out the window and at the cold, gray sky that so closely resembled her mood and wished she didn't have to do this.

"Antonia," she said finally.

"After your mother?" he asked.

"Yes, I will be Queen Antonia I."

"I don't believe there's been a British Queen Antonia, but I will verify."

"It doesn't matter; that will be my name."

"Of course, Your Majesty," Albert replied with a short nod. "I will convey that to the staff working on the coronation."

"When will that be?" she asked.

"Normally, it would be after the traditional mourning period of a month, but given these circumstances and how unprepared we were for them, it will be in six weeks," Albert informed. "The Princess will be there, obviously, but after that, we'd like to have her move out of the palace and into Coburn Cottage if you agree."

"Coburn is well over fifty kilometers away," she remarked.

"Ma'am, it's just the two of you now, I'm afraid. Neither of you has married. You understand."

"A monarch's duty is to produce an heir," Elizabeth replied, repeating the words her mother had said to her a long time ago; but she had also said them nearly in jest as they'd laughed as a family about the many rules they all lived by that were centuries old and oftentimes, came from an entirely different country.

"Yes, Ma'am. And when you're ready, we'll need to discuss that as well, but I trust you can handle that part on your own."

"Having babies?" she asked, surprised.

"Finding a consort, Ma'am; a husband."

"Right," she managed out, covering up the choke in her voice.

"I have a meeting with your security team after this. We're still reviewing what happened and who on the team should be held responsible. Someone missed something, and I want to know who and why."

"Yes, so do I."

"We'll be taking more aggressive security measures for the foreseeable future. We will keep you and the Princess safe, Ma'am; I promise you that."

"Victoria can move to the cottage, but I'd prefer to have her here until after the coronation. We both lost our entire family. We need each other right now."

"Of course, Ma'am."

"Is that all for today?" she asked.

"Yes, Ma'am."

"Okay," she said and waited for him to go. When he didn't, she asked, "Mr. Jameson?"

"Ma'am, I can't stand until you do." Albert motioned with an open palm toward her.

"Oh, right. Apologies." Elizabeth stood up slowly.

The Prime Minister did the same and gave a slight bow.

"Majesty," he said as he walked backward out of the room.

After he exited and closed the door behind him, she said to herself, "No one is permitted to turn their back to the Queen; I forgot that one."

CHAPTER 2

"PALMER, you're already there. Come on. This is a big story," her boss encouraged.

"I was here on vacation," Palmer argued. "My vacation is over."

"We'll pay for it. I've already got Cynthia calling your hotel and booking you a room for the next two weeks."

"Two weeks? Why would I stay here for another two weeks?"

"You're a reporter, Palmer."

"I'm a reporter who packed *one* week's worth of clothes because she wanted one lousy week away from reporting," Palmer replied, sitting on the edge of the bed and staring at her already packed suitcase.

"Are you really trying to tell me you're not at all interested in writing this story? You were there when it happened."

"I wasn't at the hospital; I was at the spa."

"You're in the country that half the world has never heard of. *I* had to look it up when the story broke."

"I got a deal on the flight and the room. I wanted to see the Northern Lights, and it was cheaper for me to go here than going to Norway or Iceland. Now, I just want to come back home. The cops are everywhere. It's like a witch-hunt out there."

"The entire royal family was just taken out in a bombing – you can't blame them for increasing security. The way I heard it, they've only found a few people they think are responsible so far, but there are a bunch still out there."

"I don't know. I'm on a flight in a few hours."

"Palmer, this could be the story of your life. You're in a long-forgotten-about country. There was an assassination of the royal line. Now, they have a new Queen who's just lost her entire family. If you can get close enough to this, there's a Pulitzer in it for you."

That had been Palmer's dream. For as far back as she remembered, she'd wanted to be a reporter. She'd started out on her high school paper staff as a freshman, worked her way up to editor her senior year, and majored in journalism at NYU, repeating those same steps. Then, she'd gotten a job at *The New York Courier* as a cub reporter on their website side. Now, at twenty-nine, she was ready to move up and on from writing what were essentially, blogs. Palmer wanted something with meat to it, something that could put her on the map, and her editor was right: this could be something.

"Fine. I'll stay," she replied.

"Great. What do you need?"

"My per diem would be nice."

"No problem. I'll have Cynthia get that taken care of."

"I might need more than two weeks. It depends on what I can do now and if I need to travel anywhere. I don't know if I'll be able to get into the palace or talk to anyone close to the royal family."

"Whatever you need. Keep Cynthia in the loop. She can extend your stay. I'd like at least a thousand words in my email by the end of next week, though. We need to get on it before something else happens. And if you can get me something quick before that, as sort of part one, that would be even better. You can still work the long angle."

"Sure," Palmer agreed. "I assume, since you've never heard of this place, we don't have any connections here I can use?"

"Not in St. Rais, no. But I do have connections in the UK. I've also got a friend in Norway, one in Sweden, and a couple in Denmark."

"Thanks for letting me know how popular you are," Palmer teased.

"I'll have Cynthia get you the names of the guys in London. They should at least know more about the history and the people. Outside of that, Google is your friend," he replied.

"Can't use Google as a source, but you're hilarious," she said sarcastically.

Palmer hung up the phone and lifted her bag onto the bed to unpack everything. Before she dove too far into her clothes, though, she pulled out her laptop and connected to the hotel's Wi-Fi. She'd already researched St. Rais for the resorts, spas, and tourist attractions, but this vacation had been a last-minute, although a much-needed one. She'd found the deal online through some travel site, thought it would be cool to visit somewhere no one she knew had been to before, and booked it. She'd had a nice, relaxing vacation, using her computer only to stream Netflix in the evenings.

This time, when she looked up St. Rais online, she went to a Wikipedia page. Starting at the top and working her way down, she learned that the country hadn't been independent for all that long, establishing independence from the United Kingdom in 1717 after a brief war over fishing rights. It reminded Palmer a lot of the Boston Tea Party that would occur not long after. In this case, when the British realized the island wouldn't be as plentiful and, therefore, wouldn't be worth the trouble of sending more soldiers in the freezing-cold winters, they let it go, and St. Rais was named. Palmer continued to scroll through the pages regarding its history, focusing specifically on the ones about the monarchy.

When St. Rais broke away from the UK, the people there didn't create a government for the people by the people as the United States would later do. They chose a relative of Sophia of Hanover, the mother of King George I, who was the King at the time of St. Rais gaining independence. The first monarch of St. Rais was King Edward I. He had two sons. It went on and on from there until King Maxwell I took the throne. Martin would have then succeeded him, and later, little Edwina would have been the very first Queen to rule outright, not through marriage but by birth and by law. Palmer closed her eyes as she looked at a picture of the now-deceased little girl with her father, the future King, his wife, the future Queen Consort, and their even younger son, Anthony, the Prince and the first male heir that wouldn't have superseded his older female sibling only because he'd been born male.

Palmer's phone went off, indicating she had an email. She'd loved not hearing that sound while on vacation. To-day, though, she grabbed for her phone, opened the app, and checked Cynthia's email, which had the information for her per diem, her hotel stay, and a list of contacts for her in several Northern European countries.

"Time to get to work," she told herself.

***

"Can you get me in?" Palmer asked.

"They're guarding the palace more now than ever; you're not getting a visit. You probably wouldn't have before, but you're definitely not getting in to see the new Queen now. There are even rumors they'll be relocating the Princess after the coronation because they have no heirs until the Queen gets married and has children," the correspondent she had never worked with but knew of informed.

"Jonathan, I'm in St. Rais to work the story. I need a source," she replied, leaning back against the pillow in her hotel room.

"I can get you to a friend of a friend who knows someone who works in the palace. Best I can do. Will that help?"

"It's something. I'll take anything," Palmer replied.

Then, she hung up and immediately called the contact Jonathan had just provided.

"Hello. My name is Palmer Honeycutt with *The New York Courier*. Your friend Jonathan gave me your number. I'm looking to get in contact with someone in the St. Rais palace. He said you might be able to help me with that."

That phone call led to another call, which led to an email, which led to another phone call. It was the part of reporting most people didn't understand – the legwork. Palmer liked the legwork probably more than she liked the actual writing. She also preferred to have an idea of where her story was going before she got started, even just an inkling. Right now, she knew there had been a terrorist incident, but that was it – any reporter out there could report on that. She wanted to find something no one else could or would find. That was what would win her the Pulitzer.

"Okay. I can get you the number of someone on the Queen's staff. How's that?" the sixth person she talked to offered.

"That would be amazing. Who is it?"

"I've got a name and a number. Do you have a pen," he asked in a thick Scottish accent.

"Always," she replied.

Palmer jotted down the information he provided and looked at the time. It was after nine at night. She wouldn't be able to call tonight, so she ate a late dinner in her room and decided to go down to the hotel library, which was a large room off the side of the lobby. Palmer hadn't borrowed a book yet, but she'd used the space for some relaxation a few times. As she passed the bar on her way, she saw the three TVs all covering the story. She stopped walking, decided to order a drink, charging it to her room, which was now being paid for by *The Courier*, and watched.

"All was quiet at the palace today. The Queen's office issued another statement of condolence to all those who lost friends and family at the children's hospital bombing. We don't expect to hear much more from Her Majesty in the coming days as her focus must be, according to her office, on her duties and the remainder of the mourning period, the safety of her nation and its people, as well as her coronation. Sources are saying that the coronation will be a simple affair, and under the circumstances, many agree that that is the appropriate choice."

Palmer watched the female reporter on the screen

speak into the oversized microphone as she stood outside a modest-sized palace, compared to Buckingham, which, of course, made sense: St. Rais was a lot smaller and an often-forgotten-about country. Then, a video of the new Queen, whom Palmer had thus far only seen a few pictures of, appeared on the screen, walking alongside the woman she knew was the Queen's younger sister, Victoria.

"She's beautiful," Palmer said to herself as she watched the Queen smile and laugh with her sister.

It must have been a recent video because the Queen looked unchanged in her appearance, but it was definitely before she'd lost pretty much her entire family because she was glowing with happiness. She had perfectly quaffed long blonde hair, parted in the center and flowing over her shoulders. Palmer had also seen her eyes better in pictures; they were a bright blue. She resembled her sister, but where Victoria was nearly rail-thin, the new Queen had a few curves, which Palmer thought suited her well.

"Shame, what happened, isn't it?" the bartender asked her as he placed her white wine down on the bar in front of her.

"Yes, it is," Palmer replied. She looked at him as he turned more fully to the screen to watch the story unfold as she had done. "Hey, I'm a tourist. I don't know all that much about this place. Would you mind if I ask you a few questions about the history of St. Rais and the royal family?"

"I have customers, but if you can give me a few minutes, I can," he replied.

Palmer smiled and said, "Perfect."

CHAPTER 3

"I DON'T want to move to Coburn, Lizzy. We have to stick together," Victoria told her.

"I know. It's temporary. And Coburn is only *called* a cottage. It's a mansion, Vicky. You'll have everything you need there, and I'll visit when I can. You can come here, too."

"Are you *ordering* me to move there as my Queen or *asking* me as my sister?"

"Asking. I won't order you to do anything. You *are* my sister, and this isn't the sixteen-hundreds, Vick," Elizabeth told her with a smile as they sat on the love seat, facing her fireplace.

"David offered to move here for me," Vicky shared. "From London."

"He has a job there," Elizabeth replied.

"He said he can work from anywhere. He wants to be with me, Lizzy. I needed him here for the funeral. I've hardly been able to go anywhere, and he's not on the authorized list to come here yet. Can you—"

"I'll get him added," she interrupted. "And you two can't live together unless you're engaged, Vicky. You know that. As much as I hate the outdated rules, we can't have a scandal right now."

"There's a guesthouse at Coburn. He can stay there. No one cares about the cottage, Lizzy. Besides, all eyes are on *you* right now. They won't even notice I'm not around or that I'm with a British guy all the time."

"You know you're going to get a hard time about falling for a Brit, right? Plenty of guys available here, in St. Rais," Elizabeth replied.

"I don't care," Vicky stated simply. "I love him."

Elizabeth smiled warmly at her sister and said, "You

know what? I don't care about the whole living-together thing. Martin was going to bring the monarchy into the twenty-first century. He and Dad worked with Parliament to get the law passed so that Edwina would rule next regardless of whether or not a boy came after. They both understood the importance of relevance, and relevance comes with keeping up with the times. If you love David, and he wants to move here – it's fine with me. But, Vicky – it's *your* life." Elizabeth turned her face to Victoria's. "You don't need my permission to live with your boyfriend or even to get married. If and when David proposes, if you say yes – that's all that matters to me."

Victoria smiled back and said, "Thank you. For what it's worth, I think you're going to be a great Queen, Lizzy."

Elizabeth turned back to the fire and replied, "I don't know. I've been trying to remember all the things Mom taught us as kids; everything I've read about what I'm supposed to do; how I'm supposed to do it. I feel like I forgot so many things because I never really needed to remember. It's not the Middle Ages anymore. It's no longer the whole heir-and-the-spare thing because kids die young. Even if it was, though, Mom and Dad had Martin *and* Alexander."

"You and I were superfluous," Victoria added, turning toward the fire as well.

"You and I *were* because they loved each other," Elizabeth corrected.

Victoria nodded and softly said, "You're right."

"But Martin was trained," Elizabeth continued. "He was groomed for this. Alexander was, too, just in case, until Martin got married and the kids came along."

"I don't think I've ever seen a more relieved face than our brother's when Lyla announced she was pregnant." Victoria chuckled. "Alex did *not* want to be King. If anything, he would've wanted to be Queen." Her laughter continued.

Elizabeth joined in softly, letting the sound and the rumblings from it in her chest take away some of the pain even momentarily.

"As modern as Dad was, he wasn't *that* modern," Victoria added.

"Right," Elizabeth mumbled mainly to herself. "Hey, do you think that if Alex would've been born first and he would've been the future King, Dad would have—"

"Let our gay brother be King?"

"Yes, I guess that's what I'm asking."

"I don't think so. There's a reason Alex never came out to Dad."

"Trust me, I know," Elizabeth replied, sighing.

"How are *you*, Lizzy?" Victoria asked, placing a hand over her sister's in her lap.

"I'm okay," she said.

"Are you, really? It's bad enough that we lost everyone, Lizzy. You lost…"

"I don't really want to talk about it," Elizabeth said as her sister faded out.

"Okay. We don't have to talk about that, but you're also about to be named Queen Elizabeth at your coronation. It's a lot, Lizzy."

"I meant to talk to you about that: I'm not using Elizabeth as my name."

"What? Why not?"

"There's been a couple of them already, and they're pretty well-known."

"Well, you're not going to be Queen Louise. Or, Queen Victoria – there was one of those already, too, and she's pretty famous. Plus, Victoria is mine; you can't have it," her sister teased.

Elizabeth smiled and replied, "I know. That's why I'll be Queen Antonia."

"After Mom," Victoria said softly.

"She was a far better Queen than I'll ever be."

"She was a Queen Consort, Lizzy. You will be the very first Queen of this nation. Do you realize that?"

"And I'd give it away in a heartbeat if it would bring even one of them back."

"I know." Victoria nodded. "That's why you'll make a great Queen."

***

"Ma'am, we can have someone take care of this," the palace staff member said.

"Victoria's already been through here, right? Teagan's family, too?"

"Yes, Ma'am. They've removed the items they wanted to take with them. Whatever remains is for you to decide what to do with," he replied.

"Thank you," she said.

The guy bowed slightly and opened the door for her. Alex and Teagan's house was a manor, located only about twenty minutes away from the main palace. It wasn't an old property; it had only been built in the nineties. The manor was also fairly small as far as houses for royals went, but it was what they'd wanted. The four-bedroom modern house used to be one of Elizabeth's favorite places in the world. Now, it only reminded her of what she'd lost.

Teagan Gentry had been her best friend since primary school. They'd met at age five when Elizabeth was shy and knew she was different than the rest of the kids. Teagan had been outgoing and befriended her when no one else would. They'd grown up together after that.

Elizabeth walked around the kitchen first, figuring that would be the room that least had to do with Teagan, who never cooked, but then she saw a picture of Teagan and herself on the refrigerator, and she had to go into the living room instead. There, she found furniture that also reminded her of Teagan. Alex's bookshelf next to the TV contained a photo of him with his wife on their wedding day, along with every book he'd ever read. The tears began in earnest as she made her way down the hallway, skipping the guest bathroom, bedrooms, and linen closet and heading to the other two bedrooms in the house instead.

They'd gotten married at least in part because Alex

never wanted to come out to their parents or the country. One of their cousins had come out publicly, and for all his positive traits, their father wasn't exactly waving a pride flag. When their cousin's news wasn't taken very well, Alex decided to keep his own sexuality to himself. Being only three years older than both Elizabeth and Teagan meant he'd also spent a lot of time with Teagan growing up. Teagan knew who he was and agreed to marry him all the same. As a result, they'd slept in separate beds, and oftentimes, Alex spent nights outside the manor with men he trusted. It was an arrangement that worked for everyone. Well, it worked for *almost* everyone.

"I've laid the items I'd like to keep for myself on one of the beds. Everything else can be donated or kept in the archives," Elizabeth said, exiting the house.

"Yes, Ma'am." The staff member nodded.

Elizabeth was driven back to the palace in her bulletproof car, led by another bulletproof car, and followed by yet another one in an attempt to disguise which car she could be in. For weeks now, security had been tighter than even she imagined it would be. She also wondered if it was worth it all. Maybe the country *should* be without a monarchy. Parliament ran the nation. The Prime Minister was in control. What was the point? What was *her* point? If she found a way to give it all up, wouldn't it make a lot of people happy? Then, Elizabeth realized. If she gave this up, she'd be giving in to the people who killed her family; who tried to end her line. She'd be giving them exactly what they wanted, which wasn't fair. There *were* people in this country who supported the monarchy. She would be the Queen they needed, the Queen they deserved.

***

"Rebecca, this is too much. I said simple."

"I know, Ma'am. It's still a coronation. It must be fit for a Queen."

"It's disrespectful."

"It's not, Ma'am. This is what happens: when one monarch dies, another succeeds him or her. This coronation is as much a celebration of your father's life as it is of your succession. It's a way to show the nation we are strong, and the monarchy will survive even in the most troubling of times."

Elizabeth turned to her private secretary and asked, "You've always been a strong proponent of the monarchy, haven't you?"

"Yes, Ma'am."

"May I ask why?"

"You never have before," Rebecca replied.

"I know."

"May I sit, Ma'am?"

"Yes, Rebecca. Sit down." Elizabeth patted the spot on the sofa next to her. "We're alone now. You can call me Lizzy."

"It's hard to remember to go back and forth sometimes." Rebecca chuckled a little. "Your grandmother Louise was the patron for two institutions that benefitted my family. The St. Rais Cancer Society saved my mother's life when she was a child and had leukemia. The Wesley Rehabilitation Center saved my older sister Chelsea when she was struggling with drugs and alcohol. The monarchy isn't just a family of figureheads – it's an institution that supports the nation, not the other way around."

"I suppose that's true."

Rebecca's phone rang. She stared at the readout for a second and then looked up at Elizabeth.

"I'm sorry, Ma'am. I thought I set it to silent."

"It's okay. Do you need to get it?"

"No, it's not important."

"Rebecca, I know this isn't exactly the best time, with everything that's going on, but if I wanted to get away and just go somewhere with light, and I mean *light*, security, would that be possible?"

"I don't think so. You know how things are right now."

"I do. And I don't want to put myself or Victoria at risk, but I need some space. This place is suffocating me."

"Where would you go if I *could* arrange it?"

"School."

"Lizzy, you can't go back to school right now."

"I don't mean as a student. I understand that my days of trying to earn an advanced degree are over. I would just love to go back to my little house off-campus."

"The whole country knows that's your house, Elizabeth. It's not nearly as secure as the palace."

"I'm aware. I need it, though, Rebecca."

"Would you be willing to go if security was close by but not in the house with you?"

"Can you work up a plan, and I can take a look at it?"

"I will do my best, Ma'am," Rebecca replied.

"Thank you," Elizabeth said, grateful.

She'd been one-year shy of achieving a degree that no longer mattered but was something she cared about. As fifth in line to the throne, she wasn't obligated to perform royal duties and could have pursued a career. Now, she had one and would have to give up school and her plans to become a Ph. D in Physics. She still loved the idea of returning to her off-campus home that had been more like a cottage than Coburn Cottage. It had one bedroom, a wood-burning fireplace, and a small backyard with a garden. It had also been hers. Elizabeth hadn't been there since before her flight to London and had things she needed to pick up beyond going there for the respite she desperately needed. She could only hope that she'd be permitted to go on her own, without an army of guards, which would've defeated the purpose altogether.

CHAPTER 4

"WHO gave you my number?" Rebecca asked.

"It's a long story. It took me a while to get to you. I had to go through about six people," Palmer replied.

"And you believe I will do *what*, exactly?"

"I'm looking to do a story," Palmer told her. "I was hoping I could interview you."

She placed her phone on the café table between them, hovering her finger over the record button.

"If you're looking for a story on the bombing, I wasn't there," Rebecca replied, sipping her tea as if unaffected.

"I'm not doing a story on the bombing. Well, I *am* – I've sent *that* story off to my editor already, though. That's the intro piece."

"Then, what exactly is your angle, Miss Honeycutt?"

"I've been doing man-on-the-street interviews for the past few days. There's an interesting mix in St. Rais. Most people I interviewed are actually *for* the monarchy. They genuinely believe it provides value beyond just a family of figureheads."

"You're an American... Are you an anti-monarchist yourself?"

"No, I'm an American: I'm apathetic about the whole thing," Palmer replied, shrugging.

Rebecca lightened and laughed a little.

"That *does* sound very American of you."

Palmer smiled, hoping she was making headway with the palace staffer.

"It wouldn't matter if I was pro or anti anyway. I'm a reporter; I keep my opinions out of my articles."

"Very well," Rebecca said, nodding. "So, what exactly are you going to be writing about?"

"I'd like to do a long piece on the history of St. Rais. That would be the start of it, anyway. Your nation's war for independence is similar to the Revolutionary War; our countries were both fighting with the same country. And I find it fascinating that while America went anti-monarchy, St. Rais stuck with it. Beyond that, I'd like to include interviews with palace staff, pro and anti-monarchists in St. Rais. And my biggest hope of all would be to get a sit-down with the Queen."

"That's not possible," Rebecca replied instantly, shaking her head rapidly from side to side and bringing her teacup to her lips.

"I understand her security is tight. Security is more than welcome to vet me. I'm not a huge fan of providing my questions in advance, but I'll do that if it's necessary. And I don't have to record the interview; I can just take notes."

"Her Majesty is incredibly busy. I'm sure you understand."

"I'm sure *you* understand I still have to try," Palmer replied. "I write for one of the most popular newspapers online and in print in the entire US. We have distribution in St. Rais as well. There are copies of my paper available on that stack right next to *The Wall Street Journal* and *The New York Times*. I won't pull my piece into any particular leaning – that would be unethical – but I will be fair in what I write. I won't misquote or take things out of context; I'm not that kind of a reporter," Palmer explained. Then, she slid her business card across the table. "Would you at least get this in the hands of someone close to the Queen and let her make the decision?"

Rebecca gave her a polite but stiff stare, picked up the card, and nodded.

***

Palmer hadn't left the meeting with an agreed-upon interview, but she felt good about her chances. Her contact said that he could get her a meeting with someone who worked with Elizabeth when she was Her Royal Highness, Princess of St. Rais, as well as her younger sister, Victoria. She wasn't exactly certain of what Rebecca's title was, and the woman failed to provide it to her. Palmer hadn't wanted to press the issue. She was five days into the story, and at this rate, things were going fine but not at the pace she'd prefer. She had a lot of notes and several recordings from people she'd met while traveling around the capital of St. Rais, and she'd even stood outside the fence of the palace where flowers, signs, and candles had been laid for the people who'd been lost so that she could take pictures as well as interview a few of the locals.

Palmer's favorite spot to get honest responses to her questions, though, were always bars. In St. Rais, they were called pubs, and she'd already gone to several, choosing to sit near the rowdiest group of men and women in the place. She'd struck up a few conversations, stirred the pots until the topic of the monarchy or the bombing came up, and then, she'd listen.

"I liked King Maxwell," one man had said before he finished his pint. "When the fishing unions got into a fight over rights, he came out on our side. He visited, shook our hands, asked questions, and got to know us."

"His son was a twat," a woman had added. "He wouldn't have made a good King. I'm not saying I'm glad he's dead, but I would love to have seen little Edwina take over one day. She was a feisty little girl; always giving her parents these little glares and not curtsying when she was supposed to. That's who I wanted leading the country."

"But your Parliament and Prime Minister are actually the ones leading the country," Palmer had reminded.

"I've always believed the King was more involved than just shaking hands and kissing babies," another man had replied. "He had weekly meetings with good old Albie, but he also had meetings with key members of Parliament, including the opposition. I don't know what the Queen's going to do, but maybe she'll do the same."

In another pub, Palmer had found a group of staunch anti-monarchists and had been more careful there.

"It's all bullshit, isn't it? We came from a country ruled by someone who got the job because he was born into it, and then St. Rais went and did the same damn thing; even letting the same fucking family rule. If you want my opinion, America got it right. Sure, you're fucked up now, but the idea of a government run by the people and not someone born into the right family is a good one."

"So, you would prefer the monarchy be abolished?" she'd asked the guy.

"Legally, yeah. There's never been enough of a ruckus to put it to a vote. This whole bombing thing only makes people like me look like nutjobs. They've put our cause back at least a decade. Had they just gone about it the right way – petitioned their representatives to get it into Parliament for a vote – we might have stood a chance."

"It's not that big of a deal," an older man with snow-white hair and matching beard, causing him to resemble Santa Claus, added. "They don't *do* anything, but they're not harming anything, either."

"They're using our tax dollars to support their life-styles," the other guy remarked.

"You think Parliament isn't abusing our tax dollars, too? What government in the world isn't full of some kind of corruption or abuse? Name one, and I'll buy your next round," the older man rebuffed, lifting his own half-glass. "King Maxwell was better than our previous three Prime Ministers combined. Besides, his father helped keep us out of a war before you were even born, kid. Parliament didn't do that. Our PM didn't do that. The King did."

"I thought you wanted them gone," the younger man said, nodding to Santa.

"I don't care either way," the man replied. "I'll be long

dead before any decision is made on that. I just don't think it's worth all the fuss."

***

Palmer hadn't started forming her story yet, but she had compiled her notes into categories and themes using one of her favorite apps on her computer. It allowed her to list things and then examine the keywords, mapping out those themes for her automatically and allowing her to get an idea of where the interviews and facts were taking her story. When she turned the map from text-based to visual, she found a few things sticking out. One was that everyone admonished the bombers and what they'd done, regardless of whether they were pro or anti a royal family. That made Palmer feel better about humanity. The second thing she noticed was that even the rational anti-monarchists seemed to at least think the former King was an okay guy, more man about the people than any royal in other countries. The third thing she noticed was that people were unsure of their new Queen, who was about to celebrate her coronation.

"She wasn't brought up for this," one woman had commented.

"She wanted to be a doctor or something. I'm not sure how that will make her a good Queen," a man had replied when she'd asked him a few questions outside the palace.

"I'm sure she'll be fine, but that's only assuming she can move past this horrible tragedy. We lost a King; *she* lost a father. We lost Princes; she lost her brothers," another woman had told her.

Palmer decided that her story would have short sections on the history, the bombing, and the former king, but the crux of her story, assuming she could pull it off, would be about the new Queen and how she adapted to her unexpected role, the loss of her loved ones, and the growing pressure of an entire nation now resting on her shoulders. Palmer pulled up a bio for the Queen on the palace's official website and read the blurbs to herself. Most of it, she already knew, but some of it was news to her. Elizabeth was, what St. Rais called, an Honors Scholar of the First Degree in physics. As of the writing of the bio, the woman was only a year away from a master's degree and planned to pursue a Ph. D in theoretical physics from the nation's top university. The biography also touted the charities Elizabeth was the patron for, including food banks, an organization that helped victims of domestic abuse, a program that supported girls in STEM, and others. As Princess, she wasn't required to perform many royal duties, so she wasn't interviewed often or even seen at many events outside of weddings.

The people Palmer had interviewed had been right: Elizabeth hadn't been raised for this. As she looked up Martin's pedigree on another page, though, it was obvious that he *was* raised for this. Alexander seemed to be the typical modern-day second-in-line. He partied a lot in his early twenties, was seen with a different woman on his arm every few months, and did his required stint in the army for two years before leaving, while Martin remained in for four extra years.

***

A few hours later, after enjoying dinner in the hotel restaurant, Palmer returned to her room to continue her research when her phone rang.

"Hey, what time is it there?" she asked, answering the call.

"Night there, so it's morning here. I just wanted to check in. When exactly are you coming back?"

"I told you, I'm working a story. I don't know when I'll be back," Palmer replied.

Then, she heard the sigh and waited for the frustrated comment that would follow.

"Palmer, what are we even doing?" Anna asked.

"You told me you needed space," Palmer reminded her.

"I didn't expect you to flee across the country to a

place I hadn't even heard of until you mentioned that's where you were going."

"I didn't *flee*. I told you months ago I needed a vacation. We were supposed to plan something together. Then, you asked for an open relationship."

"An open relationship, not a breakup. I could have gone with you."

"I didn't want you to, Anna. I wanted to go somewhere on my own."

"I know. You wanted to think."

"What am I supposed to do when my girlfriend says she wants to sleep with other people? You wanted space. I gave it to you."

"I'm just trying to figure things out, Palmer."

"So am I," she explained.

"I know we agreed not to talk about what we do with other people, but are you really there for a story, Palm? Or did you meet someone? I know it's not fair for me to ask. I just—"

"You're right: it's not fair. I told you I'd agree to the whole open thing while you sort through whatever's going on with you, but only if you don't tell me what you do with other women, and I don't have to tell you what I do with other women, either."

"So, there have been others?"

"You're joking, Anna."

"I'm sorry. I know it's not fair. I just need to know, Palm."

"Why now? Why do you need to know, all of a sudden, if I've slept with someone else?" Palmer paused as she realized. "Because you *have*, haven't you?"

There was a silence. That was how Palmer knew her girlfriend of over a year had slept with another woman.

"You said you didn't want to know."

"I was hoping there would be nothing *to* know. I thought you were going through some kind of a phase."

Anna was six years younger than her. When they'd

met, she was just out of college, and Palmer was her first serious girlfriend out of school. Anna had asked for some time to explore things, and Palmer had thought she needed that exploring because of her age and lack of experience. She'd only slept with one other woman outside of Palmer, so it made sense she'd be interested in searching, but that hadn't stopped Palmer from being hopeful that Anna wouldn't actually sleep with anyone else and would come back to her and they would re-enter the monogamous part of their relationship.

"I met her at work, Palm."

"Are you two dating, or is it just sex?" Palmer asked.

"We're dating," Anna replied.

"Does she know about me?"

"She knows I'm in an open relationship, yeah."

"And does she care?"

"She said it's fine while we're seeing where this thing goes but that eventually, she'd like it to just be the two of us if it gets that far."

"You asked if I'd found someone because you were hoping I *had*, weren't you? If I'd met someone, you'd be off the hook; you could end things with me and not feel guilty about it."

"That's not—"

"Anna, let's just call this what it is, okay? We tried. We were together for nine months before this whole open-relationship thing. That's not a bad run."

"I didn't call you to break—"

"Maybe not, but it's what's happening either way, Anna. I want someone who wants me; *only* me. I tried this open thing, but it's not what I want. I want a commitment. If you don't want that, or if you want that with someone else, it's just better to end things now." *She* sighed this time. "I'm here for a story for the next few weeks, most likely. Can you just grab whatever I have at your place and take it to mine? You can pick up your stuff there and leave the key on the way out."

"Sure, whatever you want," Anna said softly. "Palmer, I'm sorry. You know I love you, right?"

Palmer closed her eyes at those three words and replied, "Yeah, just not enough."

CHAPTER 5

"THEY want you to meet with the Prince of Denmark?"

"Yes," Elizabeth replied.

"And?" Victoria asked.

"And, I'm not doing it."

"Lizzy, what are you going to do here? It's not like you've ever looked for a boyfriend. Now, people are throwing single, suitable men at you. If you don't want a Prince or a Duke, you'd have to find a commoner on your own. No one's going to throw one of *those* at you."

"Don't say 'commoner.' It makes you sound—"

"Like a Princess? I *am* a Princess. That's how we sound," Victoria interrupted. "Lizzy, if you don't find someone, settle down, get married, and pop out a kid or two, you know what happens, right?"

"Yes, you'll become Queen when I die," Elizabeth replied. "You *are* getting married and popping out kids. The country will have an heir."

Victoria reached for her sister's forearm as they walked the private garden at the back of the palace property and stopped their progress.

"Are you really not going to even try?" she asked. "You know *I* don't care, right? The country won't care, Lizzy."

"Maybe it's better if I help get us through this period of instability, wait until you and David are married and you have your first baby, and then abdicate."

"What?" Victoria's expression showed shock. "No! Why would you do that? I'm even *less* prepared for this than you are. I am convinced the country forgot I existed until

35

this happened. Most people in the UK couldn't name all of Queen Elizabeth's children. It's the same here. It's like, 'There's Martin, Alexander, Elizabeth, and the fourth one. Who's the fourth one, again? There *were* four of them, right?'"

Victoria's imitation of a St. Rais citizen probably wasn't far off, but Elizabeth wouldn't be telling *her* that.

"Vicky, you know I…"

"I know. I know."

"This wasn't supposed to happen," Elizabeth said as she looked around the garden. They were walking alone, but security lined the solid fence on the inside and, likely, around the outside as well. "Dad should still be here."

"They should *all* still be here, Lizzy."

"I'm supposed to be at school. You should be introducing Dad to David and trying to convince him you should marry a Brit."

Victoria chuckled a little and said, "He's coming next weekend. We're going to talk about the future then."

"I'm glad you have him, Vicky."

"You need someone, too, Lizzy. You shouldn't have to do this alone. Even if you never get married or have kids because the country needs heirs, you should think about finding someone for *you*."

"I have to get through a coronation and an investigation into the bombing first. Then, maybe I can think about figuring out what comes next." She sighed as they resumed their walking. "I knew Dad worked hard, but I had no idea *how* hard. I have so many meetings already, and I know people are going easy on me because of what happened."

"You'll get the hang of it, and I'll help you however I can," Victoria promised. "If you need to delegate something to me, do it. I'm kind of hoping David proposes soon. And if he does, we'll be married. He'll be part of this family, and I'll put him to work, too, Lizzy. Whatever you need, we're here for you."

"God, we'll have to plan a wedding, too, won't we?"

Victoria stopped walking. Elizabeth turned around and returned quickly to her.

"What's wrong?" she asked.

"I just realized…" Victoria's eyes welled with tears. "Lizzy, Dad won't be there. No one will be there for my wedding; for yours, either, one day."

"Oh." Elizabeth wrapped her arms protectively around her younger sister in what she was hoping was a comforting hug. "I'll be there in person, but they'll all be there in spirit. You're going to make a beautiful bride. And if you want me to, I can give David the speech Dad would have given him. Remember the one he gave your first boy-friend?"

Victoria laughed through her tears and said, "Yes, he tried to pull out that deep voice to scare him."

"It worked. He brought you home early, didn't he?"

"Yeah," Victoria replied, pulling out of the hug now. "Small, Lizzy. Can I please have a small wedding?"

"I'll do the best I can, but you *are* technically heir to the throne right now – weddings for direct heirs aren't ex-actly *small* affairs."

"Maybe David and I can have a long engagement. You can meet someone and get married first. Then, when you're pregnant, he and I can get married, and I won't be the heir anymore," Victoria suggested as she wiped her eyes.

Elizabeth allowed herself to laugh and said, "We'll see."

***

"Ma'am, may I have a moment?" Rebecca asked, en-tering Elizabeth's office.

"Come in," Elizabeth replied. "Can you give us a mo-ment?" she asked her head of security.

Then, she stood, allowing him to stand as well. He bowed and left her with Rebecca.

"Have a seat," she told Rebecca, sitting down herself.

Rebecca sat across from her and asked, "Any news?"

"They believe they've identified the man responsible for running the faction of anti-monarchists. They've not been able to find him yet, but they're working on trying to get a location and to bring him in."

"That's great news," Rebecca offered back.

"I want him to tell me why," Elizabeth added. "Do you think he will?"

"If he does, Ma'am, I doubt it will be enough."

"I suppose you're right."

"May I present you with something, Ma'am?"

"Present me?"

"Yes. I wasn't sure I was going to, but – I don't know – she asked that I give *you* the choice, and I think that's the right thing to do."

"What are you talking about, Rebecca?"

"There's an American reporter in St. Rais. She got my phone number from someone. I'm not sure who, but she asked me for a meeting, and I went because I was curious."

"You met with her?" Elizabeth leaned forward in her chair.

"Ma'am, I said nothing. It wasn't an interview. She didn't record me, and she didn't take any notes, either. I'm not even sure she knows what my position is on your staff. We met at a café. She would like to do a story."

"On the bombing?"

"No, and that's what's most interesting: she's more interested in our history, the monarchy, and presenting you to the world, I think."

"*Me?*"

"I did my research," Rebecca continued. "She's a reporter for *The New York Courier.*"

"*I* read *The Courier.*"

"Yes, Ma'am. As do a lot of people in St. Rais. When I spoke with her, I didn't get the feeling that she would portray you in a negative light, would insert her own opinion, or that she would cause us any problems."

"What's her name?" Elizabeth asked, now curious.

"Palmer Honeycutt. She was born in Pennsylvania; the daughter of a high school teacher, and her mother owns a small restaurant in Pittsburgh. She went to New York University, majoring in journalism. I've emailed you some of her articles from college and added a few *Courier* links as well. She seems like an ethical, fair journalist, Ma'am."

"You want me to talk to her?"

"She only asked me to give you the choice. She said she'd let us review her questions in advance and that she wouldn't record you if that would be a problem."

"What's in it for us, Rebecca? She gets her story. What do we get out of it?"

"I think she'd give you a real chance to tell *your* story, Ma'am. She seemed genuine to me. She was here on vacation when the bombing happened. I don't think this was something she planned on doing, and her paper didn't send her here. She just happened to be in the country already."

Elizabeth sighed and said, "It's been a long time since I've done an interview, and I wasn't Queen then."

"We've been receiving requests left and right for your first interview as Queen. *This* is an article. It could be a nice warm-up for a TV interview or your Christmas address to the nation if you don't do a TV interview prior to that."

"I'd forgotten all about that," Elizabeth said, closing her eyes.

"Maybe just read through her articles. If you're interested after that, let me know. I have her business card. I can handle the arrangements."

"What about the other arrangements you were working on for me?"

"Security said they've checked out the house, and the press hasn't been around much recently since you're here at the palace. They believe that if we can get you out of the palace at night unnoticed, you could have some privacy there. But they'll only agree if you promise not to leave the house until you're ready to return to the palace."

"That's fine." She nodded.

"I'll make the arrangements. Are you thinking a long weekend?"

"That would be perfect," Elizabeth replied, smiling at her secretary. "Thank you, Rebecca."

"Of course, Ma'am."

After Rebecca left her alone in her office, Elizabeth moved behind her desk. She had hardly used this desk in her lifetime. It had been a gift from her mother when she'd turned sixteen, but she preferred a relaxed environment when she studied, so she'd chosen to sit in front of her fireplace with her books back then. Now, she was Queen of a nation, but she couldn't actually find it in herself to move her stuff into her father's old office or suite of rooms in the palace, which many people here had asked her to do. It was the custom of the new monarch to sit behind the same desk as the old monarch and to sleep in the same bedroom. It also wasn't *just* the custom. It was for security reasons as well: there were secret exits and entrances in those rooms, allowing the monarch to be safely moved when needed.

Elizabeth needed more time, though. Until then, she was perfectly safe in her old rooms. In fact, she might even be safer since many people would have assumed she'd moved already. She opened her computer, clicked on Rebecca's email, and proceeded to the first link. She read article after article from Palmer Honeycutt's college years. Then, she moved on to the puff pieces from *The Courier*. Eventually, she clicked on Palmer's biography and saw her professional headshot. Palmer Honeycutt was younger than Elizabeth had expected. She might be thirty years old, but could be a few years younger. She had short brown hair that nearly met her shoulders and some pretty deep brown eyes. Her smile seemed genuine, though posed, but Elizabeth found herself smiling at the photo.

"She's beautiful," she said to herself.

She leaned back in her comfortable desk chair and thought about whether or not she was ready to subject herself to a reporter; to an article that may or may not paint her positively. That would be the risk she'd face if she chose to sit down with Miss Honeycutt. Actually, maybe she was a *Mrs.* Honeycutt. Who knows? The photo had only been from the shoulders up, so there was no way to see a ring or its absence. Surely, a beautiful and successful woman like Palmer Honeycutt was married by now. Elizabeth squinted at herself, wondering why she was thinking about the marital status of a reporter she'd never met.

CHAPTER 6

"GOT anything yet?"

"Not enough," Palmer replied, sipping on her white wine at the hotel bar as she spoke to her editor on the phone.

"What's the angle?"

"I'm planning something about the new Queen, but I need to get to her first. I had a meeting the other day with someone who works at the palace. She said she'd get my card to someone close to the Queen. I'm still waiting."

"I know you, Palmer. You're not *just* waiting. What else you got?" he pressed.

"I've got a pro versus anti-monarchy thing, but I'd prefer that be on the side, not the main course."

"How much more time do you think you need?" he asked.

"If I don't hear from my contact by the end of this week, I'm not going to hear from her at all. I'll come back then and write from the office."

"And if you get the interview?"

"Big *if,* but if I do, it depends on what she agrees to. I'd like to set it up so we can talk multiple times."

"A get-to-know-you meeting, then a touch-the-surface meeting, a dive-a-little-deeper meeting, and–"

"Yeah, you get it," Palmer cut him off, smiling at a woman who had been looking her way for most of the night.

"If you're there beyond next week, we're moving you out of that hotel, Palmer. That place is expensive as hell."

"It wasn't when I booked it," she replied.

He chuckled at her and said, "Just get the job done

quickly so I don't have to have Cynthia find you a Holiday Inn Express."

She disconnected the call and thought about walking over to the woman who was attractive and alone, sitting by the window that overlooked an amazing view of the city. Anna had been a mistake; Palmer had known it when she'd first asked her out. Anna was young but mature, and she'd liked her immediately. So much so that she'd given into Anna's persistent advances at the end of their first date and they'd slept together. Two months later, they'd told one another they'd loved each other and started talking about next steps. They'd done the weekend-away thing, choosing to spend time in Vermont skiing. They'd gone to Palmer's cousin's wedding together. Anna had also met her parents. Everything was going well, and Palmer had planned to ask Anna to move in together at the same time Anna had decided she needed to open up their relationship. Suddenly, things were *not* going well.

Now, it was over, and Palmer was drowning her sorrows at a bar in a tiny, forgotten-about country. She could go over to that woman who still had her eye on her, strike up a conversation, and ask if the woman would be interested in going to her room and having a little fun just for the night. She *could* do that, but she didn't want to, knowing she would only wake up with regrets later. So, she asked for her bill to sign her wine to her room, and just as she was about to leave, her phone rang for the second time that night.

"Honeycutt," she greeted tersely as she reached for the jacket, which she'd hung over the back of the chair.

"Miss Honeycutt, this is Rebecca Watt."

"Miss Watt," she said, taken aback. "Hello."

"Yes, hello," Rebecca replied.

"What can I do for you?" Palmer stood frozen in place.

"Her Majesty has agreed to a meeting."

"She has?"

"Yes. But please be advised that she's only agreed to a meeting, not an interview."

"I see."

"It will be entirely off the record, and if she decides after the meeting that she'd like to talk further, we will let you know."

"So, this is a get-to-know-me kind of a thing," she stated.

"Yes, you understand."

"I do." Palmer nodded as if Rebecca would see it through the phone. "When? Where?"

"A car will pick you up at your hotel tomorrow. You'll be driven to an undisclosed location; for the Queen's safety. There will be a heavy security presence. You understand."

Rebecca kept saying those words, 'You understand,' as a way of saying Palmer had no choice *but* to understand.

"I do."

"The car will be there tomorrow night at seven."

"Tomorrow *night?*"

"I assume that won't be a problem. The Queen is very busy. She was only able to–"

"No, it's fine. I just wanted to make sure I heard correctly. I'll be waiting at seven."

"Very well."

Rebecca disconnected the call, and Palmer smiled.

"Excuse me," a woman with a British accent spoke from behind her.

"Oh, sorry," Palmer replied, turning around to face the woman she'd been eyeing from before. "Am I in your way?"

"No, but I was wondering if you had to leave so soon. I was hoping you might like to have a drink with me." She smiled in a way that told Palmer she'd definitely done this before.

"I'm afraid I can't; I'm sorry. I have to get going."

"Are you here for another night? Maybe we could try again tomorrow."

"I have plans tomorrow night." Palmer thought about being polite and telling the woman maybe they could share a drink another time, but decided to leave it at that. "Have a good night."

***

Palmer had never met a Queen before. She'd been sent a list of instructions from Rebecca, explaining what to do when she did. Women do a small curtsy. Men do a small bow. She *could* simply shake the Queen's hand in the usual way, but that seemed lazy. The correct formal address to use was 'Your Majesty,' and after that, she should refer to her as 'Ma'am.' She didn't have to obey the rules, but technically, she shouldn't sit until the Queen sat. She should walk slightly behind the Queen if they did any walking. That seemed like nonsense, but she'd follow the rules tonight. She needed to secure a real interview, one that could be on the record, to get her the article she longed to write. Palmer was ready to get back home. She wanted to see if Anna had done as she'd asked and left her stuff and her key in her Manhattan studio apartment. She wanted to start moving on with her life.

"Miss Honeycutt," a man dressed in a black suit and tie asked.

"Yes, that's me." She stood up from the chair in the lobby.

"I'm here to take you to meet someone," he explained, giving her a nod.

"Of course," she replied, realizing he wasn't about to announce who she was meeting with in the middle of a crowded hotel lobby.

"Follow me, please," he requested, glancing around the space, likely to ensure they wouldn't be followed.

Palmer did. The sliding glass doors parted, opening to the cold night outside. Sure, it was cold in New York this time of year, but she'd never experienced cold like this before. She wrapped her arms around her body, wishing she'd bought an even warmer coat than the one she'd bought when she'd arrived and realized her jacket wasn't going to cut it in St. Rais as fall turned to winter.

The man opened the door to the black car that was

waiting just outside and motioned for her to climb into the vehicle. How was this guy only dressed in a suit? She was already freezing, and she'd been outside for all of nine seconds. Gladly, she climbed into the back seat of the car, seeking warmth more than anything else.

"Is it *Miss* Honeycutt or *Mrs.* Honeycutt," a voice came from beside her.

Palmer expected to turn to see Rebecca sitting next to her. Instead, she saw a Queen.

"I'm not married," she replied simply, choosing to answer the question rather than ignore it to ask what was going on. "Your Majesty; I meant that I'm not married, Your Majesty."

Elizabeth sat next to her as the car took off. It was a town car, and they were completely alone in the closed-off back seat of the vehicle.

"I wanted to make sure I addressed you properly," the Queen explained.

"And *I*, obviously, didn't do a good job of that," she said, giving her a shy smile. "I'm sorry. I've never met a Queen before."

"I've never *been* one before," Elizabeth replied. "And since it's just us back here, and we're supposed to be getting to know each other anyway, why don't you just call me Elizabeth, and I'll call you Palmer?"

Palmer nodded and said, "I'd like that."

"Seat belt." Elizabeth pointed to Palmer's lap and continued, "I understand you were here as a visitor before you were here as a reporter."

Palmer didn't know if she should face forward. They *were* driving, after all. She buckled up, sat straight, and turned her head toward the Queen.

"I was, yes."

"Not quite used to our winters, are you?"

Palmer took in the Queen's smile. It was sweet and endearing. Palmer liked it.

"No. Things get cold where I'm from, but not *this*

cold. I bought this coat when I got here."

"That's a nice brand. It's made here, actually," Elizabeth said.

"It is?"

"Yes," the Queen replied simply. "What have you seen of St. Rais?"

"I spent most of my time at the resort, if I'm being honest. I got a really good deal on the trip, but I *have* gone around the city a bit. I took a little river cruise that opened to the sea. That was nice."

Elizabeth turned to her and said, "You're freezing right now, but you took a *river* cruise?"

"I stayed indoors on the boat," Palmer explained. "I knew it would be cold, but I saw the edge of the water as we were boarding, and it was already starting to freeze over."

"We're at the end of the season. The boats will stop running the tourist cruises next week when it's far too cold for them to make it down the river and into open water. If you have a chance, you should get a tour guide to take you up into the hills. They're not exactly mountains this close to the city, but they're high enough. You can camp out under the stars."

"I don't think I have *nearly* enough long underwear for that," Palmer replied, her eyes growing wide when she realized she'd just used the word 'underwear' in front of a Queen.

"The tour guides provide the equipment. They also talk to you about the Northern Lights. I've heard it's very peaceful."

"You've *heard?* You've never been yourself?"

"No, but I know people who have. I do have a nice skylight at my house, though – I see them most nights when I fall asleep."

"The palace has skylights?"

"No, not the…" Elizabeth faded then. "Never mind. When do you return to the States?"

"I don't know yet."

"Does it depend on your story?" Elizabeth asked.

"Yes," she replied.

"You know, I may be a new Queen, but I'm not new to this life."

"Life?" Palmer checked.

"Royal life; where people want to know everything about me and my family. Sometimes, they want to know so much that they make things up and call them truths."

"I'm not one of those people," Palmer replied, staring at the Queen intently. "That's not me."

"I didn't ask for your phone. Can I assume our conversation is *truly* off the record?"

"It's in my pocket. You can have it if you can get to it. I think I have about eighteen layers you'd have to get through first, though," she said, looking down at the thick jacket.

"I'll trust you."

"It's also turned off," Palmer told her. "I'm only interested in hearing what, if anything, you'd like to tell me. I understand this is just a meeting." She glanced out the dark, tinted windows. "I do *not* know, however, where we're going."

"Nowhere. We'll be back at your hotel in just a moment."

"Huh?" Palmer asked, turning back to the Queen in confusion.

"It's easier for security if I just remain in this car before returning to the palace. We'll drop you back at the door to the hotel momentarily."

Palmer nodded in disappointment. She hadn't passed the Queen's test, or this conversation would have gone on a lot longer.

"I understand."

"Understand what?" Elizabeth asked her, looking confused.

"I've been in this car all of a minute. I assume this is it."

Elizabeth smiled softly and said, "I'll have my private secretary reach out to you to arrange a more proper interview."

Palmer lifted an eyebrow and asked, "You will?"

"Yes." Elizabeth looked past Palmer out the window. "I see we're here, Palmer. Have a nice evening," she added.

The car came to a stop. Within seconds, Palmer's door was opened for her, and the freezing air rushed into the vehicle.

"You're only wearing a light coat. How do you put up with the cold?" she asked the Queen as she unbuckled her seat belt.

"I was born here. It's in my blood. This *country* is in my blood," the woman replied. "Have a nice night, Miss Honeycutt."

For a moment, Palmer wondered at the change in name but remembered there was a man holding the door open for her.

"Thank you, Ma'am. You as well."

CHAPTER 7

PALMER Honeycutt wasn't at all what Elizabeth had expected. Her plan had been to chat with the woman for a minute, drop her back off at the hotel, and ask Rebecca to call her the following morning, telling her that she wouldn't be able to do the interview. While sitting in that car with Palmer, however, Elizabeth felt oddly comfortable with her. It had helped that Palmer was obviously nervous and so freezing cold, and therefore, very entertaining to Elizabeth. It had also been nice to have even just one minute with someone who wasn't concerned about her safety, security, or her coronation. Elizabeth had decided in that moment, when Palmer had turned back to her confused as to why she was getting dropped back off at the hotel, that she would do the interview. She didn't trust her as she would an old friend, but she believed Palmer to be an ethical journalist who kept her own opinions out of her writing. That was all Elizabeth needed from a journalist writing a story about her.

***

"Your Majesty, we'd prefer she only be allowed in the public wing of the palace," her head of security told her the next day.

"She's a reporter. She'll go through security. What do you expect her to do?"

"Ma'am, we have to be prepared for the unexpected."

"I understand, but my office will be fine."

"Ma'am, if you insist on an office, might I suggest your father's private office, your *new* office? We have plans for– "

"My own private office will be fine. You may have a tank and the army just outside the door if you'd like."

50

"I'd prefer two men inside, along with Rebecca and Thomas."

"Thomas and Rebecca will be in the other room," she replied, referring to the Director of Public Affairs and her secretary.

"Very well, Ma'am," the head of security said, bowing his head. "I'll make the arrangements."

"Is it true?" Victoria asked as she entered Elizabeth's office unannounced, as was *her* custom.

"Is *what* true?" Elizabeth asked back. "Thank you, Sven," she added, dismissing the security head.

When he left the room, closing the door behind him, Victoria sat in the chair opposite Elizabeth's desk.

"Are you actually considering giving some American an interview?"

"I am. Why?"

"An interview, Lizzy? Why? The American press is brutal. You're going to give her all she needs to write some exposé about our family."

"It's not an exposé."

"How can you be sure?"

"I'm taking precautions, Victoria," she replied.

"Precautions? Has Thomas approved her?"

"He has."

"Who is she?"

"Her name is Palmer Honeycutt. She works for *The New York Courier*, not some tabloid magazine. And it's an article, not a TV interview. I'll be fine."

"Are you sure, Lizzy?" her sister asked, looking concerned. "I think it's too soon."

"It will always be too soon, but we have to move forward however we can, Vicky. If we were any other family, we could take as much time as we needed to grieve and mourn, but we're not any other family. We don't have that option. *We* have to put on brave faces, keep our chins level with the ground, and not show emotion out there. *We* have to support the nation that supports us."

"I guess so." Victoria glanced out the window. "Should I be there with you? I can, you know."

"I'll be okay, but thank you. I'd prefer you spend your time with David, planning for the move to the cottage and your future."

"They're worried about me even being at the coronation. Did Sven tell you?"

"It's not an option. You'll be there, Vicky."

"I know; that's what I've been saying. But they haven't caught the guy they're looking for. They're worried he'll try something there, and if he does, it could take both you and me out."

"There's always cousin Ernie," Elizabeth said of her second cousin and only other member of their family that was still alive *and* of ruling age, meaning he wouldn't require a regent.

"He lives in Greece now. People can't stand him."

"He's still technically next up after you. He has two young sons."

"They've never even set foot on St. Rais's soil, Lizzy," Victoria objected.

"All I'm suggesting is that if, heaven forbid, something did happen to both of us before there are heirs, there are other options."

"Ernie isn't an option. He sells yachts to rich people."

Elizabeth laughed and said, "I'm aware."

"Are you really sure about this interview thing?"

"I am," she replied, nodding confidently.

"Okay. If *I* can't talk you out of it, and Rebecca can't, then no one can."

***

"Your Majesty," Palmer greeted her with an awkward curtsy when she entered the room behind Rebecca, Thomas, and two security guards.

"It's nice to see you again, Miss Honeycutt," Elizabeth greeted, holding out her hand for Palmer to shake.

Palmer gave her a relieved expression and took it.

"We have two chairs set over here for the interview," Thomas spoke, moving into the room and over to the chairs that had been placed across from one another in front of her desk. "You're allowed to take notes but not record the interview in any way. We reserve the right to review your notes prior to your departure. Any questions?"

"No. I understand the rules," Palmer replied.

"We'll be just down the hall if you need anything, Ma'am," Thomas said.

"Thank you. I'm certain we'll be fine."

"Shall I have tea brought in, Ma'am?" Rebecca asked.

"Miss Honeycutt?" Elizabeth checked, looking at the newcomer.

"I'm more of a coffee girl myself." Palmer raised a hand. "American. We had that whole Boston Tea Party thing, so we went with coffee as our national beverage."

Elizabeth laughed at that and said, "Coffee, Rebecca?"

"Of course, Ma'am." The woman nodded.

Rebecca and Thomas left them alone then, and the two guards remained for a moment longer, likely at the request of the security head.

"Miss Honeycutt, do you intend to harm me in any way today?"

"What? No," Palmer replied. "I mean, no, Ma'am."

"Gentlemen." Elizabeth gave them the nod to go. "You may leave us. We'll be fine on our own."

The guards bowed and left the room, closing the door behind them.

"I apologize for the security," she said, motioning for Palmer to sit.

"It's fine. I get it. I didn't mind the strip search."

"The what?" Elizabeth asked, wide-eyed.

Palmer laughed as she continued to stand next to the chair.

"I'm kidding," she replied. "Metal detectors and a light pat-down. I've had worse at the airport."

"You scared me," Elizabeth replied.

"Sorry, I thought it was funny."

"You're not sitting down," Elizabeth noted.

"Neither are you."

"You read the rules, didn't you?" she asked.

"I did. Rebecca sent them to me."

Elizabeth sighed and said, "Have a seat, Palmer."

"Is that an order?"

"I'm not *your* Queen," Elizabeth replied. "Besides, these are customs, not laws. This is not an off-with-your-head type scenario."

"Okay," Palmer replied with a smile. "But if this is some sort of trick to make the American look like an idiot, I'm not going to be very happy." She sat in the chair. "Elizabeth."

Elizabeth sat down as well, gave the woman a polite smile, and asked, "Where do we start?"

"If you don't mind, I'd like to ask a lot of questions that I *can* find the answers to on the internet. They may seem tedious, but unless I hear it from you, I'd like to avoid printing what other sources have already posted."

"That is music to my ears, Palmer," Elizabeth replied. "You are aware that I might decline to answer a question?"

"Sure." Palmer shrugged a shoulder.

The door opened, and Jenny entered carrying a tray with an antique coffee pot with matching cups and the standard accoutrements. She gave a short curtsy and placed the tray on the table.

"Shall I pour, Ma'am?"

"I think we can manage that ourselves. Thank you, Jenny," she replied.

Jenny walked backward to the door then left the room. That custom needed to change. The poor woman had nearly run into a small table by the door because she couldn't turn her back to the Queen.

"I know we haven't agreed to anything beyond today, but I only have an hour with you today, and I have a lot more questions," Palmer spoke. "At the end, do you think we can talk about the possibility of a follow-up interview?"

"How do you take your coffee?"

"Oh, wow. The last woman to ask me that is now my ex-girlfriend," Palmer blurted out. Then, she covered her mouth in surprise. "I am *so* sorry. I have no idea why I just said that."

Elizabeth stared at her for a moment before she nodded. "Can I guess?"

"How I take my coffee, or why I just blurted out something like that out to a Queen?"

"The first one," Elizabeth said, smiling at her.

"Go for it."

"You seem like a busy woman."

"I guess," Palmer said.

"Not much time for things like cream and sugar, so black is my guess."

"Black is fine, but I also wouldn't mind a sugar packet."

"Cube."

"Huh?"

"Sugar *cubes*. We're civilized in this country. Our sugar comes in cubes," Elizabeth teased.

Palmer laughed lightly and said, "Right. One of those would be great. But I can do it."

"I've got it." Elizabeth stood. When Palmer went to stand up as well, she added, "You can keep sitting. Some of these customs have got to go."

"Which ones?" Palmer asked.

"Is this on the record?"

"It can be if you want it to be," Palmer said, readying her pen above the notepad she'd pulled from her shoulder bag upon sitting down.

"You came here on vacation. Do all reporters bring notebooks with them even when they're on vacation?"

"The good ones do."

Elizabeth poured them each a cup of coffee. Then, she added a sugar cube to Palmer's and stirred it in before passing her the cup. She made her own coffee with a splash of cream and sat back down across from the reporter.

"Can I ask you a question?" Palmer asked.

"That's why you're here, isn't it?"

"Not an interview question. It's just that these chairs are the straightest-back chairs I've ever sat in, and I flew *economy* over here. How do you deal with them?" she asked, shifting uncomfortably after placing her coffee cup on the small table next to her.

Elizabeth couldn't help but smile at the woman's attempt.

"If you'd prefer, we can move to the sofa behind you," she offered.

"Yes, that would be amazing."

"Were our spas not satisfactory for you, Miss Honeycutt?"

"What do you mean?"

"Did they not help you relax; work out your tired muscles after that economy flight?"

"They did. Why do you ask?"

"Because it seems like you're wound a little tight," Elizabeth told her.

They stood nearly simultaneously and migrated to the small sofa in her office. Elizabeth sat on one cushion, leaving the other to Palmer, who sat down carefully, coffee in hand.

"I'm interviewing a Queen. The closest I've ever come to this was the president of my *university*."

"Your article about the professor accused of sexual harassment?"

"How do you–" Palmer stopped. "You did your research."

"I did, yes." Elizabeth took a drink of her coffee. "So, are you ready to begin? I'm afraid I can't extend our time beyond the hour. I have a meeting with the Prime Minister."

"Yes, let's get started."

CHAPTER 8

"WHEN was the first time you realized your life was different than most people's?" Palmer asked.

"Oh, I was probably about four, I suppose."

"What happened?"

"I went with my parents to visit the school I'd be attending. My older brothers went to an all-boys school, so I had to attend elsewhere. My mother had also gone to my school, but she wanted to visit to make sure it was where she wanted to send her two girls. I watched other kids get picked up by their parents in cars that weren't black and driven by men in suits. I saw people walking around, not bowing or curtsying to each other. I asked my mom about it."

"What did she say?" Palmer asked, softly smiling as she'd been doing for the entirety of this interview.

"She said we were very lucky because we had people who took us places, helped us find great schools for our education, and respected us enough to bow. I don't think I was old enough to understand much else, but the next time I noticed the difference was when I got to primary school, and no one would talk to me."

"No one?"

"Well, one person did, but most of the children knew who I was, and because they were so young, I think they thought princesses were for Disney movies, not for their classroom. It's also likely that their parents told them to leave me alone as a sign of respect or custom, not realizing the impact that kind of isolation could have on a five-year-old."

"Who was the person?"

"I'm sorry?" Elizabeth looked up at her after staring down at the coffee now cold in her hands.

"You said one person talked to you."

"Oh, my friend Teagan."

"Teagan *Gentry*?" Palmer checked, recognizing the name.

"Yes," Elizabeth said softly.

"Your sister-in-law."

"Yes. We were friends long before she married Alex. Teagan is, in fact—" She stopped herself. "Teagan *was*, in fact, my only close friend outside of my siblings."

"I am so sorry, Elizabeth," Palmer said and meant it.

"So, am I," she said.

The door opened, and Rebecca entered the room.

"Your Majesty, the Prime Minister has arrived."

"It's been an hour?" Elizabeth asked, making Palmer feel pretty good about the fact that she'd lost track of time during the interview. "I had no idea. Palmer—" She stopped again. "Miss Honeycutt, I'm sorry I have to cut this short."

"You didn't. It's been the hour you agreed to."

Elizabeth stood. Palmer placed her cup on the table, reached for her bag, and slid her relatively blank notebook inside, along with the pen her mother had given her for Christmas one year, that was her favorite pen in the universe, and stood as well.

"Thank you for the time," she said, not knowing what else to say.

"Of course. Thank you for coming. I'll have them return you to the hotel. I assume we have your winter coat in a closet somewhere."

"They took it when I came in, yeah."

"Good. I wouldn't want you to freeze."

"You know, it's the pants that are the problem for me. The coat just only goes down so far."

"They make long underwear, too; the people who made your coat."

"I know, but I don't need it back home, and I'm only here for—" It was Palmer's turn to stop.

She had no idea how much longer she'd be here, but it

likely wouldn't be long. This interview was nice, but it wasn't all that informative to her story. It also wasn't a very good interview; she'd taken no notes of substance. It had been more of a conversation between two people getting to know one another than an actual interview.

"Ma'am? The Prime Minister?" Rebecca persisted.

"I should go," Palmer said.

"Right," Elizabeth replied and added, "Please don't walk backward to the door." She winked at Palmer. "I don't want you to run into the table there."

Palmer laughed a little and said, "You heard her give me permission, right?" She looked to Rebecca. "I don't want anyone out there thinking I'm a rude, inconsiderate American who refused to follow the customs."

"I heard," Rebecca said with a smile. "And I'll show you out now, Miss Honeycutt."

"Okay. Well, thanks again."

Elizabeth nodded politely. Then, Palmer was in the hallway, being ushered down it by Rebecca, who left her with one of the guards she'd seen earlier. He located her coat and escorted her to the waiting town car outside. She climbed in, enjoying the heat immensely.

Not long after, she was back in the lobby of her hotel, wondering what the hell she was going to do with the interview she hadn't really done.

***

A few hours later, Palmer had showered and was sitting in front of her laptop, staring at the blinking cursor. She'd learned things about St. Rais, about its new Queen today, but somehow, she still had nowhere to start. There was a knock at the door, which was unexpected since she'd eaten dinner down at the restaurant tonight and hadn't ordered anything sent up. She made her way over, checked the peephole, and saw the bellhop.

"Yes?" she asked through the door just to be safe.

"Miss Honeycutt, there was a package left downstairs for you with instructions to have it brought up straight away. Shall I leave it?" he asked.

"A package?" she asked back before she opened the door. "For *me*?"

"Yes, Ma'am." He passed her a long, flat box.

She didn't have any money in hand to give him a tip.

"Can I tip you later? I–"

"Not necessary, Ma'am." He nodded and headed back down the hallway.

Palmer closed the door and walked back over to the bed. The box was plain and white. It did have a small card inside an envelope on the top, though. She pulled it out and read it to herself.

"In case you decide to stay for a few extra days. Stay warm."

It was signed with only a letter. It was the letter E. Palmer opened the box and saw a very nice, warm-looking pair of long underwear, along with a pair of thick gloves and a matching scarf and hat. The Queen had given her some winter gear to keep her warm. Palmer couldn't help but smile as she sat down on the bed, but the smile disappeared when she realized she had no way of thanking Elizabeth. The Queen was a master at dodging questions she didn't want to answer, including the one Palmer had asked about the potential for a follow-up interview. It wasn't like Palmer could call her. She could call or email Rebecca and ask her to pass along the message, but it wasn't the same. Just then, her room phone rang.

"Hello?" she asked, assuming it was maybe the front desk confirming the package had been delivered.

"Palmer?"

"This is–" Palmer recognized that voice. "Elizabeth?"

"Yes," she replied, chuckling a bit. "I'm sorry to be calling so late."

"No, it's fine. It's not too late."

"It is for me, I'm afraid. I've suddenly turned into the

oldest twenty-five-year-old I know, but I have to be up early tomorrow, so it's early to bed for me tonight."

"I'm glad you called," Palmer admitted. "I just got your gift."

"I know. I had the driver wait to make sure."

"I was going to email Rebecca and ask her to send you my thanks."

"Does that mean you'll be staying in St. Rais long enough to *need* them?"

"To be honest, I didn't exactly get much out of our interview today." She leaned back against the pillows. "I wasn't able to get to a lot of my questions."

"Oh, I see."

"I just enjoyed talking to you. Is that okay for me to say?"

"It is if that's how you feel," Elizabeth replied.

"I've been staring at my computer screen, trying to figure out what to write. That rarely happens to me."

"Writer's block?"

"Yeah."

"Would it help if we continued our conversation?"

"Now?"

"I was thinking tomorrow," Elizabeth replied. "I have some time tomorrow afternoon."

Palmer sat up and said, "If you have time, yes. It would be great to continue the interview."

"Can you come to the palace around five?"

"Morning or night?" Palmer checked.

"Evening, Miss Honeycutt. I wouldn't ask you to deal with the four in the morning cold of a St. Rais winter just to get here by five."

"Well, I have all the gear now. I should be fine, right?" Palmer said before she could stop herself.

Was she flirting? Was Palmer flirting with a Queen?

"I suppose you do," Elizabeth replied. "I'll ask Rebecca to make arrangements. I'll see you tomorrow, Palmer."

"I'll see you tomorrow. Elizabeth?"

"Yes?"

"Sleep well," Palmer said softly.

Elizabeth didn't say anything for a moment.

"You too," she finally replied.

The call ended. Palmer hung up the phone and looked down at the box and the items in it, thinking about how nice it was for Elizabeth to arrange for someone to pick these things up for her and have them dropped off at the hotel. She read and reread the note a few more times before she got up and tucked it into the small pocket of her shoulder bag to save. Something told her she would want to remember the day a Queen bought her a nice gift.

Then, an idea for a different article came to her. It might not be one she'd actually turn into her editor, but it was something she wanted to write. She moved back to her laptop and typed *The Day I Met a Queen* at the top of the page. Leaning back against the pillows again, she tried to put into words her thoughts and feelings about meeting Elizabeth for the first time. She started with the minute in the car and continued with the interview today, but as she typed, Palmer knew she wouldn't turn this into her editor after all. This wasn't an article. It was a journal entry, and she was smiling the entire time she wrote it.

CHAPTER 9

"WHAT time do I have to be there?" she asked.

"Seven," Rebecca replied. "But, Ma'am, you have to get ready first. We should start soon."

"I told her five," Elizabeth told her.

"Ma'am, it'll take an hour just to do your hair and makeup, and then we have to get you into your dress, and– "

The door to her bedroom suite opened, revealing Jenny, who curtsied and announced, "Your Majesty, Miss Palmer Honeycutt has arrived. Where would you like me to escort her?"

"You've known me since I was six years old, Jenny; please call me Lizzy. Or, at the very least, Elizabeth." She looked at Rebecca. "You're a terrible example."

"Ma'am?" Jenny asked.

"In here is fine."

"Ma'am?" Rebecca asked her. "Your office would be more appropriate for an interview."

"I have to get dressed, don't I?" Elizabeth asked. "Send her in, Jenny. Thank you." She turned to Rebecca then. "It's fine, Rebecca."

"Elizabeth, I get that you like this woman; that she might make a nice friend for you, and you could use more friends, especially now, but she *is* still a reporter."

"You're the one that told me I should meet with her."

"For a quick interview. You've done that."

"And she asked for a follow-up." Elizabeth looked toward the open door of her bedroom. "When am I leaving for the house, Rebecca?"

"Tonight, Ma'am."

"After the dinner?"

"Yes, once the dinner finishes, we'll take you out through the private garden and down the block to the waiting cars. We'll report to anyone who asks that you're in the palace, working on plans for the coronation."

"What happens *after* the coronation? What lies will we tell people when I need to get away then?"

"None, Ma'am. You are the Queen – you are free to rest and relax when needed, Elizabeth. We're doing this now because we need to keep you safe until–"

"I marry a man and pop out an heir and a spare so that my petrified younger sister doesn't have to reign after I die, or that my crazy cousin Ernie doesn't take the throne and run this country into the ground?"

"Your Majesty, Miss Palmer Honeycutt," Jenny said.

Elizabeth stared at the door again where Palmer was standing beside Jenny, with both hands on the strap of her cross-shoulder bag.

"Rebecca, Jenny, can you please give Miss Honeycutt and I a moment alone?"

"Ma'am, your dresser and–"

"Send them in when they need me," she interjected.

"Very well."

Once Rebecca and Jenny were gone, with the door closed behind them, Elizabeth looked down at the floor.

"I assume you overheard."

Palmer didn't say anything for a moment, causing Elizabeth to look back up at her.

"Is this your room? I guess I should say *rooms*, huh?" She walked into the small sitting area, which was to the left of Elizabeth's actual bedroom. "It's nice, but – I don't know – doesn't seem like *you* to me. That's probably rude to say, though, isn't it?"

"Palmer?" Elizabeth persisted.

"I didn't hear anything, Elizabeth." Palmer stared at her, silently telling Elizabeth that she *had* heard something, but she wouldn't say anything about it.

"Yes, these are my rooms." She motioned with an

open palm. "You've seen my office, which is through that door." She pointed. "This is my sitting room. My bed is through there. The en suite is through the door on the right. The closet is on the left."

"I've seen movies about royalty before. Is your closet as jam-packed with shoes and jewelry as all the rest?"

Elizabeth laughed and said, "Not as much, no. The crown jewels are locked up and only pulled out for formal occasions like tonight."

"I wore jeans; I didn't know this was formal," Palmer said, looking down at her casual wear. "I didn't bring a lot of clothes with me."

Elizabeth laughed again, motioned for Palmer to sit on the sofa in front of the perpetually burning fireplace, and joined her moments later.

"I have a dinner tonight. It's my first as Queen."

"Tonight?" Palmer asked. "Should we have postponed?"

"I wasn't sure how long you were staying," Elizabeth told her.

"Oh, I don't know. I'm staying until I finish the story, however long that takes. I will have to move into a Holiday Inn Express soon because the paper won't pay for the resort much longer, but I can talk any day."

"I'm busy for the next several days," Elizabeth told her. "Maybe it's just best that we talk now. Would you mind talking while I get dressed?"

"Not if you're okay with it," Palmer replied.

Elizabeth glanced at the fire and said, "You'll get to see the tiara."

"I will? I've never seen a real tiara."

"Yes, it's customary for the royal ladies to wear tiaras to formal events after six."

"After six?" Palmer asked. "It's *that* specific?"

"It is."

"Wow."

"The dresser will be in soon, along with the hair and

makeup person. So, if you have any questions you think I might not want to answer with them in here, you should probably ask them now."

Palmer thought for a second and replied, "You know what… Would you care if I just kind of watched the whole thing? It could be nice to include how the Queen gets ready in the piece."

"Somehow, I doubt that's what your editor is looking for," Elizabeth said.

"Would it be okay with you if I interviewed members of your staff over the next few days since you'll be busy? Maybe you and I could have another follow-up interview whenever you're *not* busy."

"Palmer, how long can you really stay here? You must have a life to get back to in New York," Elizabeth said instead.

"This is my job. I travel for it sometimes." The woman shrugged a shoulder.

"Your family?"

"They live in Pennsylvania. I try to visit when I can, but I mostly make it home for Christmas. They come to the city occasionally. I have a younger sister. She's got some special needs, and they spend all of their free time taking care of her, so it's not always easy for them to get away."

"What's your sister's name?"

"Camilla. She's my favorite person. I wish I got to see her more often than I do."

Palmer lit up when speaking about her sister. It made Elizabeth light up, too.

"How old is she?"

"She's fifteen. My mom was a little older when she had her, and there were some complications. She goes to a special school, has friends, and seems to be doing well."

"Ma'am," Rebecca said upon reentering the room.

"Are they ready?" Elizabeth asked with a tinge of disappointment in her tone she hoped neither Palmer nor Rebecca had noticed.

"They are, Ma'am."

"I'm sorry, Palmer. I thought I'd have more time."

"It's okay. I can still hang out, right?"

"Of course," Elizabeth replied, smiling. "Do you want to see the tiara?"

Palmer laughed a little.

***

While her hair and makeup were being worked on, Elizabeth answered some questions Palmer called *softball* questions. Elizabeth answered them but found herself laughing more often than she probably should be. When her tiara was placed atop her head, Palmer stared at Elizabeth in the mirror. Their eyes connected, but after a long second, Elizabeth had to pull hers away.

"Miss Honeycutt, I have to put on my dress now," she spoke.

"Oh, sorry. Right. I'll just wait outside."

"Thank you," Elizabeth replied.

Palmer left the room, giving Elizabeth and her dresser space. Once she was in the dress and had another once-over completed by everyone, it seemed, Elizabeth made her way back out to the sitting room, where she found Palmer on the sofa, looking into the fire.

"Wow," Palmer whispered when she turned to see her.

Elizabeth had chosen a black dress. It was appropriate since it was still the mourning period. She also had a white pearl necklace on that her mother had given her on her eighteenth birthday, along with the matching earrings. Her long hair was pulled up in a style she could only call the *Breakfast at Tiffany's* look, with her tiara sitting at just the right angle. She hadn't yet put on her gloves, but she *had* put on the black two-inch designer heels.

"Are you ready yet?" Victoria asked, entering the room dressed in a black dress and heels of her own.

"Lucky you, Miss Honeycutt. You get to see *two* tiaras

tonight," Elizabeth said, nodding in Victoria's direction. "This is Victoria, my sister."

"Excuse me?" Victoria said.

"This is Her Royal Highness, Princess Victoria Elizabeth Georgina Hanover of St. Rais." Elizabeth looked at her sister. "Is that better?"

"And *this* is?" Victoria asked, nodding to Palmer, who was still sitting down.

"Oh!" Palmer exclaimed and stood up, giving a slight bow. "I tried the curtsy before; I was really bad at it. Any chance I can get away with a bow?"

"This is Miss Palmer Honeycutt, Victoria. She's the reporter I told you about. And, Miss Honeycutt, you can also just shake her hand."

"*You're* the reporter?" Victoria asked.

"I'm also a Yankees fan, and I'm not too bad at karaoke if everyone's had a couple of beers before I go on," Palmer replied.

Elizabeth laughed. Then, she looked at her sister again, who was glaring at Palmer.

"I don't get baseball," Victoria finally said. "I prefer football."

"American or–"

"American football is not football. You play it with your hands. How is that *foot*ball?" Victoria questioned.

"They kick it sometimes," Palmer replied.

"Majesty, Your Royal Highness, you'll be late for your dinner," Rebecca said in her attempt to rush them all out the door. "I will have Jenny escort Miss Honeycutt out."

"It was nice to meet you, Your Highness," Palmer added, offering another bow in Victoria's direction. "Your Majesty, thank you for your time this evening."

Elizabeth couldn't help but laugh at Palmer's formality. It did *not* suit her, and that was what made it so great.

"It was nice having company around," Elizabeth said. "Rebecca, can you please see that I get Miss Honeycutt's personal number? I'd like to call her to arrange another follow-up since this one got interrupted, and I'd prefer not to have to call her at the hotel."

"Of course, Ma'am," Rebecca replied.

Palmer smiled. Then, Elizabeth and Victoria were escorted out of the room.

"Lizzy, be careful," Victoria whispered as she walked down the hall.

"What are you talking about?"

"With the reporter."

"What about her?"

"She's a *reporter*," Victoria reminded.

"Yes, I realize that."

"Lizzy, you're treating her like a friend."

"Is that so wrong, for me to have a friend? The one I had is gone now, Victoria."

"I know. But this is different; you didn't grow up with Palmer Honeycutt. She isn't a member of this family. She's an American reporter who's doing a story on you."

"How are things with David, Victoria?"

"Fine, deflect. You're good at that," Victoria scolded. "I'm only trying to look out for my sister. In case you haven't noticed, Lizzy, I'm all you have left. And you're all *I* have left. David doesn't count; he's not family yet. He doesn't feel the losses we feel in the same way. No one else can."

Elizabeth knew Victoria was right: she *did* need to be careful with Palmer. The problem was that every time Palmer was supposed to ask her the hard-hitting interview questions, they ended up having a conversation instead. Those conversations made Elizabeth smile and laugh, and she hadn't had that since before a bomb went off in front of a children's hospital. She'd be careful around Palmer, but she wasn't quite ready yet to give up having a companion around that just made her laugh.

"Miss Honeycutt?" Elizabeth asked into the phone hours later.

"Elizabeth?"

"Hello."

"It's after eleven," Palmer said.

"I know. I apologize for the late hour."

"It's okay. I was up. Is everything okay?"

"Everything's fine. I was just on my way somewhere."

"You're not at home?"

"I'm *going* home, actually. I was wondering if you could join me there tomorrow?"

"I thought the dinner was at the palace. I'm confused."

"If I give you an address, Palmer, can you swear to me you won't tell anyone I'll be there? It's imperative. You know about my heightened security."

"What? Of course."

"Do you have a pen?"

"I'm a reporter; I *always* have a pen."

CHAPTER 10

PALMER had been picked up from her hotel lobby again. Before exiting the building, she'd wrapped herself up tight in the coat she'd purchased, wearing the long underwear given to her under her jeans, and donning the gloves, scarf, and hat as well. She also pulled the fur-lined hood up over her head since she'd felt the biting wind every time the sliding glass doors of the lobby opened to let someone in or out. The trip to wherever she was going would at least be by heated car. When another man in a suit and tie – but this time, also wearing a long black wool coat – entered the lobby, she knew her ride was there. It wasn't someone sent by the palace, though. It was a car she'd ordered through the hotel.

Palmer had asked the hotel to get her a car to take her to an address about a block away from the one provided to her by Elizabeth, per the Queen's instruction. Before they'd hung up last night, Elizabeth explained that she didn't want to send a palace car to pick her up since those were recognizable vehicles and would draw attention. Palmer hadn't minded ordering a car of her own, and once she climbed in it, feeling the heat rush over her exposed face, she let down her hood, buckled up, and settled in for the ride.

When the car arrived at its destination, she bundled back up and climbed out. There wasn't any snow on the sidewalk, but there was snow covering grass everywhere else except for the street. She hadn't been outside the city, so this was her first time seeing a bit of a university campus dotted with older buildings and houses. While St. Rais technically became independent only a few hundred years ago, people had settled here long ago. The first ones to do so were the Vikings, who made use of their long boats to pillage any land they could get to. They'd claimed this island as their own, and later, around the time the Romans were attempting to conquer Britain, some of those people who had heard the rumors about those Romans fled and created their own settlement on St. Rais. That was how St. Rais became a little mix of the UK and Norway. Presently, St. Rais was also a haven for people wanting to leave their hectic lives in Sweden, Denmark, Iceland, and Finland, among others. Only recently, St. Rais had started marketing itself more as a tourist destination that no one was taking advantage of. It was cheaper than Iceland and with similar features. It was cheaper and less crowded than the cities people usually visited in the UK. One could have amazing views of the Northern Lights more often than they could in Norway or other Northern European countries and pay less for the privilege. That was what had drawn Palmer here; the marketing to tourists.

Now, she was approaching a small house that rested between two other equally small houses, with only a thin strip of snow-covered grass separating them. The yards were the size of postage stamps, and all three houses had smoke billowing through chimneys, likely more to keep the place warm than for anything else. Palmer stood in front of the address she'd been given, deciding to look around first to make sure she hadn't been followed. Then, she knocked on the door.

"Come in," the voice came from inside.

Palmer tried the door, which was unlocked, opened it, and looked inside.

"Palmer, come in. It's freezing out there," Elizabeth said from just inside the door.

Palmer closed the door behind her.

"I know; I just had to walk here."

"I'm sorry about that," Elizabeth offered in response.

"I checked to make sure no one followed me here."

Elizabeth smiled at her and said, "Security followed you from the hotel, Palmer. Don't give up being a reporter for spy work. And you can take off your coat now. The fire's going. You'll burn up if you leave all that on."

"Oh, right."

Palmer used the time she *hadn't* been taking her coat off to take in the more casual-looking Queen. Elizabeth was wearing a pair of jeans today that hugged her well. She had a beige cable-knit loose sweater and wasn't wearing any shoes but covered her feet in what looked to be thick wool socks. The woman looked amazing. Of course, she'd looked amazing in that dress the previous night, too. The tiara, the heels, the dress itself had all been fine, but *Elizabeth* had been breathtaking. Palmer shook off her coat, watching as Elizabeth, the Queen of a country, took it from her to hang on the sturdy coatrack.

"How is everything working out for you? Are the gloves all right?" she asked Palmer.

"I'm wearing everything you got me. I'm still cold, but I think I'll just be cold until I head back to New York."

"It takes time to adjust to these temperatures," Elizabeth replied, taking Palmer's hat, gloves, and scarf and placing them on the table next to the door. "I've made coffee. That should warm you up."

"What *is* this place?" Palmer asked her.

She looked around, finally pulling her eyes away from the casual Queen to notice a comfortable yet small-looking living room. It was furnished with a sofa that had a quilt draped over the back of it. In front, there was a relatively small television mounted to the wall, with floor-to-ceiling packed bookshelves on both sides. There were many books sitting on the floor beneath the television as well. On the wall with the front door, there was a woodburning fireplace with stacks of firewood on either side. The far wall had two doors and a few framed photos. The wall to her right led to what looked like the kitchen and maybe, something else.

"This is my home," Elizabeth explained. "Not exactly a palace, is it?"

"It's still bigger than my apartment," Palmer replied.

"How big is your apartment?" she asked, smiling at Palmer.

"It's a studio. I barely have enough room for the bed," Palmer told her, exaggerating a tad but not by much. "I chose to live in Manhattan, though; I knew what I was getting myself into. And it works for me. I don't need much space."

"Neither do I," Elizabeth replied. "Before everything happened, I lived here. I was in school, on my way toward my degree at the university, and planning to stick around to get my Ph. D."

"In theoretical physics, right?"

"That's right." She nodded. "This was really all the space *I* needed. I was usually in class, in the library, or here studying."

"No one bothered you in school?"

"Fifth in line, remember?" Elizabeth replied. "Most people were too busy focusing on my brother and his growing family or Alexander and his wedding to Teagan. Victoria and I were mostly forgotten about once Edwina came along. It was nice. I could disappear into my studies, and security could relax. Now, I have to take a covert vehicle in the dead of night just to get here because this place isn't nearly as secure as the palace."

"Why *are* you here, then?"

"As odd as this may sound, the palace is a bit suffocating to me. My closet there is probably bigger than this whole house, but I much prefer this place."

"It's nice. Feels comfortable." Palmer looked around and took in some of the book titles and the photos on the wall, recognizing a few with Elizabeth and her family, including one with her and her sister and another with Elizabeth and Teagan. "This place feels more like you."

"Would you like the tour?" Elizabeth offered. "It won't take long."

"Sure."

"Let's start with the kitchen. The coffee should be

done," Elizabeth said, walking past Palmer to head to her right.

What the hell did Elizabeth smell like? Heaven? Actual heaven? Whatever it was, Palmer was certain she'd never smelled that delicious scent before, and that included every other time she'd been around this woman.

"This is the kitchen. It's small. I'm usually cooking for one or maybe two people, though, so it works out just fine."

"You cook?" Palmer asked.

"Palmer, do I need to say that this is all off the record? I just realized I never asked that, and if–"

"Everything we talk about is off the record until you say otherwise," Palmer assured her, placing a hand on Elizabeth's forearm. "Oh, sorry. I didn't–"

"It's okay," Elizabeth replied.

"Elizabeth, are you sure you're safe here?" Palmer took in the tiny kitchen with its boiling kettle and empty coffee mugs awaiting their water and likely, instant coffee. "I like this house – it's a lot more welcoming than the palace, where I have to go through three layers of security once I get inside, and that's after another two before I get through the gate – but it's not nearly as safe."

"Are you worried about me?" Elizabeth asked as she began to pour the water into the cups.

"Of course," Palmer replied. "I took a palace car through the gate to see you both times, and they still swept the thing with dogs and mirrors to make sure there wasn't a bomb attached. Where is security around here?"

"Well, they followed you here covertly in unmarked cars. There's a guard at the backdoor as well. The back garden is fenced in and has security cameras, as does the front door. The house immediately next to this one has at least six more guards in it until I leave. Once I made the official move back into the palace, the press left this place alone. And the university is on a break this weekend, so the town is pretty much deserted outside of the locals who don't care when I *am* here. I'm about as safe as I can be outside the palace walls." She passed Palmer her cup after adding a sugar cube.

"Shouldn't you be *inside* the palace walls, at least until they catch that guy they keep talking about on the news?"

"I'm only here for the weekend, Palmer. I needed to get out of there for a bit. We've made every effort to make sure no one knows I'm here."

"Your chimney is literally churning out smoke," Palmer pointed out.

Elizabeth smiled as she picked up her own coffee and said, "That's normal. My neighbors usually take care of the house when I'm not here. They often build a fire."

"Seems like you have it all figured out, then," Palmer said.

"Trust me, I don't," the woman replied. "Let me show you the other rooms. The kitchen is eat-in." She pointed at a small two-person table. "I don't have a dining room, but I've never really needed one, either."

They walked back into the living room and then straight to the wall with the two doors.

"This is the restroom, and this is my room." Elizabeth walked past the bathroom without opening the door but *did* open the door to her room. "It's also fairly small, but how much does one really need in a bedroom? A bed, right?"

Palmer smiled as she took in the small room that was much smaller than the woman's bedroom at the palace. In fact, the room at the palace had a king-sized bed. This room didn't look like it could even fit one of those in it.

"True," Palmer said.

"Not what you expected for a Queen, huh?" Elizabeth asked, leaning into the open doorway.

"I try not to *expect* much. That way, I might be pleasantly surprised, but I'm not usually disappointed."

"Are you disappointed now?" Elizabeth asked.

"Why would I be?" Palmer asked back.

"I don't know. I'm sure I'm not the Queen you'd prefer to be interviewing." Elizabeth made her way with her coffee back to the living room. "Please, have a seat."

"Elizabeth," Palmer began. "I never thought I'd be interviewing a Queen. And I'm *definitely* not disappointed to be interviewing you."

"My sister told me to be careful with you," Elizabeth said.

"She doesn't like me very much, does she?" Palmer asked, sitting down next to Elizabeth on the sofa that was indeed comfortable.

"She doesn't care for reporters. There was an incident when she was sixteen and rebellious."

"I can understand that; not all reporters are good or ethical."

"But you are," Elizabeth stated rather than questioned. "I can tell that about you."

"I've had great mentors." Palmer took a sip of her coffee, which was delicious and warm, and rushed through her body, taking out the last remaining chill. "I just listened to what they taught me. Would I love a Pulitzer for whatever story I end up writing? Yes. But I'll go about it the right way. If not, it's just not worth it to me."

Elizabeth gave her a soft smile and said, "I'll put more wood on the fire."

"Here. Let me. You sit. You're here for rest and relaxation," Palmer reminded, standing up.

"You're a city girl… What do you know about keeping a fire burning?" Elizabeth asked, laughing as Palmer stood in front of the giant woodpile.

"Put wood in the fireplace. What more do I need to know?"

"You've never been camping, have you?" Elizabeth asked.

"No," Palmer said, turning around and pointing to herself. "City girl."

"Maybe we should work on changing that while you're here."

CHAPTER 11

"ARE you hungry? I should've offered you something when you got here." Elizabeth stood up from the sofa.

"I'm okay. Although, I *would* like to see you cook sometime."

"Why?"

"I don't know. I've never seen a Queen cook before."

"Well, I *can* cook, so if you want something for lunch, I can make it. I can make you whatever I have here. If you want something else, I'd have to send someone for it, go out to the backyard, and have them sneak it in."

"I'm not picky, but I'm also not starving."

"Come on. We can talk while I make you something because I *am* hungry. I skipped breakfast, and the dinner last night was a little too fancy for my taste."

"Too fancy for a Queen?" Palmer asked as she followed Elizabeth into the kitchen.

"I just became a Queen a few weeks ago. Before that, I was a college student."

"You were a Princess," Palmer said.

"Technically, yes, but also not really." She opened the refrigerator. "Did you know that my mother wasn't royalty? She and my father met when they were at university."

"I think I read that somewhere."

"She grew up here," Elizabeth said, pulling out a few items to make them a meal.

"Here, as in…"

"This house," Elizabeth explained. "This house belonged to my grandparents. The neighbors I mentioned before are actually my cousins, on my mom's side."

"She grew up *here*?"

"She did. They all shared this one-bedroom house together until she went to university. Then, she met my father and moved into the palace after they got married. When my grandfather died, my dad inherited the throne, and he moved her parents and siblings into a nicer place owned by the family. But my mom kept this place, and when I went off to school, she told me I could live here."

"Humble beginnings," Palmer said. "Can I help at all?"

"No, you can just sit over there and stay out of my way," Elizabeth replied, offering Palmer a playful smile.

"Yes, Your Majesty," Palmer replied sarcastically.

"You can better ask your questions over there."

"If I'm asking questions, I need my notebook and pen. One second."

Elizabeth began working on their meal as she waited for Palmer to return. When she did, Elizabeth glanced over at the woman who was opening her notebook to a fresh page and removing the cap from her pen.

"That's a fancy pen," she noted.

"It was a gift. I love this pen. It might be the best gift I've ever gotten," Palmer replied. "Well, that I've ever gotten from non-royalty."

"Right." Elizabeth laughed a little.

"Tell me about your mom," Palmer requested, and Elizabeth realized this was now the interview.

"On the record?"

"If you don't mind," Palmer said.

"I don't," Elizabeth replied. "My mother was an amazing woman. We were so lucky to have her as our mother. She somehow had this way of making being royal – which isn't always a good thing – fun or not as claustrophobic as it can feel, while also teaching us how important it was to do our duty to our country."

"But you said she didn't grow up royal."

"She didn't. She grew up poor, and because of that, she benefitted from several of the charities the royal family supports. People often assume we take tax dollars from the country to line our pockets or to renovate our many properties, but the truth is that much of that money goes right back to the people."

"Through charities?"

"Yes. The palace was built by the first King of St. Rais using his own fortune. That fortune was maintained over the years and passed down from generation to generation. Unlike other countries with monarchies, St. Rais doesn't pay members of the royal family anything. While it's true, we have free room and board, if you want to call it that, we receive no salaries. Any tax dollars that are, let's say, tagged for the royal family go straight back to the people. In fact, by law, we are required to report all of that publicly."

"You are?" Palmer asked as she took notes. "What, like a publicly-traded company?"

"Basically, yes," Elizabeth confirmed.

"Can I ask why people seem to think the monarchy here is a bad thing, then?" Palmer asked.

"You'd have to ask them," Elizabeth replied, stirring the food in the pot she'd placed on the stove. "We have many benefits; I can't and won't lie about that. Last night, I went to a dinner wearing millions of dollars in jewelry, and even though the food wasn't my taste, it was provided to me for free by a renowned St. Rais chef."

"That's what the people see, isn't it?" Palmer asked.

"Yes, it is."

"They should see *this*," Palmer stated.

"What?"

"You, cooking in this small kitchen for a guest; using food from your fridge in the home your grandparents raised their kids in."

Palmer's phone buzzed. She removed it from her pocket, looked down at the screen, gave an unreadable expression, and put the phone back into her pocket.

"If you need to take a call, you can use my room," Elizabeth offered.

"It's a text, and I'm okay. Thanks, though. Back to you."

"Okay. Back to me," she agreed.

"Can I write about this place, Elizabeth? I won't include the address or anything you don't want me to, but this is the side of you your people should see."

"We are *on* the record," she replied.

"I'd like to ask some questions about your family. Would that be okay?"

"Yes," she said but felt the lump in her throat as soon as she did. "You know about my mother already."

"Well, I suspect there's a lot more to know about her, and I *would* like to know more about her, but maybe I can dive into that more later."

Elizabeth looked over at Palmer and nodded at her. "Go ahead, then."

"What kind of father was the King?"

"Oh, *there's* a question." Elizabeth chuckled. "It won't work if I lie, so I'll be honest with you, Palmer. I'm sure Rebecca and Thomas will want to ream me for this."

"Do they know I'm here?"

"No, I didn't tell them. Only security knows you're here."

"O-k-a-y… I wish you well, then. I hope the lecture you get is a short one."

Elizabeth smiled and said, "I can handle it. I've been getting lectured since before I could walk."

"By?"

"Everyone," she said, still chuckling. "I suppose, it started with my nanny, then my tutors, and my teachers. My mother and father lectured me, too, of course."

"What about?"

"How to be a proper Princess. I was a little kid; I wanted to run and play, but we had certain rules about that. I was told to be careful more times than I can remember. Martin had it worse than all of us, though."

"Because he was next in line?"

"And the oldest. My father did the best he could, I'm sure, but he put a lot of pressure on Martin and Alexander.

Victoria and I didn't have nearly as much to do or worry about. On top of that, they were the two boys. They're required, as are all boys when they reach eighteen, to join the military for two years. Victoria and I were able to go straight to university without risking our lives."

"Was your dad strict because he was just being a dad or because he was King?"

"A little of both," Elizabeth replied honestly. "I think, had the circumstances been different, he would have been a stern father. It was just in his character. But circumstances weren't different, and he was a King raised by a King who then fathered a future King. He raised us how he thought he had to in order to prepare us to fulfill our duties to the country."

Elizabeth plated the food she'd prepared, turned off the stove, pulled sparkling water out of the refrigerator, and sat everything down on the table.

"Now, we eat, and no more interview questions until we're done. Agreed?" she asked Palmer.

"Deal," Palmer said with a smile.

They ate in silence for a few minutes, which felt oddly comforting to Elizabeth. At the dinner the previous night, she'd had to remember to start the conversation with the man on her right first. Then, when the second course arrived, she struck one up with the woman on her left. Neither person had said anything to her until she'd opened the conversation. It was an old and tired custom that she wanted to get rid of as soon as possible. Now, she was sitting silently with Palmer, and she didn't feel like she *had* to talk to her. She did, however, *want* to talk to her.

"What was life like growing up in Pennsylvania?" she asked.

"Worlds away from growing up here in a palace, I suspect," Palmer replied.

"How did your parents meet?"

"Blind date. A friend they shared set them up when they were in their mid-twenties."

"Blind date? That's kind of terrifying, isn't it?"

"Imagine being the guy that would show up to a blind date with *you*," Palmer teased. "He'd have to bow and walk backward if he had to make a trip to the bathroom at dinner."

Elizabeth smiled but didn't laugh at the joke. "It obviously went well for them: they're still together, and they have two children," she said instead.

Palmer laughed lightly and said, "Actually, their first date had been a disaster. My mom said she found my dad annoying. My dad said my mom came off as stuck-up."

"Really?"

"Yeah. And that would have been the end of it, but they were at that same friend's Fourth of July party in Philadelphia, which is kind of a big deal there, and started talking. At the end of the night, they exchanged numbers, and they've been together ever since."

"That's sweet," Elizabeth replied.

"It is. They still seem happy together even though it's been thirty-one years and things haven't always been easy."

"Your sister?" Elizabeth guessed.

"That too, but my dad's a teacher; my mom owns a small restaurant. Neither of those jobs brings in much money. I had to get a scholarship to NYU because we couldn't afford it otherwise, and when my sister showed up, she needed a lot of help. Her medical expenses and school add up, but they've stuck together through it all. It's a lot to handle, and I help when I can, but I don't exactly make a lot of money myself, and I live in an expensive city, so it's not as much help as I wish I could provide."

"But you love what you do? You love the city?" Elizabeth asked as she ate.

"I love what I do. I *like* the city enough. It's where I need to be right now, but if I found something else in journalism that I had to move for, I'd consider it, too. New York is an intense city. That's one of the reasons I needed a vacation to a place like St. Rais."

"*One* of the reasons?" Elizabeth asked, taking her final bite.

"Yeah, well, my girlfriend and I weren't doing so well, either. That was probably my main motivation for getting away."

Elizabeth took a long drink from her water before asking, "Is this the ex you were talking about before?"

"She is *now*, yeah. That was actually her texting me earlier. I asked her to drop my stuff off at my place and take whatever she'd left there before she dropped off the key. She was just letting me know she'd done it, so I guess that's it." Palmer took a sip of her own water and added, "Can I ask you something?"

"Sure."

"You heard the part about my ex being a woman. Does that bother you? I mean, is that okay?"

"If she hurt you, Palmer, then I'd say, no, it's not okay," Elizabeth replied. "But I think you're asking me if it's a problem that you date women."

"I'm a lesbian, yeah."

Elizabeth shook her head and replied, "It's not a problem."

"Good," Palmer said. "So, I'm done eating. It was delicious. I will now happily report to the world that you, Queen Elizabeth, are a great cook."

"Queen Antonia," Elizabeth corrected.

"What?"

"I'm taking my mother's name when I'm coronated. I'll be Queen Antonia I."

"So, should I call you Antonia now?"

"No, Palmer; that's just my formal name. You can always call me Elizabeth, or Lizzy even, if you'd like when we're alone." She smiled at her. "Or, if Victoria is in the room. She'd hate that."

Palmer laughed.

CHAPTER 12

"WAS Martin interested in being King, or was it just that he was born into it?" Palmer asked.

It was a couple hours after they'd shared a meal in the kitchen, and now they were sitting back on the sofa, staring at the fire as it burned, with one of them occasionally standing to add another log.

"Martin was, quite literally, born for the role of King." Elizabeth had a far-off look in her eyes. "He would have been a great one, too."

"How so?" Palmer asked.

She'd long ago set her notebook and pen on the table in front of the sofa, choosing to keep the interview more conversational since that seemed to work so well with them.

"He and my father had similar temperaments, but Martin had a bit of my mother in him, too. So, he was less stern than my father. He'd taken to learning more about the history of the monarchy in St. Rais from an early age all on his own. He used to tell Alexander and I that he wanted to be a good King, and he planned to put in the work to make that happen." Elizabeth paused. "I wonder, sometimes, if Alex would've been born first, if he would've been the same way or if he would have just been himself."

"Alexander wasn't interested in ruling?" Palmer asked.

"Alexander is interested in fun." Elizabeth met Palmer's eyes then. "Was. He *was* interested in fun. I still do that sometimes."

"It's been weeks, Elizabeth. You're not required to do anything a certain way; you know that, right?"

"Yes, I *am*. I'm the Queen. Everything I do has to be done a certain way. I can't make a mistake like that in a speech. I have the Christmas address to the nation coming up after my coronation. What am I supposed to say to the people of this country?"

"Hey," Palmer said softly, sliding over a bit on the sofa to get closer. "It's okay. You're not giving a speech right now. It's just me."

"And your story," Elizabeth replied.

"We're off the record right now, then. I can just be your, I don't know, sassy American friend."

Elizabeth smiled at her and said, "I don't have many friends."

"Why is that? *I* like you. I'm sure everyone else does, too."

"I had a few friends at university, but not many, and I didn't confide in them. The only person I confided in was Teagan."

"What's it like, having your best friend marry your brother? *That* had to be interesting," Palmer asked.

Elizabeth looked off at the fire again and said, "Palmer, if you don't mind, I think I'd like to be done answering questions for the day."

"Oh. I didn't mean that as a reporter. I was just–"

"I know; off the record. I'm just tired, I think."

Palmer nodded, taking the hint that it was time for her to go.

"Okay. I'll let you get some rest. I just need to call for a car to pick me up," she said.

"I'm sorry. I don't mean you have to go. I–"

"No, it's fine. I *should* go. I've monopolized far too much of your time off today. I hadn't planned on staying this long anyway. I should be getting back to the hotel." Palmer reached for her phone and dialed the number she had for the car service. "Hello. I'd like to get a car right now to pick me up." She gave the man the address down the street as her pick-up spot and hung up the phone. "They'll be there in fifteen minutes. It'll take me ten to walk there, so I should get going."

"You don't have to go, Palmer. I'm sorry. We were having a conversation, and I was rude to you."

"You weren't." Palmer stood. "I should get back and transcribe my notes anyway. I have to give my editor an update, and I could use some rest myself."

"Okay. If that's what you want," the woman replied, standing up, too.

"I just need to put on my coat, shoes, gloves, hat, and scarf. That should take about thirty minutes." Palmer laughed at herself to try to lighten the tension that had just entered the room that had been so relaxed only minutes ago.

"I'm sorry for the walk in the cold." Elizabeth followed her to the door.

"It's okay. It'll help me get acclimated, I guess."

"Why is that important? You'll be going home soon, right?" she asked.

Palmer turned to look at her and said, "I don't know. I guess I was just trying to find the positive in trudging through the snow and ice for the next ten minutes."

She slid on and tied her shoes, put her coat on, zipped and buttoned it, wrapped the scarf around her face, and reached for her hat. Elizabeth grabbed it before she could, though, and slid it over Palmer's head, pulling it down to cover her ears.

"Make sure to pull your hood up, too," Elizabeth told her.

"I will," Palmer managed out, swallowing. She then put on her gloves, reached for the doorknob, and added, "I'll see you soon?"

"Yes, soon," Elizabeth replied.

***

"Ma'am, I have a message for you," the bellhop said through the door.

"Message?" Palmer asked, opening the door to him.

"Yes, the front desk received this for you a few

minutes ago. I was instructed to bring it to your room." He handed her an envelope. "Have a nice evening."

"Let me go grab you–"

"Not necessary, Ma'am, but thank you," he replied and walked off down the hall.

"I need to start remembering to grab the money *before* I walk to the door," she muttered to herself as she walked toward the bed with the envelope in hand.

She opened it, revealing a one-page letter inside. Setting the envelope on the bed, she read the letter.

Miss Honeycutt,

I hope you can find it in your heart to forgive me for my rudeness earlier. I'm finding it difficult, I'm afraid, to keep things straight in my head where you're concerned. One moment, you're a reporter, asking me questions for an article. The next, you're a new friend, trying to get to know me. This is a position I have never found myself in, and I didn't respond well this afternoon when you asked about Alexander and Teagan. For that, I apologize. I hope that it does not make you think poorly of me. I also hope you don't rush off back to New York and remain in St. Rais so that we may speak again. I will help you finalize your article however I can, but I'd also like it if you'd join me in at least one day where we aren't reporter and source but two friends getting to know one another. If you would be amenable, I'd like to arrange for something for the day after tomorrow. You may feel free to call or email Rebecca with your response at your earliest convenience. If your answer is no, I will understand, but I would be remiss if I didn't try.

Sincerely Yours,
Lizzy

Palmer read the letter all the way through a second time, finding it adorably formal, but loving how Elizabeth had signed it with Lizzy. Truthfully, Palmer had walked away from their afternoon together a little discouraged, but not at all upset with Elizabeth who was understandably going through so much in her life right now. She wondered why Elizabeth didn't just call her. She had Palmer's number. Palmer couldn't call Elizabeth herself since her number had been private. Maybe Elizabeth had needed to write things down. Palmer understood that. She also knew that this letter was written by the Queen's own hand. That said a lot to her. If Palmer wasn't mistaken though, this letter was written in ink she knew all too well.

"I left my notebook and pen there," she said to herself. "Shit."

She checked her phone. It wasn't too late to call Rebecca, but she smiled when she got another idea.

Miss Rebecca Watt,

If you would be so kind as to pass along my formal acceptance of Queen Antonia I's invitation for the day after next, I would forever be in your debt. Please let Her Majesty know that I am available, if needed, by phone at any time should she require anything from me before we meet again. If you will also please pass along news of my change in accommodations to Her Majesty, I would greatly appreciate it. I will be departing from my current lodging tomorrow morning at standard check-out time and will be making my way over to the stately Holiday Inn Express approximately twelve kilometers from the palace gates and will be there for the remainder of my stay in St. Rais. I await the details of our departure the day after tomorrow. Have a pleasant evening.

Sincerely,
Miss Palmer Honeycutt

Palmer sent off the email, hoping Rebecca would forward it to Elizabeth. She wondered at Elizabeth's expression when she read it. Would she laugh? Would she think Palmer was making fun of her letter? She had a moment of regret but then decided that what's done was done and went down to the restaurant for her final very nice meal that the newspaper would be paying for before she'd be back to either standard room service or having to fend for herself.

"You're back," the woman from the other night said when Palmer sat down at the table next to her in the restaurant.

"I am," Palmer replied, picking up the menu despite not needing it to place her order.

"I was hoping I'd run into you again," the woman said. "I'm Sylvia."

"Palmer." She gave her a polite nod. "I see, you're already done with your meal," she noted, nodding at the empty wineglass and padfolio with the check sitting on the table.

"I was considering sticking around for another drink, and now you've just given me a reason," Sylvia replied with that same smirk.

"I was just going to grab something to take upstairs. I figured it would be faster than room service."

Sylvia gave her a glare and said, "You aren't interested, are you?"

"No, I'm not. But I *am* flattered."

"Not into women, or you already have someone?"

"Into women, don't have someone, but I'm kind of nursing a broken heart," Palmer replied.

"Well, I'm not looking for a girlfriend. I'm on vacation," Sylvia told her.

"I'm not looking for one night," Palmer said as the waiter approached. "Can I get the filet, medium rare, asparagus, and the house salad to take up to my room?" she asked him.

"Of course. If you'd like to give me your room number, I can have it sent up to you."

"That's okay; she's staying," Sylvia replied for her. "She was just trying to be polite and turn me down easy." The woman winked at Palmer. "If you change your mind, I'm in room 1203. I'll be here through the weekend."

"It was nice to meet you, Sylvia," Palmer said.

"You too, Palmer," she replied, standing up to go.

"Can you actually make my order for here and bring me your house white as well, please?" Palmer checked.

The waiter nodded and was on his way. Palmer had had the perfect chance to get Anna out of her system. Sylvia was a very attractive and obviously assertive woman, and Palmer could have had her underneath her in a heartbeat had she wanted to. As the waiter brought her a glass of water, Palmer realized it wasn't Anna whom she needed to get off her mind. With the exception of wondering about her stuff and her apartment key, she hadn't really thought all that much about Anna since their breakup. She *had*, however, been thinking a whole lot about a certain Queen, and that was a problem.

CHAPTER 13

"MISS Honeycutt," Elizabeth greeted Palmer as soon as she climbed into the SUV.

"Why are you always surprising me in cars?" Palmer asked while she laughed. Then, she heard a throat clear. She looked ahead into the middle row of the SUV, where she saw Rebecca already turned around, staring at her. "I mean, hello, Your Majesty. It's nice to see you. You too, Miss Watt."

Elizabeth laughed and said, "Rebecca, can you tell them we're ready?"

"Yes, Ma'am," Rebecca replied, turning toward the front of the vehicle to tell the driver they were ready to leave.

"I enjoyed your email," Elizabeth told Palmer.

"I enjoyed your letter, Ma'am," Palmer replied.

"Rebecca will leave us when we get to the palace. She just wanted to be here to go over the rules with you in person."

"Rules?"

"Yes, the rules, Miss Honeycutt," Rebecca said firmly, turning back around to her. "I assume you brought everything I asked you to?"

"Yes, the security guard put it in the other car."

"Very well. Her Majesty, *against* the advice of her head of security, head of public affairs, her private secretary—"

"Oh, don't forget, Victoria," Elizabeth interjected, holding up her hand.

"Yes, Her Royal Highness, Princess Victoria also objects."

"To what? Where are you taking me?" Palmer asked Elizabeth.

"You'll see," Elizabeth replied.

"The rules, Miss Honeycutt," Rebecca persisted. "You will have two guards assigned to your person. Her Majesty will also have guards. Even though you may feel like you're alone, security will be close by. Anything that is said between the two of you today or tomorrow will *not* be included in your interview. You agreed to this not being about your article, and it is, therefore, entirely off the record."

"No problem," Palmer replied.

"She understands, Rebecca," Elizabeth told her secretary. "Please stop scaring the woman."

"Ma'am, I must advise against this again. If you want a night with your friends, we can arrange something at the palace. I can phone your university friends, and—"

"Rebecca, it's done. It's been planned," Elizabeth replied.

"Fine," Rebecca said. "I'll give up."

"Should I be worried?" Palmer whispered to Elizabeth.

"No, everything's fine. She's just protective."

"Does she think *I'm* going to do something to you?"

"No, she's worried about whoever killed my family, Palmer. Everyone is."

"Then, shouldn't you be at the palace? We can go there. It's safer," Palmer replied. "I don't want anything to happen to you."

Elizabeth smiled at her and said, "I know. That's why I trust you."

They drove on for several minutes in silence until Rebecca got out of the SUV after asking Elizabeth one more time to reconsider her plans. Elizabeth declined yet again, and they went on with the driver and now three security guards in their vehicle, along with the ten to fifteen more in the following cars. Elizabeth watched as Palmer stared out her window, tinted so that no one could see inside the car but light enough for them to see out. Every so often, Palmer would smile at something she saw until they made their way out of the city and in the direction of the hills.

"Ma'am, can you tell me where we're going?" Palmer asked.

"I already told you." Elizabeth smiled when Palmer turned to her, confused. "The other day; I told you we should remedy–"

"Camping?" Palmer interrupted. "You're taking me camping?"

"Yes," Elizabeth smiled. "My family owns a large plot of land at the top of that hill." She pointed off to Palmer's side of the vehicle. "I've never actually been there."

"You've never been, but you own it?"

"My family owns a lot of property on St. Rais, Palmer. I've never had any reason to go up here. The last time I went camping with my family, I was seven, and it was at the state park on the other side of the island. We didn't sleep in tents, but it was fun. I've never actually been to the top of this hill and just stared up at the Northern Lights. I thought maybe you'd like to do that with me."

Palmer smiled as she said, "I'd be honored." Then, her eyes went wide. "Wait. Are *we* sleeping in tents?"

Elizabeth laughed and answered, "Yes, we are. It's going to be authentic."

"It's going to be cold," Palmer replied.

***

"Your Majesty, we've secured the perimeter," the guard said after opening her car door. "Your tent has been set up as well."

"Thank you, Magnus," she replied, climbing out of the vehicle. "Can you see that Miss Honeycutt's bags, as well as my own, get placed inside?"

"Of course, Ma'am," he said, bowing his head as she exited the vehicle.

"Your Majesty?" Palmer said from inside the SUV.

"Yes?" Elizabeth turned around and looked back inside, smiling at the confused woman.

"It's like, negative twenty out there, isn't it?"

"Fahrenheit or Celsius?" Elizabeth teased.

"Does it matter?"

"About nine degrees or so," Elizabeth replied.

"You're avoiding my question," Palmer said.

"The tent is about fifty meters away."

"What's that in feet?"

"One hundred and sixty-four," Elizabeth said. "Now, get out of the car."

"Did you just do that in your head?" Palmer asked, sliding out of the SUV.

"Yes. Now, let's go. The sun is going to be setting soon. If we want to walk around a bit, we need to do it now, or it'll be too dark."

"You want to walk around here? You said fifty meters to my tent and, I assume, a nice warm sleeping bag and space heater," Palmer replied.

"Don't you have winter in the States?" Elizabeth asked.

"Not like *this*," she replied, rubbing her hands together.

"Come on. Let's go to the tent."

"Tent, singular?" Palmer asked.

"Is that not okay?" Elizabeth asked back as they trudged through the snow. "There are tents for the security personnel; I can ask them to bunk together and give you your own tent. I—"

"It's fine. I just thought *you'd* want your own space," Palmer replied.

"I don't think camping in my own tent is nearly as fun as camping *with* someone," Elizabeth told her.

"Well, take me to it first, then. I'd like to warm up before we go on this little hike of yours, if that's okay. Plus, I need to change. You didn't tell me to wear my long underwear."

Elizabeth laughed as they arrived at their tent, which was surrounded by several others.

"Go on in. I'll wait out here," she said. "Magnus will have brought your bag in already."

"I should probably tell the paper they're paying for a night in a hotel I'm *not* staying in," Palmer said as she unzipped the tent and went inside. "Oh, my God, it's so warm in here!"

Elizabeth laughed further and then explained, "The same company that made your clothing makes these tents. They're very warm on the inside. Sleeping bags are as well. I promise, you won't be cold, Palmer."

"Ma'am, we'd like to know if you are in for the evening," Magnus said from behind her. "We have several fires going and can bring your dinner to you in your tent."

"Magnus, I'd like to walk a bit with Miss Honeycutt. We won't go far or be long." She glanced in the tent's direction. "Miss Honeycutt hasn't yet acclimated to our weather here in St. Rais."

"I heard that," Palmer replied through the zipped-up tent.

"I know. I said it loud enough so that you would," Elizabeth replied. "Would you give us some space on the trail? We'll follow your lead, and you can have men behind us if you'd like."

"I would, Ma'am, yes." He bowed and walked off to get his men.

The tent unzipped, and Palmer exited, zipping it up again.

"Okay. I'm ready to freeze my ass off." She looked over at a guard who had overheard her. "Sorry. I mean, I'm ready to... freeze my *butt* off?" He glared further. "I'm ready to freeze my butt off, *Your Majesty?*"

He nodded at her. Elizabeth could only laugh, though. God, she hadn't laughed this much with anyone, ever; not even... Her thought concluded when Magnus re-emerged with six men.

"Ma'am, we're ready."

"Very well. Miss Honeycutt, would you like to take a

walk with me as the sun sets?"

"I would love that," Palmer replied.

They started walking, with Elizabeth taking in the view of her country she'd never seen like that before. The hill overlooked the city, giving her an amazing view of its skyline and the palace just beyond it. It was mostly dark outside than not this time of year, so they relished in the sun as it stood in the sky. It always looked so beautiful when it set. Elizabeth sat outside many nights at her house and at Alexander and Teagan's place, too, watching the sunset. Tonight was different, though. Elizabeth was walking with Palmer, a woman she didn't yet know well but so enjoyed talking to and, somehow, knew she could trust with just about anything.

"Palmer?"

"Yes, Ma'am?"

"Just call me Lizzy; I beg you," she replied, chuckling at her new friend. "Magnus?" she said loudly.

"Yes, Ma'am?"

"I've given Palmer permission to call me either Elizabeth or Lizzy instead of Her Majesty or Ma'am. Please tell your men not to glare at her anymore. *You* are also welcome to call me Elizabeth, if you'd like."

"Ma'am," he replied.

"You'll get him next time," Palmer teased.

"No, I won't," Elizabeth replied softly. "His father served my father. He's a traditionalist. Also, why are you walking behind me?" she asked, turning her head slightly to see that Palmer was about one step behind her.

"Following the rules."

"Palmer, come on. You know I'm trying to stop some of these outdated customs. Back when that one began, people thought royalty descended from God or, in many cases, gods. I'm human, just like you. Walk beside me, please."

"Okay... But maybe you should make another announcement that you've given me permission so I don't get in trouble again." She moved up next to Elizabeth.

"You'll be fine. I'll protect you," *Elizabeth* teased her this time.

"Look at this, Elizabeth," Palmer said softly as they arrived near enough to the precipice to stand comfortably and look out at the city and the sun setting behind it. "It's gorgeous."

"Yes, it is," Elizabeth replied.

"You've really never been up here before?" Palmer asked.

"No. When we take our annual holiday, we go a few kilometers from here. There's a nice lake where the boys fish. Victoria and I mostly sit around and read." She stared out at the city. "When we *took* our holiday. The boys *would* fish," she corrected herself.

"You can still take holidays there. Victoria will go with you." Palmer tried to make her feel better. "Hey, this is amazing. Thank you for bringing me here."

Elizabeth turned to her and said, "It's going to get better, but we should get inside the tent for now. Did you notice the flap up top?"

"No, what?"

"You're going to like it," Elizabeth said, smiling at her.

CHAPTER 14

"IT'S a skylight," Palmer said when Elizabeth pulled back a flap at the top of their four-person tent. "It's going to freeze in here."

"I did bring a small heater, and you can climb inside your sleeping bag. I'll close it for now, though," Elizabeth replied, zipping up the flap that had a screen they could see through but that wouldn't allow bugs inside. "I promise, you will be warm. You can take off that coat now. You'll end up overheating if you keep it on."

Palmer unbuttoned and unzipped her coat, laying it beside the sleeping bag that had been placed out for her already alongside her bag, and she'd kicked off her shoes.

"Palmer, hat, gloves, scarf can all come off, too." She smiled and removed her own outerwear.

"Are we going outside anytime soon?"

"I thought we could spend some time in here, if that's okay. I have lanterns, and there's food. It's basic stuff for sandwiches, but the guys can cook us something over the fire if you'd like. I can also ask them for coffee."

"Maybe later," Palmer replied. "This is nice, Lizzy."

"That might be the first time you've called me that," Elizabeth said with an appreciative smile.

"Felt a little weird, honestly." Palmer slid fully clothed down into the sleeping bag, looking up at her. "It's going to take some getting used to."

"Well, I appreciate the effort."

"I think my paper is going to kill me," Palmer stated out of the blue.

"What? Why?"

"Because I've hardly written anything, and I specifically agreed tonight is about you and me as friends, not about the article. They're paying me to do nothing."

"You know you can stay at the palace, right? I mean, if you wanted to remain in St. Rais, and tell your paper they don't need to pay for it."

Palmer looked over at her, sensing something was shifting between the two of them.

"There are several guest rooms I think you would find adequate."

Was the Queen blushing?

"*Adequate* is the Holiday Inn Express, Lizzy. The palace is five-star all the way. Besides, I'm glad to be out of the resort. There was this other guest I kept running into. She…"

"She what?"

"Was very *bold*; let's just say that," Palmer replied, looking away from Elizabeth.

"Bold?" Elizabeth shook her head.

Palmer could see the shadow on the side of the tent made from the lantern light.

"She wanted…"

"Oh," Elizabeth began. "She wanted to sleep with you."

"I got that impression, yes." Palmer then looked back, wanting to see Elizabeth's reaction.

Elizabeth's expression was unreadable mostly, but her cheeks were flushed. Palmer had no way of knowing if it was because of the topic of conversation or the cold outside.

"You didn't want to?"

"No," Palmer replied. "I mean, I thought about it. After Anna and I broke up over the phone, I thought about going out and just having rebound sex, but… I don't know. That's never really been my style. It didn't feel right."

"Anna and you were together for a while, right?" Elizabeth slid down into her own sleeping bag.

They both stared at the ceiling of the tent then.

"About nine months before she opened things up."

"Opened things up?"

"She wanted to see other people. Anna is a lot younger than me. She's twenty-three."

"That's how old Victoria is."

"Well, I'm twenty-nine. It's only six years, but we started dating when she was just out of school. We're just in two different places in our lives."

"Do you love her?" Elizabeth asked.

"I *did*," Palmer replied. "I don't think I'm in love with her anymore, though, no. It hurt me when she said she loved me but thought we should date other people. To me, that's not love. I don't judge other people for wanting what they want, but I want one person; a commitment. If she didn't want that with me, then it wasn't meant to be. It took me a while to sort through the pain of her with someone else. Then, I just kind of went through the motions."

"How does that work?" Elizabeth asked.

"How does *what* work?"

"If she's with other people."

"Are you asking if we talked about it?"

"I suppose... Do you know who, how many, or anything like that? I don't know how it works with open relationships."

"Never been in one yourself?" Palmer turned her head to see that Elizabeth was watching her.

"No," Elizabeth replied.

"Makes sense. I don't know many guys that would have the balls to be with a Princess and then ask her if they could see other people," Palmer said.

Elizabeth looked toward the ceiling again.

"I'm sorry. I seem to keep saying the wrong things to you when it comes to this topic," Palmer added.

Elizabeth turned her head back and said, "No, it's not that." She closed her eyes for a moment before opening them again. "Yes, dating is hard when you're in my family." She inhaled deeply. "So, you and Anna?"

"I didn't know who she was with or what they did. Based on the conversation we had when we broke up, though, it sounds like she didn't go crazy. She slept with someone recently, and I ended it."

"Were *you* with anyone else? I mean, if she could be, you could be, too, right?"

"I could have, but no," she answered honestly.

"And you two still…"

Palmer smirked at her and said, "Yeah, we did. Well, in the beginning, we did. But as it kept dragging on and on, we basically stopped. We were pretty much just friends in the end who kissed occasionally."

"I'm sorry, Palmer."

"It's fine. Like I said, it wasn't meant to be. Maybe she was meant for the woman she met at work. Maybe she'll find someone else altogether. It's really not my concern."

"What about you?" Elizabeth asked.

"What *about* me?"

"You and love."

Palmer sighed and said, "Right now, I'm focusing on two things in my life. One is my work. The other is lying here with you, hopefully staring up at the Northern Lights soon." She gave Elizabeth a shy smile.

"Oh, that reminds me!" Elizabeth exclaimed.

Then, she shifted out of her sleeping bag, reached for her small suitcase, which looked more appropriate for a fancy hotel room than a tent in the middle of nowhere, and pulled something out. She turned around and held out Palmer's notebook.

"I left it at your place. Thanks," Palmer said, taking it. "Did you happen to find my—" Elizabeth held up her pen. "Pen."

"I did. I used it for my letter."

"I thought so," Palmer concluded.

"I felt bad using some of the ink, so I bought a replacement cartridge and a few extras for you. I have those in my bag. I can give them to you tomorrow."

"That's expensive stuff. You didn't need to do that."

"I wanted to," Elizabeth replied. "The more you write, the longer you stay in St. Rais, right?"

"You want me to stay awhile?" Palmer asked.

"I'd *love* for you to stay for as long as you can," Elizabeth replied.

"Ma'am, we need to talk to you," Magnus said outside beyond the tent.

"Magnus, what's wrong?" Elizabeth asked.

"Princess Victoria and her escort were out at dinner tonight."

Elizabeth shot up and unzipped the tent instantly, letting in the freezing air. Palmer shot up out of her sleeping bag, reaching for her coat to lay over her chest and arms.

"What happened?"

"The Princess is fine, Ma'am, as is her escort, Mr. David Wilson, but there were protests waiting for them outside the restaurant where they were eating. Anti-monarchists shouted and threw objects. The Princess is okay, but she was hit in the shoulder by a rock. The man who threw it was apprehended, as were a few other protestors who attempted to attack Mr. Wilson when he went after them to protect the Princess."

"Oh, my God!" Elizabeth exclaimed. "Where are they now?"

"The Princess and Mr. Wilson are back at the palace. The royal physician is checking on her now."

"I have to go. We have to go. I'm sorry, Palmer." Elizabeth turned back to her, looking terrified.

"Hey, it's fine. Of course, we have to go. I just need to put on my shoes and my coat, and we're out of here."

"Magnus, have everything packed up. We'll meet you at the SUV," Elizabeth told him.

"Yes, Ma'am."

Elizabeth zipped the tent back up. Then, her head fell to her chest. Palmer scooted over to her, placing a comforting hand on the small of her back.

"Are you okay?"

"She could have been killed," Elizabeth managed out. "My sister could have been killed tonight."

"But she wasn't, Lizzy. She's okay. She's going to be okay," Palmer told her, lowering Elizabeth's head to her shoulder and placing a kiss on the top of it, feeling immediately protective of this person she'd come to care so much about already. "Let's get dressed, and you can go see her. I can ride back to the hotel in one of the other cars so you can get to her faster."

"No. Please come with me," Elizabeth requested, lifting up her head to look into Palmer's eyes. "Please, Palmer."

"Yeah, okay. I'm there. Whatever you need," she said.

CHAPTER 15

"VICTORIA, are you okay?" Elizabeth asked, rushing into Victoria's palace suite.

"Lizzy, I'm fine," Victoria told her.

"The doctor gave her something for the pain," David added.

Elizabeth moved to the sofa to sit down on the other side of her sister. David was on Victoria's left and holding her hand, staring at his girlfriend with concern.

"What happened?" Elizabeth asked him.

"We were out at dinner. Security cleared it. They said they used the restaurant before, and it would be okay."

"I wanted one lousy night out. We've been stuck inside because of these people, and I wanted a date night with my boyfriend," Victoria said, sounding slightly slurred.

"While we were inside, people were gathering outside. Security interrupted us during the meal and said we needed to go. We tried going out the back way, but the protestors were there, too. A few of them started throwing things. I tried to shield her, but she got hit."

"I'm fine. It's just a little bruise," Victoria replied.

"What is it really, David? Where's the physician?"

"He left already. He said she has to take it easy for a few days but that she should be fine. He wants me to put ice on her shoulder a few times a day, but we got lucky, Your Majesty."

"You're going to marry my sister one day, David. Call me Elizabeth or Lizzy."

"Elizabeth," he said, nodding. "We got very lucky to-night."

"Lucky? She's high on pain medication. I'd hardly call that lucky," Elizabeth replied.

"They could have had guns," he added.

"I don't want to think about that," she replied. "Are *you* okay?"

"I'm fine. I got hit in the leg, and when I realized she'd been hit, I went after the guys. But I only have a few scrapes on my arms; it's *her* I'm worried about."

"David, thank you."

"For what?" he asked.

"For protecting my sister. She's all I have left. I don't know what I'd do if I lost her, too."

"Oh, you *love* me, Lizzy," Victoria said, giggling.

"I *do* love you, you stubborn idiot. No more going out until we can get this whole thing sorted."

"I don't want to be caged up, Elizabeth. I hate it," Victoria told her, turning her head to look at her now. "And it's not fair. *We* didn't do anything wrong."

"I don't think you should be at the coronation. You should move to the cottage as soon as you're healed, or better yet, we can send you somewhere unknown for a bit. We have enough properties that people don't know about."

"What? No way. I'm going to be at my sister's coronation."

"Maybe we can talk about this another time," David suggested.

"Yes," Elizabeth agreed. "I should let you get her to bed. She should rest."

"I'll take care of her," he said.

"I'll make sure the doctor returns first thing tomorrow to check on her," Elizabeth added, standing up to glance down at her sister.

Victoria stood up with David's help and gave Elizabeth a smile.

"I'm fine, Lizzy. I promise. Also, why is that reporter standing in my room? Am I *that* stoned? Am I seeing a reporter standing in my room, David?"

"There's a woman over there, yes," he confirmed.

"I was with Palmer when I got the news, Victoria."

"Palmer is a funny name," Victoria giggled.

"Vicky!"

"What? It is."

"She's right," Palmer said. "It *is* a funny name."

"See?" Victoria said, pointing with her good arm at Palmer. "She agrees with me."

"I'm glad to see you're okay, Princess," Palmer added.

"I'm Her Royal Highness now. When Lizzy became Queen, she gave me a promotion."

"Vicky, get some sleep. We'll worry about titles and everything else later, okay?" Elizabeth kissed her sister's forehead, adding, "I love you, Victoria Elizabeth Georgina Hanover."

"I love you, too, Elizabeth Antonia Victoria… What are your other middle names? It's a long list; I forget."

"Sleep now, baby sister," she said, kissing the same spot again through her smile.

***

"I really am glad she's okay," Palmer said as the door to Victoria's rooms was closed behind them.

"God, me too." Elizabeth breathed out for the first real time since she'd gotten the news.

"I can walk you to your rooms if that's okay. Then, I can see myself out. Or, if I have to have an escort, I can—"

"Will you stay, Palmer?" Elizabeth interrupted. "You certainly don't have to. It's probably wrong of me to ask, but my heart is racing like crazy right now, and I think I could use a drink and just, I don't know, *someone*."

"I can stay," Palmer replied, nodding.

"Majesty, how is Her Royal Highness?" Rebecca asked as she rushed toward them down the wide hallway. "I came back to the palace as soon as I heard."

"She'll be okay. David's taking care of her right now, but would you mind asking the physician to check on her again first thing in the morning?"

"Of course, Ma'am. Is there anything else I can do?"

"Palmer, do you like whiskey?" Elizabeth asked.

"Can't say I drink it often enough to know."

"Can you ask Jenny to bring us a bottle of our best whiskey to my room, Rebecca? Along with two glasses? Oh, and Palmer's bag will need to be brought up as well."

Rebecca glared at Palmer before nodding.

"Rebecca, you have nothing to worry about with me. I promise," Palmer said.

"Forgive me for not just believing that," Rebecca replied. "I haven't seen this article you're writing yet."

"You can see it before it goes to print if that makes you feel better," Palmer replied.

"Yes, it would." Rebecca nodded. "I'll have Jenny bring the whiskey and some food. Did you even eat dinner?"

"No, we'd hardly done anything at all, but I needed to check on her."

"Of course, Ma'am. I'll send up some food as well. Would it be all right if I stayed in one of the rooms tonight in case she needs me?"

"You may have your pick, Rebecca. And if you'd like, steal a glass of that whiskey for yourself as well."

Rebecca smiled a small smile before she disappeared down the hall and around a corner.

"Let's go. I suddenly find myself entirely too exhausted to stand," Elizabeth said, and they walked down the hall toward Elizabeth's room.

When they arrived in Elizabeth's suite, Palmer stood off to the side while Elizabeth headed straight into her bedroom. Before she opened a drawer to find something more comfortable to wear, she turned back around and headed into the other room.

"Your bag will be brought in soon. You can change out of your clothes into something more comfortable if you'd like. I'm going to do that now if that's okay with you."

"Oh, yeah. That's fine." Palmer shrugged.

"You can sit down, Palmer. I'll be right out." Elizabeth smiled softly at her.

"Okay."

She watched Palmer move to the sofa opposite the fireplace. Then, she went into her bedroom, closed the double doors behind her, and found some pajamas to change into. She didn't bother to take down her hair, which was now messy from being outside, lying on the ground, and rushing to the palace. When she pulled the doors open to her sitting room, Palmer was being handed a glass by Jenny, who then placed Elizabeth's glass on the table, looked up, and gave Elizabeth a curtsy.

"Your Majesty, I have your drinks and some light refreshments as well." Jenny motioned toward a table of meats and cheeses next to the open bottle of whiskey.

"Thank you," Elizabeth replied. "Is Miss Honeycutt's bag also on the way?"

"It's been placed by the door, Ma'am. If you'd like me to take it to one of the guest rooms for Miss Honeycutt, I'd be happy to."

"It's okay. You can leave it here for now. I suspect, Miss Honeycutt would like to change out of her outdoor clothes and into something more comfortable to enjoy her drink," she replied.

"Yes, Ma'am."

Elizabeth rolled her eyes at the woman she had grown up with who still wouldn't call her by her first name. When Jenny left them alone, Elizabeth moved to grab Palmer's bag and placed it beside her.

"You can change in my room," she offered.

"Okay. Thank you," Palmer replied, standing up.

Elizabeth flopped unceremoniously onto the sofa, reaching instantly for a slice of Swiss cheese and prosciutto. She was so hungry; she couldn't wait for Palmer to finish changing. She at least resisted taking a drink.

"I'm back," Palmer replied.

Elizabeth turned to look at her. Palmer was standing there, closing the doors behind her, wearing a plain white T-shirt with a pair of black sweatpants.

"Sorry, I didn't know what to wear. Rebecca just told me I was supposed to pack a bag."

"No, it's fine. You look great," Elizabeth replied, clearing her throat. "Drink?"

"I don't know that I've ever just drank whiskey," the woman said, sitting back down next to Elizabeth.

"You haven't? Why do I have it in my head an image of reporters all sitting around after a long day of reporting sipping whiskey or bourbon?"

"If that's a thing others are doing, I haven't done it myself."

"I can ask for something else. I have a small liquor cabinet in my office."

"No, this is fine." Palmer picked the glass up off the table. "This is the good stuff, right? Not the bargain basement swill? It's got to be good to start at the top." She held up the glass. "I don't know if this is an occasion to cheers."

"It's not, but we still can. You are about to drink really good whiskey for the first time."

They pushed their glasses together, creating that clinking sound. Then, Elizabeth took a slow slip of the warm amber liquid. She watched Palmer, her eyes over the glass, doing the same thing. The woman's dark eyes nearly matched the color of the whiskey, and Elizabeth nearly choked on her drink when she realized that.

"Well?" she asked, preferring to focus on Palmer's drink instead of Palmer's eyes. "What do you think?"

Palmer lowered the glass from her lips and coughed rather loudly at the same time.

"It burns," she said.

"Oh, God."

Elizabeth placed her own glass on the table, taking Palmer's with her free hand to do the same with it, and then leaned over to pat Palmer's back as she continued to cough.

"How do you just drink that?" Palmer was finally able to ask.

"I guess it takes practice," Elizabeth replied, smiling

even though she probably shouldn't be. "Sorry, it's smooth to me."

"Smooth? I would never call *that* smooth," Palmer remarked, pointing to the glass on the table.

"How about something else, then?" Elizabeth asked, rubbing circles over Palmer's back. "I have wine in my office."

"No, it's okay. I should probably just have some water or something after that. I think that one sip is going to get me drunk."

"You don't know how to handle your alcohol?"

"Not whiskey, apparently," Palmer replied, sitting back on the sofa, which meant Elizabeth had to remove her arm and shift back over to her spot.

"There's water in that pitcher. Maybe have something to eat," Elizabeth suggested.

"To at least get that taste out of my mouth," Palmer said, leaning forward.

"Blasphemy," Elizabeth said, laughing.

"Blasphemy?" Palmer laughed as well, but it sounded a little pained, as if the coughing had hurt her throat.

"Yes, that whiskey is my family's whiskey."

"What?"

"Remember how I told you the monarchy of this country is self-sufficient?"

"Yeah."

"Part of that is because we've had the ability to maintain the fortune of the first King by investing well and owning companies."

"That's allowed?"

"It is when we don't take funds from the taxpayers, pay our own taxes properly, and report our earnings as required, which we do. We own a distillery as well as two breweries – one for the nation's most popular beer and a smaller craft brewery."

"So, you're saying all your money is in booze?"

Elizabeth chuckled and said, "Not *all*, but some."

"Did I just insult your ancestors by not liking the whiskey?" Palmer checked.

"No, but you *did* make me feel like my father."

"I did? How, exactly?"

"He introduced each of his children in turn to this whiskey; Martin was first when he reached eighteen. Alex came next. I was a few years later. Victoria was after me, obviously. Martin, Alex, and I handled it okay. I had to grow to like it, but I didn't cough it up like someone I know."

"Hey," Palmer said, slapping Elizabeth on the leg lightly.

"Victoria, on the other hand," she began, chuckling. "Spat it out in my father's face. She sputtered and coughed, and he had to rub her back and talk her through it. Then, he laughed, and we all laughed with him." Elizabeth pictured that family moment in her mind. Her mother had been there, too, asking why he felt the need to share a glass of alcohol with each of his children on their eighteenth birthday. "She still can't stand the stuff."

"Good memory?" Palmer asked, watching Elizabeth closely.

"Yes," she said. "But then, the bad ones come in. I watched the video even though they told me not to."

"The video?"

"The TV stations were there for the grand opening of the hospital. They got the whole thing on camera. Rebecca tried to tell me not to, but I just had to see it."

"Oh, Elizabeth…" Palmer slid closer, wrapping an arm around Elizabeth's shoulders.

"Palmer, I don't know what to do. You can't write that in your paper. The country needs a Queen that–"

"Hey, I told you before, there's nothing to worry about. I wouldn't do that, okay?"

Elizabeth wiped back the tears and said, "Yes."

"You believe me, don't you?" Palmer asked seriously. "That I wouldn't do anything to hurt you?"

"I do," Elizabeth replied. "Now, if you don't mind, I'd

like to get some sleep. It's early, but the events of the day have gotten to me."

"Of course. Should I find myself a room, or will Rebecca or someone want me to—"

"There's a room next to mine that's available." Elizabeth stood up and walked toward the double doors. She pulled them open, moved into her room, and pointed at the door that led to the smaller bedroom that used to house the closest servant to the resident of her room. It had been redone into a very nice guest room. "This one."

"Okay," Palmer said, standing up. She grabbed her bag and walked into the bedroom. "I guess I'll say goodnight, then."

"There is a phone in the bedroom. Call the kitchen if there's anything you need. There should be toiletries and towels in the bathroom, but if—"

"I'll be okay," Palmer interrupted. "Sleep well, Your Majesty."

"Palmer, I—"

Palmer winked at her instead and said, "I'll see you in the morning?"

"Yes, you will." Elizabeth nodded.

CHAPTER 16

THE room was nicer than Palmer had expected, but the bed was a full and not the luxurious king bed in Elizabeth's room or the very nice one in the resort. The new hotel had a full bed as well, so she might as well just get used to this until she could get home and enjoy the one nice thing she'd done for her apartment since moving in: buying the queen-sized bed and very-high-thread-count sheets. She hadn't brought her laptop on this little adventure, but at least she now had her notebook, pen, and phone. Since it was still pretty early for her, Palmer decided to handwrite some of her thoughts on the article, thinking with each note that she wrote down about when and how she'd heard it from the Queen. She wouldn't break her word to Rebecca, but most importantly, she wouldn't break her word to Elizabeth. Anything she saw or heard tonight was completely off-limits.

As she lay back against the pillows after taking a shower, Palmer thought she heard something coming from her right, Elizabeth's room, through the adjoining door. At first, she wasn't sure she'd heard right, but after a few minutes, she knew for sure: Elizabeth was crying. Palmer closed her eyes in heartbreak for the woman next door. It wasn't fair for someone like Elizabeth to be going through this at all, but definitely not all at once. She'd nearly lost her sister, her last remaining family member, tonight. It was too much for anyone. Yet, Elizabeth had been strong enough to go on not only for herself but also for her country.

Palmer thought about playing some music on her phone to drown out the sound; not for herself, but for Elizabeth's benefit. She sensed the woman had a lot of pride and wouldn't like it if Palmer heard her crying. Palmer knew she couldn't just sit there and *not* do something, though. Instead, she dropped the notebook and pen, stood up, and went to the door. She knocked softly but heard no reply. Could she get in trouble for going into a Queen's bedroom at night without having permission? She probably would have been executed for doing it a few hundred years ago, but surely, she was safe now.

"Elizabeth?" she asked softly after opening the door just a crack.

"Yes?" Elizabeth sniffled. "Is everything okay? Do you—"

"Everything's fine. I'm fine. Are *you* okay?" Palmer asked, moving into the room uninvited but praying it would be okay with Elizabeth. "It's dark in here."

"It's nighttime," the woman replied, clearing her throat. "I was sleeping."

"Sleeping?" Palmer said before she could stop herself. "Okay. I'm sorry for waking you up."

"Did you need something?"

Palmer had to think fast. She couldn't yet see Elizabeth since her eyes hadn't properly adjusted to the total darkness of the room.

"No, I just wanted to know if you'd hear it if I maybe played music on my phone. I don't have headphones, and I was thinking about listening to it a little out loud. I wasn't sure how thick these walls were."

"You can hear me, can't you?" Elizabeth asked, sniffling again.

"Yes."

"I see." The sheets or blankets moved around. "I apologize. Yes, you are more than welcome to listen to music. It won't wake me up."

"Can I sit down?" Palmer asked, her eyes adjusting enough to see Elizabeth sitting up in the bed.

"Palmer, I just want to get some rest."

"I know. Maybe I can help," she said, moving closer to the bed. "Do you want to talk for a bit?"

"Not really."

"Okay. What if I just lay down next to you?"

"That would be inappropriate," Elizabeth replied.

"No, I didn't mean…" Palmer wanted to smack herself. "Not like–"

"Palmer, I'll be fine. I'm sorry I disturbed you."

"Right." Palmer lowered her head. "I'm sorry. I'll leave you alone. Good night."

"Yes, good night, Palmer," Elizabeth said.

Palmer returned to her room, closing the door behind her and wishing she'd never even opened it up, to begin with. She'd been right: Elizabeth was embarrassed now. And Palmer hated herself for making her feel that way. She'd only wanted to help; to hold her, or just let Elizabeth talk if she needed someone to listen. Palmer slid into the now-cool sheets under the comforter, turning off the lamp by the table and deciding tonight was just not her night. She'd close her eyes and try to get some sleep. Then, tomorrow, she'd return to her hotel, and that would probably be the end of whatever this new friendship was, given the Queen's reaction to her just barging in on her in bed.

"Stupid. Stupid," she chastised herself as she stared up at the ceiling.

"Palmer?"

Palmer froze. Was that Elizabeth?

"Yes?"

"I'm sorry."

"You don't have anything to be sorry for. I barged in on *you*," Palmer replied, moving to sit up.

"No, please. Stay there."

Palmer could make out Elizabeth's form moving around to the other side of her bed.

"Would you do what you said before?" Elizabeth asked.

"Which part?"

"Lie beside me?"

"I can follow you back to bed right–"

"In here," Elizabeth interrupted.

She slid under Palmer's blanket, and the bed was small enough that Palmer felt her cold feet against her legs instantly.

"Do you not have heat in your room? Your feet are like ice!" Palmer exclaimed, moving her legs back.

Elizabeth laughed and said, "Sorry."

"Just keep those Popsicles over on your side of the bed, Your Majesty," Palmer teased.

"Yes, Ma'am," Elizabeth replied, rolling to face Palmer.

Palmer rolled to face Elizabeth, making out her features in the pale light of the room.

"Are you sure you don't want to talk?" she asked her.

"I don't get to cry out there; even with my staff and with Victoria, I have to keep it in."

"So, you cry at night in bed?"

"Sometimes," Elizabeth replied. Then, she added, "Every night, actually, since it happened."

"Elizabeth, I'm so sorry," Palmer said, wanting so badly to place a hand on Elizabeth's cheek or around her waist to comfort her.

"So am I," the woman said. "With each good memory, I see the more recent, bad ones, and I don't know how to push those away to focus just on the good."

"What if you tell me about some of the good memories until you fall asleep?" Palmer suggested.

"I shouldn't be in here. You were trying to get rest. I should—"

"Was Martin a good older brother? Did he let you hang out with him, or did he treat you like his annoying kid sister?" Palmer interrupted.

Elizabeth gave her a soft smile and said, "It depended on how old we were at the time and who was around."

"He had to protect his reputation, huh?" Palmer asked.

"Sometimes. Other times, when it was just us, he'd teach me about stuff."

"Like what?"

"Martin was a big fan of the stars. He actually got me into science."

"Yeah?"

"When I was about five, he'd take me to the telescope; just the two of us. Victoria was too young, and Alex wasn't interested. He'd point it at something, stand back, and let me look at it. Then, he'd tell me what he knew about it. I'm sure some of it was wrong or made up. He was only eleven at the time, but it felt real to me, and I liked it."

"It was your thing."

"It was." Elizabeth gave a small nod. "We started doing little experiments. Sometimes, my mom would help. Other times, it was just us. Either way, I had a lot of fun with him."

"And you ended up studying physics," Palmer said.

Elizabeth didn't say anything for a long moment.

"Not that it matters anymore, but yes."

Palmer felt Elizabeth shutting down with the thought of her loss.

"And Alex?"

"Alex?" Elizabeth asked, her tone shifting back to where it was before.

"What was he like?"

"Rebellious second in line, if there ever was one."

"Yeah?" Palmer chuckled and shifted down more into the blankets.

"He never really settled down, either."

"Well, he got married. Some would say that's settling down, right?"

Elizabeth didn't say anything in reply, and Palmer worried she'd brought up another bad memory. She moved her legs over until she could feel Elizabeth's still-cold feet.

"I can feel how cold they are from all the way on my side. Give them here so I can warm them up."

"You're always freezing," Elizabeth said, laughing but allowing her legs to be captured by Palmer's all the same.

"Outside; I'm always freezing *outside*. Inside, I'm fine."

"I must be the opposite, then. It *is* a little cold in here, isn't it?"

"Is your room warmer?"

"Probably not. I didn't add wood to my fire tonight."

"There's no central heat in this place?"

"There is. It's on, but it's likely on low. I usually keep the fire burning until after I fall asleep."

"Queens put wood on their fires even in their *own* palaces?" Palmer teased.

"This one does," Elizabeth replied proudly.

Palmer laughed a little and said, "So, Victoria... Does she really not like me?"

"What? No, she doesn't know you. She only knows your profession."

"And I'm guilty by association?"

"Yes. But, perhaps, if you spend some time with her, you'll be able to change her opinion. She wants me to have dinner with her and David tomorrow night. I think he's going to ask her to marry him soon, and tomorrow night, he's likely to ask me for her hand."

"Ask *you?*"

"I'm technically supposed to give my blessing as Queen. I've already told her they don't need it, and they're free to marry as they please, but David wants to follow the tradition."

"A royal wedding?"

"Yes, most likely," Elizabeth said. "If you're free tomorrow night, maybe you could join us for dinner."

"Me?"

"Yes, Palmer. You *are* the only one in here."

"It just sounds like a family thing, Elizabeth. I'm not family."

She watched Elizabeth's expression change from playful to serious.

"You are quite right. I just thought Victoria could get to know you a bit."

"Oh," Palmer said. "I wouldn't want the night to be

about *me*. It should be about your sister and David, and you, too."

Elizabeth nodded and said, "Yes, I agree. Some other time."

Palmer watched Elizabeth roll onto her back, taking her cold feet with her.

"Hey, I'd like to get to know your sister."

"Of course," Elizabeth replied.

"What about the night after? Can I join a less formal thing then?"

"I'll speak with Victoria about it, have her check her diary."

"Diary?"

"Calendar," Elizabeth explained.

Palmer slid a little closer to Elizabeth and asked, "Are your feet still cold?"

It took a moment, but then Elizabeth said softly, "Yes."

Palmer slid out from under the warmth of the blankets and walked to the smaller fireplace in her own room that she'd failed to light earlier.

"Where are you going?" Elizabeth asked.

"Since you won't let *me* keep them warm, I'm going to start a fire for us."

"That's unnecessary. I should get back to my room."

"Nope, stay right there; you are sleeping in here tonight."

"I am?" the woman asked, laughing lightly.

"Yes, you are. You're telling me the good stories until you fall asleep, remember?"

"Very well," Elizabeth replied softly, and Palmer knew Elizabeth liked that idea.

CHAPTER 17

ELIZABETH could hear something, but she wasn't sure what it was. It sounded like yelling. *Who* was yelling? Why *was* there yelling?

"What's going on?" a muffled voice asked from behind her.

Elizabeth's eyes shot open. Who the hell was lying behind her? Why was their voice muffled?

"Elizabeth, what's going on?"

Palmer. It was Palmer Honeycutt, and her voice was muffled because her face was pressed against Elizabeth's neck. Elizabeth took one second to herself to think about how that felt. Then, she rolled over, forcing Palmer to do the same. Just as she did, the door adjoining their rooms opened wide, revealing her head of security and her private secretary.

"Your Majesty!" Rebecca yelled, covering her mouth immediately after.

"Rebecca, what is going on?" Elizabeth asked, shooting up into a sitting position.

"Majesty," the man next to Rebecca said, turning away so as not to see his Queen in her nightclothes, which revealed nothing anyway. "Your breakfast was delivered as usual, but you weren't in your room."

"We thought something had happened," Rebecca said to Elizabeth. "Call off the search," she added to the security head.

"Yes, Ma'am," he replied to Rebecca. "Majesty." He turned back and bowed before leaving the room, closing the door behind him.

"Miss Honeycutt," Rebecca said in a tone Elizabeth knew all too well.

"It's not her fault, Rebecca. *I* came in *here* last night." Elizabeth stood up.

"I should probably get dressed," Palmer said.

"Yes. I'll be in my room, Palmer," Elizabeth replied. "Rebecca, would you follow me, please?"

"Yes, Ma'am," Rebecca said but didn't take her eyes off of Palmer until Elizabeth dragged her from the room.

"I'm sorry I wasn't in my room. I didn't mean to frighten anyone," Elizabeth said, moving into her closet to search for something to wear.

"Elizabeth, might I ask what, exactly, you were doing in bed with the reporter?"

"You know her name, Rebecca. And I was with Palmer because she caught me crying last night, and the only thing that stopped me was talking to her until I fell asleep."

"Oh," Rebecca said, not finding any other words. "My apologies then, Ma'am."

"Palmer is a friend. I don't have any of those, Rebecca." She turned to her secretary. "Not students from the university and not truly even my sister, whom I love more than life itself but can't talk to her how I talk to Palmer; not now that we've lost so much. It's not fair of me to put it on her, what I'm going through, when she's going through just as much."

"Majesty, she's your sister. She understands."

"Maybe so, but I'm enjoying Palmer's company. She's been, I don't know; she's been a lifeline to me, Rebecca. I don't know what I'm going to do when she goes back to New York."

"Elizabeth, you know I worry about her being a reporter and what she might write."

"I know. I did, too, but I don't anymore, Rebecca. I trust her."

"She's really a friend? You trust that she won't report anything that might put you or this country in harm's way?"

"I do. If she wanted to write an article and ruin me or this family, she could have done that already. The things she heard and saw yesterday alone could have filled a book. She could have gone back to her hotel, wrote that book, and emailed it off last night, but she didn't. She stayed with me, Rebecca. She kept me company and helped me push the bad memories away. I believe her when she says we're friends."

"She still has a job to do. It's why she's in the country, Elizabeth. She has a story to write."

"I know. I plan to talk to her about that today before she returns to her hotel. I *would* like to get dressed and eat my breakfast first if that's okay with you."

"Of course. Shall I have something brought in for her as well?"

"Please. And make sure they include coffee for her, not tea."

"Yes, Ma'am," Rebecca said, nodding.

"Thank you," Elizabeth replied.

Rebecca made her way out of the room, and Elizabeth opened the door to Palmer's room after a soft knock and Palmer's reply to come on in.

"How much of that did you hear?" Elizabeth asked.

"None. I was in the bathroom. Is everything okay?"

"Yes, it's fine. Breakfast will be in my room in a few minutes. Care to join me?"

Palmer nodded and asked, "How much trouble am I in? Is *this* an off-with-my-head type situation?"

Elizabeth laughed and said, "No, you're safe."

Palmer ran a hand through her messy hair, which somehow still looked good.

"I'll just get packed up and join you," she said.

Elizabeth smiled at her and then closed the door between them; not for Palmer's sake, but for her own. She needed a minute to herself. The past few weeks had been overwhelming and terrible, but the past several days had been surprisingly pretty good; still overwhelming, but in a completely different way.

***

"The doctor said it's fine. It's a pretty massive bruise, but no internal damage," Victoria replied. "I only needed the meds yesterday because I was a little in shock."

"I imagine so," Elizabeth replied, taking a drink of her rich red wine. "And he's sure there's nothing beyond the bruise?"

"X-rays were taken. Nothing else," Victoria assured.

"I guess that's something."

"They arrested everyone that was there. Some people are now protesting the protestors getting arrested," David said. "Victoria could have been killed."

"They don't care about that," Victoria replied. "They don't want us here anymore. There's been a lot of anti-monarchist influence coming from the UK in recent years. More and more nations with remaining monarchies as well as a Parliament are eliminating the monarchies altogether."

"That makes sense in nations where the taxpayers fund the monarchy and their economies are declining," Elizabeth explained.

"They don't trust us anymore," Victoria stated. "As much as we disclose to them about how we take the taxpayer money that *is* assigned to us, if you can even call it that, and give it all back to the country, they'll never believe us."

"What are you supposed to do if you're already telling the whole truth?" David asked as he finished his own wine, reached for the bottle, poured more into Victoria's glass first and then his own, noting with a nod that Elizabeth's was already full.

"Let's talk about something a little more positive, shall we?" Elizabeth asked.

"Yes, let's." Victoria leaned over the table toward her sister. "So, I heard from a little birdie that something rather interesting happened this morning."

"Who's your little birdie?" Elizabeth asked, pushing her plate away.

"Jenny."

"Jenny wasn't even here this morning."

"She wasn't, but Bridget was, and she heard from someone who heard from someone else that you woke up *with* a certain someone this morning." Victoria lifted an accusing eyebrow at her sister.

"And you didn't help the situation by putting an end to the gossip?"

"No, but I didn't *add* to it."

"Should I maybe run to the loo?" David asked.

"No. If you're going to be part of this family, you might as well stay," Elizabeth replied. "And on that note, don't we have something *else* to talk about at this dinner?"

David nervously cleared his throat and said, "Yes, but I was hoping to speak with you alone if you don't mind, Ma'am."

"Oh, he gave you the *Ma'am...* He means business," Victoria teased and took David's hand. "David, she knows. *I* know. Just ask her."

"Don't ruin the man's plans, Vicky," Elizabeth said, smiling at her sister. "But yes, we do both already know, David. And this family could do with some good news, so out with it."

He cleared his throat again and said, "Well, Your Majesty, I would very much like to marry Her Royal Highness, Princess Victoria, and–"

"Oh, my God! Just ask her, David!" Victoria laughed out.

"I'm trying to do this the right way, Vicky," he argued and then wiped his now sweaty brow.

"Don't let my annoying little sister get in your way, David," Elizabeth said, smiling still at Victoria.

"Can I marry your sister?" David finally asked, giving up on the formalities.

"Of course, you can. If Victoria wants to be your wife, you have my blessing." She turned to look at Victoria, who was smiling at her, likely, future husband. "And Dad would have given you his blessing, too."

"You think so? David *is* British."

"He wouldn't have held that against him once he saw how happy David makes you," Elizabeth replied.

"Thank you," Victoria said softly.

"I'm happy for you both," Elizabeth replied.

"Now, David and I will talk more later about us, but don't think I'm letting you off the hook for the whole reporter-in-your-bed thing this morning."

"It's not nearly as scandalous as you've been led to believe. We simply fell asleep," Elizabeth said.

"In the same bed, Lizzy?"

"Yes, we were talking. After what happened to you, Palmer and I were talking, and I fell asleep. That's all there is to it."

"In the old servant's quarters that we never use anymore?"

"Yes. I told her to sleep there since our plans had gotten ruined by the attack on you and David. When I couldn't sleep, I went in, and we talked. Then, I fell asleep, and we woke up to shouting because Rebecca thought something had happened to me."

"That *is* less scandalous than I'd been led to believe." Victoria shrugged a shoulder dismissively. "Disappointing."

"What exactly did you think happened?" Elizabeth asked, laughing at her sister's reaction.

"Nothing specific. I just worry about you, given the entire reason she's here is to get a story out of you about our family."

"Actually, as I told Rebecca earlier, that's not the case. Had that been the case, she would have left last night. She stayed because we're becoming friends."

"You're becoming friends with a reporter?" Victoria asked. "Is that wise? Maybe any other time, it would've been fine, but with what's going on right now... I just worry about you, Lizzy."

"I'm fine." Elizabeth took a long drink of her wine. "Besides, she'll be leaving soon anyway. Palmer has a life to get back to that doesn't include me." She swallowed hard, and not just because of the wine.

"Does that bother you?" Victoria asked.

"Bother me?"

"You're becoming friends with her, and she's leaving."

"I assume we'll stay in touch," Elizabeth replied. "I *hope* we do anyway."

"What happens if she really was just in it for the story? Or, if it's too hard to keep in touch with the time difference, your work, and hers when she gets home?"

Elizabeth didn't like thinking about that. Although, she probably *should* start thinking about it. Palmer would be leaving. It might be in a day, a week, or a month, but she would be going back to New York, and Elizabeth would find herself alone again in a country that, apparently, no longer wanted her or her role, and with only a younger sister who was about to be married. Victoria would be starting a life with David, living in Coburn Cottage, not the palace. She'd be safe there, which was important, but it also made Elizabeth feel even lonelier than she thought possible.

CHAPTER 18

PALMER had spent much of the day working on her piece. It was the piece that wouldn't be sent to her editor, but she still worked. She found it enjoyable to type out how she'd spent her time with the Queen thus far, even changing from referring to Elizabeth by title in what she was writing to using her actual name. She *did* owe her office an update, though, so she also typed up a quick email and sent it off to her editor. She had several pages of a rough draft ready to go, and she had spent much of her time combing through it to ensure she wouldn't be violating Elizabeth's trust with anything she'd typed already. Their friendship was far more important to Palmer now than the story or any acclaim that may come from it one day.

The email that had come not from work but from her ex-girlfriend, though, had been surprising. That was what currently occupied Palmer's thoughts as she sat on the uncomfortable bed in her hotel room, sipping lukewarm, overly acidic coffee from the in-room machine. Anna was asking for another chance. She missed Palmer. She loved Palmer. She was ready to stop the open relationship and commit. Palmer rolled her eyes at Anna's antics. One day, they were happy. They were in love. They were planning a future together. The next, Anna was telling her she wanted to see other people. When Palmer had agreed reluctantly, Anna ended up finding someone else. They ended their relationship. Now, Anna wanted to commit? It was too much to deal with and not at all something Palmer was interested in.

It should tell Palmer something that after breaking up

with a woman she'd once thought about sharing her life with, she had hardly thought about Anna at all. It was true that she was in another country, pursuing a story, and that things would've probably been different if she was in her studio apartment staring at the photo of the two of them next to her bed or going through the box of stuff Anna had left along with her key. Even so, Palmer found her mind, as well as her heart, constantly drawn to another woman.

She needed to stop this. She couldn't be feeling this way. Elizabeth was a Queen. But even if she wasn't... Even if Palmer had met Elizabeth under a different circumstance while on this trip, they'd still be headed in different directions. Palmer's was home to New York. She'd never been against long-distance relationships on principle, but she also wasn't looking for one and wanted a girlfriend she could be with more often than not. Palmer shook her head then and laughed. As if Elizabeth, the Queen of St. Rais, would ever be her *girlfriend.*

She responded to Anna's email and added a few more pages to the story she'd be turning in to the paper once complete. Then, she thought about what Elizabeth was doing at that very moment. Dinner was probably over by now unless it had gone long. Maybe the woman was working in her office. Maybe she was lying in bed. Was she thinking about Palmer? No, she was probably thinking about the family she'd lost along with the life she would have had, had some horrible person not killed most of her family. Palmer wished she had Elizabeth's direct number. She wanted to call her, to talk to her until she fell asleep if that was what Elizabeth needed to get through the night. Palmer, however, wouldn't dare call or email Rebecca to request that information. It would likely only end with yet another warning from the secretary.

Her phone dinged from its position next to her on the bed. Palmer reached for it, thinking it was likely someone from back home, given the late hour here. She was pleasantly surprised to see a private number with a text message.

She opened the app and read it. Then, she clicked on the number that had been included with it and listened to the ring.

"Hi," Elizabeth greeted.

"Is this the personal phone number of the Queen of St. Rais?" Palmer teased.

"It is, but if you give it to anyone, I can have it changed in a heartbeat."

Palmer laughed and said, "I wouldn't dare. How was dinner?" She relaxed against her flattened pillows.

"David asked me for Victoria's hand in marriage. It was quite sweet. He was very nervous."

"And you said no, obviously," Palmer teased.

"I said yes." Elizabeth laughed. "He loves my sister, and she loves him."

"I guess that's a good enough reason."

"It's the *only* reason, in my opinion," Elizabeth replied.

"I agree," Palmer said, thinking about the faceless man Elizabeth would likely soon marry and trying to shove that thought out of her mind and just focus on this conversation. "So, how are *you*?"

"You just saw me this morning. I'm the same," Elizabeth said.

"Are you? It's late. I assume you're in bed."

"I am, yes."

"Are you going to be able to sleep?" Palmer asked.

"I hope so," the woman replied. "But I was hoping I might see you tomorrow. That's why I called."

"Yeah, I'm free."

"Palmer, I know you have an article to write, but I meant as a friend. I'd like to see you again as a friend."

"That's what I meant, too, Elizabeth."

"Am I hindering your ability to do your job by asking for that?"

"Yes, but I don't care," Palmer said honestly.

"What do you mean?"

"I mean that you're more important than a story,

Lizzy," she replied. "I have a job to do, yes, but I don't know how long I'm going to be here for, and I can work on my story from anywhere. If I'm only here for another few days, I'd rather spend them with you." Palmer swallowed. "As friends."

Elizabeth was silent for what felt like a full minute.

"Would you be able to stay in St. Rais for my coronation?"

"Your coronation? That's in a couple of weeks, right?"

"It's in ten days," Elizabeth replied. "I would love it if you could stay and attend. I understand if you have to get back; your life is in New York. If you can stay, though, I'd be happy to pay for–"

"No, it's fine. I can stay," Palmer interrupted.

"You can?"

"I just need to let the paper know. They'll love a reporter being at the coronation. It would put a real bow on the whole piece."

Elizabeth was silent again.

"Elizabeth, I won't be there as a reporter. I'll be there as your *friend*. I won't write anything you don't want me to. I just meant that I'll be able to swing it with the paper that I need to stay through your coronation."

"I understand," Elizabeth said.

"Do you?"

"I'll admit that I'd prefer there be no strings with your paper. That's why I offered to pay for you to stay here. If they're footing the bill, you have obligations to them, and I'd rather–"

"You're right," Palmer interrupted. "You're right. I'll ask my editor for some time off."

"You don't–"

"It's okay. I've only taken a few days off since I started at the paper. They owe me the time. I can tell my boss I'll finish the article when I get home. The rest of my trip here will be on me."

"On *me*, Palmer. You–"

"I can't let you pay for me to stay in the country, Elizabeth. Besides, my flight is already taken care of, and this hotel isn't expensive."

"Stay in the house," Elizabeth blurted out.

"What house?"

"My house; the one you visited before. I'd let you stay in the palace, but that caused some rumors this morning. The house is empty, Palmer. I'd love for you to stay there."

"That's *your* house, Elizabeth."

"And I'm inviting a guest to stay," Elizabeth replied. "If your paper won't be paying for you to remain here, the least I can do is let you stay in my empty house. You're staying here for me, Palmer."

"Are you sure?" Palmer checked, uncertain if she should impose in this way but also secretly wanting to stay somewhere Elizabeth considered home.

"Of course. You can move there tomorrow if you'd like. I can't join you there, but if you could come to the palace afterward, maybe we could have lunch."

"Okay. I'll talk to my editor and make sure it's okay with him."

"Palmer?"

"Yeah?"

"Thank you. You have no idea how much this means to me. Sometimes, it's so lonely here, even though the building is filled with people."

"I know," Palmer said softly. "And you don't have to thank me. If I'm being honest, I'm not quite ready to leave St. Rais yet."

"You're not ready to go home?"

"I'm ready to wear clothes I haven't been wearing every day for the past few weeks." She laughed at her own joke and then sobered. "But no, I'm not ready to go back home. I'm still hoping I'll get to see the Northern Lights with you on that hill."

"I'm sorry we weren't able to last night," Elizabeth replied.

"Me too," Palmer said.

"But I don't know if I'll be able to get away to do that again, unfortunately, Palmer. I don't want to make you any promises I can't keep."

"It's okay. I know you're busy. There's the country, the coronation, the investigation into what happened with your family, the attack on Victoria and David, and probably a royal wedding soon. It would be a lot for anyone."

"You're keeping me together through all of it," Elizabeth said seriously. "You are, Palmer. I don't know how, but you've helped me so much since we met."

"If I've helped at all, that makes me very happy. I hate to think of you in that room alone," she said. "You're really in bed already?"

"Yes."

"Are you going to be able to sleep now?"

"Probably," Elizabeth replied.

"Do you want to talk for a while?" Palmer asked her.

"Yes," she said. "Is that okay?"

"What do you want to talk about?"

"You. I'm so tired of talking about me. I feel like that's all I've been doing lately."

"Okay. I can talk about me. Give me a topic, though."

Palmer stood, pulled back the thin blanket and sheets, and slid beneath them.

"Okay… What was your least favorite subject in school?"

"Oh, that's easy, but you're not going to like it." Palmer chuckled as she settled against the pillows.

"Why not?"

"Because it's science."

"What? How can you not like science?"

"My dad is a science teacher," Palmer replied. "And get this: when I was in grade school, he was *my* teacher. When I finally made it out of that school and into high school, he became a high school teacher. I literally had my father as my science teacher from second grade through tenth. Then, finally, I took chemistry, and he wasn't a chemistry teacher."

Elizabeth laughed and asked, "Was he a tough grader?"

"No, he was fair, I think. It's just annoying to have your dad as your teacher. I had to ride with him to school each day and wait until he was done so that I could leave, when everyone else left after their last class. I was so happy when I got my driver's license and this old beat-up Ford so I could finally drive myself."

"We don't get licenses here until eighteen, so you were lucky."

"*You* have a license?"

"No, members of the royal family don't get them, but we can still drive. We rarely drive ourselves places, though."

"I never took physics. I finished chemistry, met my requirements for graduation, and left science behind in college."

"That's so unfortunate; science is amazing."

"I'll take your word for it." Palmer laughed.

"Did you have any pets growing up?" Elizabeth asked.

"I had a dog while I was growing up. Her name was Flash."

"Flash?"

"Yeah. She was the slowest dog in the world, lazy as could be, but we didn't know that when we got her as a puppy. It ended up being a funny family joke."

They talked like that for the next few hours until she could hear Elizabeth's words slowing as she spoke more softly into the phone.

"Your Majesty, I think it's time for bed," Palmer said with her own eyes closed from exhaustion.

"You're probably right. It's late."

"I'll see you tomorrow?" Palmer asked, hopeful.

"Yes. And Palmer?"

"Yeah?"

"You can save this number and use it if you'd like."

"I'd like that," Palmer said, smiling.

CHAPTER 19

"WE don't have an extradition treaty with them, Ma'am," Albert told her. "If we want him back on our soil, we can't risk him leaving St. Rais."

"Where is he now? Why can't we find him?" Elizabeth asked the Prime Minister.

"We believe he has a small faction of loyal supporters in the northeast."

"And he's staying with one of them?"

"He's likely moving from place to place so as not to get caught. We can only search places lawfully, which means we have to have cause to enter homes if we don't have permission. We could ask Parliament to issue a temporary order to allow us to search without cause."

"No, that would only give the anti-monarchists another reason to hate the monarchy. As much as I want this man and all of his followers responsible caught, I won't break the law in doing so."

"If you'll permit me, Ma'am; I wanted to say that you are an honorable woman. You will make a good Queen for this country."

"Thank you, but I'm not so sure." Elizabeth sighed.

"I worked with your father, Ma'am, and you're quite on par. He was also raised and *trained* to be King. You had to take this role on under unimaginable circumstances and with very little guidance or help. It's interrupted your life, and you haven't faltered. That's quite impressive in my book."

"Well, thank you, but it's still early."

"Shall we talk about the coronation?" Albert offered.

"Yes," she said.

"The ceremony itself is simple. It should take under five minutes. Your speech will be given to you by tomorrow for your review and approval. I will speak before you, and my speech will also be given to you for you to review, but I've already included words regarding my faith in you and in the monarchy as both strong and relevant today."

"Thank you."

"Rebecca will go over more specific details with you, and you'll rehearse the processional in a few days. Security is already hard at work at the cathedral, ensuring your safety as well as the safety of everyone else attending. There will be people outside and on the road leading up to the building. Security will review anything you need to know with you, but they've already cordoned off the areas and ensured people will not be in close proximity to the building or the road."

"That's sad that that has to be done."

"It will be a no-frills ceremony, per your request."

"It's appropriate," she said.

"There are a few matters of State we should discuss as well," Albert added.

***

By one in the afternoon, Elizabeth was exhausted. She'd had five meetings already and had another few to go after lunch, but lunch was the one thing she was actually looking forward to. Palmer was scheduled to arrive any minute, and Elizabeth couldn't wait to see her. Talking to Palmer for hours last night had allowed her to have a restful night's sleep. In fact, the past two nights had been the best sleep she'd gotten since before she'd lost her family.

"Your Majesty, Miss Palmer Honeycutt has arrived," Jenny announced, opening the door to Elizabeth's sitting room.

"Thank you, Jenny. Send her in."

Jenny gave a curtsy and left the room. Palmer entered and closed the door behind herself.

"Hi," she greeted with a smile.

"Hi," Elizabeth replied, smiling at Palmer, too.

For some reason, a blush crept up her cheeks. Elizabeth lowered her head to try to keep Palmer from noticing.

"So, are we eating in here?"

"Yes, they'll bring it in shortly. I asked them not to until you arrived. Please, have a seat." Elizabeth motioned with an open palm to the small table over by the bay window. "I've been eating here alone most days. It'll be nice to have some company."

"This company is tired," Palmer replied.

"I kept you up last night." Elizabeth nodded. "I'm sorry."

"No, it's not that." Palmer chuckled as they both walked to the table. "I *did* stay up late last night, but I had to talk to my editor about the piece this morning, tell him I'm taking some time off around your coronation, and then check out of a second hotel in as many days. I have my stuff out in the hallway. I didn't know what else to do with it."

"I'll have a car take you to the house after lunch. You can make yourself at home there. I was able to remove most of my clothes from the wardrobe, so please, use whatever space you need. I've asked my staff to make sure it's fully stocked with wood, food, and coffee, of course."

"You didn't have to do that. I could have gone shopping."

"I wanted to," Elizabeth said as she sat down. She noted Palmer didn't wait for her to sit down first, which made Elizabeth smile. "You'll also have a car at your disposal, and two security officers will be staying in the house next door should you need anything."

"*I* don't need security," Palmer remarked.

"It's *my* house, Palmer. It's better to be safe. People know I'm at the palace leading up to the coronation, so nothing should happen there, but I don't want you to be alone in case something does."

"Thank you. I hadn't thought about that, honestly."

"Of course," she replied.

The door opened, and Jenny came back in with a cart carrying their lunch. She pushed it over to their table and began placing their food, tea, and coffee for Palmer in front of them. Palmer and Elizabeth were silent until Jenny left with a thank you from Elizabeth.

"Are you no longer here for the paper?"

"Technically, I'm working today and tomorrow, but the day after, I am no longer here on the paper's dime. I promised my editor I'd have a rough draft of the story for him to review. I'd like to give it to you and Rebecca today to check it over first, if that's okay. It's not done yet. It's rough, but I think it'll make *The Courier* happy. I hope it makes you happy, too," Palmer added. "I am on my lunch break, though, so anything we say or do is off the record."

"That's good to hear. Are you hungry?"

"Yes, I skipped breakfast."

They ate in comfortable silence for a while. Then, Palmer asked a few questions about what she could expect at the coronation, and Elizabeth did her best answering but reminded Palmer that she'd never been to one herself. After they ate, they sat on the sofa. After that, Elizabeth brought up the video on the television of her father's coronation. Palmer asked if she was sure she wanted to watch this, but Elizabeth needed to watch it. Her own coronation was in nine days, and she needed to know what to expect for herself. She wanted to watch her father go through the same process and do her best to emulate him if she could.

"He's so young there," Palmer noted.

Elizabeth's father was walking down the middle aisle of the cathedral draped in reds and purples.

"He is," Elizabeth agreed.

"How old was he when he became King?"

"Twenty-seven."

"Not much older than you," Palmer replied.

"No, but he was born for this."

"So were you." Palmer looked over at her then. "You don't see it, do you?"

"See what?" Elizabeth asked.

"How good you are at being Queen."

"I've been Queen for a few weeks. It's impossible to evaluate that."

"Hey, look at me for a second, please," Palmer requested.

Elizabeth turned to her.

"It's true that it hasn't been long, but I've spent a lot of time with you since this horrible thing happened to your family, Lizzy. It was your *family*. For some people, it was their King or their Prince, but for you, it was your father and your brothers. It was your sisters-in-law and your niece and nephew. It was the people you loved most in the world, and they were taken from you. You're forgetting that I've interviewed people on the street. I talked to people on your staff. I *know* who you are, Elizabeth. I know you're an amazing Queen. I know you care about your people when some of them don't even want you to. And I know you love your sister more than life, and you'd do anything to protect her, including pushing her away when you need her most because it could keep her safe. I know you put her happiness above your own, just like you do with everyone else. I know your staff loves you. They know how much you appreciate and care for them because it shows, and they love you, Elizabeth. I know you could have just given up after what happened. They know it, too. They know you could have abdicated, phoned it in, or just disappeared, and you haven't." She took Elizabeth's hand in her own and squeezed it. "You are so strong. When I was assigned this story, I did a lot of research on this place. I found out that St. Rais is a martyr in the Roman Catholic church. She was the daughter of a Christian priest living in Egypt. You probably know all this, but *I* only recently discovered it. When she was twelve, she was sent to live in a monastery. One day, when there was widespread persecution of Christians, she went to a well for water with other nuns. Walking there, they noticed a ship with a group of nuns, monks, and other Christians in chains, being abused by someone with a name I can*not* pronounce." Palmer laughed a little. "Rais screamed at the abusers and told them to kill her, too, if they were killing Christians. They took her prisoner. She was one of the first to die. When the unpronounceable-name guy yelled something about spitting on the Christian God, Rais had stepped up and spat in that guy's face. She literally spat in his face. She was tortured and beheaded for standing up for her people; people who just wanted to worship their God in peace."

"It's been a very long time since I've heard that story," Elizabeth said softly.

"I think you need to hear it now, then. Your country was named after this woman for a reason, Elizabeth. She was a strong woman, who fought for what she believed in, and you're doing the same thing now. You believe in this monarchy for this country, and you've taken on the burden of your new role. You say you weren't raised for this, but I think your mom and dad knew exactly what they were doing with their children, raising the four of you. They knew Martin could be King, and they probably understood Alexander would never be able to do it. Victoria wouldn't be a good Queen. But *you*, you, Elizabeth, you will be an *amazing* Queen. Your parents knew that, and they gave you exactly what you needed to be able to do this job."

Elizabeth's eyes welled with tears.

"Thank you," she said. "I really needed to hear that."

"I'll say it any time you need it, okay?" Palmer replied.

"Even when you're back in New York and you've forgotten all about this place and your time here?" Elizabeth asked, wiping the fallen tears from her cheeks.

"How could I ever forget this place or my time here? How could I ever forget you, Elizabeth?" Palmer entwined their fingers. "I'll never forget any of this."

"I won't, either," Elizabeth said.

CHAPTER 20

PALMER would equate staying in Elizabeth's house to staying in an Airbnb. Someone lived in the house normally, so it was comfortable and cozy, but that someone *wasn't* Palmer, so it was a little strange to be staying there alone. Elizabeth had arranged for the fire to be lit prior to Palmer's arrival and for the security guards to introduce themselves immediately after. Palmer had first gone into the kitchen to check her food and beverage options. Finding everything more than satisfactory, she went into Elizabeth's bedroom for the first time. *That* was the strangest part.

Elizabeth's room was small. The bed looked modest and comfortable despite its size, but sleeping in it would be weird. Maybe she'd just sleep on the sofa. No, she couldn't do that. The sofa was more love seat than sofa, and Palmer was five foot seven. She'd have to sleep in the fetal position and right next to the fireplace, which would burn her up. The bed would have to do. Her bag was placed just inside the bedroom door. She made her way to the living room, where she stared at the intimidating number of books. She walked by the bookshelves, trying to discern any kind of organization system, but not being able to find one, she figured she could pull a book down and put it back later. Even if she placed it incorrectly, Elizabeth wouldn't likely notice.

Palmer grabbed two books on physics. One seemed like an introduction, which would be more her speed. The other had a lot of pictures. Maybe that would help. After flipping through the pages of both and not retaining anything, Palmer gave up, put them back, and grabbed a novel she hadn't read. She'd been a big reader as a kid, but once she'd gotten a job, reading for pleasure had been something she'd had to either do without or do with very little of and only when she could get it. She opened to the first page of the book, and something fell out. Worried she'd messed up a bookmark for Elizabeth, she reached down into her lap and discovered it wasn't a bookmark; it was a picture. She stared at the image of Elizabeth and her friend, Teagan. Teagan was kissing Elizabeth's cheek. Elizabeth looked happy. It seemed like it had been taken a few years prior. Palmer closed her eyes at the thought that Elizabeth would never see her best friend again. Then, she slid the photo into the back of the book, planning to read at least the first chapter and decide whether or not to continue, but on the page under the title and author, Palmer found handwriting.

When I read this, I thought of you and me.

Love, T

Palmer read the title again and then went to the back of the book to read the description.

"When love is forbidden between them, will they find a way through space and time to be together?" Palmer read the last line of it out loud to herself. "What the…"

She stood up, placed the book back on the shelf, and paced the living room. Not finding an answer to an unasked question in there, she went into the bedroom again to pull out her laptop and get some work done and then search for something to watch on Netflix. Then, Palmer noticed two more pictures. One was on a small shelf on the wall opposite the bed. It was again, of Teagan and Elizabeth. The way Elizabeth was staring at her friend made Palmer's stomach rumble. The other picture was on the tiny bedside table and was again of the two friends.

"Friends?" Palmer asked herself.

They had to be friends and only friends. Teagan was married to Elizabeth's brother, for crying out loud. There's no way they'd have an affair. There was no way Elizabeth was gay or bi or anything other than ramrod straight. She was a Princess. She was going to marry her Prince and will now marry a man and make him her King Consort, the first one in this country. That was the plan. What Palmer was seeing in the pictures and reading into some writing in a book was her own wishful thinking that Elizabeth could or would ever fall in love with a woman. Well, Palmer didn't care about her falling in love with *any* woman. One woman, though, would be nice.

"I cannot feel this way," she told herself.

She rushed into the bathroom, turned on the shower, threw off her clothes, and climbed into the still freezing cold water. She screamed, not being able to handle the cold for long, and rushed out, reaching for a towel on the rack to bundle herself up in. She could *not* be falling in love with a Queen.

***

"How are you sleeping at the house?" Elizabeth asked two days later. "I'm sorry I wasn't able to phone or check on you. Things have been hectic here."

"It's okay," Palmer said. "I've been sleeping great, and everyone's bent over backwards to take care of little old me. Security has come in twice a day to make sure the fire is still going; like I can't toss a log on the thing to keep it lit."

"I *did* tell them you'd never been camping," Elizabeth teased. "This is it," she added, looking up and in front of them. "It's no Notre Dame, but it dates back to around the same time."

They'd just walked into the cathedral, where Elizabeth would soon host her coronation. Palmer had never been to Notre Dame prior to the fire or since, but this place was nice on the outside, and it was gorgeous on the inside.

"Can you believe how they made this place and other places like it? My mother had a thing for architecture. She actually went to university for it and would have been an architect had she not met my father. With only elementary drawings, stone masons meticulously directed the construction of the greatest medieval cathedrals all over Europe, and we managed to get one of our own in St. Rais. Did you know that the practices of intuitive calculation based on simplistic mathematical ratios were closely guarded secrets? They were passed down from generation to generation."

"I did *not* know that," Palmer replied, staring at Elizabeth and no longer the clerestory windows and the alter up ahead. "It's beautiful."

Elizabeth turned to her and smiled.

"I'm glad you're here. Although, it will likely be very boring for you. I have to practice walking slowly, taking things someone hands me, and then check the sound for my speech. I'd understand if you'd like to meet me for dinner after instead of enduring this tedium." She chuckled.

"I'm good here," Palmer replied. "You don't have to entertain me, Elizabeth."

A throat cleared from behind them.

"Your Majesty," Palmer corrected.

"Majesty, it's time," Rebecca said.

"Yes, of course." Elizabeth met Palmer's eyes. "Soon, there will be no going back. I will be *officially* a Queen."

"You already are," Palmer replied, winking at her. "Can I sit anywhere?"

"The back would be preferable as security is still running the dogs through the pews up front," Rebecca answered.

"Okay."

Palmer sat in the second to last row of pews. She watched as Elizabeth walked slowly down the middle aisle. Her chin was level with the floor; her hands were positioned just so. This woman was a Queen. How she couldn't see it was completely beyond Palmer. The bishop placed a crown on Elizabeth's head. Then, she moved to the seat that was acting as her throne for this rehearsal.

"Coronations have been practiced in St. Rais since the first King," Rebecca explained, sitting down next to Palmer. "Many European countries have done away with them entirely, or if they *do* have them still, they're simple ceremonies. Sometimes, the new monarch takes an oath in front of their Parliament or legislative body."

"Can I ask why *you* still do it this way?" Palmer asked.

"As a reporter or as a guest of Her Majesty?"

"Guest," Palmer said, shaking her head at Rebecca's continued mistrust.

"There are many traditions we take from our British and Norwegian ancestors. That, for example," Rebecca nodded toward where Elizabeth was being handed what looked like a small replica oar, "That is meant to represent the Vikings who settled here. The crown contains an English symbol, the three lions. We still have a coronation because it's important for us to acknowledge the accession of our new monarch. In this case, it's vital we acknowledge Her Majesty, Queen Antonia I. She is the very first Queen by birth this nation has ever had, and given the tragedy, people must see a strong monarchy. *She* will give that to us."

"You have faith in her, don't you?" Palmer asked.

"I do. Don't you?"

"I do," Palmer agreed, nodding. "She's good at this. She's going to be an amazing Queen. I just hope people give her a chance to show them what good she can do."

"And you?"

"What about me?" Palmer asked, forcing her eyes off of Elizabeth and onto Rebecca.

"Will you be sticking around to see all the good she does?"

"Until after the coronation," she answered. "I'm not sure what you mean, exactly. She told you I'm not here as a reporter anymore, right? I sent you the piece I—"

"She did. And I read the article – you did right by our young Queen."

"Thanks?" Palmer asked rather than stated because she wasn't certain she should take that as a compliment.

"Palmer, the Queen seems to enjoy your company quite a lot."

"I enjoy hers, too." She shrugged a shoulder.

"But you will be leaving her for New York soon."

"I can't help that. I don't live here; I live in New York.

My job is there. My family is in Pennsylvania."

"I understand. I'm not asking you to move across the world. I'm merely asking you to remain her confidant if she requires or requests it."

"Oh, God. Yeah, of course. I don't want to just leave and never talk to her again. I couldn't do that. I–" Palmer stopped herself, realizing she might be going a little too far for the private secretary. "I hope *she* wants to keep in touch. I wouldn't mind coming back for a visit, and if she's ever in the States, I'd expect her to let me know so we can meet up. I'd offer to let her stay at my place in the city, but it's way too small for a Queen and her staff. *I* barely fit." Palmer laughed lightly.

"I believe that you are a good person, Palmer."

"I hope so. I try to be."

"Elizabeth has always been a good judge of character. I should have known that if she approved of you, you were worthy of that approval."

Palmer turned her body to Rebecca and said, "I'd never hurt her, Rebecca. I'd never do anything to hurt her."

"Good," the woman replied, nodding.

"Is this loud enough?" Elizabeth's voice came from the microphone attached to the pulpit. "Louder? Softer? Can you hear me back there?" She smiled wide in Palmer's direction.

"I can hear you," Palmer spoke loudly. "Loud and clear, Your Majesty."

CHAPTER 21

"IT'S not the top of the hill, but it's safer, and this close to the coronation, security really didn't want me leaving the palace," Elizabeth explained.

"No, it's great," Palmer replied. "Freezing cold, but it's great."

"The space heaters and every winter coat in the country aren't enough for you, Palmer?" Elizabeth laughed, looking over at her.

"I think I'm just meant for warmer weather," Palmer said.

"I hope that's not true," Elizabeth blurted out before she thought about it.

Palmer turned to her then and asked, "Why's that?"

Elizabeth tried to look away from Palmer's eyes, but she couldn't. They were piercing through her, and the swirling colors from the Northern Lights only made them more mesmerizing. Elizabeth hadn't been able to get away before her coronation, but she *had* been able to put together a view of the Northern Lights from the palace roof. It wasn't the same, but she hoped that it was something Palmer would remember forever. Her staff had been kind enough to place large space heaters in a circle around two comfortable lounge chairs, which the women had pushed together. Beneath their heads were fluffy pillows. Over their thermal wear, they had a thick blanket. They'd been staring up at the colors moving about the sky for the past several minutes, and neither of them had said anything since the nearly nightly show began. To Elizabeth, it was a perfect reason to stay up late.

"Because if you can't handle the cold, you might not come back to visit me," Elizabeth said finally.

"There's always the summer," Palmer replied, turning to look back up to the night sky.

"The lights aren't as prevalent in the summer."

"I wouldn't be coming back for the lights, Lizzy," Palmer stated, sliding a little closer to Elizabeth.

"Cold?" Elizabeth asked, moving closer to Palmer.

"Yes, but I'm not all that cold. I just like to be dramatic," she replied. "This is one of the coolest things anyone's ever done for me. I say *one* of the coolest because the coolest thing was the camping attempt the other night. You are responsible for probably the best couple of weeks of my life, Elizabeth."

Elizabeth swallowed and said, "I don't know if that's a good thing or a bad thing. What does it say about your life if one of the best things in it was a camping trip where there wasn't any actual camping?"

"It's about who I'm spending it with," Palmer replied. "I think I'd go to the dentist voluntarily and have a root canal if *you* came with me."

"Oh, don't bring up the dentist on a night like this. No need to ruin the evening." Elizabeth laughed a little. "Can I tell you something?"

"Yeah," Palmer replied.

"When it happened…" She paused to try to make sure she could get it out right. "When I lost my family, I remember thinking as my plane landed that I'd never smile again. I'd never laugh. I'd never have another happy moment. I'd never allow myself to enjoy anything ever again because none of them would be able to enjoy another moment."

"Elizabeth…" Palmer said softly.

"I miss them every second of every day."

"I know." Palmer's hand, inside the thickest of gloves, met Elizabeth's, and their fingers automatically entwined.

"After it happened, I focused only on the monarchy. It was about getting me into the best position possible to be a believable Queen; to be strong, and show the anti-monarchists that we were a good thing for this nation, while showing the traditionalists that *I* would be good for this nation. The only feelings I cared about were the citizens of St. Rais and Victoria's. I blocked everything else out until I was alone in bed and no one could hear me." Elizabeth felt tears well in her eyes but knew the air around them was so cold and dry that they would never escape. "Then, I met you, Palmer. I met you, and I smiled, and I laughed again, and I felt so guilty at first. I still do, if I'm being honest."

"You have nothing to feel guilty about," Palmer replied.

"I understand that logically, but it's not entered my heart yet, and I'm not certain it ever will. It will likely dissipate, but it won't disappear completely, and that, I'm afraid, has to be okay because it is the hand I've been dealt."

"I'm glad I've made you laugh. And trust me, this is hard for me to say, but if I had to give up making you smile or laugh because it meant I had no reason to stick around St. Rais and interview you about what happened – I'd give them back to you in an instant, Elizabeth."

Elizabeth turned to her and noticed Palmer was looking back at her. Her expression was as serious as it was genuine.

"We can't turn back time, but we can find a way to make the most of what we have now."

"Which is?" Palmer checked, her eyes searching Elizabeth's face.

"This." Elizabeth smiled warmly. "You and me, staring at the Northern Lights. I assume you know some of the stories of the lights? There are tour guides and pamphlets everywhere in St. Rais."

"I heard some of the myths, yeah."

"In Norse mythology, which is what we tend to follow in St. Rais, the aurora was a fire bridge to the sky built by the gods. Do you know the *science*, though?"

"Not really, no. If my dad ever taught me, I tuned it out," Palmer replied, turning back to the lights.

"The Sun is ninety million miles away from Earth, but its effects extend far beyond its visible surface. There are storms on our Sun that send charged solar particles across space in our direction. When the charged particles from the Sun hit atoms and molecules in our atmosphere, they excite those atoms, and they light up." Elizabeth smiled as she took in Palmer's expression as the other woman watched the lights. "When those charged particles strike atoms in the atmosphere, electrons move to higher-energy orbits, farther away from the nucleus of the atom. When an electron moves back to a lower-energy orbit, it releases a photon, or a particle of light. Different gases give off different colors when they are excited. Oxygen, for example, gives off the green color; like right there." Elizabeth leaned over and pointed at a particular swirl of green with her free hand. "Nitrogen is blue or red in color."

"Like there?" Palmer asked, pointing with her free hand.

"Yes," Elizabeth replied, realizing that the reason they both had to point with their *free* hands was that their other hands were still entwined together under their shared blanket. "I suppose, this makes the aurora not as mysterious as it used to be, but even though I know the science behind the lights, I can still sometimes see a fire bridge built by the gods."

Palmer turned toward her again and softly said, "That's beautiful."

"Yes, it is," Elizabeth replied, looking into Palmer's eyes.

***

"I'm glad you decided to stay," Elizabeth told her.

"It's after two in the morning. I could go back to the house, but–"

"No, it's far too late," Elizabeth interrupted her. "Besides, I have everything you could need here."

"Clothes to sleep in?"

"Of course," Elizabeth replied, nodding. "Are you ready for bed *now*?"

"It *is* late," Palmer said.

"Right. I should get some sleep as well."

"What does your day look like tomorrow?" Palmer asked as she stood up from the sitting room sofa and stretched.

"Pretty busy. Victoria, David, and I are going to talk about their move to Coburn Cottage as well as the wedding over lunch. Other than that, my day is filled with tedium," she replied.

"I guess I'll go back to the house and do some reading or something," Palmer said.

"I'm sorry, Palmer. I realize I asked you to stay here for me and hardly have any time for you. And when I do, we can't leave the palace." She brightened then. "I've not given you the full tour of the palace, though, have I?"

"No. How rude is that, by the way?" Palmer teased.

"Very rude. Unforgivable," Elizabeth replied, standing up as well. "Would you allow me to remedy that tomorrow night after dinner?"

"Dinner?"

"Yes, we can eat in the formal dining room. You haven't seen that, so we can start our tour there if you'd like."

"Formal? What about *me* says formal?"

Elizabeth took in Palmer's jeans and a hooded sweatshirt.

"True."

"Hey," Palmer chastised. "You were supposed to say something like, 'Oh, Palmer. I know your trip was only supposed to be a week *and* was supposed to be a nice, relaxing vacation, so you wouldn't have possibly thought to bring with you a formal gown and heels.'"

"You *do* know that I have many formal gowns."

"I know they wouldn't fit me. Do I have to dress up

to sit at the formal dining table?"

"Of course not," Elizabeth said. "Come on. I'll find you something that *will* fit, and we can get you squared away in the guest room."

Elizabeth moved toward her bedroom.

"Hey, Elizabeth?"

"Yes?

She stopped and turned to Palmer.

"I can stay in any of the guest rooms tonight," Palmer began, moving toward her. "Or, I can stay with you."

Elizabeth swallowed.

"Correct me if I'm wrong, but when I slept over before, you slept better."

"I did," Elizabeth confirmed.

"I can just be there. If you're worried about people seeing us in the morning, just tell me what time to get up so they won't bring in your breakfast before that. I can go into the other room then. I'll feel bad about messing up a bed I didn't sleep in because someone will have to make it after I go, but at least, they'll think I slept in there," Palmer said. When Elizabeth didn't say anything right away, she added, "Or not. It was just an idea. Inappropriate, I know. I'm–"

"It's fine, Palmer. I appreciate it," Elizabeth interrupted.

"No, I shouldn't have suggested it. I–" Palmer stopped herself. "I just hate the idea of you lying there crying yourself to sleep, Elizabeth."

"As do I," Elizabeth replied. "I'll find you something to sleep in. Toiletries are in the guest bathroom, like last time."

"Right. Got it."

Palmer turned to head toward the door adjoining the rooms.

"And, Palmer?"

"Yeah?" Palmer asked.

"Come back in here when you're done?"

Palmer met her eyes, gave her a soft smile and a nod,

and then opened the door. Several minutes later, she was still wearing her jeans and sweatshirt as she re-entered Elizabeth's bedroom. She reached for the pajamas Elizabeth had placed on the corner of her own bed, disappeared for a moment, and then returned changed for the night.

"This is what you meant, right?" Palmer asked.

"Yes," Elizabeth said.

She'd already slid under the blanket. When Palmer did as well, on her own side of the bed, Elizabeth thought about moving closer to the edge of the bed to give Palmer as much space as possible, but she didn't. She stayed where she was, staring up at her ceiling as if a beautiful, smart, kind, and amazing woman wasn't lying in her bed next to her.

"Good night, Palmer," Elizabeth said after several moments of awkward silence became too much.

"Good night, Lizzy," Palmer replied.

Then, Elizabeth reached for the switch, turning off the bedside table. Minutes later, she closed her eyes. Hours later, she woke up, finding her body wrapped around Palmer's and not moving an inch for fear she'd wake the sleeping woman, and this rare moment of bliss would be gone.

CHAPTER 22

PALMER sat on the sofa, adding to her own, personal piece on meeting a Queen. It was good for her. She needed to be able to document her feelings for Elizabeth in what she'd probably refer back to when she was old and gray, living alone with her three cats and reminiscing on the time she went on a vacation and ended up falling in love with a woman she could never have.

She'd never been one to believe a person could fall so fast. In her previous relationships, it had taken some time before she'd been able to see what she felt for what it was; love. Anna was the fastest, but Anna had said it first, and Palmer had said it back before she'd even thought about whether or not she actually felt it. She did. She had felt it. But saying it was what made her understand that was what those feelings were. And look how that had turned out.

Now, it had been a few weeks with a woman, and Palmer was ready to call it love? No, that wasn't right. It was probably a crush or infatuation. Elizabeth was a gorgeous woman. Maybe it was just lust. Palmer hadn't been with anyone since Anna, and toward the end of their relationship, they hadn't been having sex at all. She probably just needed to get laid. She'd go home in a few days and maybe get on one of those apps or something and have some fun like every other person her age seemed to be doing these days.

She looked up from her laptop, staring at the book on the shelf where she'd found a picture and a message. She hadn't said anything to Elizabeth. She didn't want her to think she'd been snooping through her stuff. Elizabeth had enough going on. She didn't need to add Palmer invading her privacy to the list. Still, though, as she stared, she wondered about that message. She closed her laptop after saving her work, stood up, and placed more wood on the fire. Then, she forced herself to go into the kitchen and make a snack instead of going to the bookshelf, which was what she really wanted to do. Having made and eaten a sandwich and coffee, Palmer had no more reasons to hole up in the kitchen, so she returned to the living room and stared at the books again. She made her way over and reviewed the titles again. Most of the books were academic in nature, but there was a small section on the very bottom shelf that looked more fiction than fact. Palmer sat on the floor and pulled out all seven of the books. She stared at the title of the first one.

"*The Love I Never Had?*" she read out loud to herself.

She opened to the first page, and finding no photo or other items contained inside and no message, she dropped it to the floor and reached for the second book in the pile. This one was called *Seeing Her*. While there was again, nothing inside and no message, as Palmer flipped through it quickly, she noticed there was writing inside the book itself. Making her way back to chapter one, she flipped until she found words underlined.

"*She was the most beautiful thing I'd ever seen. And no matter how many times I tell her, she never believes me,*" Palmer read out loud again.

She continued flipping, finding dialogue between characters, sentences and, sometimes, whole paragraphs underlined in black pen. Other times, the color of the ink was blue, though, and the lines were darker, as if the person who'd placed them there had pressed harder into the pages.

"*I loved her in a way no one else ever would, and I see her in a way no one else ever can because of that love,*" Palmer read to herself.

That was the last piece of underlined text. Palmer moved back to the first book to see if she'd missed something, and she had. There were several more sections underlined in two different-color inks.

"You make me feel like I can do anything; BE anything I want."

Palmer moved on to the third book and then the fourth and fifth. By the time she got to the sixth book, she looked up to see she'd been sitting on the floor for a couple of hours now. She needed to get ready for her dinner with Elizabeth. She re-placed all the books in the exact spots she found them, but as she took a shower, she couldn't help but think about the picture of Elizabeth and Teagan and the books. It was clear to Palmer what it all meant, but she'd thought it before and had dismissed it as wishful thinking on her part. Elizabeth wasn't gay. She and Teagan had been best friends; closer, likely, than her and Victoria because they'd been the same age and had grown up together even before Teagan had married Alexander.

Palmer dried her hair with the old blow-dryer that looked like it had been through a war, and for some reason, that only made her love Elizabeth more. The woman was a Princess when she'd lived here. She could have bought a million hair dryers, probably, but she used one she had for years. It was endearing, but Palmer needed to stop thinking about the words 'love' and 'Elizabeth' going together. She needed to not use the word 'endearing' when describing her. Even if Elizabeth and Teagan *had* been together before Teagan had married Elizabeth's brother, Palmer didn't stand a chance. She was leaving for New York after the coronation. Elizabeth was Queen of a country. Whatever Palmer was feeling would dissipate when she got home, back to her normal and anything-but-royal everyday life.

***

"Hi," Elizabeth greeted, smiling at her, and that smile

nearly broke Palmer.

"Hey," she replied, pushing down her desire to reach out for the woman standing in front of her.

Elizabeth was wearing a very flattering green dress with matching short heels. Her hair was down, framing her face in loose curls. Her face wasn't bare, but the makeup was light and highlighted her beautiful features. This look was *not* helping Palmer's feelings in the slightest.

"You look nice," Palmer added.

"You do too," Elizabeth replied.

"I'm wearing a pair of jeans and the nicest shirt I brought with me."

"I'm only wearing *this* because I'm still in my work clothes, so to speak. I plan on changing if that's okay with you."

"Why? You look great," Palmer blurted out before she could stop herself.

Elizabeth's cheeks turned a light shade of red, and Palmer's heart raced in her chest.

"I'd like to be comfortable for dinner. This dress and these shoes aren't that. Would you mind giving me a moment?"

"Sure," Palmer said, sitting down on the sofa.

Elizabeth disappeared into her bedroom but left one of the double doors open. Palmer stared at the wall, trying hard not to look in that direction.

"Palmer, would you mind?" Elizabeth asked.

"Huh?" Palmer asked back, turning that direction but keeping her eyes closed in case Elizabeth wasn't fully dressed.

"I can't reach the zipper. Normally, I'd have someone come in and—"

"No, it's fine. I've got it," Palmer interjected, stood, and moved into the bedroom.

Elizabeth was facing a full-length mirror. She'd already kicked off her shoes, leaving her barefoot. Palmer slid up behind her, and their eyes met as Palmer reached for and then pulled down Elizabeth's zipper to where it ended at the small of her back. Palmer swallowed, her throat suddenly dry. She wanted to touch the skin she'd just revealed so badly, it hurt not to, but she'd never do that; not to this woman. Elizabeth's skin looked so soft. Palmer's lips ached to kiss down her back, slide the dress off her shoulders, and nibble on every inch of skin she revealed as she did.

"Thank you," Elizabeth spoke, but her voice was different than a moment ago, softer somehow.

"No problem," Palmer replied, forcing herself to step back.

When Elizabeth didn't wait for Palmer to leave the room to step out of her dress after it fell to the floor, Palmer looked away.

"I'm going to wait out there," she said, turning to go.

"Okay. I'll be right out," Elizabeth replied, but her tone sounded almost disappointed.

No, that had to be wishful thinking, too. She needed to get a grip. Elizabeth needed help getting out of her dress. Palmer was just right there. That was all. God, maybe she should go back to the hotel. Staying at Elizabeth's house, amongst her personal things, was making Palmer crazy.

"I'm ready," Elizabeth said a few minutes later after she emerged from her bedroom wearing a pair of jeans and a light-blue sweater that only brought out her eyes and made Palmer want to stare into them all night long.

"Lead the way," Palmer replied, motioning toward the door.

***

"You have a bowling alley in the palace?" Palmer said an hour and a half later after they'd finished dinner and ended their tour here.

"We do. It was my mother's idea, actually. This space used to be storage, but she had four children that couldn't always just go outside and play with other kids. She didn't want us to play video games or watch TV, either, so there's a court outside where we could play a variety of things, and she had this built for the winters. There's also a small putting green next door. My father used that mostly, but he taught my brothers how to golf as well."

"Not you?"

"I wasn't interested. Neither was Victoria, but we bowled together a lot. It would be boys versus girls most of the time." Elizabeth chuckled. "I haven't been down here in a few years, though. We all grew up. Martin and Lyla moved into Desmond Manor when they got married. Alex and Teagan moved into their house. I moved into mine. Victoria was at university."

"Do you want to bowl now?" Palmer asked.

"I should warn you; I'm quite good."

"Well, you had a bowling alley in your house; I'd expect you to be better than me. I've only bowled maybe ten times in my life."

"Really?"

"I wasn't very good, so I didn't go much." Palmer shrugged a shoulder.

"Would you like me to teach you some tips and tricks?" Elizabeth asked, smiling.

"If you have any," Palmer replied.

"Oh, I have tons."

"Let's do it, then."

Elizabeth pressed a few buttons, causing the machine to bring down the pins. They each selected a ball. Elizabeth helped Palmer, who had initially chosen one that would be too heavy for her, and she lent her an old pair of bowling shoes that fit okay. Then, Elizabeth demonstrated good form and let her first ball roll down the lane, hitting eight of the ten pins.

"A little rusty, huh?" Palmer teased.

"Oh, shut up," Elizabeth said, chuckling. Then, she promptly knocked down the remaining pins and added, "Your turn,"

Palmer stood, picked up her ball, lined herself up, and

waited. Elizabeth came up behind her and placed her hands on her hips. Softly speaking into Palmer's ear, she gave her instructions and then took a few steps back. Palmer missed her touch instantly, but she refocused on the pins ahead of her and rolled her first bowling ball in nearly a decade. She knocked down four pins, which wasn't terrible, but when she turned around to smile at Elizabeth at her success, Elizabeth wasn't smiling back. She'd moved to sit in one of the chairs and only gave Palmer a nod. Then, she forced a smile. Palmer turned back, a little defeated but determined not to let that get her down. She bowled again, hitting another three pins. When she turned around again, the woman still had that forced smile on her face.

"Well done," she said, but it wasn't the happy woman she'd just been talking to a minute ago.

"Your turn," Palmer said, sitting down next to her.

Elizabeth stood without a word, waited for the pins to drop, and bowled.

CHAPTER 23

ELIZABETH didn't sleep well that night. Palmer had offered to stay again, but she'd thought it wrong to ask Palmer to share her bed solely for the purpose of her getting a decent night's sleep and not crying again at her loss. Palmer had already done so much for her. Elizabeth owed at least three nights of good sleep to her as is. The first night, when they'd ended up in Palmer's bed, was one. The second came with their hours-long phone call, and the third had been the previous night, when Elizabeth had woken up holding on to Palmer from behind, wishing she had the courage to just be herself for once in her life.

"Hey, do you think we can avoid getting married at the cathedral?" Victoria asked her. "I think, if I was still sixth in line, it wouldn't have mattered, but now that I'm next, technically, the tradition is that I get married there."

"You can get married wherever you want, Vicky," Elizabeth said without much energy.

"Don't sound so enthusiastic," Victoria replied.

Elizabeth sighed and said, "I'm sorry. I've had a weird couple of days."

"Weird how?" Victoria asked.

"I don't know. Just weird."

"That's helpful," Victoria said sarcastically. "Is there anything I can help with? I know the coronation is pretty much set, but is there anything *you* need? Besides the wedding, Lizzy, I'm kind of in limbo here. I'm not used to this, honestly. I was supposed to go to graduate school, but– "

"You should. You should go to school."

"I'm getting married, Lizzy."

"After the wedding, you should go back to school. I

mean, if that's what you want to do – you should do it. Don't let this get in your way."

"*This*? You mean losing our entire family?"

"I meant you being second in line."

"Is there something you're not telling me? Got your eyes on someone who's going to help you make a *new* second in line so that *I* don't have to do the job?"

"What? Of course not," Elizabeth said loudly. "When would I have even found the time? I've hardly been able to breathe these days."

"You've found time to hang out with the reporter."

"Palmer; I know you know her name, Victoria."

"I do. And you've found time to be with her."

"She's only here for a few more days. I–"

"Have to spend as much time with her as possible before she goes?"

Elizabeth cleared her throat, leaned forward on her sofa, and said, "Yes, something like that. Can you fault me for wanting a friend, Victoria?"

"Of course not, but I *can* worry about you and what happens when that *friend* goes home, I go to Coburn, and you're here alone."

"I have staff."

"Alone, Lizzy. You and I both know we love the staff, but they work for you; they're not your friends. Even Rebecca, who loves you, still works for you. She's not a friend."

"I'll be fine. I'll make friends in time, and Palmer and I will keep in touch. We've even talked about her coming for a visit in the summer."

"Really?"

"Well, I asked her if she'd consider visiting one day, and she doesn't seem to enjoy our harsh winter, so I suggested the summer."

"You'll see her once a year, if you're lucky; maybe twice."

"So? We can talk on the phone or video chat."

"In all that copious free time you keep telling me you *don't* have? *And* with the time zone difference? Lizzy, you'll be lucky to talk to her once a month."

"You and David were long-distance, and you made it work."

Victoria's eyes went wide, and she said, "Lizzy, David and I were dating. We were a couple. We're getting married. Besides, he lived in London, not New York."

"I just meant that…"

"What? What did you mean?" Victoria leaned in close. "Lizzy, do you *like* Palmer?"

"What? No. Of course not." Elizabeth stood up.

"You know that's okay, right?"

"I don't know what you're talking about. What's okay?"

"If you like her."

"Of course, I like her. She's my friend. I wouldn't make time for her if I didn't like her."

"But you're not interested in her in a romantic way?"

"No, I am not." Elizabeth looked at her feet.

"But you just compared your relationship with her to my relationship with my *fiancé*."

"I only meant that in reference to the distance," Elizabeth argued.

"Sure." Victoria stood up. "Listen, if you *were* interested in Palmer, it would be okay."

"You were just telling me I'd be lucky to even remain friends with the woman. Now you're trying to tell me it would be okay to feel something more?"

"I'm not telling you the logistics would be easy; I'm saying the feelings are okay, Lizzy. You're allowed to feel how you feel. Of course, you don't feel that way… but if you did, it would be okay."

"No, it wouldn't," Elizabeth replied.

"He's gone, Elizabeth." Victoria squeezed Elizabeth's forearm gently. "Dad's gone."

"It doesn't matter," she said, shaking off Victoria's

touch. "I have a dinner with the Prime Minister and his wife to get ready for. I should go."

"When do you see Palmer next?"

"She'll be at the coronation."

"When does she leave?"

"The day after," Elizabeth replied. "She booked her return flight yesterday. I had hoped she'd be able to stay longer, but that was selfish of me. She has a life to get back to."

"You know how we usually take vacations for the holidays after the Christmas address?"

"Yes," she replied.

"Maybe you should take one."

"We go as a family. I assumed you and I would go. David is welcome as well, obviously."

"I think you should go somewhere, Lizzy. Where you pick is up to you, but I've heard New York City is a nice place to visit."

She gave Elizabeth a soft smile and left the room. That idea, of course, was a ridiculous one; Elizabeth couldn't just leave the country. She would be a newly made Queen in a nation that may or may not even want her family around anymore. She had to remain in St. Rais for stability alone. There was also the fact that security would be next to impossible in a city like New York. Of course, it would also be unlikely that an anti-monarchist would follow her all the way there just to make an attempt on her life. Then, there was the other obvious reason for her not to go. Palmer had her life to get back to. She had a family and a job and friends to meet up with. She wouldn't want Elizabeth following her around New York City, asking her to take her to the Statue of Liberty or the Empire State Building like some tourist. No, she'd stay at the palace for the holidays. She could take a vacation later, after they found the man responsible for murdering her family.

***

"I tried to call last night," Palmer said.

"I know; I got your message. I was unable to get back to you until now. I'm sorry."

Elizabeth hated lying to Palmer. The truth was that she'd watched Palmer's number appear on her phone screen. She'd then watched it disappear and become a missed call. Then, she'd checked the short voicemail and the follow-up text message, and she hadn't replied because she didn't know what to say. The closer she got to Palmer Honeycutt, the closer she *wanted* to get to her, and Palmer was leaving soon. Her heart couldn't stand to be broken again.

"No problem. I know how busy you are."

"How are you?" Elizabeth asked.

"I'm good. I actually went to that massive library in the city and just looked at the thousands of books today. I had lunch at the restaurant next door; that one that serves the best klippfisk in the country, apparently."

"*You* ate klippfisk? What did you think?"

"It's salty," the woman replied.

Elizabeth laughed and said, "Yes, it's salted, dried, and pressed cod. I'm surprised you tried it."

"Well, I wanted to eat traditional food while I was here."

"There's an American place on the next block. You should go there tomorrow and have a burger. Tell me if it's anything like what you have back home."

"Tomorrow is your coronation. Am I uninvited now?"

"Oh, I'm losing track of my days." Elizabeth sighed. "The day after then, because you are still invited."

"The day after, I'm on a plane, Elizabeth."

"Right," Elizabeth said. "Next time."

"Next time," Palmer agreed softly before adding, "And next time I'm here, maybe you can go out more, and we could go together."

"I hope so," Elizabeth said. "Are you excited to get back to New York?"

"Yes, but I'll only be there for a couple of days. I'm

going to visit my family for the holidays."

"You have more time off?"

"No, I'll be working from there. I have a new assignment that I can write from anywhere, and I'll use any free time to find my next piece."

"I'm glad you'll have time with your family, Palmer."

"Me too. My parents have a nice three-bedroom place in the suburbs. It's pretty peaceful most of the time unless the Steelers are playing."

"Steelers?"

"American football," Palmer replied.

"Oh, I'm a *real* football fan."

"I know," Palmer laughed. "But their neighborhood is in Steeler country."

"I hope you have a good time."

"What are *you* doing for Christmas?"

Elizabeth shifted the phone from one ear to another and lowered herself into the bed to get more comfortable.

"The Christmas address is first on my list. Well, I guess that *is* my list; I'll just be here after that. I think Victoria and David are going to take a trip together."

"Why aren't you going with them?"

"Because they're engaged. I highly doubt Victoria wants her older sister as a third wheel."

"It's the holidays, Elizabeth. It's time for family."

"I don't have much family left," she said, feeling sorry for herself.

"All the more reason to be with the ones you *do* have left."

"I don't know. I think I would like some time alone. I might see if security will let me stay at the house for a week. I still have some packing up there left to do."

"Don't just stay here by yourself. I hate to think of you like that over Christmas."

"I'll be okay. I'll think of all the Christmases that came before this one, and I'll think of you having time with *your* family, and I'll be okay. Can we change the subject?"

"I guess." Palmer let out a deep breath. "I got the dress you sent me for tomorrow."

"Were your measurements correct?"

"Yes, thank you. I don't have anything I could wear here, but I don't know that I have anything at home I could wear to a Queen's coronation, either."

"It's not every day one needs a coronation dress, is it?"

"No, it's not." Palmer laughed. "Are you nervous?"

"Yes."

"Don't be. You're going to crush it."

"Crush it?" Elizabeth laughed.

"Yes, your speech is good. You've mastered the slow, purposeful walk. You're going to be great."

"You're coming to the dinner afterward, yes?"

"I'll be there."

"I've placed you next to me at the table."

"Is that allowed? I'm not important enough for that."

"You're important enough for *me*, Palmer."

"I should probably get some sleep if I'm going to look halfway decent tomorrow," Palmer said.

"Oh, okay," Elizabeth replied.

"Do you need to keep talking?"

"No, I'll be fine. I'm tired. I'll be able to get some sleep tonight."

"Are you sure?"

"I need to get used to you not talking me to sleep, Palmer."

"That makes it sound like I'm boring," she joked.

"You *are* anything but boring."

CHAPTER 24

"WELL, there's a new Queen in town," Victoria said.

"Oh, hello," Palmer replied.

"Hello. You got the seat on the right, I see."

"I just sat where she told me to sit," Palmer replied, looking at the people taking their seats for dinner at the round tables in the giant banquet hall. "Is it not right?"

Victoria glared at her playfully and said, "No, it's right." She nodded then. "So, I talked to my sister this morning, and she mentioned her plans to spend Christmas alone in her little house."

"I know. I tried to talk her out of it."

"Did you try to talk her *into* anything?"

"What? No."

"I suggested she go with David and I to London. His family will all be there, and I'll be meeting most of them for the first time. I also told her I'd skip that, and she and I could have the holiday together, but she turned me down."

"She told me she wanted to be alone. I guess we just have to accept that."

"You're a reporter, Palmer. I didn't take you for a quitter," Victoria said.

"Excuse me?" Palmer replied.

"Ask her to join you in New York for the holidays."

"What?" Palmer asked. "I'm not going to be there. I'll be in Pittsburgh."

"Great. I don't care. Take her with you."

"I can't take her with me; she's a Queen. She–"

"The entire family always takes two weeks off this time

of year after the Christmas address. Everyone knows this. Elizabeth should be taking time off. She was forced to jump right into this thing. She needs to take time away from it."

"I agree, but I can't just invite her—"

"Yes, Palmer. You *can* just invite her."

"What about security concerns?"

"No one needs to know *where* she's going, and she'll have some security go with her. She'll be safer there than she is here. Besides," Victoria leaned over the empty seat that Elizabeth would soon fill, "I want my sister to be happy, Palmer. *You* make her happy."

Palmer nodded and gave Victoria an awkward smile. Then, trumpets sounded, and the announcer, who had already announced the names of several Dukes and Duchesses along with Victoria and her escort, David Wilson, announced Elizabeth's arrival into the ballroom.

"Her Majesty, Queen Antonia I," he yelled.

Elizabeth walked in, and Palmer saw what she'd seen earlier at the coronation – Elizabeth was a Queen. She was a Queen long before she'd had to take the job, and she'd forever be a Queen in Palmer's eyes, even if she gave it up one day. Her long deep-burgundy dress with purple sash contributed to her looking the part, but her confident and kind expression was what sold it to the room of dignitaries, lords, and ladies. Palmer stood up with the rest of the room as Elizabeth made her rounds. She stopped at one table to greet another King and Queen. Then, she made her way to her table, where Palmer was waiting.

"Your Majesty," Palmer said, giving her the requisite curtsy.

"Miss Honeycutt," Elizabeth replied, smiling at her knowingly.

***

"You're in the papers, and I'm *not* the one getting the scoop," her editor said.

"I didn't think it was that big of a deal," Palmer told

him, looking back to see that Elizabeth was drinking her whiskey and staring at the fireplace. "I told you, I needed the time off."

"Palmer, *this* is the story. You should have been writing about this. Everything on the record, and with pictures. Instead, I'm reading about an American woman accompanying the new Queen to her coronation dinner in *The Times*. *The Times*, Palmer."

"I had no idea *The Times* would pick this up. The dinner was a private thing. I didn't know there were reporters there."

"*You're* a reporter," he replied.

"I was off-duty."

"What is going on with you, Palmer? This is a once-in-a-lifetime story: *A reluctant Queen takes over from her fallen father.*"

"I sent you my piece."

"And we'll print it. It's fine, but it could have been more. It could have been better."

"I promised her," Palmer stated.

"Who?"

"The Queen."

"Promised her what?"

"That I'm here as a friend now."

"Well, why the hell did you do that?"

"Because I am; I'm here as a friend. You have your story. It's a good one. But today is off-limits."

"This is bullshit. But if you said off the record, we'll stay away from it. I don't need a lawsuit from an entire country on my hands here. We'll talk when you get back, though, Honeycutt."

"Yes, sir," she replied, hanging up after.

"You're in trouble because of me, aren't you?"

"What? No," Palmer replied, moving to sit down next to Elizabeth. "It'll be fine. I just didn't know there was a reporter from *The Times* in the ballroom tonight."

"There wasn't. There weren't any reporters there at all."

"*I'm* a reporter," Palmer argued.

"Any reporters working tonight," Elizabeth corrected, glancing over at her. "You *weren't* working, right?"

"No, Lizzy; I wasn't working. *The Times* must just have a source or something. I was off the clock, and that's what I just told my boss."

"And that's why you're in trouble," Elizabeth concluded.

"It's a slap on the wrist; I'll be fine. I'm allowed to have a life outside of the paper."

"Still, I'm sorry," Elizabeth offered, looking back to the fire and finishing her whiskey.

"You don't have to be sorry." Palmer watched as the fire flickered in Elizabeth's eyes. "Hey, are you okay?"

"Yes, I'm fine."

"I can tell when you're lying, Elizabeth," Palmer replied.

"I'm not lying."

"Please look at me," she requested. "What's wrong?"

"You're leaving tomorrow," Elizabeth stated. "In a few minutes, you'll tell me you're tired or that you have to pack. You'll take a car to the house, and I'll be here alone. You'll get on that plane, and I don't know when or *if* I'll ever see you again."

Elizabeth's eyes welled with tears that Palmer wanted to make disappear.

"I *will* come back, Lizzy. I promise you; I'll come back."

"I can't put this on you, Palmer. It's not your fault I'm alone. I'll need to remedy this feeling in some other way."

Palmer licked her lips and said, "You could try to meet someone."

"Someone?"

"I don't know. I assume you need to…"

"What? Have babies now?"

"It's not the Middle Ages, but that's how this works, right? You have to have an heir. It was the same for your dad and his dad before him."

"Other monarchs haven't had an heir."

"But you want kids, don't you?" Palmer asked.

"I didn't always. I was focused on school and a potential career before, but I think now I do." Elizabeth smiled. "Do you?" she asked Palmer.

"I do, yeah," Palmer said. "I was hoping for at least one or maybe a couple; I don't know. I'd have to meet someone to share them with first."

"Anna?"

"I told you, I turned her down when she asked to get back together."

"I know, but you'll be home soon. Maybe things will be different."

"Things *will* be different, but not because of Anna."

"Then, why?"

"Because of you," Palmer admitted. "You've changed my whole world, Elizabeth."

"I have?" Elizabeth asked as a tear rolled down her cheek.

When the second one began to fall, Palmer couldn't stop herself. She wiped it away softly with her thumb. Elizabeth's eyes closed as she did that and didn't open again until Palmer's touch was gone.

"Come back with me," Palmer suggested.

"To the house?"

"No, I'm staying here tonight."

"You are?" Elizabeth asked.

"Yes, I am. I wore a dress for you today, Your Majesty. The least you could do is let me sleep in that giant, comfortable bed."

Elizabeth chuckled a bit and said, "What about your stuff?"

"It's in the guest room already. Security had someone bring it up. Is it okay that I stay? I kind of just invited myself because it's my last night and–"

"Of course, it's okay," Elizabeth interrupted. "But if you weren't talking about the house... What were you talking about?"

"Come with me for the holidays. Victoria said you take two weeks off every year. Come to the States after the Christmas address thing. I'll be in New York for a couple of days first to check on my apartment, do laundry, and buy gifts for the family. Then, I'm driving to Pittsburgh. If you want, you can fly straight there."

"What about your family?"

"What about them? My parents think the more, the merrier, and my sister would love to meet a Queen. When I called her the other day to tell her about you, she was so excited that I had a Queen as a friend. She'd love to meet you."

"I can't impose on your family like that, Palmer."

Palmer leaned in and said, "If you don't want to go, just say no. But you don't have to worry about imposing or my family not wanting you there. *I* want you there, Lizzy. If you can make it happen, I'd love it. I'm not ready to say goodbye to you, either, in case you haven't noticed."

"Where would I stay?"

"With me." Palmer swallowed at her own response. "It's not a huge bed like this one, but it'll fit both of us. If you'd prefer to stay in a hotel, though, I can send you a list of the good ones. There's one only five minutes away, where security could stay. I don't know the protocols for this stuff. Do they stay in the adjoining room if you're in a hotel or something?"

"You really want me there? Victoria didn't put you up to this?"

"She mentioned that I should invite you."

Elizabeth's look changed to disappointment before she said, "So, you're doing this out of some sense of obligation."

"Elizabeth, I would have asked you sooner had I actually thought I could."

"What do you mean?"

"You're the Queen of a country. I didn't think I *could* ask you to come to visit me."

"Of course, you can." Elizabeth wiped another tear off her own cheek.

"Well, then I am. Will you come?"

Elizabeth stared into the fire again and said, "I'll have to discuss it with security, but I'd like to go with you."

"I can't wait to tell Camilla. She's going to freak out." Palmer laughed a little, letting out the breath she'd been holding in since this conversation began.

"Don't tell her just yet. I have to make it through the Christmas address first."

"It's just a speech, right?"

"It's a speech that closes one of the most tumultuous years in the history of this country and sets the tone for the next year."

"Oh, so no big deal, then," Palmer joked.

Elizabeth laughed before turning serious again and said, "How am I supposed to address a country when some of them don't even want me here?"

"I'm no speechwriter, but I'd say acknowledge that."

"Acknowledge it?" Elizabeth turned to her.

"Yeah. If there's an elephant in the room, I always think it's better just to say it. There's no point in hiding it when everyone knows it's there, right?"

"What do you suggest I do?"

"You can either come down hard and tell them you're here to stay, and they need to get used to it, or you can risk asking their opinion."

"What do you mean?"

"Tell them about the history of the monarchy in St. Rais. Explain about the money; how you make your own and give back to the community. Tell them you understand how some people don't think a monarchy here is relevant, but you are, and give them the reasons why."

"We've done that before."

Palmer stood up abruptly and asked, "Have you ever asked them?"

"Ask them what?"

"Elizabeth, if you had to live without a title, without being a Queen, would you want to?"

"I want to support my country, my people, but I don't care about titles. The title just allows me the opportunity to do that."

"And if that was taken away?"

"I'd feel like I let my family down, but if that's what the people wanted, I don't think I'd have a choice. It's important to me that if there is a monarchy, the nation can at least in part agree that it should be here."

"I have a crazy idea that will likely make Rebecca and everyone else around you want to send me back to the States immediately and never let you talk to me again, but if you're up for listening to it, I think you might like it."

CHAPTER 25

THEY'D stayed up most of the night reworking Elizabeth's Christmas address speech to include Palmer's crazy idea. At first, Elizabeth worried that the three whiskeys she downed and the bottle of wine Palmer drank might have been clouding their judgment. Then, she'd woken before Palmer and read it again, her mind sober and alert.

"Well?" Palmer asked.

She'd appeared behind the sofa and leaned over the back of it, placing her head right next to Elizabeth's, who could feel her warm breath that was minty fresh thanks to the toothbrushing she'd just done in Elizabeth's bathroom.

"It's still crazy."

"But?"

"But… I have to get it approved by about a million people."

"You're the Queen; you're in charge."

"Not really. You know that's not how it works," Elizabeth said as Palmer walked around the sofa and sat down next to her. "I have very little actual power. Parliament is involved here. So is the Prime Minister. Plus, this risks Victoria and David's titles as well as the titles of any of their children and their children's children."

"Do you think Victoria will care?"

"I don't know, honestly. This hasn't ever been something we've discussed."

"Is that all that worries you?" Palmer asked.

"No," Elizabeth replied. "But we don't have time to go into all my worries right now. You have a plane to catch, Miss Honeycutt."

"Oh, we're back to that, huh?" Palmer laughed.

"I don't think there is any going back, Palmer," she said.

"No, I don't think there is," Palmer agreed. "I should get changed."

"I'll be here when you're ready."

Secretly, Elizabeth hoped it would take Palmer hours, days, weeks, or even months to get ready. She didn't want Palmer to leave. There was still so much for Elizabeth to learn about the woman. There was still so much for them to do together. Realizing the one person she'd come to count on since the loss of her family was about to leave, forcing her to be on her own with all of this again, Elizabeth let the tears fall freely down her cheeks. Victoria had David. Elizabeth would have no one.

"Hey, what's wrong?" Palmer asked, emerging from Elizabeth's bedroom, wearing her patented sweatshirt and jeans, pulling her bag and warmer winter gear lying on top of it behind her. "Elizabeth, what—"

"Nothing. It's nothing." She wiped her cheeks. "Sorry. Where were we? Do we have enough time to just go over it again?"

"Don't do that," Palmer said, sitting down next to her and taking the papers they'd printed the previous night from Elizabeth's hands, dropping them onto the table. "What's wrong?"

"You're leaving," Elizabeth answered honestly. "I think I just realized how much I'm going to miss you."

"You're still coming to visit me soon, though. Right?"

"I'll speak with security; I don't know for sure. They might not like that idea, or the Prime Minister might—"

"Don't do that," Palmer said again. "Don't try to make other people the reason you won't do something, and don't push me away just because I have to get back home. We made a plan, Lizzy. You'll come for Christmas and stay with me. I'll do my best to make it back in the summer."

"But what about after that?" Elizabeth asked, letting it all out now, no longer fearing what might happen if she kept in her tears. "It's going to be too hard, Palmer."

"Bullshit," Palmer argued, glaring at her. "Don't pull

this crap, Elizabeth. I just met you. This isn't it. We'll figure it out, okay?"

Elizabeth wiped her tears away again and decided to tell her, to finally tell her. Palmer had earned that much.

"Palmer, I have to tell you something," she began. "It's about Teagan."

Palmer leaned back on the sofa and asked, "How long were you two together?"

"What? How did you–"

"I was staying at your house, Elizabeth," Palmer interrupted. "I didn't mean to, at first, but I noticed things. The pictures in your room, for one. They looked a lot like some I've taken with previous *girlfriends*." Palmer then looked over at Elizabeth. "I saw the books."

"The books?" Elizabeth met her eyes. "Oh, *the* books." She turned away again. "I meant to take those with me, but every time I looked at them, I couldn't move."

"Tell me about her; about the two of you?"

Elizabeth cleared her throat, stood, and went to the small table by the window to get herself a glass of water. Filling one and taking a long drink, she finally decided to tell the whole story.

"Teagan and I met in primary school, like I told you. We *were* best friends."

"Until?"

"We were fifteen," Elizabeth answered and took another drink as she stared out the window into the wintery morning sky. "She went to kiss me on the cheek, but I moved my head on accident. I was just turning toward her because she was laughing, and our lips touched. It was innocent, but I left the encounter thinking about the next. That's how it began."

"That's sweet," Palmer said with a soft smile.

"It was. By the time we were sixteen, we were kissing for long minutes and calling it practice for when we'd kiss boys."

"And *did* you?" Palmer asked.

"We both tried it. It was easier for her. She wasn't a Princess, but I kissed boys at a couple of parties. Nothing compared to kissing *her*, though." She thought back on those first few kisses. "By the time we were seventeen, we were together. I called her my girlfriend in private, and she called me hers. She was my first in every way, and I loved her."

"How long were you together?"

"Until she died," Elizabeth replied.

"What? She was married to—"

"Alexander and I had a problem in common," Elizabeth interrupted. "Teagan allowed us to solve it, for the most part."

"What does that mean?"

Elizabeth turned to face her and said, "It means, Alex and I were both gay. And while our father had many positive traits, supporting two gay children wasn't one of them."

"What did he do?" Palmer asked, looking angry.

"Nothing. He didn't know."

"Then, ho—"

"We knew our father. We knew *his* father, too. They were fairly conservative, devout in their faith. Our mother was better, but also devout. When you add that to the fact that we were royals and meant to carry on the line, it didn't compute for either of us to tell him. Dad made several comments over the years about homosexuals. He wouldn't have wanted two out of his four children to be gay."

"You can't help who you are, Elizabeth."

"I know that. Alex knew, too, but we both made the decision that it would be better for us if Dad didn't know. Martin was going to be King one day. He was much more progressive. Gay marriage was only just legalized here last year, and while monarchs don't vote and don't choose political sides, Dad made his opinion known on the matter. He didn't want it to pass. Alex and I made and stuck with our decision."

"So, your gay brother *married* your girlfriend?"

"Yes, he did. Alex didn't want a husband. He much preferred to date around, and he always chose men who were discreet. Teagan wanted to be with me, but we couldn't without facing my father's wrath and maybe even the country's, too. She and Alex never slept together. They had separate rooms, and she and I got together whenever we could. It was a lot easier when she was in school with me, before they moved into their house, but we made time for each other."

"The books?"

"Those were from when we were in school. She'd buy one and highlight things that made her think of me. Then, she'd give it to me to do the same. I kept some of them at my house. She had the rest. I went to the house she and Alex shared after and took them. I haven't had the heart to open them and read them since she died, but I have them to remember her by."

"Elizabeth, you lost your family *and* the woman you loved in one day?"

"Part of me will always love Teagan Gentry, Palmer, but after she married Alex, something changed with us." She moved back to the sofa to sit down next to Palmer. "It was like that ceremony and that vow before God and country made me see her differently. I know that's not fair to her; she did it for me. It was a way for us to be together, for Alex to marry and avoid any speculation about his own sexuality, and no one really cared about me as the third-born once Martin had the kids. I had a lot of time before I had to get married or people would start wondering why I wasn't. I figured I could use school as an excuse and then a career, and eventually, people would give up, including my parents, and Teagan and I could be together in our own way. But things changed."

"How so?" Palmer asked softly.

"We stopped being romantic, for one. We had to arrange to spend time together. As second-born, Alex was required to perform royal duties alongside Martin. He would bring his wife, obviously, and Teagan seemed to enjoy that part of the deal. I normally wasn't required to attend or didn't want to have to find my own date, so I was left alone a lot. About six months ago, she started to talk about this friend she'd met at one of the functions, and how they'd hit it off. They started spending time together, and I thought she was cheating on me, and technically, Alex, too. We fought over it. She was risking everything. I yelled. She told me nothing had happened but that she was starting to have feelings for her. I yelled some more." Elizabeth let a few tears fall. "We were each other's only. She wanted to explore, but she'd locked herself into this family and had no way out. I loved her and couldn't understand how she'd want to be with someone else in the way we'd been together."

"God, I'm sorry, Elizabeth."

"Three months before it happened, we were still technically together, but things were different. I think she was with me because she felt trapped, and I was with her because I'd never known anything else. I thought I'd spend the rest of my life with her. And when Rebecca told me they were all gone, I thought of her first." She started crying in earnest. "I thought of my girlfriend first; not my father or my brothers or Lyla or even the kids. I thought of Teagan and how I'd never know if we were going to make it past what we were going through. How wrong is that?"

"It's not wrong. You can't help how you feel or what comes to your mind when something like this happens. Come here," Palmer said, pulling Elizabeth into her side, wrapping her comforting arm around her as Elizabeth's head went to Palmer's shoulder. "I am so sorry. I wish I could take away all this pain. I wish I could find a way to give her back to you."

"She didn't want me, Palmer. She wanted someone else at the end. I could tell. I could see it in her eyes; feel it when she kissed me."

"Maybe you could have worked it out. I don't know. I–"

"She told Alex the day before it happened that she wanted a divorce, Palmer. Don't you see? She wanted to be free of him. Being free of him meant she could be free of *me*. She'd be able to be with whomever she wanted with no strings; have the life she wanted. She could marry a woman, have a family, and settle down. I never thought I'd do that. I couldn't give that to her. I was too scared."

"You don't have to be scared now."

"I'm terrified," Elizabeth replied, wiping the tears from her cheeks again. "I am terrified, Palmer."

"Why? You can be whoever you want to be now, Elizabeth. As terrible as it is that you lost them all… you can be yourself now."

"No, I can't." Elizabeth stood.

"Why not? What's holding you back?"

"I'm the Queen of St. Rais, Palmer. I have—"

"Your Majesty," Rebecca said, entering the room. "Oh. Ma'am, is everything okay?" she asked when she saw Elizabeth's tear-streaked face.

"Yes, everything's fine. What is it, Rebecca?" she asked tersely.

"Miss Honeycutt's car is waiting outside to take her to the airport, Ma'am."

"Oh," Elizabeth spoke softly, looking down at Palmer now, who still sat on the sofa.

"I can take a later flight," Palmer said.

"Ma'am?" Rebecca asked.

"No, it's fine. Palmer, you should go. You have to get home."

"Elizabeth, we're talking about something pretty important here."

"You need to get home, Palmer. You've only stayed this long because of me."

"There's another flight that leaves in the afternoon. I can—"

"Rebecca, will you have someone help Palmer with her things?" she interrupted Palmer, looking at her secretary because she couldn't look into Palmer's disappointed eyes.

"Yes, Ma'am." Rebecca left the room.

"Don't do this, Lizzy." Palmer stood up. "Let's finish this conversation. There's more to say here."

"I told you the story because I thought you deserved to hear it. You've been a great friend to me, Palmer. Now you know. I would ask that you don't tell anyone."

"I would never," Palmer said. "But there's more, isn't there? There is for me, at least."

Elizabeth swallowed, allowed a few more tears to fall, and then looked toward the floor.

"I have to take a shower. I have meetings today."

"I am asking you not to push me away," Palmer replied. "You at least owe me *that*."

Elizabeth nodded rapidly, knowing Palmer was right but not being able to do anything about it.

"I'll message you about the Christmas address to tell you if I'll be giving the speech we worked on together. Have a safe flight, Palmer."

"Will I see you over Christmas, at least?" Palmer asked as Elizabeth breezed past her toward her bedroom.

"I'll let you know." Elizabeth closed the double doors behind her, rushed into her bathroom, and turned on the shower to drown out her tears.

CHAPTER 26

"YOU'RE back?" Anna asked.

"Anna, what are—"

"I tried calling and texting after you emailed me back. You never responded."

"That should've told you something," Palmer replied.

"I've been coming by the apartment every day, knocking like an idiot. I made a mistake, Palmer. Can we please talk?"

"Anna, I told you, I don't want to get back together. I just got home yesterday. I'm still jet-lagged, I have Christmas shopping and laundry to do, and then I have to drive to Pittsburgh."

"Why are you driving?"

"Because I planned on driving long before I decided to stay in St. Rais, so I didn't book a flight. Now, the prices are astronomical, so I'm just going to power through with some caffeine and then sleep until the new year."

"Can I come in? I feel like your neighbors are going to call the cops on me. I've been coming here every day, remember?"

"This is New York. No one cares enough to call the cops." Palmer inhaled deeply and let it out through her nose. "You can come in, but just for a minute, Anna."

"Yeah, fine. That's fine." Anna moved into the apartment.

Palmer regretted the decision immediately but closed the door behind her ex-girlfriend anyway.

"What did you want to say?" Palmer asked.

"I figured out what I want, Palmer." Anna shrugged as she turned around to look at her. "I thought I needed to, I don't know, find myself, which is such a cliché and should be something I do in my forties or something, but I don't need that. I don't want to be with other women. I want to be with you."

"Anna, you said that in your email and in your texts. I told you I don't feel the same way. I'm sorry. I don't want to get back together with you."

"You said you loved me in the email."

"I said I *loved* you. Yes, I did love you."

"You don't anymore?"

"Anna, you told me I wasn't enough for you. You needed someone else or, possibly, multiple people. I tried. I did. I tried *because* I loved you. When I went on my vacation, I thought about what I would say to you when I got back. I kept going back to the fact that you needed someone else, and I wanted one person."

"I can be that person now, Palmer." She moved into Palmer's space.

"No, you can't. You're not that person for me, Anna. And I'm not that person for you, either." Palmer stepped back. "I'm sorry, but I just woke up, and I have a million things to do."

"No, I get it," Anna said, looking down at the chipped hardwood floor. "Were you with someone else over there?"

"You don't get to ask me that, Anna."

"I know." The woman looked back up. "You're right. I'll go."

Palmer sighed and said, "You were with someone else, Anna. *You* did that. I didn't. I wasn't with anyone else, okay?"

"Yeah, okay. I guess I thought it would make it easier, knowing, but it just makes me feel like more of an asshole." She laughed at herself.

"I'm sorry."

"Don't be. It's on me. All of this is on me, okay? Don't

ever think you weren't enough for me, Palmer. You were. You'll be enough for someone else, too. They'll just be smart enough to keep you."

With that, Anna left.

***

It had been three days since Palmer had returned home, and after a stern lecture about what it takes to be an investigative reporter from her boss, a visit from her ex-girl-friend, three loads of laundry, five hours of Christmas shopping for her parents and her sister, along with the secret Santa gift she needed to get for the office gift exchange, Palmer was more than exhausted. She regretted not getting a flight when there had been good deals earlier in the fall, but she'd been so focused on her failing relationship with Anna and her desire to go on a vacation that she'd wanted to save up money for her solo trip and not for a flight. It was only a six-hour drive, seven or eight with breaks and the weather, which wasn't great but wasn't nearly as cold as St. Rais.

Strangely enough, she found herself missing that level of cold. There was just something about it that, even though she complained a lot, she enjoyed being all layered up, walking through the city trying to find something to eat or a place to check out. Of course, that was probably more about St. Rais than the weather, but Palmer couldn't focus on that right now. She'd thought about Elizabeth the entire flight home, refusing to let any tears fall until she arrived home. When she'd flopped onto her own bed, she thought about how she missed Elizabeth's. When she tried to make coffee, she thought about how she liked the instant stuff she'd found in St. Rais and the fancy stuff she always got at the palace. When she cranked up the heat, she thought about how she missed the fires that didn't just provide warmth but comfort as well. She missed St. Rais. And she missed Elizabeth more.

Palmer hated the way they'd left things. They were finally getting somewhere. Finding out about Elizabeth and Teagan only made Palmer think that she hadn't been crazy in what she was feeling. There was a small chance that Elizabeth had felt it, too. But if Elizabeth felt something, she wasn't ready to admit it, and Palmer couldn't just wait around St. Rais hoping she would one day. Teagan had essentially done that, and their relationship had fallen apart at the end.

Palmer packed everything she needed into the rental car and hit the road. Elizabeth hadn't reached out, but Palmer had sent an email with the details of her visit to Pittsburgh should Elizabeth decide to come, after all. Palmer missed her like crazy. There were three days until Christmas, and she hoped beyond hope that Elizabeth would call her and say she'd be there soon. If she didn't, Palmer didn't know what would happen to them. Would she still visit in the summer? Would things ever be the same with them? Would their friendship or whatever it could have been just end, after the best weeks of Palmer's life?

She stopped for gas and snacks about halfway to Pittsburgh and checked her phone for messages just in case. Not finding any, she couldn't resist taking a moment to do a quick Google search, typing 'Queen Antonia' I into her phone. The Christmas address was hours ago now, if it went according to the schedule Elizabeth had given her. Finding the YouTube link posted by the palace, she clicked on the video, leaned back in the driver's seat, and watched Elizabeth, who was sitting behind a desk Palmer didn't recognize, looking regal and confident as ever.

"My fellow citizens, this has been a trying year for all of us. As I am sure you could imagine, giving this speech is not something I thought I'd ever have to do. My father delivered this speech every year for many years. My grandfather did before him, and so on and so on. The plan was for my brother Martin to deliver this speech, and then his young daughter Edwina would take the throne and carry on the tradition one day. It's a hard thing for us to consider taking over one after the other because it means we lost someone we loved. In this case, I lost many people I loved, as did others. Mothers and fathers lost sons and daughters, brothers and sisters lost siblings, friends lost friends. And all because a group of people in St. Rais no longer believes a monarchy is necessary. I've longed believed not only in the necessity of the monarchy but also in its relevance even today. I recognize that some of you – perhaps, even many of you – would disagree or find that statement self-serving, but I assure you it's not. The monarchy of St. Rais is unlike any other monarchy in the world. We are not funded by our taxpayers. We've said this before, but I believe after the events of this year, that it may bear repeating. This building I live in, the houses owned by my family, the staff that works so hard for us, and everything else is paid for out of the money my family has earned and invested for generations. While it is true that tax money is diverted in our name toward our interests, our interests have *always* been in bettering the lives of the citizens of St. Rais. We supply all of you with every bit of information you need to see that this is true, and yet, there are people who still doubt us and our intentions enough to commit an act of terrorism, murdering fifteen people. They'd planned to murder more as well. Their plan would have killed my sister, Victoria, myself, and several others who are only doing their jobs in providing our security. I find it hard to swallow that we, in St. Rais, have to commit these types of acts when we have a democratic government where votes can be cast, speeches can be made, and campaigns can begin in earnest. There is the right to free speech, and if there is the desire to remove the monarchy of this country, all that would be needed is an act of Parliament brought about by the citizens of St. Rais. I love my country. I was raised to believe that being a member of the royal family was my duty, as it was my father's before me and all of my siblings. However, if this nation no longer believes in that duty, it might be time for a change." Elizabeth paused. She was really about to do this. "I have consulted my sister as well as the Prime Minister and key members of Parliament in this decision. I cannot simply step down as your Queen. Because it is my duty, I would be letting down my ancestors if I abdicate. That would also only put my sister in the same position I'm in now. So, instead, I've asked Parliament to bring about an emergency vote of confidence in the monarchy. In two months' time, there will be a nationwide vote. Every citizen who meets the legal and age requirements will be allowed to vote on whether or not the monarchy should remain in St. Rais. If the vote is no, Victoria, myself, and the rest of our family will be stripped of our titles, and there will be a plan put in place by Parliament and the Prime Minister for the nation after the monarchy is dissolved. However, I am hopeful that you still find value in our charitable works and our support of this country. If the vote is that the monarchy remains, I will continue on as your Queen, and I will do anything and everything I can in support of this amazing country. Now, I will leave you with this message. Each Christmas, despite what has gone on during the year, it was the King's duty – and now my own – to express my sympathies to those who are alone or have been driven from their homes by war or violence, as well as those who have been lost to the same things. For harmony in St. Rais to return, we must find the healing power of tolerance. Friendship and love must be allowed to play a part in our society. We must work together despite our differences. We must celebrate these holidays with those we love because they are sometimes taken far too soon." Elizabeth's eyes welled with tears. "Please welcome in the new year with a new hope for peace and prosperity for all. Happy Christmas to everyone. I wish you joy and happiness, love and safety."

That was it. The video ended. Palmer couldn't wait; she called Elizabeth immediately.

"I'm sure you're busy or asleep. I just wanted to tell you how unbelievably brave and strong you are, and that I am so proud of you, Elizabeth. I haven't told my family that you're not coming yet, which means they're saving a place for you. I hope I don't have to tell them that you've changed your mind. If I don't get to see you, though, Merry Christmas, because that's how we say it in America. And... I don't know... I guess I'll just say that I miss you." She hung up when she'd left her message.

Then, she left the gas station parking lot and hit the highway again. Three hours later, she pulled up to her parents' house. Before she could get out of the car, a text message came in. Palmer rushed to check it, but before she looked, she said a silent prayer that it wasn't Elizabeth canceling her trip officially. It was from a number she didn't recognize, but she opened the message in her app anyway. She laughed a little when she saw it was from Victoria. Elizabeth *was* sleeping. The whiskey she'd consumed after delivering the address had gotten to her, but Victoria said Elizabeth would be on a plane headed to Pittsburgh tomorrow. She'd even included the information for the private plane she'd be taking and the time of her arrival at the small airport, about an hour away from her parents' house. Elizabeth was coming, after all. Palmer would be seeing her tomorrow, and she could *not* contain her smile.

CHAPTER 27

WHEN her plane touched the ground, Elizabeth let out a deep exhale. The last time she'd been on a plane, she'd gotten the worst news of her life. This time, she felt as if she'd fled her country after giving them the news that she and her entire family would give up the crown and everything that comes with it if a vote passed. It was true that the family always took this time off during the holidays, but it still didn't feel right that she did it this year. She'd wondered what her father would think about her decision to put it to a vote, and she didn't have to wonder long. She knew he would be displeased. Her father could be kind and loving one minute and strict and angry the next. He'd never been abusive in the strictest sense, but he had a way with words that made his children understand when it was time to back down from whatever they were asking for or wanted from him. Their mother had applied balance for much of their lives, but after her death, their father had gotten worse. His entire focus moved to Martin and the future of the monarchy he saw in his son and his grandchildren. It struck Elizabeth, at times, how he had no issue with a woman on the throne and showered Edwina with both affection and faith in her future as Queen, but that he *did* have problems with the idea of anyone who wasn't heterosexual ever becoming a monarch.

She knew her mother would be supportive of her decision, especially given the circumstances. Not only had Elizabeth lost most of the people she loved in the world, but there was also an attack on the only family member she had left shortly after. Until the agencies found the man they were searching for, along with his most dedicated followers, her family was still at risk. Victoria and David would be married soon. Children would follow thereafter, and likely, quickly, given how much those two seemed to want them as soon as possible. Elizabeth didn't want to risk more loss for herself, for her family, or for her country. Victoria had understood her decision and had, in the end, supported it. She'd admitted being rather fond of her title, but that if Elizabeth felt this was the right thing to do to at least curb some of the unrest and put the vote to the people, she'd go along with whatever those people said.

Elizabeth had visited the gravesite of her family prior to leaving for America. Security had been on full display, but she'd needed to talk to her parents, her brothers, her sister-in-law, her niece and nephew, and lastly, Teagan, who had been buried next to Alex because no one knew the truth. Now, no one would ever know. Elizabeth knew only ashes were buried there, but it was still a place she could go to talk to them; to let them know they were and would never be far from her thoughts and that she only hoped she'd make them all proud.

She'd been holding on to so much guilt and anger at what happened. The guilt was survivor's guilt, and she knew she'd have to talk to someone about it one day, but today was not that day. The anger was directed at the people responsible for taking her family from her, but also at Teagan. Was it fair? Elizabeth didn't know. It was how she felt, though. Teagan had been the only woman she'd ever loved; the woman she thought she'd spend her life with. It was unconventional, to say the least, but it had worked for them. Alex had been protected. Elizabeth and Teagan had been able to be together without anyone else knowing. Then, it had all changed. Now, it was all over.

Elizabeth had checked the message Palmer had left for her, and it had made her smile just hearing the woman's voice. Palmer's words, though, were what had helped her make the ultimate decision to come to the States for the holidays. Prior to Palmer's voicemail, she'd still been going back and forth. They hadn't left things in a good place. It had been Elizabeth's fault, so she was carrying that guilt now, too. She'd known what Palmer wanted to talk about. It had been that elephant in the room for a while now, so it would make sense for Palmer to want to address it. She, likely, hadn't done so right away to save Elizabeth from having to deal with one more thing.

"Your Majesty," Palmer said with a smile as Elizabeth deplaned.

"Palmer? What are you doing here?"

"I'm picking you up," Palmer replied. "I got permission from security to meet you out here."

"I was going to go straight to the hotel," Elizabeth said as her feet hit the pavement. "I would have called you to—"

"Yeah… forgive me for not believing you," Palmer interrupted her. Then, she held out a single white-and-yellow flower. "For you."

"A plumeria? How did you know?" Elizabeth asked.

"You had a bunch of them in your rooms. And when you gave me the tour of the palace greenhouse, they were the only flowers you touched. I took a guess that they might be your favorite."

"They are. Do you know why?" Elizabeth asked, bringing the flower to her nose.

"I don't, no."

"Besides being beautiful, plumerias have many different meanings to cultures around the world. To some, they're revered and worshipped. They're sacred. To others, they represent death and funerals. Others still, see them as a representation of perfection. My mother saw them as representing new beginnings. She's the one that built the greenhouse. The plumeria only grows in warm climates. You've *seen* our winter. Without a greenhouse, she wouldn't be able to see her favorite flower very often."

"They were your mother's favorite?" Palmer asked as security officials and other people tried to get bags off the plane and into a waiting black SUV.

"They were. She told me a story about them when I

was a young girl, and I thought it was so cool, they became my favorite as well. At night, plumerias release a fragrance that attracts moths looking for nectar. Only there is no nectar; it's a trick. The plumerias know that they need the moth to pollinate them to survive, so they bring them near with the scent and give the moths nothing in return, but the moths pollinate them by going from flower to flower in search of their prize." She smiled widely. "Not great for the moths, I'd wager, but it's fascinating to me how plants know exactly what they need and how to have that need fulfilled, and they create the mechanisms to do it."

Palmer smiled at her and said, "You and my dad are really going to get along."

"We are?" Elizabeth asked.

"Wait until you see their backyard." Palmer took a step into Elizabeth's space. "Can I hug you?"

"What?" Elizabeth asked, taken aback by the question.

"We're in public. I didn't know if it would be okay, but I want to hug you, Elizabeth. I've missed you." Palmer shrugged a shoulder.

"Oh. Yes, you can hug me."

Palmer's smile widened, and she moved a step closer. Then, her arms went around Elizabeth's waist, and Palmer pulled her flush against her own body. For a moment, Elizabeth forgot what a hug was, but finally, she moved her own arms around Palmer's neck and moved more fully against her. When Palmer's face pressed to Elizabeth's neck, Elizabeth dropped her own onto Palmer's shoulder and breathed her in.

"I missed you," Palmer repeated against Elizabeth's coat.

"I missed you, too," Elizabeth replied.

***

"You know you don't have to stay at the hotel, right?" Palmer asked.

"It wouldn't be right to stay with your parents."

"Why not?"

"Because I have a security team with me. Where would they sleep? On the sofa? The floor? On the dining room table?"

"No, but *they* could stay at the hotel. *You* could stay with me."

Elizabeth met Palmer's eyes and said, "In the same bed, Palmer? What kind of message would that send to your parents or your younger sister?"

"That's not what you're really worried about. But we're not alone right now, so we can talk about *that* later." Palmer lifted an eyebrow at her. "And *I* could sleep on the sofa."

"I'm not making you sleep on the sofa in your own home, Palmer."

"It's not my home. I grew up there, Elizabeth, but I'm twenty-nine years old – I don't consider their house my home anymore."

"Well, *I'd* sleep on the sofa in your studio apartment if we were going there. I wouldn't make you–"

"That's not my home, either," Palmer stated.

Elizabeth turned in her seat and said, "That's where you live."

"But it's not my home. It's where I sleep at night. It's got some furniture in it and a few personal things, but not even all that many. It's not home, though."

"Then, you have no home, Palmer? I don't like the sound of that."

"Home isn't a place, in my opinion. It's not the things you own, either. I've always believed your home is wherever your people are. If my parents move to a different house, my home goes with them. It goes with my sister, too." Palmer's cheeks turned a light shade of pink then. "Home will be wherever the woman I love is one day. That's my hope, at least."

"That's a nice hope," Elizabeth replied, giving her a smile.

"Yeah, it is." Palmer nodded in the direction of Elizabeth's window. "We're here."

Elizabeth turned around to see that they'd pulled up to the hotel.

"I'd like to shower, change, and unpack if that's all right with you. When am I expected at your parents' house?"

"It's not like that." Palmer chuckled at her. "You're not expected to *be* anywhere or *do* anything, okay? We'll have dinner out tonight since my mom will be cooking for Christmas Eve and Christmas Day. You're invited, of course, but the restaurant is a casual one, so wear jeans and a sweater or something."

"I feel like I don't even need my coat here. It's so warm," Elizabeth teased.

"It gets colder at night. Wear the coat, smart-ass," Palmer replied, tugging on the garment until Elizabeth's face was next to her own. "Can I come back here with you after dinner?" she asked softly just as Elizabeth's door was opened for her. "We need to talk."

"Won't your parents miss you?"

"No, it'll be fine." Palmer kissed Elizabeth's cheek. "I will text you the details for dinner, but I'd like to pick you up here and bring you if that's okay."

"I don't know if security would like that," Elizabeth replied.

"Does anyone know you're here?"

"No, we told the country I'm at Coburn Cottage with Victoria and David."

"Then, let me pick you up. They can follow us or lead the way or both if they want." She kissed Elizabeth's cheek again. "Please."

Elizabeth could only nod. Palmer's touch was so soft, so warm, and so hard to pull away from.

"I'll see you in a few hours, then," Palmer told her. "Your Majesty," she added when the security officer leaned into the SUV to offer his hand to Elizabeth.

"I look forward to it, Miss Honeycutt."

As Elizabeth showered, she couldn't get her mind off Palmer's more overt advances. In St. Rais, she'd been reserved with her touches, almost reverent with Elizabeth. In part, due to her respect for Elizabeth's position, no doubt, but also in part because of Elizabeth's recent losses. Now, it was as if Palmer had decided to make her intentions obvious. Elizabeth hadn't ever been able to share touches like that with Teagan unless they were alone. It had been exciting to be kissed on the cheek and pulled into Palmer's embrace with others around them to see that someone cared for her. Someone cared for Elizabeth, and it appeared, Palmer wasn't worried about whatever had been worrying her in St. Rais. She no longer cared about Elizabeth being a Queen, the distance between where they lived, or the fact that Elizabeth had had a very long relationship with someone who was now gone. Elizabeth smiled at the thought that Palmer Honeycutt might try to kiss her soon. She might even want to do more, and Elizabeth wasn't sure she'd be able to resist. She just wasn't sure she was ready.

CHAPTER 28

"YOU brought me another flower?" Elizabeth asked, laughing as Palmer handed her a single flower.

"It's a dahlia. I'm sure you even know its Latin name, but I know it as a dahlia. It means dignity and elegance. It made sense for you, I thought."

"Where are you getting these?" Elizabeth laughed a little, bringing the flower to her nose.

"Most dahlia species don't have a scent. Did you know *that*? They're just beautiful. Another reason I thought you should have it," Palmer said.

"Thank you, Palmer."

"You'll see later where I get them, but we should get going. Security let me come up here to get you, but the guys on shift are waiting downstairs."

"Let me get this in some water first. Come in," Elizabeth said, motioning for Palmer to enter the hotel suite. "You look comfortable." She added as she turned back to Palmer.

"*I'm* wearing what I told you to wear. You're wearing a dress," Palmer noted. "We talked about this, Elizabeth…"

Elizabeth laughed and said, "I'm meeting your parents and your sister for the first time. I shouldn't be *too* casual."

"My sister won't be at dinner. She's at school until tomorrow. My parents will pick her up then, but you need to know your audience, Your Majesty. My mom runs a restaurant. My dad is a teacher. I don't think I've seen my mom in a dress in years, and the most dressed up my dad ever gets is wearing a tie with his short-sleeved button-up shirt. Did you even *bring* jeans?"

"Yes, I brought jeans."

"Then, put them on."

"You don't like my dress?" Elizabeth asked.

Palmer raked her eyes over the blue cocktail dress that went so well with Elizabeth's perfect eyes. Palmer very much liked that dress. She just also wanted to tear it off her.

"Your dress is beautiful. *You* are beautiful in it, but I like it when you're comfortable. Don't dress up for my parents. Just throw on a pair of jeans and a shirt or something."

Elizabeth nodded and dropped the dahlia into a glass with water in it next to the plumeria from earlier.

"I'm starting quite a collection," she said with a smile, glancing at the flowers.

"I'll help you add to it while you're here," Palmer said.

"What's gotten into you?" Elizabeth asked.

"What do you mean?"

"You seem different."

"Different *bad?*" Palmer asked, swallowing hard.

"Not bad; just different. Do you really want me to change?"

"You don't have to if *you* don't want to, but no one else is going to be dressed up."

"Maybe I shouldn't go, Palmer."

"What? Why?" Palmer sat on the end of the bed and looked up at her.

"What is security going to do while we're eating?"

"What do they *normally* do when you eat? Stand around, right?"

"I haven't been to a restaurant in a while; since I was fifth in line and in school, and no one cared about me."

"We're going to an American restaurant for burgers and fries in a Pittsburgh suburb where no one even knows about St. Rais, most likely, let alone its Queen. You'll stand out more if you're dressed up. I have a hat in my car. You could wear that, too. You'd be totally incognito, and security could back off a bit."

"You have a hat in your car?"

"It's a Pittsburgh Pirates hat. It's not exactly a tiara, but I think a tiara might make you stand out a bit, too." Palmer smiled at her before she reached both hands out to take Elizabeth's and pull her in closer.

"Another American football team?"

"No." Palmer laughed. "The Pirates are baseball. Don't tell my dad, but I'm now secretly a Yankees fan. I was converted when I moved to New York, but I still like the Pirates, and I make sure to bring the hat whenever I come home."

"I do not understand American sports," Elizabeth said, looking off into the distance, but she didn't let go of Palmer's hands. Instead, she entwined their fingers and let them dangle between them. "I'll change. Can you give me a minute, or will we be late?"

"We'll be fine. Maybe save the dress, though."

"For?" Elizabeth asked, pulling back so she could find clothes to change into.

"I don't know. I'm sure I'll find some reason to get you to dress up while you're here." Palmer stood up. "I'll wait outside."

"Can you unzip me first?" Elizabeth asked, staring into Palmer's eyes.

"How did you get into the dress, to begin with? Did someone from security—"

"No, I did it myself," Elizabeth replied, turning her back to Palmer. "I just want you to do it."

Palmer's eyes met Elizabeth's in the mirror above the desk. She slowly unzipped the dress, but before she stepped back, she lowered her lips to Elizabeth's shoulder and kissed her bare skin.

"We're talking later," she told the woman.

Then, she backed up and left the room, waiting for Elizabeth out in the hall more out of necessity than to give Elizabeth the privacy to change. Palmer let out a deep breath she'd been holding in. There was just something about Elizabeth being *here*, on Palmer's turf, that made her feel like she could finally be herself in every way. And part of her loved wooing a woman. She liked buying the flowers, planning dates, making a woman feel like she was special. And Elizabeth was definitely special. Palmer knew she needed to take it easy. She was coming on a little strong; strong enough that Elizabeth had noticed. Then, she realized that Elizabeth not only hadn't pushed her away or asked her to stop, but she *had* asked Palmer to unzip her dress for her. And it had taken everything in Palmer to not look at Elizabeth's back but to keep her eyes on Elizabeth's instead.

***

"I'm sorry. Palmer told us to treat you like anyone else, but I wasn't sure if we should or not," Palmer's mom said as she shook Elizabeth's hand.

"Mom, it's fine." Palmer had her hand on the small of Elizabeth's back, guiding her into the booth first. "We don't want anyone to know she's here anyway, so her name is Elizabeth, and she's not a Queen tonight, okay?"

"Okay," her mom replied, sitting down.

"It's nice to meet you," Palmer's father said as he sat down next to his wife. "Palmer's told us a lot about you."

Palmer slid into the booth after hanging Elizabeth's coat, along with her own, over the hook between two booths.

"All good, I hope?" Elizabeth asked.

"We know about what happened to your family, sweetie. We're so sorry you have to go through this," her mom said.

"Me too," Elizabeth replied. "I'm happy to be here, though. Thank you so much for allowing me to join your family for the holiday."

"Of course. The more, the merrier," her mom said.

"Told you so," Palmer said to Elizabeth, who looked over and smiled at her.

"You know you're welcome to stay with us, though. You don't have to stay at a hotel."

"I know. Palmer told me, and I appreciate that, but I

come with a security team, and they need a place to sleep, too. I didn't think it was fair to ask them to sleep on the floor or for you to put them up."

"Palmer tells us you're a Ph. D candidate in physics," her father said.

"I would have been one day, I think. I had one more year of school to get through before I could go for a Ph. D, though."

"Hello there, folks. I'm Steven. I'll be your server tonight," the waiter said as he approached their booth, notebook in hand.

"Hi, Steven." Palmer's dad looked down at the menu for a moment. "I don't think we've had a chance to look at the menu yet."

"Can I get you something to drink while you think about what you want?"

"Honey?" her father said to his wife.

"Iced tea," her mom said.

Palmer glanced at Elizabeth.

"Oh. I'll have the same, I guess."

"Lemonade," Palmer requested.

"Same for me," her father added. "You know, if you two mix your drinks together, you'll make an Arnold Palmer."

"I'm sorry?" Elizabeth said, shaking her head in confusion.

Palmer placed a hand on Elizabeth's thigh and laughed at her father, who was one of the biggest nerds she'd ever met.

"Don't worry about it. Do you want an appetizer?"

"I don't know. Whatever you order, I'll try."

"Yeah? They have an artichoke spinach dip I like, and Mom usually gets the mozzarella sticks."

"Okay," Elizabeth said.

"Have you ever had a mozzarella stick?" Palmer asked, smiling at her.

"No," Elizabeth replied.

"We should have taken her someplace nicer," her mother said.

"Oh, no," Elizabeth replied. "No, this is perfect." She smiled at Palmer's parents. "This is exactly what I wanted."

Elizabeth's hand moved on top of Palmer's, and she entwined their fingers. Palmer smiled and knew she was blushing but couldn't do anything about it.

"We should get the blooming onion appetizer," her father said. "It's deep-fried, terrible for you, and delicious."

"Maybe no onions," Palmer suggested.

Then, Elizabeth turned to look at her. The smile she had dimmed only for a second before it went wide again.

***

"Your parents are lovely," Elizabeth said as they walked to her hotel room door.

"They're good people, yeah."

"Please thank them for dinner again for me. It wasn't necessary for them to pay. I'll treat them later in my trip."

"They don't mind, but I'll tell them," Palmer said as they arrived at Elizabeth's door. "So, can I come in with you? We haven't really had any time to just talk."

Elizabeth unlocked the door but turned around instead of walking inside.

"Palmer, I think I'd like to be alone tonight if that's okay. I flew here, and with the time difference, I–"

"No, you're right. I get it. I just said the same thing to my ex a few days ago."

"What? Anna?" Elizabeth asked.

"She stopped by my apartment when I got back. I told her I was jet-lagged when she wanted to talk, and now I'm doing the same thing to you. Why don't you call me when you wake up tomorrow? My parents are picking up Camilla. I'll have most of the day to myself. We can do some tourist things in the city if you want; if security thinks it's okay."

"Anna wanted to talk to you?" Elizabeth asked.

"Yeah, the conversation lasted all of five minutes."

"Did she…"

"Elizabeth, I'm here." Palmer took Elizabeth's free hand and added, "I'm here, okay? Now, get some sleep. We can talk later."

"Okay." Elizabeth nodded. "I'll see you tomorrow, Palmer."

She leaned in and kissed Palmer on the cheek.

"Good night, Your Majesty."

"Good night, Miss Honeycutt."

Elizabeth smiled until the door closed between them.

CHAPTER 29

"WELL, how is it?" Victoria asked.

"Different than I thought it would be," Elizabeth replied.

"How so? Is the food terrible or something?"

"No." Elizabeth laughed. "*Palmer's* different."

"Oh." Victoria's tone changed. "Bad different?"

"No. I don't know." Elizabeth sighed.

"Okay... Can you explain what you *do* know? Maybe I can help."

"She knows, Vicky."

"Knows what?"

Elizabeth shifted in bed.

"Knows I'm gay. I told her about Teagan before she left St. Rais."

"You told her? Why didn't you tell me that you told her?"

"I'd had a lot on my mind, and I wasn't even sure it mattered. Palmer promised she'd never say anything, and I trust her. I wasn't sure I was coming here, anyway. I guess I thought I could tell her and not come to America for the holidays, and then..."

"And then what? Never talk about it again? Never talk to Palmer again?" Victoria asked.

"I don't know. I didn't think it through. She figured it out mostly, anyway. I just filled in the blanks."

"Did she tell you how stupid you're being, staying in the closet when *you're* the Queen now and Dad is gone? I'll never understand his issue with the whole thing."

"He was religious, Vicky."

"So was Mom. And she was okay with it."

"Probably not with *it* being in her family if she knew. I mean, tell me what other monarchy had a second or third in line for the throne that were both gay."

"You and Alex both got demoted when Edwina and Anthony came along, anyway. If that asshole hadn't taken our family from us, Martin would've taken over for Dad, and he would've been a perfect cookie-cutter King. Lyla would've made an amazing Queen Consort. Little Edwina would have followed in their footsteps, and Alex could've gotten divorced because he would have been fourth in line. You and Teagan could've just been together. Who knows? Maybe Lyla and Martin would have had more kids. They were talking about it before it happened, you know? And the further down the line you go, the less people care about who you are, what you do, or whom you do it with." Victoria paused before adding, "But none of that matters anymore, Lizzy. You're gay, and *you're* the Queen. You can show the country that love is love, and it doesn't matter if it's between a man and a woman, a man and a man, or a woman and another woman. Gay marriage passed in St. Rais. You wouldn't be alone."

"There's no point going through all that if I'm not going to be Queen in a couple of months."

"There is if you've found someone," Victoria argued.

Elizabeth rolled onto her side and said, "I haven't."

"Don't lie to me, Lizzy. But more importantly, don't lie to yourself. You like Palmer. In fact, I think you might be falling in love with her."

"Palmer is an amazing woman. I—"

"Don't give me some line about how she lives there, and you live here, or how you're the Queen and she's an American. None of that crap matters when you care about someone, Lizzy."

"I cared about Teagan," Elizabeth replied.

"You loved Teagan, but that relationship had run its course. Neither of you wanted to admit it, but that's the truth. I'm convinced she married Alex in a last-ditch chance to try to make it work between the two of you, which ended up breaking the two of you up."

"We were still together."

"You just hadn't said the words, Lizzy, but you two hadn't been in love for a long time. Look, I know it's hard for me to relate or identify; I've had one serious boyfriend before David, but it was never like how it was with you and Teagan. You two grew up together. You were best friends first. Then, you were together for years – it's got to be hard to end something like that. And then you lost her so abruptly." Victoria sighed. "I wish I could bring Teagan back to you just so you could get the closure you need to move on, because Palmer is great, Lizzy. I can tell she cares about you. And I can see that you care about her, too. Just don't push her away. Don't make excuses. Just be with her while you're there; see how it goes. And if you think it could be something, the two of you will figure it out, okay?"

"I don't know."

"What are you so afraid of?"

"Teagan wanted to leave me. What if Palmer does, too?"

"Well, we're all afraid of that, aren't we? David and I are engaged to be married – we'll *be* married soon, and there's always a chance he could leave. There's a chance *I* could, too. You can only love someone and hope that you grow together, not apart, right? Mom and Dad grew together. Growing up, I could always tell how she changed him for the better, and he changed her for the better, too. Even though he could be an asshole sometimes, he never was with her. In every relationship, there's that chance they could leave, Lizzy. But that doesn't mean you give up trying to find someone."

"What if I'm not ready?"

"Do you like her?"

"Yes," she admitted out loud for the first time.

"Is she worth it, Lizzy? Is she worth the risk?"

"Yes."

"Then, if you're not ready for something – whatever it

is – you tell her. And if she's the kind of person that's worthy of you, she'll understand, and she'll wait."

"I can't ask her to wait for me."

"You can let her make the decision for herself."

"What if I'm never ready?"

"You will be, Lizzy. You will be."

***

"I can't believe *that* was what you wanted to do," Palmer said the next day.

"I've never been to see a movie at an American movie theater before."

"Is it any different than theaters in St. Rais?"

"No, but I rarely got to go to those. We have the small theater in the palace, remember? It wasn't until I went to university that I saw a movie in a theater, like everyone else, for the first time."

"Really?" Palmer asked, shielding both of them from the cold rain with an umbrella.

The weather was cold but not freezing enough for snow, so as the rain began to fall, Palmer had taken an umbrella out of the car and held it over both of them. That meant they had to walk closely together as they exited the theater, but Elizabeth didn't mind.

"When we were growing up, our father didn't like when we socialized with other kids," Elizabeth explained. "His father raised him in a bubble, so it was what he knew."

"I'm not sure I would've liked your father very much," Palmer admitted, taking Elizabeth's hand and giving it a squeeze.

"Well, I'm not sure I would've let you meet him." She squeezed the hand back and held on to it.

"Why not? I can dress up from time to time. You've seen me." Palmer pulled her in closer. "I did the whole title-curtsy thing until you told me not to."

Elizabeth laughed and said, "It's not because of you,

Palmer. My father wouldn't have understood you. There's a reason the world doesn't know much about St. Rais. He and the monarchy worked, in part, to keep the place separated from everywhere else. I don't know if it was the right decision, but me being friends with an American reporter wouldn't have made sense to him. He wouldn't have liked it."

"In the same way he wouldn't have liked your relationship with Teagan?" Palmer asked, opening the door for Elizabeth and helping her inside the car.

Elizabeth waited until Palmer was in the driver's seat before she spoke next, "I don't really know how to answer that."

"Why not?" Palmer asked, starting the ignition. "I was thinking, we could grab dinner somewhere. Is that okay?"

"Dinner anywhere is fine. And I don't know how to answer that question, Palmer, because I don't know how I'd describe our relationship; yours and mine."

Palmer turned to her and said, "I think you do. I think you have to admit it to yourself, and that's hard, but I think you know how to describe what we're doing; what we have or *could* have."

"Americans, certainly, are direct, aren't they?" she replied, laughing more as a stall technique than anything else.

"Look in the back seat," Palmer told her.

Elizabeth squinted in confusion before turning to look in the back seat.

"I don't know these," she said, picking up a small bunch of pale-colored flowers.

"They're forget-me-nots," Palmer explained, pulling the car out of the parking lot. "According to my dad, they mean two things."

Elizabeth sniffed the flowers and held them out in front of her. Palmer took her free hand and moved it into her lap, entwining their fingers again.

"They mean true love," Palmer added. "And don't forget me."

Elizabeth stared at Palmer as she drove.

"Which one of those applies to me?" she finally asked.

"I think that depends entirely on you," Palmer replied.

They drove on for a while until Palmer pulled into another parking lot. Their day had been cut short due to Elizabeth sleeping in way later than she'd planned. Palmer hadn't seemed to mind, though. She'd just picked her up at the hotel later and was fine with security following them everywhere they went. Security, for their part, had been keeping their distance, and for the first time in a very long time, Elizabeth felt free: free from her worries about her country, about her family, about herself, and even free from her guilt and anger at her losses. Before they got out of the car, Palmer, without words, brought Elizabeth's hand to her lips and kissed the outside of her palm. They said nothing of it. When they got inside the restaurant, Palmer placed her hand again on the small of Elizabeth's back and ushered her to their table.

After they'd eaten their dinner, Elizabeth insisting on paying this time, Palmer stood up and helped her with her coat. Elizabeth took Palmer's hand this time, not being able to wait for Palmer to initiate the contact and also wanting Palmer to know that she loved holding her hand. And she hoped they had more chances to touch like this; she knew she wanted that. She wanted to hold Palmer's hand, and she wanted to do more. God, she was finally able to admit to herself that she wanted more with Palmer Honeycutt, who had taken her completely by surprise in St. Rais, and was now doing it again in Pittsburgh, Pennsylvania; a place Elizabeth had never thought she'd see but was now so glad she had.

"So, what do you want to do now?" Palmer asked when they climbed back into the car.

"Do you have to go back to your parents' house just yet?"

"No, they took Camilla out to dinner tonight. They'll probably be home a little later."

"Do you want to come back to my hotel, then?"

Palmer turned to her and softly said, "Yes."

"Would it be okay if we stopped by your parents' house first, though?"

"Sure. But, why?"

"So that you can get your stuff, Palmer. I'd like you to stay the night with me."

Palmer softened and asked, "You *did* have a hard time sleeping last night, didn't you? It's why you slept in so long today."

"Palmer, you misunderstand," Elizabeth began, taking Palmer's hand and placing it into her own lap this time. "I don't want you to stay because I need help sleeping. I just want you to stay."

CHAPTER 30

"HEY, Cami," Palmer said into the phone. "Yeah, I'm with a friend right now, but I'll be at Mom and Dad's tomorrow to see you."

"Okay. Mom said you were with the Queen."

"I am. We're going to hang out tonight, but she's very excited to meet you tomorrow."

"She is?" Camilla asked.

"She is, yeah."

"Does she have a tiara?"

Palmer turned her head to look at Elizabeth and said, "You didn't happen to bring a tiara with you, did you?"

"I *did*," Elizabeth replied.

"Wait. You did? Why?"

"For your sister, of course," Elizabeth replied as if it was a stupid question. "It's one of my old ones. I thought it might fit her."

"You actually brought a tiara for her to try on?"

"No, I brought one for her to keep," Elizabeth responded. "What kind of person would I be if I gave your sister a tiara to wear but not to keep, Palmer?"

"You can't just give–"

"Palmer?" Camilla interrupted.

"Sorry, Cami." She refocused on her sister. "Elizabeth *did* bring a tiara for you to try on. How cool is that?"

"It's awesome. I'll get to meet her tomorrow?"

"Yes, but it's late now. Mom told me she's trying to get you to get some rest."

"She is, but I wanted to talk to you first."

"You need to get some rest if you're going to meet a Queen, don't you?"

"I do. If I go to sleep now, morning will come faster."

"That's right. I love you, Cami."

"I love you, too."

"Sleep well, Camilla."

"Okay."

There were some sounds that Palmer was used to. They indicated Camilla was passing the phone back to their mother.

"Hey, honey," her mother said.

"Hey, Mom."

"Are you okay where you are?"

"We're just at the hotel."

"And you're going to stay there tonight?"

"Yes."

"With Elizabeth?"

"Yes, Mom." Palmer laughed.

"I'm sensing there are things your father and I don't know. I sure would appreciate an update."

"Tomorrow, okay? I can't right now."

She looked over at Elizabeth, who was staring at her.

"Fine. The mother is always last to know."

"Don't be dramatic," Palmer said, laughing. "I love you, guys. We'll see you tomorrow."

"Love you, too, honey."

Palmer hung up the phone, placed it on the table in front of the sofa, and wrapped her arm around Elizabeth's shoulders.

"Is everything okay?"

"Everything's fine. Cami just wanted to say goodnight to me."

"She loves you."

Elizabeth placed her head on Palmer's shoulder.

"I love her."

"It shows."

"Please tell me you're not really giving my sister a tiara?"

"I am. It's her Christmas present, actually."

"So, it's fake, right?"

"What? No." Elizabeth lifted her head and shook it at Palmer. "I've had a tiara since birth, Palmer. My head got bigger; they didn't. So, they just sit there, and eventually, they get donated to a museum or become part of the palace tour. I brought the one I had when I was her age. It's very real, and it's hers to keep."

"That's too much, Elizabeth."

"No, it's not. She's your sister. I want her to have it."

Palmer kissed Elizabeth's forehead and said, "My parents are going to shit a brick."

"Oh, my God!" Elizabeth exclaimed through her laughter as she placed her head back down on Palmer's shoulder. "Is that an expression here? That's terrible."

"We're not known for our class in America, Lizzy."

"I suppose not," Elizabeth said, placing an arm over Palmer's middle and settling into Palmer's side.

It was the closest they'd been since they'd met. Sure, Palmer had woken up in the middle of the night and found Elizabeth spooning her in her sleep, but this was different. They were both fully awake right now, and Palmer wasn't comforting Elizabeth this time; they were just enjoying being wrapped up in one another while watching a movie they'd ordered on the TV.

"Is it okay that you're staying here tonight? Your parents and sister aren't disappointed?"

"My parents are asking questions I've yet to answer, but my sister is so excited to meet *you*, she doesn't even really care that *I'll* be there."

Elizabeth turned her face up but didn't move her head from Palmer's shoulder.

"They're asking questions?"

"My mom just wanted to know what I wasn't telling her. I'll talk to her tomorrow. It'll be fine."

"About us?"

"Yes."

"And you don't have the answers?" Elizabeth checked.

"No, I don't. I have… feelings."

Elizabeth *did* lift up then and looked into Palmer's eyes.

"So do I," she admitted. "But I don't know if that makes it harder or easier."

Palmer smiled, cupped her cheek, and said, "Well, it at least lets me know I'm not the only one in this thing; whatever it is."

"I want you to stay tonight, Palmer, but I'm not ready for–"

"It's okay. Neither am I."

"You're not?" Elizabeth's arm moved from Palmer's middle to her thigh.

"No, I'm not." Palmer shook her head. "I want to, though."

"Me too." Elizabeth gave her a shy smile. "I just need time."

"I can give you that."

"You don't have to. This is all so unfair to you."

"How's that, exactly?" Palmer shifted so she could see Elizabeth's face better.

"Because I come with all this baggage, and it's recent baggage." Elizabeth sat up more. "Palmer, I don't even know what I can offer you."

"This is pretty good so far," Palmer replied.

"*This* is temporary," the woman argued, shifting out of Palmer's grasp.

"*This* is enough for now, Elizabeth. I know things are complicated; I'm not naïve."

"I know you're not. I just worry I won't be enough for you, Palmer. I worry I can't give you what you deserve. I couldn't give Teagan what she deserved, and it made her look elsewhere. I–"

"Hey, can we just watch this movie, please?" Palmer reached for Elizabeth's hands. "I just want to sit here with you and finish this movie. That's what I need, okay? Then, we can go to bed. If you don't want me in there with you, I'll sleep out here."

"What? No, I want you in bed with me, Palmer. I want

to hold you tonight. I sleep so well when you're next to me."

Palmer pressed her forehead to Elizabeth's and said, "Then, that's what we'll do. We don't need to worry about anything beyond tonight for now, okay? I'm not going to pressure you into having all the answers. We'll come by those together when we need to."

"Are you sure?" Elizabeth asked her.

"Yeah, I'm sure. I don't want to let you go, Elizabeth. I can't, okay? I just need to be with you tonight. We'll figure it out."

"Okay. We'll figure it out." Elizabeth repeated after her as Palmer kissed her forehead.

They sat on the sofa, curled up together until the movie ended. Palmer wouldn't be able to tell you the plot, but if asked later how to describe how good it felt having Elizabeth there next to her, breathing against her neck, that Palmer would remember. After that, they changed into their pajamas in different rooms, and it reminded Palmer of her first year in the dorm at NYU, when she and her roommate hadn't known how to operate in a rectangular room with no walls. Palmer had ended up changing behind the door, using it to shield her body, and her roommate had taken to changing behind the dressers they had stacked against the wall.

After they brushed their teeth next to one another in the bathroom, sharing smiles throughout, Palmer made her way into the bedroom. The bed was a king-sized one, nice and spacious, but she kind of hoped they wouldn't use all that space. Elizabeth slid in first. Palmer moved in next to her. Then, they rolled on their sides, facing one another.

"We haven't talked about the whole Christmas address vote thing," Palmer began as she wrapped an arm around Elizabeth's waist possessively.

"Do you want to now?"

"I don't know. It's a big deal."

"It *is*, yes."

"How are you feeling about it?" Palmer rubbed circles on Elizabeth's back over her shirt.

"Scared," the woman replied.

"What did the Prime Minister say?"

"At first, he was against it. He thinks the monarchy provides an outlet for people at times – there's another form of government almost, without there actually being a form of government in the monarchy."

"I don't think I'll ever fully understand how it all works," Palmer said.

"You're an American; you haven't grown up in a country with a monarchy. In fact, if I remember correctly, your Founding Fathers, as you call them, made it illegal for the government to grant titles of any kind."

"That sounds like us," Palmer said.

"He understood why I wanted to do this, though," Elizabeth added. "Given everything that happened, putting it to the people to decide the fate of the monarchy is the right thing to do. If we take no public funding for our own benefit and we aren't lawmakers or part of any official government body, maybe they're right: maybe we *are* irrelevant. If that's what they say in their vote, I'll renounce my title, and so will Victoria."

"Should I ask what you're hoping for?" Palmer asked, sliding her hand under Elizabeth's shirt to rub her warm, soft skin.

Elizabeth's eyes closed, and she answered, "No, because I honestly don't know myself. One moment, I can't picture my life any other way. The next, I think of the freedom I'd have. I could finish school, get a job in physics, and maybe get married and have kids one day."

"With a woman?" Palmer checked.

Elizabeth's eyes opened.

"I won't marry a man, Palmer. I may not be as brave as you – I'm not out, and I am ashamed of that fact – but if I do ever get married, it would be to a woman. I won't lie to myself, even if I've been lying to everyone else."

"You have nothing to be ashamed of, babe." Palmer slid a little closer to her. "Nothing. No one else has the right to shame you when they don't know your circumstances. How many young women grow up third in line to a throne with a father who makes it clear being gay is not an option? How many people have lost all that you just lost on top of having to take over for a King? Your choices are your own. And I'll support you in them, for whatever that's worth."

Elizabeth's eyes grew watery.

"And if they vote to keep the monarchy and I remain Queen?"

"Then, you remain Queen." Palmer looked at her with confusion.

"What about us, Palmer?"

"Oh," Palmer replied, rubbing Elizabeth's back again. "We're not worrying about anything beyond tonight, remember?"

Elizabeth nodded.

"Can you sleep?" Palmer asked.

"Yes. But can I hold you? I held you that one night, and I don't think I've ever slept better."

"You want me to be the little spoon?" Palmer teased.

"Yes," Elizabeth confirmed.

"Okay. I will happily be your little spoon."

Palmer rolled over and felt Elizabeth slide up against her back. Elizabeth's arm wrapped around Palmer's waist, and Palmer slid it under her own shirt, pressing Elizabeth's hand against her stomach. She let the tension leave her body when Elizabeth's face went into the crook of her neck, and Elizabeth kissed her there.

"Good night, Palmer."

"Night, beautiful."

Palmer could swear she could feel Elizabeth's smile against her skin.

CHAPTER 31

"SORRY, I have some work to do today."

"It's okay. You warned me," Elizabeth replied, sipping on her tea.

"How is it?" Palmer asked, smirking at her.

"American," Elizabeth said, smirking back. "But your mother was very kind to get this for me."

"You have to tell her if you don't like it. If you don't, she'll keep buying it and make it for you every time you come over."

"Every time?" Elizabeth repeated in question form, making sure to meet Palmer's eyes.

"Yes, every time." Palmer winked at her.

"Okay... Are you ready for the real tour?" Palmer's father asked as he entered the kitchen where Palmer had set up her desk for the afternoon to get some writing done, and Elizabeth had joined her because she didn't want to be apart from her any more than she had to be.

"Yes, of course."

"Grab your coat," he said, zipping up his own.

"That won't be necessary," Elizabeth replied, standing up.

Palmer laughed and explained, "Dad, she thinks that because the winter she's used to is so harsh, our winters are basically summer."

"Oh, really?" he teased. "You've never been through a Pittsburgh winter. It's true that this year we're having a mild one, but it's normally worse. I remember the snowstorm in seventy-eight: twenty-seven inches of snow in three days. About twenty people died that year."

"What's twenty-seven inches in centimeters?" Palmer asked Elizabeth.

"Sixty-eight point six," she replied.

"Sixty-eight," Palmer's father said at the same time. "I rounded down," he added.

Palmer lifted an eyebrow at Elizabeth, then looked at her father and said, "You two leave me alone and go do your nerd tour."

Elizabeth stood up. As Palmer's father moved to open the sliding glass door, she leaned down and gave Palmer a quick kiss on the cheek.

"Don't work too hard," she said softly.

She watched Palmer's smile grow. Then, she turned to see that Palmer's father was giving her that patented Honeycutt lifted eyebrow. She'd been caught, and now she was about to spend alone time with this man.

"After you," he said, motioning to the now-open door.

Elizabeth followed him into the backyard down a sidewalk path that had already been shoveled and then salted. It was cold, but her borrowed sweatshirt with 'NYU' on the front was enough to keep her warm until they arrived at the greenhouse.

"This is amazing," she said once they were inside.

"The school where I teach subsidized it once I took over the AP botany courses."

"AP?" she asked.

"Oh, sorry. It's advanced placement. They're classes that bright students can take in high school. They take a test at the end of the year, and if they score high enough, they can skip courses in college when they get there. I started teaching botany two years ago. The school's actually only a half-mile through the woods behind our house. It's very convenient for me to get to work, but when I was able to get a grant to build the greenhouse, as long as I use it for the students, the school helped me make it a part of the curriculum. Now, the students can come to the greenhouse and see plants they'd likely never get to see otherwise."

"You have hibiscus?" Elizabeth asked, walking over to one of the rows where she noticed the pink flower.

"I do. That one wasn't easy to get growing here, even in the greenhouse." He stood behind her. "Palmer thought you might like this place. I see she was right."

"My mother had a greenhouse. Her favorites were plumerias, but she taught my sister and I about a lot of flowers. The hibiscus means rare and delicate beauty." She touched just one of the petals with the tip of her finger.

"It's possible, my daughter will give you one of these later," he said, chuckling. "She appears to be on a mission to make my thriving greenhouse a barren desert."

"Oh, I'm sorry." Elizabeth turned to look at him. "I'll ask her to stop."

"No, don't." He waved her off. "For starters, flowers are meant to be seen. I give them to my wife all the time. And to Camilla, of course. I'd give them to Palmer, but–"

"She's more of the giving kind when it comes to flowers?"

He smiled and said, "Yes, she takes after me that way, I guess."

"She's very sweet," Elizabeth said, smiling.

"She is, yes," he said. "What's *your* favorite?"

"Sorry?"

"You said your *mother's* favorite was the plumeria."

"Oh, the plumeria is mine as well," Elizabeth replied. "Although, it's probably my favorite because it *was* her favorite, so I don't know. Maybe it's time to find a new one." She smiled at him. "It might just be the next one Palmer gives me."

"Until she gives you another one?"

"Are we about to have a conversation about Palmer?" she asked, meeting the man's eyes.

"I don't know. *Should* we have a conversation about Palmer?" he asked back.

"She must have gotten her directness from her mother." Elizabeth laughed.

"You've noticed that, huh?" he asked back. "Yes, my wife wears the pants in our marriage. I am man enough to not only accept but acknowledge how well it works for us. That includes her directness; she's not someone who messes around when there's a direct line to something."

"What would you like to know?" Elizabeth asked as she walked to the next row of fragrant flowers.

"The two of you are more than friends," he said.

"We haven't really stated *what* we are to each other," she replied.

"You don't have to; it's pretty obvious. You seem to know her pretty well already, and we noticed the holding hands at dinner the other night, not to mention the kiss on the cheek before we came out here, and the fact that she stayed in your hotel room last night."

Elizabeth swallowed hard at the mention of the hotel room and said, "We haven't... We didn't... I mean, I–"

Palmer's father laughed loudly and said, "Palmer is almost thirty years old, Elizabeth. We know how this works."

"Maybe Palmer should be the one to talk you," she said, trying to sidestep this whole conversation.

"She will. Well, she'll probably talk to her mother first. I guess what I'm curious about is how this is going to work with you two; assuming there *is* something with you two."

"Things are complicated," Elizabeth admitted. "I'm not... out." She met his eyes again.

"We'd never say anything. I knew Palmer was a lesbian before she did, I think. I kept my mouth shut until she sat us down to tell us." He gave her a kind smile. "We can keep a secret."

"Palmer is so different than anyone I've ever met," she said. "And my world has changed so completely the past few months."

"How does my daughter fit into all of that?"

"I don't know yet," Elizabeth replied honestly. "I

don't know if she can or if she even wants to."

"She wants to," he stated. "I can tell. Besides, I can also see her from the kitchen table right now. She's turned around at least ten times to check on us since we've been back here."

Elizabeth chanced a glance only to meet Palmer's eyes. Palmer quickly turned back around. Elizabeth and Palmer's father both laughed.

"She's beautiful," Elizabeth said more to herself than anyone else.

"She takes after her mom that way."

Elizabeth returned her attention to the flowers and began walking around the space.

"Do you know the Silene viscaria?" he asked, nodding toward flowers that were bright rosy pink, appearing in long-whorled spikes. "They grow on cliffs and rocky places. Their common name is just viscaria."

"I don't know them, no."

"They mean an invitation to dance. I know Palmer isn't one to receive flowers, but I know she likes to dance."

"She does? She never told me that. There was a dance at my coronation dinner, and she declined the Duke of Nottingshire's offer."

"She would, wouldn't she," Palmer's father laughed lightly. "I doubt she wanted to dance with a duke of anything. She probably wanted to dance with a Queen."

Elizabeth nodded slowly.

"Why don't you take some of these to her later?" he offered, passing her some sheers that had been on the table nearby. "I taught her everything I know about dancing, and even my wife will tell you, I've got moves," he joked.

***

"Camilla, let the woman breathe," Palmer's mother said as Camilla continued to show Elizabeth pictures of her friends from school on her iPad.

"It's okay," Elizabeth said. "I'm enjoying the show," she added for Camilla's benefit.

"Oh, no," Palmer said.

"What?"

"My show! Do you want to see my show? Mom recorded it."

Elizabeth turned to Palmer in confusion.

"She was in a play last year. She calls it her show. It's an hour long. You just signed yourself up for some fun," Palmer explained.

"What was the play, Camilla?" Elizabeth asked, placing a hand on Palmer's thigh and giving it a playful shove to punish her for making fun of her sister.

"It was about history. I was Betsy Ross. I made the American flag."

"Yeah, can I see?"

"I had four lines," Camilla said as she scrolled through the iPad, searching for the video.

"Camilla, why don't you leave the iPad with Elizabeth for the night? She can watch your show while you get ready for bed," Palmer's father suggested. "It's bedtime, sweetie."

"But Elizabeth is here," Camilla replied.

"I'll be here tomorrow, too," Elizabeth told her. "It's Christmas."

"Christmas is here!" Camilla yelled.

Elizabeth had noticed her volume increased and decreased erratically at times. She was such a happy kid that Elizabeth found Camilla's happiness rubbing off on her, and she liked it. As hard as it was, being around a family when she'd only just lost her own, there was still something so comforting in being with *this* family.

"Yes, Santa comes tonight," her father replied.

"She still believes in Santa," Palmer whispered into Elizabeth's ear. "Don't ruin it for her."

"Never," Elizabeth said, smiling at Palmer. "Camilla, if you let me borrow the iPad, I'll watch your show tonight. We can talk about it after presents tomorrow."

"Yay!" Camilla gave her a big hug before practically jumping off the sofa and bursting up the stairs leading to the bedrooms.

"I'll put her to bed," Palmer's father said.

"I'm tired, too. And we have to get the gifts down here under the tree," Palmer's mother said. "You get her in bed. I'll get the gifts under the tree. Then, I'll go in and kiss her goodnight."

"Sounds like a plan," he replied like a man who had done this at least twenty-nine times before. "I'll say good-night now, ladies."

"Night, Dad," Palmer said.

"Good night," Elizabeth added.

"Elizabeth, honey, I know security is just outside, but you will be safe here tonight. Please stay in Palmer's room. Camilla is usually up so early on Christmas morning... I'd hate for you to have to go to the hotel tonight only to turn right back around, and I definitely don't want you to miss her seeing her presents for the first time. She's the reason we still make such a big fuss at Christmas."

"It's true. She's happy no matter what she gets," Palmer added. "I could buy her a pencil with a unicorn eraser, and she thinks it's the best thing in the world."

"You didn't, did you?" Elizabeth asked.

"No, I didn't. But it doesn't matter what *I* got her – you got her a freaking tiara. No one can compete with that," Palmer replied.

"You two fight over your gifts for Camilla all you want. Just do it quietly, please. You know she wakes up easily," Palmer's mother told them. "And, Elizabeth, please stay."

Elizabeth gave her a nod. Then, they watched Palmer's parents follow their daughter upstairs.

"Will you?" Palmer asked. "If you can't, I understand, but I need to stay here tonight."

"I just need to tell security to go back to the hotel," Elizabeth replied. "I'm sure they'll give me a lecture."

Palmer turned to her, slid a hand over her cheek, and

said, "I won't let anything happen to you."

"It's still early," Elizabeth told her. "Want to watch a movie with me in bed?"

Palmer smiled and said, "Yes."

"Good. I have a play to watch. Camilla is Betsy Ross. Did you know?" Elizabeth said, standing up.

"Not again," Palmer sighed out.

CHAPTER 32

"PALMER! Palmer!"

"What the hell?"

"'Hell' is a bad word," Camilla said.

Palmer opened one very tired eye and asked, "Cami, what time is it?"

"Christmas time. Santa was here. I went downstairs already."

"Okay. Go get Mom and Dad," Palmer replied, closing her eye.

"Don't go back to sleep! We have to open presents!"

"They'll still be there when I wake up, Cami."

"What's going on?" Elizabeth asked against Palmer's neck.

Palmer opened both eyes then and saw Camilla staring down at her in bed with another woman.

"Cami's here," she said.

"Oh," Elizabeth replied, rolling away immediately.

"You were holding Palmer," Camilla said, pointing at them.

"Cami, can you give Elizabeth and me a minute? We'll get dressed and then meet you downstairs, okay?" Palmer requested.

"Did you watch my show?" Camilla asked Elizabeth.

"I did," she replied. "Palmer and I both watched it."

"The whole thing," Palmer grumbled.

"What was your favorite part?" Camilla asked.

"When you said the color white on the flag represented purity and innocence," Elizabeth told her.

"Palmer, what was your favorite part?" Camilla asked with such a wide smile on her face that Palmer couldn't deny her younger sister.

"When you said, 'Let the thirteen stars in a circle stand as a new constellation in the heavens.'"

"George Washington said that in real life," Camilla began. "But *our* George Washington got sick, and I got to say his line."

"You did an amazing job, Cami," Elizabeth replied. "Do you think Palmer and I could just have one minute to get dressed? Then, we'll come downstairs and watch you open your presents."

"Presents!"

Camilla smiled first, then laughed, and ran out of the room without closing the door behind her.

"She really is adorable," Elizabeth said, rolling back over to snuggle against Palmer's chest.

"And early. It's only six," Palmer replied.

"She's got that wide-eyed innocence that people usually lose by the time they're her age, Palmer. It's so nice to see it, you know?"

Palmer wrapped an arm around Elizabeth's shoulders and pulled her in closer.

"I know. I love it. I just love it after ten AM." She kissed Elizabeth's temple. "We should get up, or she'll just come back in."

"I'm borrowing your hairbrush again," Elizabeth told her.

"Borrow whatever you want." Palmer slid out from under her and ran her hands rapidly over her face. "Okay. I'm ready. Time to be jolly."

"Jolly?" Elizabeth laughed.

"Yes, jolly. It's Christmas." She turned around and winked at Elizabeth.

"Hey, Palmer?"

"Yeah?"

"Merry Christmas," Elizabeth said with a smile.

"You said *merry*. We're converting you to our American ways." Palmer moved quickly to tickle Elizabeth's sides.

Elizabeth moved onto her back, and Palmer moved to straddle her, continuing to tickle the woman. Elizabeth laughed and laughed. Palmer smiled down at her and stopped tickling her until she stopped laughing. Then, Elizabeth just stared up at her, and if the door to Palmer's bedroom weren't open, Palmer would've leaned down and kissed her. She'd been thinking about kissing Elizabeth practically every moment of every day since she'd first uncovered Elizabeth might actually *want* her to kiss her.

"I'm so glad you're here," she said instead, running her hands over Elizabeth's stomach over her borrowed sleep shirt.

"So am I. I didn't know how much I needed this until I got here."

"We should get down there," Palmer told her as Elizabeth began running her hands up and down her thighs and under the shorts she'd put on to sleep in. "Because that feels really good."

"Yeah?" Elizabeth asked, using her fingernails to drag teasingly over Palmer's skin.

"Yeah. And I'm trying to behave myself since the door is open, so let's go." She gave Elizabeth's stomach a playful smack. "Oh! Before you get up… hold on."

"Get up. Stay here. Get up. Stay here," Elizabeth teased.

Palmer jumped off the bed, made her way down the hall, and returned with what she'd been after. She sat down on the side of the bed and turned to Elizabeth.

"I picked this one last night for you. It didn't come from my dad's stuff. My mom grows her own herbs for work and cooks with them here, too. I remember she told me once that rosemary means remembrance," Palmer explained, holding out the sprig of rosemary she had left in the bathroom the night before to give to Elizabeth this morning. "It's not as pretty as the flowers I've given you, but I wanted to give you something today to remember your family. I hope that's okay."

Elizabeth looked at the small token and then met Palmer's eyes. Palmer watched her smile softly.

"Thank you," she said.

"I'm sorry you can't have this Christmas with them. But, Elizabeth, I'm so glad you're here, spending it with me."

Elizabeth nodded, taking the rosemary from Palmer's hand, sitting up, and then placing the gentlest of kisses on Palmer's lips.

"Where are you guys?" Camilla's yell came from not all that far away.

They pulled back, laughing at Palmer's sister.

"Let's go, Your Majesty. The Princess awaits."

***

"Do you like it, Cami?" Palmer asked.

"It's beautiful," the girl said.

As expected, Cami had liked all of her gifts, including the magic set and VIP membership to the fan club for her favorite boy band of the moment that Palmer had gotten her. It came with an autographed picture that she knew Cami would love. Her sister had loved the gifts their parents had gotten her and the ones that had come from Santa, but her favorite gift of all had been the tiara that Elizabeth had not only given her but had added to it Princess lessons from herself and remotely, from Victoria. She'd even gotten Victoria to record a sweet video for Camilla that included when, where, and how to wear a tiara. Then, Elizabeth had taught her how to wave, how to sit, and how to sip her tea, which Camilla did *not* care for.

Palmer's parents had received gifts from Elizabeth as well. Her father had been given a membership to the Dad Science Lab, which was a monthly science kit delivery specifically for dads to share with their kids, as well as a book signed by a prominent botanist. He'd loved it. Palmer's mother had been given a box of St. Rais exports that were hard to come by, as well as a promise to send them to her as often as she'd liked if she decided she wanted to use any of the ingredients in her restaurant. Elizabeth had also gotten her a cooking-with-kids kit. She'd thought of everything. Palmer's father would get to share science with his daughter, and her mother would get to share her love of cooking with Camilla.

"Palmer's turn," Camilla said, pointing to Palmer, who was holding the gift Elizabeth had placed in her lap.

"You didn't have to get me anything," Palmer told her.

"It's Christmas." Elizabeth smiled at her simply. "And I wanted to."

Palmer tore open the very nice wrapping paper, acting like Camilla, who only moments earlier had torn every gift open within seconds. Palmer doing it earned a laugh from Camilla, which was what she was going for.

"Plane tickets?" Palmer asked. "To St. Rais?" She turned to Elizabeth.

"They're open-ended; you can come whenever you want. I thought you and your family might like to come in the summer."

"My *family*?" Palmer checked all the tickets. "You got us *all* tickets?"

"Yes," Elizabeth said. "You are all welcome to stay with me in St. Rais whenever you'd like." She turned to Camilla. "I know Princess Victoria would love to meet you, Cami."

"She would?" Camilla asked hopefully.

"And I'd love to show you all my country if you can get away." She looked at Palmer's parents.

"We've never traveled internationally," Palmer's mother admitted. "Cami doesn't even have a passport."

"I think ours are expired, too. We got them when we thought we'd take a vacation to the Caribbean, but Camilla had needed us, so we'd had to cancel."

"St. Rais is beautiful in the summer, and not cold," Elizabeth noted, turning back to Palmer again. "There's something else in there just for you." She nodded toward the box.

Palmer looked down as well and found a small box within the larger one. She opened it and smiled.

"No way..." she said. "Mom, it's a lifetime supply of ink cartridges for my pen." She laughed and looked at Elizabeth. "This is amazing. Thank you."

"I know how important that pen is to you," Elizabeth replied.

"It is." Palmer smiled over at her mother, who then smiled back at her.

Palmer leaned into Elizabeth and whispered, "I know you could have just gotten me a different or better pen, but you didn't because you know this one is important to me because *she* gave it to me. Thank you for understanding that."

Elizabeth smiled in response.

"Elizabeth's turn," Camilla said, clapping.

"Oh, yeah," Palmer's father added. "We didn't know what to get a Queen, so Palmer suggested we just get something for *Elizabeth*. I hope that's okay."

"You got me a gift?" Elizabeth asked, surprised. "You didn't have to do that."

"We wanted to, honey," Palmer's mother said. "Here you go." She passed Elizabeth the box.

Palmer watched as Elizabeth opened the box revealing their gifts. Elizabeth laughed.

"A movie theater gift card?"

"You said you never go," Palmer replied. "I thought we could all go together tomorrow if you're interested. There's a new movie Camilla has been wanting to see."

"Can we?" Camilla asked.

"Of course," Elizabeth replied. "And a bowling gift card?"

"It's a totally different experience when you have people around you drinking bad beer, yelling, and bowling right next to you. Let's see how you do then, Your Majesty," Palmer teased.

Elizabeth laughed and said, "You're on. Camilla's on my team. Thank you all very much."

"Of course, honey," Palmer's mother said.

"Elizabeth's turn," Camilla repeated.

"I opened my gifts, Cami," Elizabeth said sweetly.

"There's one more, actually," Palmer said, passing her a red-and-green gift bag with gold tissue paper. "This one's from me."

"You got me a gift?"

"You got *me* a gift," Palmer reminded.

"Open it! Open it! Open it!" Camilla clapped again.

"Okay. Okay." Elizabeth laughed and looked inside the bag, pulling out the paper. "What is it?"

"Just read the first page," Palmer suggested, leaning into her.

"*My Time with a Queen?*"

"I've been writing it since the day I met you. I thought you might like to read it," Palmer explained. "It's all the stuff I couldn't or didn't want to include in the piece for the paper."

Elizabeth turned to her and asked, "This is about you and me?"

Palmer nodded and said, "Yeah. I had it printed for you and bound."

"Palmer, this…" Elizabeth stared down at the document again.

"Is boring," Camilla concluded. "You got her paper?"

"Camilla," her father said.

"She wrote her a story, Cami," her mother explained.

"Can you read it to us?" Camilla asked then.

"Actually, kiddo, this one is just for Elizabeth and me, but I'll write you another one, okay?"

"Can it be about *me* meeting a Queen?"

"Sure." Palmer laughed.

CHAPTER 33

"Hey, Palmer?" Elizabeth asked.

"Yeah?" Palmer turned to her.

"Can I borrow you for a minute?"

"Just a minute. We're watching *A Christmas Story*," Camilla said, glaring at Elizabeth.

"I'm not her favorite anymore, am I?" Elizabeth asked Palmer, who'd moved to stand next to her.

"She just gets hyper-focused on things sometimes. It's fine. What's up?"

"Can we go into the greenhouse?"

"Yeah, let me grab my coat," Palmer replied. "And do *not* make fun of me; it's cold on the way there."

Elizabeth laughed. Then, she looked at Palmer's dad, who winked at her.

"Camilla, it's going to be bedtime soon. Prepare yourself," he said.

"Are you staying over again tonight, honey?" Palmer's mother asked her.

"I was going to ask Palmer if that would be all right. Is it okay with you?"

"Of course, it is." The older woman smiled at her and squeezed her shoulder. "We're so happy to have you with us. Palmer seems so happy with you here, too."

"She an amazing woman," Elizabeth said.

"Yes, she is. But so are you, sweetie." Palmer's mom kissed Elizabeth on the cheek. "We'll get Camilla up to bed soon and get some sleep ourselves. You and Palmer can have some space tonight."

"That's not necessary. I've missed being around a family. And this has been amazing. You don't have to disappear on my account."

"Honey, you're not *around* a family. You're part of it now. I don't know what my oldest daughter's plans are, but I *do* know that my youngest's involves you being around for a very long time." Mrs. Honeycutt smiled warmly at her. "And I think my husband and I would like that as well, in case you're curious."

Elizabeth could only nod. She was, yet again, speechless.

"Ready," Palmer said as she re-entered the room.

"Good night, ladies. We'll see you in the morning. Merry Christmas," Palmer's mother said.

"Oh. You guys are going to bed?" Palmer asked.

"Yes, it's been a busy day for us and Camilla. We'll see you tomorrow."

"Okay. Good night," Palmer said. "You ready?" she asked Elizabeth.

Elizabeth took Palmer's hand, and they made their way outside, walking the path to the greenhouse side by side. When they got inside, Palmer turned on the lights, illuminating the colorful space, and let go of Elizabeth's hand. Elizabeth walked to where she'd left her gift, picked it up, and turned back, handing it to Palmer.

"This is for you," she said.

"What's this one?" Palmer asked.

"Viscaria."

"And what does it mean?"

"Dance with me."

Palmer smiled and said, "You talked to my dad, didn't you?"

"He told me you liked to dance, which surprised me because at the coronation ball, you–"

"Wanted to dance with *you*, Lizzy." Palmer placed the flower on the table. "Only you."

Elizabeth swallowed and pulled her phone out of her pocket.

"I brought this."

"Our soundtrack?" Palmer asked.

"Yes."

"Do you have a song picked out already?" Palmer asked.

"Yes."

"Then, I would love to dance with you, Lizzy."

"This is better than at the ball anyway," Elizabeth said, pulling up her music app and searching for her song. "You would've been dancing with a Queen at my coronation, and we would have had to do some type of waltz; all eyes would have been on us." She pressed play. "Now, it's just the two of us, and you can hold me close if you want."

"Oh, I *want*," Palmer replied. "What song is this? I don't recognize it."

Elizabeth sat her phone down next to the flower she'd just given Palmer and answered, "*A Love that Will Last.*"

"Come here," Palmer said, taking off her coat, hanging it on the only chair in the room, and holding out her arms.

Elizabeth walked into them, pressing her body against Palmer's fully before resting her head on her shoulder, turning her face into Palmer's neck. Palmer's arms wrapped tightly around her as the slow, almost jazz ballad played in the background. Palmer's head rested against Elizabeth's shoulder, and they swayed back and forth, mostly using the dance as an excuse to hold on to one another. Outside the greenhouse, Elizabeth heard light tapping sounds; too light to be rain.

"It's snowing," she said when she opened her eyes to look outside.

"I've seen snow before," Palmer muttered against Elizabeth's neck. "I've never danced with *you* before."

Palmer's lips touched Elizabeth's skin, and Elizabeth shuddered at the contact.

"Sorry," Palmer said, pulling her lips back a bit.

"No, don't be," Elizabeth told her. "Will you do it again?"

Palmer pressed her lips to Elizabeth's neck again, lingering this time. Her hands also moved from around Elizabeth's waist to rub up and down her back over her sweater.

"Under, Palmer," she whispered into Palmer's ear.

Palmer slid both hands under Elizabeth's sweater and the shirt beneath. Her lips continued to place kisses on Elizabeth's shoulder and neck.

"You feel so good," Palmer said so softly, Elizabeth almost didn't hear her.

"Palmer, I…"

"It's okay. This is enough." She kissed her again.

"No, that's not…" Elizabeth leaned back to pull Palmer's face up, cupping her cheeks. "I have no idea what the future holds, but today has been the best day I've had in a very long time, and it all started with waking up next to you." She pressed her forehead to Palmer's. "Thank you for sharing your family with me on a day I thought I'd be spending alone." Elizabeth kissed Palmer's nose. "And thank you for your gift. I can't wait to read it." She kissed her cheek. "And thank you for being so sweet and so patient with me." She kissed Palmer's other cheek. "And, God, I just need to kiss you right now."

Palmer's lips formed a small smile, and Elizabeth leaned in to kiss it. When their lips finally pressed together for their first real kiss, Elizabeth gasped and pulled back before she smiled and pressed them together again. She parted her lips to let Palmer know what she wanted. Palmer didn't disappoint. Her hands on Elizabeth's back pulled Elizabeth in tighter as their lips danced together. The song had ended already, but Elizabeth had wisely placed it on repeat and was now enjoying the slow start to it again as Palmer's tongue moved into her mouth tentatively until Elizabeth met it with her own.

When Palmer moaned, Elizabeth sighed internally. She had only ever kissed one other person like this in her life, never letting any of those early kisses with boys get this far. It had been so long since she and Teagan had shared a kiss like this, and as the snow fell outside the greenhouse, the temperature inside the room went up. Palmer's lips were fire. Elizabeth wanted more of them. She wanted them everywhere on her body, all at once. Palmer's tongue was searching, exploring, and would then pull out, and Elizabeth would do exploring of her own. It was perfect, and she wanted more, but she wasn't sure she was ready for more yet.

She worried she'd have to slow things down and that Palmer might be disappointed, but before she even had the chance, Palmer's hands on her back slowed and stilled, and her lips pecked Elizabeth's once and then again before she kissed her forehead.

"I know," she said softly.

"You know?" Elizabeth asked, surprised she could even string two words together.

"We need to stop."

"I don't want to," Elizabeth said. "I'd love to keep kissing you all night." She moved Palmer's dark hair behind both of her ears.

"Will you at least stay over tonight?" Palmer asked, sliding her hands out from under Elizabeth's sweater and placing them on her hips instead.

"I'll call security and ask them to bring–"

"You don't need to. I have everything you need here. Just stay. Please. Tomorrow night, if you want, I can stay with you at the hotel." Palmer kissed her sweetly.

"Okay," Elizabeth replied. "You're not upset I'm basically acting like a sixteen-year-old virgin and making you go this slow?"

Palmer smiled at her and said, "No, but I would like to kiss you more tonight when we get to my room."

"Yeah?" Elizabeth smiled at her.

Palmer nodded and looked around the greenhouse. Then, she moved away from Elizabeth, apparently found what she'd been looking for, clipped a flower, and returned, handing it to Elizabeth.

"Heliotrope," she explained. "My dad told me this one means devotion." She kissed Elizabeth's cheek. "That's what you have from me, among other things."

"Other things?" Elizabeth asked, looking up from the purple flower.

"Yeah, like my heart."

Elizabeth held on to the flower as she pulled Palmer in to kiss her again. The song played for the third time. They swayed together until the snow outside began to really pile up, and then Palmer gave Elizabeth her coat, insisting she wear it until they were inside. They walked, hand in hand, back up the path to the back door of the house. Elizabeth made Palmer a cup of coffee to warm her up, choosing a cup of tea for herself.

"You need to teach my mom how to make it right," Palmer reminded.

Elizabeth took a few sips. Then, she moved to sit between Palmer's legs on the chaise portion of the sofa. Palmer wrapped her arms around Elizabeth's middle.

"Can we finish the movie we were watching earlier? I've never seen it. I'd like to know how it ends."

"You've never seen *A Christmas Story*?"

"No."

"It's always on this time of year. I'm sure we can find it. We might just end up at a different part, maybe even back at the beginning." Palmer reached for the remote.

"That's okay. I don't really want to go anywhere for a while anyway."

Palmer found the movie on a different channel, near the beginning, and they just lay like that, with Elizabeth between Palmer's legs, her head resting against Palmer's chest, feeling her heart beating fast and loving the feeling of being this close to someone again.

"Are you asleep?" Palmer asked as the credits rolled.

"No," Elizabeth muttered.

"Liar," Palmer said, chuckling.

The vibrations moved through Elizabeth's body, and

she turned a little on her side to snuggle in closer.

"Babe, I'd love to let you sleep on me like this, but my family would have a pretty big surprise when they come downstairs tomorrow."

"I know. You're just so comfortable."

"Come on. I'll be just as comfortable upstairs."

"I like that you call me *babe* now," Elizabeth told her, forcing her eyes open.

"Yeah?"

"Yeah. I've never been a *babe* before."

"Oh, you've *always* been a babe. Trust me on that one," Palmer replied.

And Elizabeth laughed until they made it to Palmer's room to get some sleep.

CHAPTER 34

"I'M going to miss you," Elizabeth said.

"Me too," Palmer replied, running her hands up and down Elizabeth's sides. "Is it okay for me to kiss you in here?"

"I asked them to give us some privacy. We'll be alone until you…" Elizabeth faded out.

"Hey, it's going to be fine." Palmer kissed her forehead. "We know what this is now, right?"

"Real," Elizabeth said.

"Yeah, it is," she confirmed.

She and Elizabeth were standing alone on the small plane that would take her back to St. Rais.

"I know you have work, but you did say once you could write from anywhere. Is there a chance you could maybe come back to St. Rais sooner than the summer?"

"I can see," Palmer replied. "And you can maybe come back here after the vote, depending on how that goes."

"God, I wish you could be there for that."

"Me too. I'll try, okay?" Palmer promised. "Until then, we'll just take it day by day, babe. Call me when you're safe in the palace."

"I will." Elizabeth pulled Palmer into her. "Palmer, I…"

"I got you these for the road," Palmer interrupted her. She handed Elizabeth a bunch of flowers. "They're salvias. Blue means that I'm thinking of you."

"And the red ones?" Elizabeth asked.

"Forever mine."

Elizabeth smiled at her and nodded.

"I'll see you as soon as I can," Palmer added.

"Okay."

Palmer leaned in and kissed her slowly. Elizabeth held on tightly to the flowers. The other ones Palmer had given her before were already stowed and pressed between the pages of Palmer's piece. Elizabeth had agreed that she'd wait to read it until the plane ride back, even though she'd told Palmer she'd wanted to read it straight away.

"There are words I want to say, but I don't want to say them with goodbye," Palmer said as she pulled out of the kiss.

"I'd say there's always later, but you and I both know that's not true." She cupped Palmer's cheeks and added, "I love you."

Palmer hadn't been expecting that, but the moment Elizabeth said the words, Palmer smiled.

"I love you, too," she replied.

Elizabeth kissed her quickly and suggested, "Don't say goodbye right now. Let's just say we'll talk later."

"We'll talk later," Palmer replied, kissing her once more. "I love you," she added, trying out just how good it felt to admit that to the woman she'd been in love with for a while now.

"I love you, too," Elizabeth said, nodding. "I have to go."

"I know. Call me later. I don't care what time it is."

"I will."

"Okay. I love you."

Elizabeth laughed and said, "I love you, too. Now that we've said it, are we going to say it a million times?"

"Yes," Palmer said, kissing her quickly and then backing up a few steps. "I love you, Your Majesty," she teased.

"I love you, too, Miss Honeycutt. Now, get off my plane," Elizabeth said playfully.

"You say 'I love you' to a Queen *one* time, and she kicks you off her plane." Palmer winked at her.

"Go before I try to take you with me."

Palmer finally got off the plane, but she didn't leave right away. She stayed on the tarmac until the plane moved down the runway and took off. She watched it for a while until she could no longer see it. Then, she climbed into her car and cried.

***

"Hey, sweetie. Did Elizabeth's plane get off okay?" her mom asked.

"Unfortunately," Palmer replied, flopping down on the sofa.

"You've got it bad, don't you, kiddo?" her mom asked.

Palmer looked at her mom, who was getting ready to leave for work.

"I told her I love her today."

"You did?" She sat down next to Palmer.

"Yeah."

"And did she say it back?"

"Yes." Palmer smiled. "She said it *first*, actually."

"Well, that's good." Her mom patted her leg. "When can you see her again?"

"I don't know. I'm on thin ice at work already."

"Why?"

"Because I fell in love with the woman I was supposed to be writing about, and all the juicy stuff got left out of my piece."

"Juicy stuff?" her mother asked, lifting an eyebrow at her.

"Not that. We haven't done that yet. We just kissed for the first time the other day, Mom."

"Taking things slow?"

"Wouldn't *you*? She's a Queen of a country, and she lives thousands of miles away. Plus, she just lost pretty much everyone she loved, including an ex-girlfriend. Well, they were still technically together when Teagan died, but it was over before then, I think. At least, that's how Elizabeth describes it."

"Okay. Okay. Hold on. Your father told me Elizabeth isn't out back home."

"She's not. She was in a very long-term relationship with her brother's wife."

"What?" her mother asked, shocked.

"It's not like that. Her brother was gay, too. He and Teagan – that's Elizabeth's lifelong best friend and long-term girlfriend – got married because it allowed Teagan and Elizabeth to be together, and for Alex – that's Elizabeth's brother – to not have to worry about finding a real wife."

"Honey, this sounds like a soap opera."

"It sounds worse than it is, but she and Teagan were together for a long time. And it's not like they broke up; Teagan died, Mom."

"But Elizabeth told you she loves you, honey."

"She did, and I believe her. It's just... I don't know if she's ready for everything with someone."

"Are you talking about sex? And if you are, and you're not willing to wait for that sweet, beautiful young lady to work through what–"

"Mom, no," Palmer interrupted her. "It's not just sex. I mean, it *is* sex, but–"

"Palmer Jane Honeycutt, you will not pressure that–"

"Mom, I wouldn't." Palmer laughed at her mother being ridiculous. "I'm not like that."

"You better not be, or your father and I would be very disappointed in you."

"Mom, I love her. I've waited all this time already. I'd wait as long as she needs me to wait for that."

"Then, what are you worried about?"

"I want a girlfriend, Mom."

"Are you two not girlfriends?"

"I don't know what we are. There's so much going on for her right now. She might not even be a *Queen* in a few weeks. Then again, she might be one forever."

"It's not the Queen thing that you're worried about, though, is it?" her mother asked.

"I don't want to be a secret, Mom. I won't marry some man – gay, too, or not – just so I can be with the woman I love. And I won't just make up some excuses for why two *friends* would be so close or spend so much time together."

"You want her to be out with you?"

"Yes. Eventually, anyway."

"And you don't think she'll be able to do that?"

"Her dad was an asshole about the gay thing," Palmer explained. "I think he really messed Elizabeth and her brother up about it. I mean, Alex was willing to get married to a woman because he didn't want to come out to his dad."

"That's terrible, honey. And as much as we love Elizabeth – and we do – you have to do what's going to make you happy in the end. Elizabeth was very sweet with your sister, and she obviously cares about you. When the time is right, I think you need to tell her what's important to you in a relationship. And keep in mind, she might not be able to give you everything, but relationships *are* about compromise. It's rarely black and white. You might need to give a little in one area or for a time, at least."

"I know," Palmer sighed. "Mom, I miss her already."

Her mother laughed and said, "Yeah, you're in love, kiddo."

"It's both amazing and terrible, isn't it?"

"Only when they're away, sweetie." The woman stood up. "Now, I have to get to work. Your father is upstairs, playing video games with Camilla, if you want to join them."

"Actually, can I go to work with you? I could use a distraction."

"Sure. But you know I'll put you to work."

"Doing the paperwork or waiting tables?"

"Worse: my bartender called out sick."

Palmer laughed and replied, "I haven't bartended in a while. Are you sure?"

"I'm sure. Plus, you can keep your tips. Sounds like you're going to need a whole lot of travel money."

Palmer rolled her eyes and stood up.

***

Hours later, Palmer had a giant wad of cash in her pocket from a very good night of bartending. When she got back to her parents' house, she made her way to Camilla's room. Her sister was sound asleep, so Palmer walked over to her piggy bank, opened the bottom as quietly as she could, and shoved the cash inside, closing it back up and walking over to her kid sister's bed. She brushed the hair off Camilla's face, said a silent prayer for her sister's happiness, and went back to her own room.

She readied herself for bed, then checked her phone for the hundredth time, even though Elizabeth wouldn't have gotten home yet, and slid under her covers. She smelled Elizabeth on the pillow she'd used and pulled it toward her, missing the woman she loved more than she thought possible. She wasn't sure what time it was, but her phone started vibrating in her hand, waking her from sleep. Her eyes snapped open when she realized she was getting a call.

"Hey, babe," she said sleepily.

"I woke you up," Elizabeth stated the fact.

"It's okay. Are you home?"

"I just landed. I couldn't wait to call until I got to the palace."

Palmer smiled at that and said, "I miss you, too."

"I read it, Palmer."

"Yeah? What did you think?"

"That you fell in love with me a while ago, huh?" Elizabeth laughed lightly.

Palmer laughed as well and said, "Yes, I did."

"I did, too," Elizabeth admitted. "I fell in love with you a long time ago, too.'"

CHAPTER 35

"MAJESTY, the polls are a mixed bag," the Prime Minister explained. "The north seems to be going against the monarchy, as we suspected, but the south appears to support the monarchy. There are some small villages in the east we don't have any polling data from, and the west is fifty-fifty right now."

"So, what you are saying is that we don't know?" Elizabeth concluded.

"Not yet. But there are still two weeks until the vote. We'll do another poll in a week. It'll be closer. We should get better data."

"Nothing like living in limbo," she said on a sigh. "I know this has put you in a difficult position, Albert. Thank you for your support and your understanding."

"Ma'am, as an institution, I find the monarchy lacking in most countries. In my youth, I wasn't sold on it in St. Rais, if I'm being honest. I wasn't always a huge fan of your father's; God rest his soul. I *am* a fan of yours, though. I do believe you will be a great monarch for this country. You have the ability to relate to so many young people, but you have the wisdom associated with someone who's lived as well. St. Rais is known as the forgotten-about European country, and I think you'd change that for us in a way that *I* cannot. I hope the nation gives you a chance, but if you don't mind me saying so, you are a remarkable person for even putting this in their hands. We're living in uncharted territory. As far as I know, and I could be wrong, but I've never heard of a sitting monarch asking their people to vote on whether or not they should keep their title."

"We're not like most countries, and we're definitely unlike any other monarchy. When it comes down to it, Albert, that's all this is – it's a title. It's one I was handed because I was born into a certain family, and I've inherited this newest one. It's not one I believe I've yet earned. And if the country votes to take that title and everything it comes with away, I will honor that." Elizabeth stood up. "Now, I'm afraid, I have to cut this meeting short. My sister is returning from her holiday with her fiancé, and we're having dinner."

"Of course, Ma'am." He stood up and gave her the requisite bow.

"You might not need to do that for much longer, and you know I don't mind if you don't now, right?" she asked.

"Yes, Majesty. But I don't bow because of tradition; I bow as a show of my respect."

"Thank you," she said as he backed out of the room and then left.

"Who came up with that? So stupid," she said to herself, referring to the whole walking backward thing.

Elizabeth checked her phone and found she had a missed text from Palmer. She giggled at it and typed her reply as the door to her suite opened.

"Who are you laughing at?" Victoria asked as she walked in.

"Your Majesty, Her Royal–"

"She knows I'm here, Jenny," Victoria interrupted the introduction.

"Sorry, Jenny. Thank you," Elizabeth said.

Jenny left the two of them alone.

"Where's David?"

"He's working. He had a lot to catch up on after vacation, and he's still trying to get used to working remotely when the office is in London. What were you laughing at just now?"

"You don't miss a beat," Elizabeth said. "It's nice to see you, Victoria. Happy Christmas. How's your new year going so far?"

"Fine. How's yours?" Victoria asked, hugging her sister and then pulling out of it quickly. "Palmer?"

"Yes, she texted me. I responded."

"Was it dirty?" Victoria asked, lifting a devilish eyebrow at her.

"What? No," she replied, laughing.

"No dirty texts? What's the point?" Victoria flopped onto the sofa.

"What's the point? I don't know; it's nice to just talk to her sometimes."

"Because she's your girlfriend?" Victoria asked in a singsong, teasing voice.

Elizabeth sat down next to her and said, "We haven't used that term, specifically."

"Specifically? What have you said *generally*, then, Lizzy?"

Elizabeth smiled and replied, "That we love each other."

"Holy shit! You told her?"

Elizabeth laughed and confirmed, "Yes, I told her."

"And she said it back? Or did she say it first?"

"No, *I* said it first. She said it back, though."

"Thank God. It was so obvious."

"It *was* not."

"Lizzy, I've known you my whole life. I've seen you in the only other relationship you've ever been in. I know what it looks like when you're in love with someone."

Elizabeth lowered her gaze to her hands in her lap.

"I've been thinking about her a lot lately."

"Well, yeah, you love her."

"No, I meant Teagan. I've been thinking about Teagan a lot."

"What kind of thoughts have you been having?"

"They're kind of all over the place. I have a lot of anger toward her that I don't know I'll ever resolve now. She asked Alex for a divorce because she wanted to break up with me."

"She *said* break up?"

"No, but that was what she meant. She wanted to date other women, and divorcing Alex would have meant she was free from him and from me."

"I get why you'd be angry with her. That whole stupid marriage thing was supposed to help all three of you."

"Dad would have gone through the roof when he found out they'd only gotten married to hide Alex and I."

"Probably." Victoria shrugged a shoulder.

"But it's also just this intense amount of guilt that I've been feeling," Elizabeth added.

"I feel that, too," Victoria admitted honestly. "We were supposed to be killed, too. If that security guard hadn't stopped them at that airport, their plan would have killed us, Lizzy."

"I know," she said, taking her sister's hand. "But I'm also feeling guilty because of Palmer."

"Teagan was going to break up with you. Or, she did; I'm not sure how it all went down. You're free to love someone else, Lizzy."

"I've only ever loved one person like that. I've only ever *been* with one person. I thought she'd be the *only* one."

"You and Palmer didn't…"

"No," Elizabeth said. "She's being patient with me, but I don't think it's just because of me. I think *she* needs the time, too."

"Why? It's not like she's a virgin."

Elizabeth glared at her sister and said, "Thank you. That's just what I need to be thinking about right now; Palmer's sex life with her exes."

"It's a thing you have to deal with. David wasn't a virgin when I met him. I wasn't one either when he and I started dating. It's a conversation you have, and you move on. But that's not the point. Why do you think it's not just about you that she's waiting?"

"I think she knows how complicated this is, and I think she knows that taking that step is a big deal."

"And she doesn't want to unless what?"

"Unless this is it," Elizabeth replied. "I think that's what she wants, at least."

"Like, if you two have sex, she expects a ring?"

"Not like that; just that this is going somewhere."

"Well, it *is*, isn't it?"

"Can it?" Elizabeth asked.

"Oh, my God, Elizabeth! Get out of your own head. Better yet; screw Dad. Get him out of there, too." Victoria stood up. "You love this woman. She loves you. Distance aside, just be with her already. Just *be* in love and let her love you. Who cares about anything else?"

"What about being Queen of St. Rais?"

"You might not even be that in a couple of weeks. But even if you hadn't called for the vote, you guys shouldn't be worried about anything other than what it feels like when you're together. If you love each other, you figure the rest out. The distance between you should be your only concern; get that closed somehow. Then, decide how to tell St. Rais you're a damn lesbian in love with another damn lesbian." Victoria looked around the room. "Where's dinner?"

"They're bringing it up now. Victoria, answer me honestly. Do you really think I can just come out?"

"Yes, I do. Will there be people against you? Sure. But what's new? They're against you *now*, anyway."

"Palmer's an American."

"She's worse than that: she's an American *reporter*." Victoria sat back down. "But we can't help that, can we? Just like we can't help who we love. I mean, I'm marrying an Englishman. Dad would *not* have been the happiest about that."

"No, but at least David is a *man*," Elizabeth replied. "Dad still would've walked you down the aisle. Dad didn't even think I should *get* an aisle to walk down."

"I'll walk you down the aisle," Victoria told her. "To Palmer or to some other woman; I'll be there. David will be there. You can ask him to walk you if you want. *We're* your family, and we'll support you. I don't care what Dad would have said or done. You deserve love, Lizzy, and you deserve everything that comes with that."

"You are wise beyond your years, Victoria."

"I had Mom," Victoria said, smiling. "And I have the best older sister in the world who's finally met someone I actually approve of."

"You didn't approve of Teagan?"

Victoria let out a deep laugh and said, "No. Teagan was your *first* love; I never believed she'd be your *forever*. But you're stubborn sometimes, Lizzy. There's no talking you into or out of something you're not ready to see or admit."

Elizabeth laughed and said, "I suppose that's true."

"Now, I'm starving. David made lunch today, and he's no cook," Victoria said.

"How are things otherwise?" Elizabeth asked.

"Well, as second in line, I have royal duties that take up a lot of my time. If I'm not second in line in two weeks, I've got to figure out what I'm going to do with my life."

"School?"

"I'm thinking about graduate school, yes, but if I'm not second in line, I might not go in St. Rais. I might see what else is out there for me."

"Even if you *are* second in line, we can work out a schedule that allows you to go to school when and wherever you'd like to go, Vicky. You know that."

"I can't just leave you here if you're still Queen; at least, not for a while. If you have kids and they start performing royal duties in a couple of decades, maybe I can take a break, but that's not going to be for a while."

"God, can you picture that?" Elizabeth stared off into the distance, seeing nothing in particular. "I could either not get married at all, and you or your kids would inherit the throne, or I could marry a woman, and our kids would take over after me." At that thought, she pictured Palmer standing next to her, and that felt... well, it felt right.

"Would *you* have them?"

"Huh?" Elizabeth asked.

"Well, it wasn't like you and Teagan were going to have kids, so we've never really talked about this. Would you be the one to have them? It wouldn't matter either way, except for the whole crown thing."

"I don't know. I guess I'd want to have them myself. Truthfully, I haven't allowed myself to plan or dream this stuff before. You're right about Teagan: we wouldn't have been able to have kids. And I was in school, planning on spending the next decade in academia, at least, so I wasn't thinking about having kids. This is all a little new to me. I know Palmer wants kids, but I don't get the impression she wants to have them herself."

"Palmer, huh?"

"Yes, Palmer."

"When you picture those future kids, they're with her, aren't they?"

Elizabeth shook her head and said, "I know that's crazy; so much can happen between now and then."

"Lizzy, it just means you're in love, and you want a future with her. I think that's a good thing."

"I hope so," Elizabeth replied.

CHAPTER 36

"YOUR output hasn't been a lot lately, Palmer," her editor said.

"I finished that last piece on time, and I'm on track with two more," she replied.

"You let the big one go. We hardly got anything from your time in St. Rais. Where was the Pulitzer you promised the paper?"

"It would have been *my* Pulitzer. And I stand by what I wrote. I went where the story took me."

"And it took you away from the interesting stuff?" he asked. "You wrote what everyone else wrote, Palmer, and *you* had the inside scoop."

"Maybe I can add to it. The whole country is voting on whether or not to keep the monarchy, and it was the Queen's idea. I don't think that's ever happened before. I could do something on that."

"I've got Lynch on that."

"You put Lynch on St. Rais?" Palmer sat up in her chair.

"Yeah, *he'll* get me the story."

Palmer tried not to let her ego get in the way. Lynch was a good enough writer. It was just that St. Rais was hers. Elizabeth was hers. If someone at *The Courier* was going to write about her or her country, Palmer wanted to be that person. Then again, she was in too deep now. She wouldn't be able to be unbiased and write a piece about Elizabeth either remaining a Queen or being dethroned. Maybe this was for the best.

"Fine." She shrugged a shoulder.

"Where's your fire, Palmer? I expected an argument about me taking your story away." He sat up and placed his elbows on his desk.

"I wrote my story already. You didn't seem to like it. Let Lynch take it."

"What are you working on now, then?"

"I have a few ideas."

"Ideas? We have a one-thousand-word gap to fill on the online side, and I thought you were ready to have a breakout year this year, Palmer."

"I am. I've just got a lot going on right now."

She failed to mention her long-distance relationship and the fact that sleep wasn't coming as often or as consistently as it used to as a result. She wouldn't change anything about it, but it had made working a little bit harder. Well, if she *could* change something about it, she'd put herself in the same room as Elizabeth.

"Palmer, this is your job. It's your career. You're on track to be a star at one of the most read newspapers in the world. If you want it, you've got to take it."

"There's a potential labor strike in Jersey. I was going to write about that."

"Union?"

"Yeah, the one-ten."

"They've been threatening to strike for years now."

"I know, but the signs are pointing to soon," Palmer said. "I could head to Jersey tomorrow, get some interviews in, and have the first stab at it on your desk the day after."

"Get me that and try to find a new angle, not just the standard shit. I'm over the standard shit."

"Okay." She nodded.

"And I've something else for you. There's a candidate in Virginia. She's running for senate against the incumbent who's been in office forever. She's got some fresh takes on the issues *and* has the money to back her up. I think she'll be the underdog, but she stands a chance at winning. I was thinking about putting you on her campaign."

"A campaign?"

"Yes, a campaign. Can you show me something better than St. Rais?"

"Yeah, I can, but you're talking about me going to Virginia, right?"

"Yes, Palmer. I'm talking about putting you on her bus. It's going to be a long and dirty campaign; probably some juicy content in there and a chance for you to get it first. This is a good next step for you. It's what you told me you wanted when you first got here."

"It *is*, yeah. When would I leave?"

"Take care of the Jersey thing. Then, we'll get you set up to head out."

"Right away?"

"Yes, right away. Palmer, what is your problem?"

"It's just that I was going to go out of town and write my next piece. I was thinking about doing something on St. Rais, but if you're giving that to Lynch, I can think of something else."

"Out of town, where exactly?"

"Just out of town. I wanted to get out of the city and really focus on my work."

"Good. Do it in Virginia."

"This is probably a bad time to ask for this then, but if I can't work from where I was going to go, can I maybe take some time off? I could come back and then do Virginia."

"You just took time off, Palmer."

"Not much. It was a few days, really, and I've never taken time off before that."

"Correct me if I'm wrong, but while you were in St. Rais, you only worked part of the time."

"That's true, but I have more vacation time saved up. I only need a week."

"Is everything okay at home, Palmer? Is that what this is about? Something personal?" he asked.

"No, everything's fine at home," she replied. "I just need a week."

"A week?"

"Yes, sir."

"You'll go to Jersey first."

"Yeah," she agreed.

"And then only a week?"

"Yes."

"Then, I get my reporter back?"

"Yes," she repeated again.

He glared at her and said, "Okay. One week." He held up his index finger. "Then, you're back for good, Palmer. I want your best, so figure out or fix whatever you need to get your head back in the damn game."

Palmer let out a deep breath and said, "I will. Thank you. Really. Thank you."

"Don't thank me. Give me the words I need to fill my gap."

"I will."

***

"They caught him, Palmer," Elizabeth shared on the phone later that night.

"They caught him?"

"Yes. He was on a boat about to flee, and they found him. They got him *and* three of the other leaders of the anti-monarchists. He's behind bars now."

"Really?" Palmer asked, sighing with relief. "You're safe."

"As safe as I *can* be; not everyone wants a Queen. But as far as we can tell, they're the only faction that's gotten violent over it."

"Has he talked at all?"

"Just nonsense. His father blamed my grandfather for supporting the war and suggesting to Parliament that St. Rais join the cause a long time ago, and he's carried that blame. *I'd* always heard my grandfather tried to keep us out of the war and that Parliament was the reason the country had gotten involved. I guess their family lost three boys, and my father was so much like his own, and the world seems poised for another war these days; he worried that we'd be forced to get involved in a war that was *not* our own again. That's about all he's said so far."

"But he's in jail?"

"Yes, he'll spend the rest of this life there, and so will the rest of them after the trial. Albert told me they have more than enough evidence to convict."

"That's great news, babe," Palmer said.

"I feel so much better knowing I don't have to worry *as* much about Victoria and David."

"Or yourself?"

"That too," Elizabeth said, and her voice told Palmer she did feel better just knowing those guys were locked up.

"You can leave the palace now?"

"If I have to, yes. They're still working their way through homes up north to see if they find anyone else, but they're convinced the major risk is gone."

"That's so good, Lizzy."

"You sound tired," Elizabeth said.

"I am. It's late here."

"I'm sorry. I should let you sleep."

"No, don't go. I want to talk to you. I miss you."

"I miss you, too, love," Elizabeth said.

Palmer smiled and said, "So, the vote's coming up."

"A week away," Elizabeth replied.

"I have to go to New Jersey tomorrow. I'm working on a quick piece, but I was thinking about taking a week off after that."

"A week off?" Elizabeth asked.

"I bought a ticket today, babe."

"To St. Rais?"

"Yes, Lizzy. I bought a ticket; I'm going to be there in three days."

"Why did you *buy* one, Palmer? I would have sent the plane for you, or you could've used the ticket I got for you already."

"Those are for when the whole family visits in the summer. This one was just for me. And I don't mind flying coach if it means I get to see you. I don't need a private plane."

"You're really coming?" Elizabeth asked.

"Yes. I want to be there for you when you find out," Palmer said.

"I love you," Elizabeth replied.

"I love you."

"Are you sure this is okay, Palmer? You just took time off for me. I don't want you to get in any more trouble at work."

"It's fine. I cleared it with my boss."

"I get to see you in three days?" Elizabeth asked.

Palmer could hear something in her voice.

"Are you crying?" Palmer asked.

"Yes, but they're happy tears. I miss you so much already, and I didn't think I'd get to see you for a while. I really needed you here for this vote, Palmer, but I didn't want to ask because you've given me so much already."

"Hey, you can always tell me what you need. I'll do the best I can to give it to you," Palmer told her softly.

"You can do the same with me. You know that, right?"

Palmer smiled to herself and said, "I know."

"I'll pick you up at the airport," Elizabeth promised.

"Can you really do that?" Palmer laughed.

"I'll move stuff around. Just send me your flight information."

"Elizabeth, I can just meet you at the palace. Oh, I didn't book a hotel... Is that okay? I figured I'd just put my stuff in one of the guest rooms."

"Put your stuff in *my* room."

"Yeah?"

"Yeah. I'm not ready for the world to know – there's too much going on this week – but I don't care if the staff knows. I *want* them to know, actually. I've already told Rebecca and Jenny about you. Thomas and Magnus know as well. I told them all today. I wanted them to know that if you call, you get put through no matter what. And if you're here, you take priority over everyone else."

"You told them?"

"Yes."

"What did Rebecca say?" Palmer asked and laughed at the thought.

"She smiled when I told her, actually. She said she's glad I'm happy."

"She did?"

"She likes you now. You did right by St. Rais and by me in your article. She appreciated that."

"How did the rest of them take it?"

"Magnus wants me to be safe, so he said that if there's someone else out there looking out for me, he's happy about that. Thomas is trying to figure out how to keep it out of the news until if or when we want it to be news. Then, he wants to control the messaging."

"When, Lizzy."

"When what?"

"*When* we want it to become news."

"Sorry, I'm a little tired myself. What are you talking about?"

"I don't want it to be an *if*, Elizabeth. I want you. I want people to know. I don't care if you're Queen of a country or just another person on the street – I want people to know we're together; you're my girlfriend, and I love you."

"I love you, too, but there's still a lot to work through, Palmer."

"I know. I'm not asking you to come out right now. I'm just telling you what I know I'll need one day."

"Is that one day this week?" Elizabeth asked.

"No, it's not." Palmer laughed again.

"Okay. Then, let's get through this week. We can talk about it when you get here."

"That sounds good." Palmer yawned.

"Get some sleep, my love. I'll see you soon."

"Have a good day, okay? I love you."

"I love you, too."

CHAPTER 37

"HER Majesty wanted me to deliver an apology. She was unable to pick you up from the airport and asked that *we* bring you to the palace instead," Magnus told Palmer.

"Oh, okay," Palmer spoke. "I just talked to her before I took off. She said she'd be here."

Elizabeth could hardly contain herself. She wanted so badly to get out of the back of the SUV, but she couldn't resist playing this tiny prank on Palmer.

"Miss Honeycutt," Magnus said.

Elizabeth sat back from the slit in the window she'd rolled down in order to see her prank play out.

"I'll put your stuff in the back for you," Magnus added, opening the door for Palmer.

Palmer then appeared in the open doorway, seeing Elizabeth immediately and smiling.

"Oh, you've got jokes now?" Palmer said, laughing.

She climbed into the car, and Magnus closed the door behind her. Elizabeth wrapped her arms around Palmer's neck, pulling her as close as she could get her.

"I couldn't resist. Hi," she said. "I've missed you."

"I've missed you, too." Palmer leaned in and waited.

"What are you waiting for?"

"Magnus; he's putting my stuff in the back. I know he knows, but do you–"

Elizabeth leaned in the rest of the way and kissed her hard.

"He's going to put your stuff in the following car. He knows we need a minute."

"Thank God," Palmer replied, leaning in again and kissing her more deeply. "How long do we have?" Her lips moved to Elizabeth's neck.

"Not *that* long." Elizabeth laughed at her.

"I meant when we get back to the palace," Palmer said, pulling back a little.

"I have a few meetings I can't skip today. We have a lot of last-minute planning to do. We still can't tell which way the vote is going for certain, so we must plan for both eventualities."

"After the meetings?"

"I was thinking, we could have dinner with Victoria and David, if that's okay with you."

"Sure," Palmer replied, sitting back as soon as Magnus entered the car.

"As a couple, Palmer. I was thinking of it sort of as a double date."

Palmer smiled at her and said, "I can do a double date."

"I meant to ask you; a man named Lynch reached out to my office asking for a meeting. He said he works at your paper. He mentioned you by name."

"Yeah, my editor gave him the piece on the vote."

"What? Why?" Elizabeth took Palmer's hand.

"The article I wrote while I was here was okay, but it wasn't exactly what he was hoping for. I mean, I couldn't include a lot of what I saw and heard here, so it was pretty surface stuff, which is what everyone else wrote."

"I'm sorry. It's my fault. I asked too much of you."

"You've never asked anything of me I haven't been willing to give, Elizabeth." Palmer leaned over and kissed her cheek. "It's fine. I'll be on this campaign when I get back."

"Campaign?"

"Yeah, a Virginia senator."

"Politics?"

"Yes."

"You want to write about politics?"

"I used to," Palmer replied. "Honestly, when I was in school, I thought I'd end up on the political beat, but... I don't know; it's not super exciting to basically live on a bus while she goes from town to town trying to drum up votes."

"Then, why are you doing it?"

"Believe it or not, it's a step up. It's something regular to write about. And if I do a good enough job, I get off the bus and put on something else. I was hoping that one day, I could maybe get into broadcast journalism."

"TV?"

"I took a bunch of classes on it in school. My degree isn't in broadcast specifically, though. I went with the newspaper because I wanted to write, but I think I'd like to do broadcast one day."

"You certainly have the face for it," Elizabeth said, winking at her.

"Is that a compliment, Your Majesty?" Palmer teased.

"Definitely," Elizabeth replied. "And is there anything *I* can do about the whole Lynch thing? I can turn him down; tell the paper I'll only deal with you."

"No, Lynch is good. If you *are* going to talk to a reporter, there are worse ones out there. He'll treat your story right, or I wouldn't let him near you."

"You'd do a better job," Elizabeth told her. "I read the *real* story you wrote, and it is very good."

"You're biased." Palmer squeezed Elizabeth's hand. "And so am I now; that's the problem. I shouldn't be writing anything about you anymore."

"You are a very good reporter."

"My boss would disagree with you," Palmer argued.

"Then, he would be wrong. Not many people would have given up what you gave up for me, Palmer. I don't know much about journalism, but I'm pretty sure that with your talent, and what I read that you've only shared with me, you could have written something that would win you awards, get you a promotion, or whatever journalist get when they do a great job."

"I guess." Palmer shrugged. "I don't really feel like I gave up anything, though."

"You don't?"

"No, I feel like I've gained so much recently. I love you, Elizabeth, and I want to be here with you. I've never been good at taking time off before. When I finally did, I met you. I want to spend time with you this week. I want to be here when you get the news and for us to figure out what happens next."

"You will tell me, though, right? If me being who I am or *what* I am is causing you problems or isn't allowing you to have what you want in your life, you'll tell me? I don't want that for you. I've seen what that does to people. Alex, for example."

"You?" Palmer said. "You weren't able to be who you are or have what you wanted."

"I'm trying to change that," Elizabeth replied, smiling at her. "You're a pretty good start. I just don't want you to ever feel like I did, or like Alex did, because you're with me. Promise me you'll tell me."

"Okay. I will." She kissed Elizabeth's forehead. "Right now, I'm just jet-lagged and so happy to be here with you."

Elizabeth pressed her lips to Palmer's and suggested, "Let's get you to my bed. You can take a long nap."

***

"Miss Honeycutt," Rebecca greeted her when Palmer entered the office.

"Rebecca, I think you can call me Palmer, don't you?" she replied, moving into the room and looking around. "I just woke up," she added, addressing Elizabeth this time. "They told me you were in here."

"This was my father's office," Elizabeth explained.

"You're not using *your* office anymore?" Palmer asked, moving around the desk to kiss Elizabeth on the cheek. "Also, hi."

Elizabeth smiled and met Rebecca's eyes. Rebecca was kind enough to then look away.

"This *is* my office. It's the monarch's office. It became mine when my father died. I just wasn't in a good place to use it."

"And you are now?" Palmer asked, placing her hand on Elizabeth's shoulder.

"I had to for the Christmas address, but after that, I've been able to see it more and more as the office of the King, or in my case, the Queen, and not *his* anymore."

"That's great," Palmer replied. "Should I leave you two alone? They said I could come in, but I just wanted to check on you."

"No, you can stay. We were just talking about options for the palace staff if the vote goes against the monarchy. Have a seat." Elizabeth motioned to the empty chair next to Rebecca.

"The staff?"

"Yes," Rebecca said.

"But you pay them, don't you?" Palmer remembered. "They're not paid by the taxpayers."

"That's true, but many of them, including Rebecca, took their jobs to work for the royal family because they believe in the institution of the monarchy. If the monarchy no longer exists in St. Rais, some of them might not want to work here or just for Victoria and me."

"I guess that makes sense," Palmer said.

"We're trying to find ways to make sure that those wishing to leave because of that, land on their feet with jobs. Victoria and I, for example, wouldn't need security; or, at least, not as much if we're no longer royals."

"Would you still live *here*?" Palmer asked.

"No, I'd move into the house," Elizabeth replied. "Or, perhaps, somewhere else," she added with a shy smile.

Palmer smiled back and said, "What would you do with this place, then? It's yours. You own it."

"We'd explore our options, but I wouldn't want to keep it as a residence."

"Museum?" Palmer asked.

"Perhaps."

"But not to the royal family," Palmer continued. "Maybe to St. Rais in general, with only a small mention of your family. That could be good, right?"

Elizabeth smiled and said, "Could be, yes."

"If you did that, you could keep everyone on staff that wants to stay. Museums need security. They need curators. They need cooks for the cafeteria."

"You're right," Elizabeth said, turning to Rebecca then. "We don't have a national museum in St. Rais. There are village museums, but nothing at this scale."

"Yes, Ma'am," Rebecca replied.

"And Palmer's right: the staff could stay on if they chose to."

"All of this is assuming the vote goes against you, Ma'am. It might not," Rebecca replied.

"We still have to plan just in case it does. It would make sense for me to make a speedy exit from both the palace and my position."

"I hope you don't have to worry about any of this," Palmer said.

Elizabeth stared at her, trying to figure out if Palmer was telling the truth or trying to make Elizabeth feel better about the situation.

"It would be easier for *us* if—"

"I don't need easy," Palmer cut her off softly, standing up then. "I just need you." She winked at Elizabeth. "I need to go unpack, so I'll leave you two alone. Sorry for the interruption."

"I'll walk you out," Elizabeth offered, moving to stand.

"It's okay. I know my way around now. Hey, if this place *does* get turned into a museum, maybe I can give tours. I can show them the bowling alley," she joked.

"I'll meet you in the bedroom in a bit," Elizabeth replied.

Palmer wiggled her eyebrows at her, making Elizabeth laugh.

"She's good for you," Rebecca said once the door was closed behind Palmer.

"Yes, she is."

"The museum isn't a bad idea. You could give it to the country. It would go a long way."

"It would." Elizabeth nodded.

"Have you given any thought to what you'd do if the nation decides to keep the monarchy and you as its monarch?"

"Of course."

"I meant, regarding your relationship with Palmer," Rebecca clarified.

"I haven't figured that part out yet, no."

"You'll need to soon, Ma'am."

"I've got time. If the vote is that I remain, I have time before I need to start determining my next personal steps."

"Not much. Victoria is getting married. She'll have children shortly after, most likely. The country will start to wonder why you're not doing the same thing."

"They can wait, too."

"Elizabeth," Rebecca began. "You love Palmer. She loves you. That's easy to see. St. Rais can handle a gay Queen, Ma'am. I promise you that your people will support you in this."

"It might not even be an issue. Palmer and I could ride off into the sunset, so to speak, if the vote goes differently."

"You'd move to America?"

"We haven't talked about that yet."

"It seems to me that she's hoping you remain Queen."

"She's trying to be positive for me."

"Still." Rebecca stood. "If you don't mind me saying, Ma'am, she'd make a *great* Queen Consort."

CHAPTER 38

"CAN I ask you a question?" Elizabeth asked.

"Could you make it more ominous?" Palmer teased.

They were lying in Elizabeth's bed, and Palmer had her arm around Elizabeth's shoulders. Elizabeth's head was on her chest, and her fingertips were drawing lazy circles on Palmer's stomach.

"Sorry," Elizabeth chuckled against Palmer's breast. "I guess I just want to know which you'd really prefer."

"I'm a smooth peanut butter girl all the way," Palmer joked.

"Be serious," Elizabeth requested, but laughed all the same.

"You want to know if I want you to lose your crown or not, right?"

"Yes." Elizabeth lifted herself up, resting her head on her elbow, and stared at Palmer. "Rebecca seems to think you'd make a fine Queen Consort one day."

"She does not." Palmer laughed.

"She does. She said as much today."

"*I* barely make a responsible adult," Palmer argued.

"You're a very responsible adult," Elizabeth replied. "And you're kind and caring. You're smart and intuitive. Rebecca's right: you would make a great Consort."

"Is this a proposal?" Palmer lifted an eyebrow at her.

"No," Elizabeth said, smiling.

"I kind of thought *I'd* be the one doing that one day."

"Proposing? To me?" Elizabeth asked in a very high-pitched voice.

"Calm down," Palmer said, running her hand over Elizabeth's cheek. "I meant that I'd be the one proposing to any woman I'd end up with, not specifically you."

"Why is that?"

"I've just always thought so," Palmer replied. "Since I thought about settling down, I figured it would be *me* buying the ring and doing the asking."

"Not that I'm saying we're heading that direction or anything, but technically, as a Queen, the rule is that *I'd* have to ask *you*."

"You're kidding?" Palmer asked, running a hand through Elizabeth's long blonde hair.

"No, the King or Queen must do the asking. That's how it's always worked."

"Aren't you trying to get rid of some of those old-timey customs? Can *that* be one of them?"

"We might not even need to worry about it," Elizabeth reasoned. "But we have a while before you and I would be talking about that step, anyway. If the vote goes against me, I won't be a Queen anymore, and you can ask, assuming you'd want to, then."

Palmer kissed her quickly on the lips and said, "Do you really want to know what I'm thinking about this whole thing?"

"Yes, I think we have to discuss it. We love each other, and we're together, Palmer, but there *are* logistics and practicalities we should think through as well."

"Okay. Well, here's what I'm thinking." She kissed Elizabeth again. "I'm crazy about you." She shrugged a shoulder. "I love you. I want to be with you. I've never felt about anyone the way I feel about you, and that won't change because of some vote."

"I know that," Elizabeth replied softly.

"Well, if I got a vote in this thing, I'd vote *for* the monarchy."

Elizabeth pulled back, surprised, and said, "You would?"

"Every time you've talked about this, you've said, 'If they vote *for* us or *against* us,' and you meant *for* keeping you in your position and *against* keeping you in your position. That tells me you want the vote to be pro-monarchy, Lizzy. You want to stay the Queen of St. Rais. And you don't want it because you really care about some title – I'm convinced you'd be perfectly happy living in that one-bedroom house, studying physics all the time – you want the monarchy to remain because you believe it helps support St. Rais. You know what it's about, and that's not draining public funds or taking the nation to a war the entire world was already in anyway. I'll admit: I don't know where *I* fit into all of that. But it's clear to me that you know what you want. You may not want to admit it to yourself because it *does* mean you have to give up other things you want." Palmer stared into Elizabeth's blue eyes. "Then again, maybe it doesn't. You're already changing the rules so much, babe. I'm sure you could change a few more and have the best of both worlds."

"I want you," Elizabeth stated.

"I want you, too," Palmer replied.

Elizabeth sighed and rolled away, running a hand over her face.

"When Teagan started to pull away from me, I knew it wouldn't end well. I just didn't want to believe it. I kept telling myself it was normal; we'd been together forever; of course, she'd be curious about other women or another life. Her feelings for me and my inability to tell my father and St. Rais that I was a lesbian locked her into something that she wanted to get out of. I should have let her go, but I was jealous and selfish."

Palmer rolled on her side, facing her, and asked, "Because she *could* go?"

"Yes. She had choices I didn't think I had. I didn't want to disappoint my father, and I didn't want to cause

Alex any problems. Even though I had it in my mind that it wouldn't end well, I still had hope that she'd come back to me."

"You loved her," Palmer replied, placing her hand on Elizabeth's stomach.

"It wasn't just that. Teagan was all I'd ever known. She was my only girlfriend, but she was also my best friend; oftentimes, my only friend. The thought of things being over between us was too much for me to handle. When she told me she was asking Alex for a divorce, I knew I was losing my girlfriend. I was in London with Victoria at the time, meeting David. I knew the moment I returned to St. Rais, Teagan would finally end things for good."

"And you'd lose your best friend in the process?"

"I ended up losing her in a very different way than I ever expected."

"I'm sorry, Lizzy," Palmer said.

Elizabeth turned her head to Palmer and asked, "Do you know why I'm telling you this?"

"Not really, no."

"Because I thought Teagan was my only chance at love. With her gone, I didn't think I'd ever have the courage to go out and meet another woman, let alone fall in love with one, given what had happened with Teagan. What woman would want to be with me if I was too scared to tell my father, the King, that I was gay? Teagan had only done it because of our history. Another woman wouldn't have shared that with me. She wouldn't have been as invested."

"You're assuming that it takes that kind of time for someone to be that invested," Palmer replied. "I've known you a few months, at most, and I'm already invested, Elizabeth."

"Enough to move to St. Rais and be my Queen Consort one day?"

"That assumes you're willing to tell the country you love a woman. Oh, and that you'd ask me to marry you one day." Palmer winked at her.

"I might just let you ask me," Elizabeth teased.

"I might just ask," Palmer replied. "But since we have a while before we worry about that… Tell me if it's really possible that you'll be okay being out? I love you. I know it's real between us, Elizabeth. But I also know who I am, and I can't be your secret. I won't."

Elizabeth smiled at her and said, "Let's see how the vote goes. If I remain Queen of St. Rais, I'll talk to Thomas about his plan."

"To come out?" Palmer asked.

"Yes." Elizabeth nodded.

"You can't do this for me; you know that. It has to be for *you*. It has to be when you're ready," Palmer told her.

"It would be for me. I realized, when I sat behind my father's desk today, that it really *does* feel like my own now. When I talk to the Prime Minister, he sees me as Queen and treats me with respect, despite how I got the job and that I'm only half his age. I am Queen. I want to remain. I'll honor what the people want, but if I stay, I need to be honest with them about who I am and whom I love." She gave Palmer a soft smile. "And that's you. I never thought I'd get another chance at this, Palmer. I spent a few days with your family, and I was dreading it before I went because I thought I'd be so sad that my own was gone. And I missed them terribly, but yours made me feel so safe and so at home. I'm at home when I'm with you, my love."

Palmer smiled and said, "I feel the same way."

She leaned down and captured Elizabeth's lips. Every time they kissed, the butterflies in Palmer's belly fluttered and told her this was right; this was what kissing the woman of her dreams was supposed to feel like. It was supposed to feel like she was coming home. Palmer ran her hand up under Elizabeth's shirt, pausing just below her breast and waiting for permission. Before she could get it, though, there was a loud knock at the door of the bedroom.

"Is there a camera in here? Do they know I was about to get to second base and decided they needed to protect your virtue?" Palmer joked, rolling onto her back.

Elizabeth laughed and said, "There are no cameras in here. I don't know who that is. Just wait here. I'll be right back."

"Can we pick up where we left off?" she asked.

"Yes, love," Elizabeth replied, laughing.

She got out of bed, reached for her navy-blue robe, and slid it on over her white-and-blue silk pajamas. Palmer watched as she walked elegantly to the double doors and pulled them open.

"Majesty, I'm sorry to disturb you, but I thought you should know."

Palmer recognized Magnus's voice, which caused her to sit up and listen intently.

"Victoria?" Elizabeth asked, covering her mouth with her hand.

Palmer was on her feet then and making a hasty move to stand behind Elizabeth.

"No, Her Royal Highness is safe. This is about Sebastian Adrian," he explained.

"What happened?" Palmer asked, placing a protective hand on Elizabeth's back and pulling her into her own side.

"He killed himself in his cell, Ma'am," Magnus explained. "It happened about an hour ago. He made a noose and hung himself."

"What? How? There were supposed to be precautions against that," Elizabeth said.

"He used a sheet, Ma'am. His belt and shoelaces were taken away, but he used a sheet and hung himself off the end of his bed. Technically, he was sitting down. He actually just choked or strangled himself."

"He's the one that—"

"Killed my family, yes," Elizabeth confirmed.

"Thomas would like to know if you'd like to issue a statement, Ma'am. He and Rebecca are available by phone if you'd like to talk to them," Magnus told her.

"No, it's fine. It's late. It can wait until morning."

"The vote is tomorrow," Palmer reminded.

"You're right," Elizabeth said on a sigh. "I don't want this to affect how people vote either way. Does anyone outside the prison or our people know yet?"

"Not that we can tell, Ma'am."

"Should we keep it to ourselves until after the vote?" Elizabeth asked.

It took a moment before Palmer realized she was asking *her* and not Magnus.

"I don't know. Maybe you should talk to Rebecca or Thomas. I don't think I'm the right person to ask."

Elizabeth turned to move into Palmer's arms and said, "I'm asking you because I want to know your opinion, love."

"I say, you let the news out tonight."

"Really?"

"Better late at night. The evening news is already done for the day. If you hold it back, people are going to be mad about that. And if you tell them now, and they let it impact their vote in either direction, that's on them. It's *their* vote, right?"

"I suppose so."

"Don't spin it, either. That just makes it seem more important than it is. A man who murdered fifteen people killed himself because he's a coward. He doesn't deserve anyone's pity or attention. Announce it tonight. The news will get buried in the stuff about the vote tomorrow. That's what that asshole deserves. Then, no one can accuse you of hiding it or trying to sway a vote in any direction."

Elizabeth nodded, smiled, and then turned around.

"Magnus?"

"I can let Thomas and Rebecca know, Ma'am," he replied.

"Instruct them how Miss Honeycutt just explained, please, and tell them they can issue the statement without my review," she said.

"Of course, Ma'am."

"Thank you. Good night, Magnus."

"Good night, Ma'am," Magnus said with a bow.

Then, he was gone, and they were alone again. Palmer turned Elizabeth around in her arms and pulled her in for a long hug.

"You okay?"

"Is it wrong that I'm glad he's dead?" Elizabeth asked against Palmer's chest.

"Not even a little bit," Palmer replied, kissing her temple.

CHAPTER 39

THE polls were open from eight in the morning until six in the evening. Then, the officials would finalize the tally. Elizabeth couldn't sit still. She had already had two cups of tea and couldn't eat anything for breakfast. She'd never been so nervous. Well, that wasn't true. She'd been pretty nervous the moment she'd realized, after the shock of losing her family, that she was Queen of St. Rais. So much depended on this vote, though. Her entire life could change in an instant. Either way, her life would change today. If she remained as Queen, she'd keep her promise to Palmer: she would come out to her nation. She could only hope Palmer could find a way to be by her side when she did. And if she was no longer a Queen, she'd have so many options; *all* of them, really.

Elizabeth had been going over them all in her head. She could stay in St. Rais, work for a charity, and continue the work of her family, but not as a royal. She could go back to university, earn her degree, and end up in research. She could also get her degree elsewhere, maybe at a more prestigious school in Europe. She could ask Palmer if a move to America was in order. They hadn't been together long, but Elizabeth knew that the distance between them had already been so hard, and she didn't want Palmer to get into more trouble at work because of Elizabeth than the woman already was. Elizabeth didn't want Palmer to have to risk anything else on her behalf.

"So, you're clearly going crazy. Anything I can do to help?" Palmer asked, wrapping her arms around Elizabeth's waist from behind.

"Make it over already," Elizabeth replied.

"I'm afraid, it just started, babe. But we can, I don't know, do something to take your mind off of it."

"The news about Sebastian Adrian is out, but no one

seems to be noticing," Elizabeth said as Palmer's lips pressed to her neck. "Everyone in the world seems to be focusing on whether or not my family will have titles by the end of the day."

"Mmm." Palmer kissed her neck again in a different spot.

"What am I supposed to do today? It's not like an election – I can't just kiss babies or shake hands, as you Americans say. I suppose I could." She quickly turned in Palmer's arms. "Do you think I should be campaigning? Did I mess this up because I didn't make more speeches or go around the country requesting that people vote pro-monarchy?"

"Elizabeth, hey." Palmer rubbed her arms up and down. "You didn't screw it up. I think it's good you *didn't* campaign. You're not a politician. Had you done that, it would've been like everyone else out there, that is. You're a Queen. Queens do *not* campaign." Palmer smirked at her.

"Thank you for being here. I don't know if I've said that enough."

"You have," Palmer replied. "And you don't have to thank me. I want to be here. I'm pretty sure I'm about sixty percent adjusted to the cold now."

Elizabeth laughed and said, "Well, that's good. We have long winters here."

"You'll just have to keep me warm, then."

Palmer leaned in and placed a sweet kiss on Elizabeth's lips.

"That won't be a problem," Elizabeth replied.

"Let's just do something fun," Palmer suggested, pulling out of their embrace.

"Like what?"

"You have a bowling alley and a movie theater inside the palace. Let's just block out the world until the votes are in. We could use a fun day off."

"You want to bowl? You're terrible at bowling."

"Yes, but you can teach me. It also means your hands will have to go on parts of my body, so I can take the hit to my ego when you slaughter me," Palmer replied.

"Okay. Bowling it is."

***

Palmer lost all five of the games they played before they had lunch in the greenhouse. Elizabeth wasn't sure she could actually keep anything down, but Palmer had insisted she eat something. Elizabeth's rumbling stomach and her girlfriend won out, so she ate the sandwich that the kitchen staff had prepared for her while Palmer had showed her videos of Camilla, who was back at school and, apparently, bragging to her friends about her friend the Queen and her brand new tiara.

When Palmer went to the restroom after their meal, Elizabeth grabbed something to give her later. Then, they made their way to the private theater. Palmer selected a movie for them, and they settled into the comfortable seats. Elizabeth snuggled into Palmer's side, running her hands over Palmer's thigh, wrapping her arm around Palmer's middle, and finally, sliding her hand under Palmer's shirt to rest on her stomach. She dragged her fingertips across the skin she found there until she heard a gasp. She smirked and repeated the gesture. Palmer shifted a little under her touch, which made Elizabeth only want more. She moved her index finger to Palmer's belly button, moving it around and around until she lowered her hands still and placed it over Palmer's belt buckle.

She could feel Palmer's heart racing beneath her head. She could hear her breathing picking up in speed. Her hand slid a little lower but moved to the inside of Palmer's thigh and rested there. Elizabeth lifted her head and moved her lips to Palmer's neck, kissing her over and over again, feeling Palmer's pulse intensify with every touch. She knew what she wanted now. She didn't want to wait for it anymore.

"If I didn't know any better, I'd say you were trying to get me in the mood, babe," Palmer spoke.

"Why did you say it like that?" Elizabeth asked, sitting up fully.

"Like what?" Palmer asked.

"Like I *wouldn't* want that," Elizabeth replied.

"It was just a comment. I didn't mean it like that, though."

"I *do* want that, Palmer."

"Want what?" Palmer asked. "Me in the mood?"

"Yes," she said.

"Right now?" Palmer asked.

"Yes," Elizabeth replied assertively.

Palmer stood and asked, "You want that *now?*"

"Yes. Is it that hard to believe that I'd want you?"

"No, it's not, but we've been waiting."

"Do you still want to wait?" Elizabeth asked, gulping and hoping the sound from the movie still playing loudly in the room would drown it out.

"No, I don't want to wait. I want *you.* I don't mind waiting as long as you need me to."

"I don't need to wait anymore," she said softly.

"Lizzy, today is a big day."

"I know that."

Palmer looked down at the dark carpet and said, "Babe, I don't want our first time to happen because you're trying *not* to think about what's going on out there. I want you to be thinking about us and what we'd be doing in *here.*"

Elizabeth closed her eyes, realizing how she'd made Palmer feel.

"Love, that's not what this is," she said, standing up. "I'm not trying to drown out what's going on out there. I'm trying to show you how much I love you."

"You don't have to show me; I know." Palmer stood.

"No, you don't," Elizabeth replied, placing her hand in the middle of Palmer's chest. "I don't know that you ever *can* know how much I love you, but I want to try to show you if you're ready, too. Do you want to know something cool about this place?"

"What?" Palmer asked.

"This room has a secret lift. Well, you'd call it an elevator."

"Elizabeth, what—"

"It runs from upstairs where my room is, down here, and then into a tunnel. It was built during World War II in case we needed an escape route. No one ever came to St. Rais, so it goes virtually unused. When my family built the theater here, they left the lift there."

"Why are we talking about an elevator right now?"

"Because I want to take it up to my room, Palmer," Elizabeth replied, running her hand down the center of her girlfriend's chest. "I'm ready. I don't know why I'm ready right now, specifically, but I am. It's not because of what's going on *out* there. It's because of what's going on inside me. I woke up next to you this morning, and you were holding me. I could feel your breath on my neck, and I so badly wanted to roll over and make love to you."

"You did?"

"Yes. And this morning, you were behind me, kissing my neck to try to calm me down, and I wanted to take your hand and slide it—"

"Okay. Slow down," Palmer said as Elizabeth's hand met her belt buckle.

"When we were bowling, I got to hold your hips and press you up against me." Elizabeth undid the belt buckle. "And when we came in here, and the lights went down, I couldn't help myself; I had to touch you. I *want* to touch you, Palmer."

"We can. We can do that," Palmer replied nervously. "Maybe tomorrow or—"

Elizabeth pulled what she'd taken from the greenhouse out of her back pocket.

"Do you know what this one is?" she asked.

"No. What?"

"It's not very pretty, but it *is* coriander. Do you know what it means?"

"No," Palmer replied again. "I don't think my mom ever told me about that one."

"Lust," Elizabeth explained, unbuttoning Palmer's jeans with her free hand and placing the sprig of coriander inside Palmer's front pocket. "I want you, Palmer. And I'll wait if you're worried about it being about something else, but I can promise you it's not. I love you." She unzipped Palmer's jeans. "I want to make love to you."

God, it was the truth. She'd wanted it the night before, too, and probably would have, had Magnus not interrupted them with that news. She'd wanted it for longer than that, too. Today, being with Palmer, knowing that their future together could go one way or another and that Palmer was still there, that she loved Elizabeth enough to support her through this, was something Elizabeth hadn't known she needed. Then, there was how beautiful Palmer was; how sexy the woman could be with those dark eyes darkening even more at times when she didn't think Elizabeth was looking. Palmer's skin was soft. Her lips were warm and so talented; Elizabeth wanted to be touched by her and to touch her so much she could no longer hold it in. When she'd noticed the coriander in the greenhouse, she'd thought it fate. And now, all she wanted was to be with Palmer in a way she had only ever been with one other woman, and in a way she hoped she'd never be with another woman after Palmer.

"Where's the elevator?" Palmer asked as Elizabeth pulled on her shirt in an attempt to get it off Palmer's body.

"Over there," Elizabeth replied. "Keep the movie playing – I want people to think we're still in here. No interruptions for this, my love."

Elizabeth then pulled on Palmer's undone belt until they ran into the wall. Palmer pressed her fully against it, placing her hands on either side of Elizabeth's head.

"Press the up button," Palmer told her, licking her lips.

"Yes, Miss Honeycutt," Elizabeth replied, locating the hidden button with her finger, pressing it, and waiting.

CHAPTER 40

WHEN Palmer had woken up that morning, the last thing she had expected was that they'd be making out in a tiny elevator on their way to Elizabeth's bedroom to make love. She'd assumed her job today was to be a supportive girlfriend. But now, Elizabeth had her pressed against the side wall of that elevator, and her hands were cupping Palmer's ass, pulling her in closer.

"There aren't cameras in here, are there?" Palmer breathed out.

"No," Elizabeth said. "Well, I don't think so."

"You don't *think* so?" she asked as Elizabeth licked her neck.

"Can we not talk right now?" Elizabeth requested as she sucked on Palmer's earlobe.

"Whatever you want," Palmer agreed breathlessly.

When the elevator stopped, Palmer was pulled out of it and into Elizabeth's sitting room. Thankfully, the room was empty, so Palmer allowed Elizabeth to drag her in the direction of the double doors leading to the bedroom. Then, she took over. She pressed Elizabeth against one of them, sliding her hands under Elizabeth's blouse and lifting it off, revealing a pale pink bra with a tiny bow situated between Elizabeth's breasts that were heaving. Palmer stared into Elizabeth's now darkening blue eyes.

"You really want this?" she asked.

"Is that your non-clichéd way of asking if I'm sure?" Elizabeth teased.

"You're extra sassy when you're turned on," Palmer teased back.

Elizabeth's hand went behind Palmer's head, and she pulled her lips to an inch between Palmer's and her own.

"I love you. I want you. I am certain, my love," Elizabeth said seriously.

Palmer closed the distance between their mouths. She pressed the door behind Elizabeth until it relented and opened. They practically fell into the bedroom, but Palmer had enough sense to ensure the door was closed behind them just in case. She walked Elizabeth back to the bed, kicking her jeans off along the way. When the back of Elizabeth's legs hit the bed, Palmer just watched as she sat down on it, looking up at her with such want yet such vulnerability in her gaze.

After a second, Palmer moved into Elizabeth's body, standing between her spread legs, and wrapped her arms around Elizabeth's shoulders, pulling her face against her chest. Elizabeth, for her part, lifted at Palmer's shirt until Palmer took the hint and removed it herself, leaving her in only her bra and underwear. Then, Elizabeth pulled back enough to take in Palmer's body, met her eyes, and gave her the softest smile before pressing her lips against Palmer's skin between her breasts. Palmer felt that kiss *everywhere.* Her toes curled at the intimate touch of Elizabeth's hand cupping her breast over her bra. Her nipples hardened, and she wanted more.

"Lie back," she requested.

Elizabeth looked up at her.

"Lie back, beautiful," Palmer requested again, cupping Elizabeth's cheeks. "I want to touch you."

Elizabeth nodded slowly. She moved until she was lying on the bed, her head against the pillows. Palmer stood at the end of the bed and just looked at her, her Queen. Then, she undid the clasp on her own bra and let it fall to the floor. Elizabeth's eyes widened and darkened at the same time. Palmer watched her swallow. Then, she reached for the underwear she'd put on after her shower that morning, having no idea that she'd be taking them off in front of Elizabeth later. She moved onto the bed and crawled her way to the top of it in order to hover over her girlfriend.

"You're overdressed," Palmer said, trying to relieve

some of the tension that had entered the room the moment *they* had.

"You're perfect," Elizabeth replied, cupping the back of Palmer's neck.

Palmer pressed her body fully into Elizabeth's but knew she needed to feel the skin on skin, so she lifted up, allowing Elizabeth to do the same thing she did earlier. Then, she watched her girlfriend arch her back to reach for the clasp on her bra, and that pale pink garment with the tiny bow was pulled off, revealing Elizabeth's flesh-pink nipples in a nearly matching shade. Palmer sat up then, looked down at Elizabeth's body, and bit her lower lip. She'd never seen something so beautiful in her entire life.

When Palmer looked down at the matching bikinis, noticing the dark wet spot between her girlfriend's thighs, she gasped out, "Oh, fuck! Did I just say *fuck*? I'm sorry," she added.

Elizabeth laughed a little and suggested, "You can take them off if you want."

"I do want," Palmer replied.

She slid her fingers to the hem of the bikinis and danced them over the fabric, making Elizabeth squirm beneath her.

"You're so wet," Palmer noted.

"I told you, I want this, love. Take them off, please."

Palmer smirked, pulled at the bikinis until they were completely off, dropped them on the floor next to the bed, and spread Elizabeth's legs, revealing everything to her greedy eyes. Then, licking her own lips, she thought about what she wanted to do first. Remembering why she wanted Elizabeth's clothes off in the first place, Palmer moved back on top of her, pressing their flesh fully together for the first time.

"Oh, God," Elizabeth gasped out.

"Yeah," Palmer echoed, wishing she had something more eloquent she could've said to describe this moment.

Elizabeth's legs spread wider on their own, allowing

Palmer to settle more fully between her thighs, her hands moved to Palmer's lower back, and she began to move her hips, encouraging Palmer to do the same. Palmer lowered into her at the same time she met Elizabeth's lips with her own. She dragged her tongue along Elizabeth's lower lip before sliding it inside her mouth. Elizabeth moaned. Her hands lowered to Palmer's ass, which she cupped and pressed down into herself.

Palmer moaned then. She disconnected their mouths, needing air, before moving her lips to Elizabeth's neck. She licked and sucked on the skin, listening to Elizabeth's sounds as she moved her hips and her lips around her body. She lowered her mouth until her lips pressed to the spot where that tiny pink bow had been moments earlier, and she cupped Elizabeth's right breast in her hand, feeling the hard nipple in her palm. Her lips moved to Elizabeth's other breast, kissing around the nipple until Elizabeth's sounds enticed her toward the peak. Palmer sucked it into her mouth, squeezing the other nipple between her thumb and forefinger.

"Oh," Elizabeth gasped. "Yes."

Palmer thought she'd come just from that. She grunted loudly, which made Elizabeth laugh.

"Need something?" Elizabeth asked.

"Yes, you," Palmer stated, releasing her nipple with a pop and looking up at her with hungry eyes. "But we've got time, so I'll be patient."

"How patient?" Elizabeth asked seriously.

"Not *that* patient," Palmer replied.

"Good," Elizabeth said.

Palmer smiled and returned her attention to Elizabeth's breasts, loving how full and soft they felt in her palm and between her lips, but especially, how good the hardened peaks felt when she ran the flat of her tongue over them. When she lowered her lips farther, Elizabeth gave a whimper at the loss of contact between her legs. Palmer kissed her way down until she settled between Elizabeth's thighs.

She kissed and licked the inside of them, taking in the scent of Elizabeth's desire for her and feeling her own hips rock on their own against the mattress.

Palmer licked closer and closer, listening to Elizabeth's whimpers and cries for her to continue until she couldn't take it anymore. She spread Elizabeth with two fingers, seeing her fully for the first time, and licked her lips at the sight. Elizabeth was wet, swollen, and ready. Palmer had done that to her.

"I love you," she said.

Then, she slid her tongue slowly from Elizabeth's entrance to the tip of her clit.

"Oh, God!"

Palmer repeated the movement, feeling Elizabeth's legs spread wider, giving her more room to work. Her tongue continued to lap at Elizabeth's wetness until she finally sucked her into her mouth. The sensations nearly took Palmer over the edge, but she held on to the pulse between her own thighs, silently promising herself it would be addressed later; right now, her focus needed to be on Elizabeth's need. When she hesitantly slid one finger inside her lover, Elizabeth's hips lifted abruptly, and she gasped loudly. She was wide open for Palmer, so Palmer slid another finger inside and moaned against Elizabeth's clit. She was inside this beautiful, remarkable woman, and she was going to make her come.

Her thrusts started off slow, letting Elizabeth rise and fall repeatedly before she finally picked up the speed. Elizabeth's sounds grew more frequent when Palmer curled inside her, so she repeated that over and over, sucking and licking Elizabeth's clit. Elizabeth began to tighten around her fingers. Her hips began to lift higher and rocked faster and harder against Palmer's mouth. When Palmer knew Elizabeth was about to come, she moved deeper inside her and flicked her tongue against the woman's clit. Finally, she curled inside and flicked her fast, pressing the flat of her tongue down hard against Elizabeth's clit.

"Yes! Yes!" Elizabeth's hands moved to the back of Palmer's head, encouraging her to stay in place.

Palmer had no plans to go anywhere, though. She only wanted to listen and let Elizabeth take her pleasure.

"Oh, my God," Elizabeth said slowly as her hips fell to the mattress and she tried to catch her breath. "Oh, my God, Palmer."

Palmer kissed the inside of Elizabeth's thighs, one after the other, and stared at Elizabeth's sex. Noticing it didn't appear completely sated yet, she pressed her thumb to Elizabeth's clit.

"What? Oh, God!"

"Again?" Palmer checked.

"I don't think…"

Palmer pressed a little harder and then lightened the pressure before she used her thumb and forefinger to squeeze Elizabeth's clit gently. She then also moved her tongue over the bundle of nerves now-squeezed between her fingers.

"Oh, God! Yes!"

Palmer listened as she licked. Elizabeth came again, her body shuddering until Palmer finally slowed and then stopped altogether. Palmer moved up the bed, kissing Elizabeth, wanting to claim those lips again. This woman was hers. She loved her.

"I love you," she repeated her earlier words as Elizabeth's eyes welled with tears. "I love you, Elizabeth," she told her again. "I won't leave. I'm yours. You're mine."

Elizabeth nodded rapidly in response, and a tear fell from her eye. Palmer kissed it off her skin. Then, she kissed Elizabeth deeply until, surprisingly, Elizabeth flipped them over and ended up on top.

"You're mine," Elizabeth said, repeating Palmer's words now.

"Show me," Palmer requested softly.

Elizabeth smiled down at her, captured her lips, and settled her own thighs between Palmer's.

CHAPTER 41

ELIZABETH hadn't ever cried after an orgasm, even after the very first one given to her by another's touch. These tears were happy ones. They were tears that came because of her release, but not just her physical one, the emotional one as well. She let a few of them fall, and Palmer caught them with her fingertips and her lips, kissing them away but not asking why they were falling in the first place, which told Elizabeth how well Palmer knew her.

Elizabeth moved her lips around Palmer's body, kissing and nipping at her neck, her ears, and then her collarbones, listening to Palmer's sounds and sensing her hips were eager to rock and sought the friction Palmer needed. Elizabeth took her time with Palmer's body, not wanting these moments to ever end. When she finally entered Palmer, she watched Palmer relax into her touch, welcoming Elizabeth farther inside. She stroked Palmer's clit with her thumb as she lay on top and rocked against her.

"Yes, there," Palmer said, wrapping her hands around Elizabeth's neck and pulling her in for a kiss.

"I love you," Elizabeth whispered against Palmer's lips when they pulled apart for much-needed air, needing to say it again.

"Don't stop," Palmer told her.

Elizabeth wasn't sure if Palmer was telling her not to stop loving her or not to stop touching her.

"I won't," Elizabeth replied, referring to both.

When Palmer came, it was with a gasp, not a scream, and it was with her pressing Elizabeth's forehead to her own. Elizabeth stroked her until she came down all the way, whispered those three words again, and slid down Palmer's body until she took her with her mouth.

Palmer whimpered and then moaned as Elizabeth licked and sucked, bringing her to another orgasm – this time, much faster than the first. Elizabeth waited until Palmer's breathing had returned to normal before she kissed her thighs, her clit, and then her stomach, moving up her body until she met Palmer's nipples with her hands and mouth. She brought Palmer to a third orgasm by rolling her hips down into her and sucking on one nipple while squeezing Palmer's other full breast. Then, she hovered over her and stared down at the woman who had so completely stolen her heart.

"No matter what happens," Elizabeth began. "I want this forever, Palmer."

Palmer smiled dizzily up at her and said, "Whatever you want."

"I want you to touch me again," Elizabeth requested.

Palmer's eyes went wide, and she nodded.

***

"Why do I feel like we're teenagers and we're going to get caught?" Palmer asked.

"I have no idea," Elizabeth replied. "I'm kind of in charge here, so no one's going to get us in trouble."

The door to the small elevator opened, depositing them back into the theater they'd left behind hours earlier. Elizabeth flopped down onto the sofa, pulling Palmer down on top of her.

"Oh. I thought we were coming back down here because we were *done* having sex for now," Palmer said, settling between Elizabeth's thighs.

"We can still make out, can't we?" she asked. "Start a new movie and kiss all the way through it? I'm kind of addicted to your lips now."

"Just now?" Palmer teased, leaning over Elizabeth to kiss her lips.

"No, I think I've been addicted to your lips since I saw

the picture of you Rebecca showed me before we even met."

"Oh, yeah?" Palmer said. "Wait." She pulled back. "She showed you a picture of me?"

"I told you, I did my research," Elizabeth replied, kissing Palmer's neck. "That included a picture. You were very cute."

"I was?"

"Yes, you were. Still are," she added.

Palmer stared down at her and, after a long moment, said, "We should just go back to your room the usual way, babe. We can make sure the door is locked and just make love all night."

"I wish that were possible, but they'd have to interrupt me when–"

"Majesty," Rebecca said, entering the theater without knocking.

Palmer shot up and off Elizabeth instantly, moving to stand.

"I was just…" Palmer began nervously. "I mean, we weren't doing–"

"Rebecca, what is it?" Elizabeth interrupted her adorable girlfriend, sitting up on the sofa.

"Ma'am, haven't you been watching?"

"Watching what?" Elizabeth asked. "Oh, the vote? Is there an update?"

"Ma'am, it's after seven. The polls were closed at six. The votes have been tallied and confirmed."

In that moment, Elizabeth second-guessed every decision she'd made since becoming Queen. Well, she second-guessed every decision other than Palmer. Of their relationship, Elizabeth had no regrets; nothing to second-guess. Had she made the right decision? Would her father, her grandfather, or her great-grandfather want to disown her for even thinking about putting their inheritance, as well as her own, to a vote? Would they support it, given the circumstances? Elizabeth glanced over at Palmer, who sat back down beside her, taking her hand and entwining their fingers.

"What is it?" Elizabeth asked.

"Majesty, the vote was seventy-two percent," Rebecca said.

"Okay... Seventy-two percent, which way?" Palmer asked only after a moment, likely noticing that Elizabeth wasn't able to ask the question herself.

Rebecca smiled softly and said, "Long live Queen Antonia I."

Elizabeth's eyes went wide, and she asked, "Rebecca, what—"

"Your Majesty, your country voted to *keep* the monarchy." Rebecca's smile widened.

"They did?" Elizabeth asked with tears in her eyes.

"Yes, Ma'am. Now, I believe there are a few people who wish to toast alongside you, if you would be so kind as to join us in the formal dining room."

"Toast?" Elizabeth asked, turning to Palmer.

"Go. Have a drink with the people who love you."

"Where will *you* be?"

"Right next to you, if that's okay," Palmer replied with a smile.

"Always." Elizabeth smiled back at her. "Rebecca, can you give us a moment? We'll join you shortly."

"Of course, *Your Majesty*," she replied, bowing her head.

Rebecca left the theater, closing the door behind her.

"How do you feel?" Palmer asked.

"Seventy-two percent? I thought it would go the other way."

"They love you, beautiful," Palmer said. "And they believe in you. And the monarchy."

"Palmer, we need to talk now," Elizabeth replied, placing her other hand on top of their still-joined ones. "I honestly thought they'd vote to remove me. I've been planning for both contingencies just in case, but because of what happened, I think I just assumed they'd want us out."

"You were honest with them – it sounds like you and your family always *have* been – and you gave them the chance to choose what they wanted. I must admit: I'm surprised, too."

"Disappointed?" she asked, looking for Palmer's reaction.

"What? No. Why would I be disappointed?"

"Because of us," Elizabeth said softly.

"What do you mean?"

"If I'm no longer a Queen, I'd have a lot more opportunities to leave St. Rais; to be with whomever I want, and–"

"Oh," Palmer said and cupped Elizabeth's cheek. "Babe, you *are* a Queen. I knew that when I met you *and* when I fell in love with you. This whole vote thing happened, but I knew I wanted you long before the idea."

"And you honestly weren't hoping that this little idea of yours wouldn't go the other way?"

"I was hoping you'd get what you want," Palmer said, leaning in and kissing her quickly. "And *this* is what you want. I know it's hard because it was thrust upon you, and you've lost so much, but it doesn't mean you have to lose everything. I think you can be Queen and get your degree. Maybe you won't work in physics as a researcher or professor, but it doesn't mean you can't still pursue it as a hobby or something more. You could rewrite the rules, Elizabeth; make the monarchy modern. Be yourself, baby." Palmer kissed her lips again. "You were born for this."

"What about us?" Elizabeth asked against Palmer's lips.

"I'm not going anywhere."

"You're leaving in a couple of days," Elizabeth noted, pulling Palmer in closer. "And we only just–"

"We'll do long-distance for a while. We'll figure it out."

"How many times are we going to say that until we do?" Elizabeth asked.

"I don't know what else I can say, Elizabeth. I can't

just move to St. Rais; not right now, anyway. I have a job back home, an apartment, and my family is there."

"I know. I'm sorry." She lowered her head.

"But I can someday," Palmer added.

Elizabeth raised her head then and asked, "Yeah?"

"We haven't been together all that long, and if I'm not mistaken, you need to take some time after this whole vote thing before you tell everyone you're gay and that you have an American girlfriend. I don't think it's a good idea for you to come out tonight."

"No, I agree."

"Okay. So, I'll go home. Maybe you can come for a visit once things settle down here."

"Victoria's wedding will be soon," Elizabeth noted. "She doesn't want to wait. The date will be in May."

"Do you need a date?" Palmer asked.

"I'd like you to be here."

"Then, I'll at least come for the weekend."

"Only a weekend?"

"Depends on work, but I should be able to take a week in the summer: my vacation time resets in June. Camilla will be out of school. We could take that family trip here."

"That sounds nice."

"And after that, you can come to the States, yeah?" Palmer asked.

"I'll come as often as I can," Elizabeth replied.

"And that will be *very* often if I have anything to say about it," Palmer teased as she wiggled her eyebrows.

Elizabeth laughed but shoved lightly at Palmer's shoulders.

"Don't joke, my love. We're planning the entire year because we have to."

"And maybe one day, we won't have to."

"You'd really move here one day? I mean, if we're still together, and—"

"Yeah, I would. Like I said, I'm adjusting to the cold. I can write anywhere, or maybe I'll break into broadcast TV.

I've got time to figure it out. I would only move here if we were out, though, Elizabeth." She paused. "I believe you when you say you'll come out, but I can't live here with you and not really be *with* you."

"I know. Now that the vote has been confirmed, I'll speak with Thomas again tomorrow about the plan."

"Then, let's just go celebrate. I'm sure Victoria wants to celebrate with you, too. Let's have some champagne."

"We'll have whiskey," Elizabeth teased. "The good stuff." She winked at Palmer.

CHAPTER 42

PALMER had said it without really thinking about it. Would she actually move to St. Rais? As she watched Elizabeth stand in front of her staff and give what was, essentially, a victory speech as she held up a glass of whiskey, Palmer knew she would. She loved this woman. She'd been right before: she could write from anywhere. She could even try her hand at TV news. She'd stand a good chance of getting a job in St. Rais with her resume and the fact that, if she did move here, she'd be dating the Queen.

"How are you?" Victoria asked.

"A little buzzed, honestly," Palmer replied. "I had to choke down that whiskey. No offense, but it burns."

"Our liquor is smooth; I'll have you know," Victoria said, laughing at her. "And I meant, how are you with the news that your girlfriend will be remaining the Queen of a country?"

"I'm happy for her."

"And for yourself?"

"It's going to be hard, but I love your sister." She smiled as Elizabeth hugged Rebecca.

"So, you're not going to end things?"

"What? No! I just found her," Palmer replied, turning to look at Victoria.

"Good answer." Victoria glared.

"Did you actually think I'd just leave her after everything?"

"No, I didn't. I assume you value your life, and you'd know that I'd kill you if you ever hurt her."

Palmer laughed a little and said, "I hope I never do, but I'm sure I'll do something stupid one day."

"Don't," Victoria replied, winking at her. "So, how's it going to work between the two of you?"

"Long-distance for a while."

"You're all right with that?"

"I don't have much of a choice."

"Yes, you do." Victoria shrugged a shoulder. "You could end things, go home, move on, and meet someone else one day, who isn't tied to a country like my sister."

"No, I can't," Palmer replied.

"Why not?"

"Because she's the one," Palmer said easily. "I don't want anyone else. She's it for me."

"You are full of good answers tonight." Victoria laughed.

"I'm serious, Victoria. I've never felt this way about another woman before. And I don't think I ever will. I want to marry her one day."

"And she's okay with this plan?"

"We've talked about her coming out, and yeah, I know that I'd have to move here and become whatever it is I'd have to become, but I'd do it for her. Hell, I'd do it for *me*."

"What do you mean?"

"I love it here, and only part of that is because of her. This place was supposed to be somewhere I intended to spend a week, go home, and look at the pictures later to remember my relaxing vacation. But it had turned into so much more. I spent weeks diving into its history, learning about the people, and roaming around the city in the cold. I don't exactly know what the future holds. I know I can't just leave my family in Pennsylvania without a plan to see them as often as I could, but... I don't know; even working for the paper doesn't feel as good as it used to."

"I thought reporters were supposed to annoy you with their perseverance." Victoria lifted an eyebrow at Palmer. "But you never have."

"Maybe I'm more of a writer than an investigative reporter. Maybe there's something else out there for me."

"Some*thing*, right? Not some*one*?" Elizabeth's voice came from behind her.

"Rest easy, my sister. Palmer, here, was just singing your praises, telling me how much she loves you *and* St. Rais."

"She was?" Elizabeth asked, smiling.

"I was," Palmer confirmed. "And I'd kiss you right now if we weren't surrounded by a bunch of people who—"

Elizabeth leaned in and interrupted her words with a quick kiss on the lips. When she pulled back, Palmer must have looked shocked, because she started laughing.

"Everyone, may I have your attention for just one more moment?" Elizabeth asked the room. When everyone got quiet, she continued, "Most of you have already met Miss Honeycutt. She came to St. Rais several months ago on vacation, and after what happened with the King and the rest of our family, Palmer stayed to write a story. As a reporter for her paper, it was her job to get all the dirt she could and to report on it in a way that would sell papers." Elizabeth smiled at Palmer. "Fortunately for me *and* for St. Rais, Palmer has integrity. She didn't make a mockery out of me, my family, or St. Rais. She also made sure that some of the more personal things I revealed to her stayed between us. I don't know many reporters who would have done the same." She paused for a moment. "And I am so grateful." Tears welled in Elizabeth's eyes as she took Palmer's hand. "I am so grateful for Palmer. Her strength and her support have gotten me through the toughest days I will likely ever encounter in my life. Her humor and her intelligence brightened those days when I could find nothing else to be happy about. On top of that, she's given me the courage to not only ask my people if a monarchy was what they wanted but also to be myself more completely." Elizabeth squeezed Palmer's hand. "I will tell the rest of the nation in time, but given the recent events, I'd prefer to keep this just between us for now." She looked around the room of about thirty people. "You are all part of my family, so I believe that I can trust each of you." She met Palmer's eyes again. "I am absolutely in love with Palmer Honeycutt. Our relationship is new, but it is real, and it is lasting. I would request that you all treat Palmer as if she were part of this family because she is; or, I hope she will be one day, at least." Elizabeth looked around the room again. "If you have a problem with my relationship with Palmer, you are more than welcome to turn in your resignation at any time; I won't be upset with you. It's time, though, for St. Rais to move forward from the pain of what happened. For me to help us do that, I have to be myself, and Palmer is part of me in a way no one else has ever or will ever be." She pressed her forehead to Palmer's. "I love you."

Palmer felt the tears well up in her own eyes as she said, "I love you, too."

"Well, it has been quite a day, hasn't it?" Victoria asked loudly. "More drinks all around!"

The room erupted into cheers. Palmer didn't hear them, though.

"I can't believe you just did that," she said, kissing Elizabeth's lips.

"They won't say anything. Anyone in this room is someone I can trust. And even if they do, it won't matter; we'll tell the world soon enough."

"Did you mean what you said?" Palmer asked, wiping the tears off her own cheeks before doing the same to Elizabeth's.

"Every single word," Elizabeth whispered against her lips.

CHAPTER 43

"IT'S strange. I almost don't know what to do now," Elizabeth said against Palmer's chest.

"Sleep?" Palmer suggested. "It's been a long day."

"I know," Elizabeth replied, sliding in closer against Palmer's naked body. "I'm sorry."

"No, it's fine; you need to talk it out. Let's talk it out," Palmer said, kissing her temple. "What's going through your mind?"

"I feel like I just got so much work to do, but I didn't, really. It's strange. After my family was killed, I was made Queen by default. It didn't feel like my own. I still used my own office. I went through the motions of what I thought I was supposed to do. Then, I told everyone we'd put it to a vote, and everything had to just wait until that vote."

"Now, it's done. You're still the Queen of a country."

"Yes." Elizabeth rested her head on her elbow to look down at Palmer. "It's like now, the *real* work begins. My brain is filled with all of these ideas I've never had before, and it's two o'clock in the morning, and I don't know what to do about it. I'm using my father's old office now – which is a start, I guess – but I'm still sleeping in my room." She sighed. "I don't know that I can ever sleep in his old room. That was *their* room," she said, referring to her parents. "Changing out the furniture wouldn't help."

"Is someone trying to force you to sleep in there?" Palmer asked, running her hand through Elizabeth's hair, still mussed from their recent lovemaking.

"No, it's just the custom. It's what you do."

"Well, it doesn't have to be what *you* do. It's just a bedroom, babe. If you don't want to sleep there, sleep here or sleep somewhere else entirely."

"Are you adding that to the list of rules I should change?" Elizabeth teased.

"I'm not adding *anything* to your list right now. I'm only suggesting that if something doesn't make you happy, don't do it. I think you've figured out by now that being Queen is something you actually want and that it does – or it can – make you happy. That's a good first step, right?"

"Yes, I suppose it is."

"But it doesn't have to be the *only* thing that makes you happy. And it's definitely not all that you are," Palmer added. "That list you have running through your mind right now – none of that has to happen overnight. Plus, it shouldn't just be about the country. There should be other things on it for you."

"You're on it. Making this work between us is at the top of my list. You know that, right?"

"I'm glad to hear that," Palmer said, smiling at her. "But I'm not even talking about me. Where do you want to live, Lizzy?"

"This room is fine enough."

"Babe, don't limit yourself to this room. Do you even want to live in the palace?"

"Well, I can't go back to my little house; it's not secure enough. And even if we could make it that way, it sort of feels like a step back into my old life, and I'm not sure I want that."

"You guys have other properties, though, right?"

"Honestly, I love Coburn Cottage. It's too far away from the palace, though."

"How far is it?"

"About fifty kilometers."

"And before I ask, you're going to–"

"About thirty-one miles."

"You can drive that every day if you had to. People back home drive that far to get to work all the time."

"I suppose," Elizabeth replied. "But I just gave that to Victoria and David." She thought to herself for a second. "But Victoria doesn't want it. She was thinking about going to school out of the country anyway."

"See?" Palmer asked.

"I could speak with her about it, but if she says no and wants Coburn, I'll figure something else out."

"That sounds good," Palmer replied.

Elizabeth kissed her quickly and said, "The palace can be a museum, after all."

"What? How'd we get *there*?" Palmer asked.

"Well, it's two wings, for one. This wing is the residence. The other is the office wing. If I'm not living here, the top two floors could easily be converted into a museum. They already do tours in the other wing. It could be part of the experience. Then, the palace staff can remain on, and I don't need a staff at Coburn; I'd prefer it just be you and me."

"You and me?" Palmer asked.

"One day," Elizabeth said. "Security would be there, and Rebecca lives closer to Coburn than she does here. If you end up moving here one day, Palmer, we'd have a real home."

"With maybe a cook and a maid, too?" Palmer asked. "You haven't seen my apartment; I'm not the cleanest person in the world."

"Whatever you want, but I don't need much myself." Elizabeth lay back down on Palmer's chest. "Assuming we get there, our kids would grow up in a real home, not a palace with servants. I never wanted that for my kids anyway."

"I never had that as an option, but I like how I grew up. I guess I'd want that for my kids, too."

"Yeah?" Elizabeth checked.

"Yes. But none of these needs to be decided tonight, right?"

"No, you can get some sleep," Elizabeth replied, chuckling at her.

"Not what I meant. You woke me up, and now I'm thinking about a house and kids one day with you." Palmer quickly flipped them over. "And how much I already miss touching you; and I'm still in bed with you."

Elizabeth wrapped her arms around Palmer's neck and pulled her down into her body.

"What are you going to do about it?" she teased.

"Tell you how proud I am of you, that I love you, and remind you that we're going to be okay."

"Not what I was expecting," Elizabeth said, giving her a playful glare. "But I love it anyway."

"Now, I'm going to kiss you. Let's see where it goes from there, shall we?"

Palmer leaned down and captured her lips in a sweet, soft kiss.

***

"What are you so worried about?" Victoria asked.

"I'm not worried. It's just that she'd be giving up so much to be with me."

"Like what? She'd have to move, but people do that for their girlfriends all the time."

Elizabeth sat across from her sister in the sitting room of her suite. Palmer was with Thomas, who was grilling the woman with questions about her background, her job, and probably, even her sexual history, if Elizabeth had to guess. He'd said he'd needed the information to help him with his plan on helping his Queen come out of the closet and that it would also prepare Palmer for whatever she might endure from other people who had questions.

Elizabeth had wanted to attend, but Palmer had assured her she'd be fine. Elizabeth had also wanted to attend because it was Palmer's last full day in St. Rais – she'd be leaving tomorrow and wouldn't be back until Victoria's wedding in May. Elizabeth hated missing any of the time they had left together, but it was important for their future, so she'd opted for lunch with her sister to pass the time between meetings.

"She'd have to give up her job, too."

"She'd find one here."

"Queen Consorts don't work, Victoria. They have functions, charities they support, and overall royal duties, but they don't have jobs."

"I'm aware. But she's not your Queen Consort just yet, so wait until she says yes before you start worrying about all of that stuff. Besides, you can change that. She can, too. She could still be a Queen Consort and have a job. We don't take public funding, so it would be allowed. It's just never been done."

"I suppose," Elizabeth replied. "There's something else I was hoping to ask you today, and you can feel free to say no. It's just that Palmer asked me something, and it got me thinking."

"What?"

"Do you and David really want to live in Coburn Cottage?"

"What? No. He and I both want to move back to London. I want to get back to school; you know that."

"And if I said that was fine, and that I wanted to live in Coburn, you'd be okay with that?"

"*You* want the cottage?" Victoria asked, leaning forward in her chair. "What about the palace?"

"I never wanted to live in the palace. Even when we were kids, I wanted to live somewhere else."

"I remember. We'd probably sound like spoiled rich kids to anyone who heard this, huh?"

"Maybe, but it was a life we were born into, not one we sought out. I think Palmer and I have found a way that no one here would lose their jobs, and we could live somewhere and still be kept safe just in case there's ever another Sebastian Adrian out there. You and David could have what you want as well. Plus, I'd still be able to get here to work.

I'd be as normal as I *could* be, given my job."

"You and Palmer, huh? I thought that would take time to figure out, but you're including her in this plan."

"I don't know what's going to happen with us, but I do love her. I want to make the big decisions in my life *with* her now. She and I have already talked about it, and I showed her pictures of Coburn as well. We're going to visit the place when she's here for the wedding; I want to make sure *she* wants to live there, too."

"She'll love Coburn. You told me her dad loves botany. Build a greenhouse there, too, for when they visit. Her sister is a big fan of putting on shows, right? There's that sitting room that no one uses. You could build a little platform for her there; give her a place to play and act. The kitchen in Coburn is modern and really nice. Her mom would probably love to cook in there. Plus, the town is really quaint. They'd have fun visiting, I think. Palmer could write in that little sunroom off the back of the house in the summer, and there's that office upstairs for the winter. And if she does decide to pursue broadcasting, Channel Four News is in Renfro. That's only a twenty-minute drive. There's Channel Eight and Channel Seven here in town, too. She'd have options."

"You've really thought this all out, haven't you?" Elizabeth asked her.

"I have. Lizzy, I'm your sister. I love you. I want you to be happy." Victoria looked around the room. "Before this whole thing happened, you weren't happy. Maybe you liked school enough, and your little house off-campus, but you and Teagan were on your way to a slow and inevitable end. I was worried about you. When Dad asked you to go to meet David for him first, I told David not to make a big deal out of how in love we were because I was afraid it would make you feel bad. I knew things with Teagan weren't good, and I also knew that other than me and Alex, you had no one to talk to about it. Alex wasn't a lifeline; he would have been too worried about what would happen to him.

And I was away at school and then dating David, and you wouldn't have brought your misery to me because you would want *me* to be happy and not worry about it. You're always doing things for other people. You and Palmer are good together." She grasped Elizabeth's hand over the table. "If she's willing to move here one day, be your girlfriend in the public eye and then your Consort, that's such a big deal, Lizzy."

"I never thought I'd love anyone how I loved Teagan."

"And Palmer's the one?" Victoria asked.

Elizabeth smiled and said, "I've never felt how I felt when I first met her. I know that's not fair to Teagan. We met as kids, and we were friends before we figured out there was more to it, but I fell in love with Teagan as a teenager."

"And you fell in love with Palmer as a woman?"

"Yes, as who I am now. And I believe she and I can grow together, not apart."

"Then, I'll hope for that, too."

CHAPTER 44

PALMER stared at her laptop screen. Things had not been easy since she'd gotten back to New York. She had spent a couple of days at home, and then she'd packed up again to join the candidate's Senate campaign in Virginia, feeling like a nomad. Most of her time was spent with other reporters who didn't exactly want to share their scoops with the competition, and the candidate herself had been rather elusive thus far, unfortunately.

Now, Palmer was staring at her laptop, not for work but because her girlfriend was late for their scheduled video chat. The past thirty days apart hadn't been much fun for Palmer. She was counting the days until she went back to St. Rais for Victoria and David's wedding. What she'd thought she'd like about life on the road during campaign season was beyond her now. She didn't like the company. She didn't like the food. She didn't like the hotels the paper paid for. She didn't like how lonely it all felt.

"Hello, my love," Elizabeth said with a smile when they finally connected.

"Hi, babe," Palmer replied, yawning.

"Tired?"

"Yeah, sorry; it's just been a long day."

"How's the campaign going?" Elizabeth asked.

"It's pretty dull. I'm writing my stuff and sending it in, but nothing big has broken yet."

"How long are you going to do this for?"

"Another month, at least; unless my editor wises up and realizes there's nothing here. This candidate is pretty boring behind the scenes. She can turn it on for the camera, but that's about it."

"That's so long away from home, Palmer," Elizabeth said.

"Home is with you."

Elizabeth smiled wider and replied, "*My* home is with you, too."

"It's still far too long until I get to see you," Palmer said.

"I know, love. But when you're here, I promise, we'll have as much time together as possible. I've already delegated everything I can for the wedding to other people so that we can have at least a couple of days just for us."

"Thank you. I need that." Palmer noticed something. "Why are you on your phone? Are you not at the office already?"

Elizabeth smiled and said, "I asked Rebecca to get your hotel information from you to send you a little gift."

"I texted it to her yesterday, but I don't–" There was a knock on Palmer's door. The sound from the knock wasn't just on her side of the chat. "Babe?"

Elizabeth laughed and said, "Palmer, open the door."

Palmer's eyes went wide. She practically tossed her laptop aside, jumped out of bed, and yanked open the hotel door. Standing in front of her was the love of her life.

"You're here?" she asked softly, afraid that if she said it too loudly, Elizabeth would disappear.

"I am. Can I kiss you now? I've missed you like crazy."

Palmer pulled on Elizabeth's hand and hugged her first, wanting to feel her solid form against her body. Then, she pulled back and pressed their lips together.

"I missed you. What are you doing here?"

Elizabeth stared at her, running her hands up and down Palmer's chest.

"I missed you, too. And I know you've been lonely out on the road. I just asked security if I could come to the middle of nowhere, Virginia, and escort you to a much nicer house I'm renting for us for the next two days while you're here. They said yes."

"Babe, you have no idea how happy I am right now. I've been pretty miserable lately."

"I know. I could see it in your face," Elizabeth replied. "Let's get you packed up. The house Rebecca found for us has a fireplace."

"I love you."

"I love you, too," Elizabeth told her.

***

"How's Camilla?" Elizabeth asked as they lay snuggled up in bed later.

"She's amazing. Thank you for helping us find that new school for her. Her old one was fine, but this one is so much better for her. And it's closer to home, so my parents get to see her a lot more than before."

"I asked them not to tell your parents about the scholarship she got being sponsored by me. I hope that's okay. I don't want them to think I'm trying to interfere."

"They wouldn't. They're not prideful like that, but the school hasn't said anything."

"Good. I was thinking, we could maybe sponsor more scholarships for students like Camilla. It could be something we award to families who need the help but can't afford it."

"Yeah?" Palmer asked, surprised at the topic.

"You could maybe run it. It could be a foundation. I wouldn't expect it to be a full-time job, and you could have a staff and still have time to write or–"

"You want me to run a foundation?" Palmer asked.

"No, not unless *you* want to. It was just an idea. I thought it would be nice."

"It would be nice. I don't have any experience with that, though."

"You could hire people who do, and you could help them select the families. Maybe even ask Camilla to help."

"What's this *really* about?" Palmer asked, sensing an ulterior motive.

"You're coming to St. Rais for Victoria's wedding." Elizabeth sat up and turned to face her. She glanced down at Palmer's bare breasts, cleared her throat, and returned her eyes to Palmer's. "We've talked about you going, but not specifically you being my official escort."

"Yeah…"

"I want you to be my *official* escort."

"Yeah?" Palmer asked this time.

"Yes, love. I plan to tell the country about you, about us, and this wedding is a good way to do it. Even Thomas agrees that it gives us a good chance for people to see the four of us as a family."

"Family?"

"You are my family, Palmer."

"You're mine, too," Palmer said. "And I'm happy to be your escort, but I still don't know what this has to do with me running some–" She stopped when she figured it out. "That sounds like something a Queen might do, or maybe a Queen Consort."

Elizabeth softly smiled at her and said, "You don't ever have to do anything you don't want to do, Palmer. If you want to live here, we'll figure things out. I'll come here as often as I can. We can even buy a house somewhere in the States. I'll do whatever I can for us, but if you're moving to St. Rais one day, and we're thinking that the future for us could be with a wedding and with children, this would be a step in that direction. Getting you a job that a Queen Consort would typically do would show the country that we're heading in that direction. It would provide that stability of the monarchy."

"I guess it would help."

"But I want to be clear," Elizabeth added, climbing on top of her. "You don't have to have a typical Queen Consort job if you don't want it. You can write full-time or report for the news; build sailboats, for all I care. I just want you to be happy. If that means we shake up *all* the rules of the monarchy, I'm in, my love."

"You'd really buy a place in the US?" Palmer asked, running her hands through Elizabeth's long, luxurious hair.

"Of course, I would. I couldn't live there full-time, but we should have a place near Pittsburgh no matter what for when we visit your family. I can ask Rebecca to look into it when I return to St. Rais."

"This is crazy," Palmer said, chuckling. "It's only been a few months."

"And after the worst possible time, these few months have been the best months in my entire life. We can go as fast or as slow as we want here, Palmer. I won't rush you to agree to something you're not yet ready for. I just want you to know where my heart is."

"With me?" Palmer asked.

"Yes, with you." Elizabeth kissed her lips. "*Only* you, sweetheart."

"If I help these families, I can still write if I want," she said it out loud just to hear how it sounded.

"If you want to, you can even take that piece you wrote about me and turn that into something. It's beautiful, Palmer. Other people should read it."

"That was just for you."

"I'll leave that up to you, but it doesn't have to be. Either way, yes, you can write; you can not work at all. It's completely up to you."

"Right now, I'd like to make love to my girlfriend who came across the ocean just because she knew I needed her."

"She would love that." Elizabeth smiled down at her.

"And then, we can talk more about this foundation thing."

"We can?"

"It's a great idea, babe." Palmer pressed their lips together. "But less talking now. More kissing."

***

When Elizabeth left a couple of days later, they had a

plan. Palmer would be her official escort for the wedding. The office of the Queen would announce their relationship and their future plans for Palmer to relocate to St. Rais at a future point. Palmer would check out Coburn Cottage to determine if it was where she wanted to live when she moved, and she would also work with Rebecca to identify the staff she'd need for the foundation while wrapping up her work at the paper she used to love working at but could now no longer see the point. It just wasn't fun anymore. The kind of writing she wanted to do wasn't the newspaper kind these days. She didn't know *what* she'd end up writing, but she wouldn't be writing for *The New York Courier* for much longer.

After the wedding, Palmer's family would visit as planned, in the summer, giving her parents and Camilla a chance to see Palmer's future home. They'd find a guest room that they could turn into Camilla's room for when she visited, get a greenhouse set up for her father, and make sure her mom loved the kitchen as much as Victoria thought she would.

Victoria and David would be leaving St. Rais to live in London, at least, while Victoria was in school. Victoria would still perform her royal duties when necessary, but Elizabeth would attempt to keep her out of the ones she didn't want to be involved in so that Victoria and David could have as much of the life they wanted as possible.

After the summer visit, Elizabeth planned to return to the US to spend time house-hunting and touring parts of the US that Palmer had called home. Then, they'd return back together. Palmer would then make the move to St. Rais, run the foundation, and write whatever it was she wanted to write. Maybe she'd break into TV one day; maybe she wouldn't. She'd figure that out when the time came, but the idea of helping other families like her own find the right kind of schools and programs for their special needs kids made her so happy; she had no idea why she hadn't thought of it herself.

The other thing Palmer had already planned but hadn't told Elizabeth had to do with finding a way to surprise her with one of the most important questions Palmer would ever ask another person. Victoria was already helping her plot the event, and Palmer was hopeful that when it did happen – months and maybe even years from now – Elizabeth would say yes; that they'd spend their years going back and forth between St. Rais and the US, raising their children, supporting the country, and taking care of each other. She could not think of a better way to live her life than with Elizabeth by her side.

EPILOGUE

"YOU'RE coming back for Christmas, right?" Camilla asked Palmer.

"Of course, we are," Palmer replied, hugging her sister. "And then, you're coming to stay with us for your spring break."

"I am?" Camilla asked, excited. "Can I play with the horses again?"

"Absolutely. They'd like that," Elizabeth said, running her hand over the back of Camilla's head protectively. "Your horse is going to have her baby by then. You have to name him, right?"

"Can I name him Unicorn?"

"Unicorn the horse?" Palmer asked, looking at her girlfriend.

"Of course, you can name him that," Elizabeth said playfully, lightly slapping Palmer's shoulder.

"I packed you something for the flight," Palmer's mom said as she came out of the kitchen.

"Nothing like Mom's home-cooking," her father added, coming into the foyer to join them.

"You have everything you need?" her mother asked, passing Palmer the bag of food.

"Yeah, we're good," Palmer replied. "And we'll be back for Christmas, Mom. It's only a couple of months away."

"I know. I know. I think I've seen you more this year alone than I have since you moved to New York, but it doesn't stop a mom from worrying about her daughter. You'll find that out someday."

Palmer met Elizabeth's eyes and smiled at her. The year so far had flown by. After the vote in February, Elizabeth had given a speech, expressing her gratitude to the country for believing in her. The police had found another two members of the anti-monarchist faction that had some low-level involvement in what had happened to her family. They were currently behind bars, *and* they were talking, giving up more names of people involved. Outside of that, though, the anti-monarchist movement had calmed considerably. Elizabeth now believed it was mainly one man holding a generations-old grudge against an institution that, in the end, didn't even have the power to decide if a nation should go to war or not.

In May, Palmer had been Elizabeth's official escort, and the office of the Queen had made a statement that Miss Palmer Honeycutt would be relocating to St. Rais and taking a position in a new foundation sponsored privately by the Queen and her family. Palmer had left *The Courier*, and it surprised her how happy that had made her. She'd once considered that her dream job and one that she'd have forever. She'd also moved out of her apartment that she'd hardly lived in this past year in August, choosing to spend the month with her family prior to making the move to St. Rais. She and Elizabeth had found a nice house in the neighboring town that had required very little work. Elizabeth had spent a week helping Palmer decorate and make it a home for them whenever they returned to the States.

It was now September. The hoopla surrounding the Queen of St. Rais coming out as a lesbian with a girlfriend was beginning to die down. There had been the usual reactions of shock, anger, ignorance, and fear among people, but also ones of happiness and understanding. Finding out that the Queen planned to regale herself with one of the nation's newest laws one day – gay marriage – was seen as mostly a good thing. Others, of course, were not as happy about the Queen's choice of potential Consort, though that had less to do with Palmer being a woman than they'd expected and more to do with her being an American and a reporter.

For Palmer's part, she'd been gracious, supportive, and understanding of any and all reactions. She hadn't taken any of them personally and had been by Elizabeth's side when the worst of it had come in. They'd laughed together, but they'd cried together, too. They'd argued on whether or not they should respond to some particularly hateful comments when Palmer wanted to punch someone through a wall and Elizabeth just wanted to fall asleep next to the woman she loved. It was because of all of this, though, that Elizabeth finally convinced Palmer to write the real story of what had happened leading up to the bombing, the bombing itself, and the aftermath. It wasn't the personal story of their relationship as much as a commentary on what happened with a nation. Still, there were bits and pieces of their relationship mixed in when appropriate, and Palmer – the always-ethical Palmer – made sure to include mention of the fact that she was in a personal relationship with the Queen of St. Rais. The lengthy piece had been her last for *The Courier*, but it had made her editor very happy.

It had been a busy year indeed, but now they were about to catch their flight back to St. Rais, to Coburn Cottage, which would be their new home. As Palmer hugged her sister and her parents, she knew she would miss them like crazy, but she was also so excited to begin this new part of her journey with Elizabeth. She was itching to get back to the place she would now call home.

Rumors had been swirling around their potential engagement. Though they'd only known each other for about a year and had been together officially for about nine months, the people of St. Rais wanted their Queen married, and gossip about when they'd start having heirs also covered the pages of local newspapers and magazines. Apparently, when one was dating a Queen, it wasn't just parents wanting to be grandparents; an entire nation wanted the details of when, how, and who of their future children.

They said goodbye to Palmer's family and arrived at the small airport. Most people in the US didn't care much about monarchies around the world, but ever since it was announced that an American woman was dating a Queen, people started showing up at the airport to see them arrive or depart when news hit that they were in town. It was a lot to get used to for Palmer, but she just held on to Elizabeth's hand and watched the woman she loved graciously smile and wave at everyone before they climbed on board the plane.

"When we come back for Christmas, I was thinking, I could bring Camilla the tiara I got for my sixteenth birthday. Do you think that's too much?"

"Babe, her head has *not* grown since you gave her the first one." Palmer laughed as they sat down next to each other.

"I know, but it's a special one to me. It was actually one of Queen Victoria's. My mother had it fitted for me for my birthday. It just seems silly to have it sitting in a locked cabinet."

Palmer turned to her and said, "My sister is fine, and she doesn't need another tiara. The first one is crazy enough. Besides," she added as she took Elizabeth's hand. "Don't you think you might want to save it?"

"Save it? It's just going into the museum."

"Save it, babe," Palmer repeated with an expression that told Elizabeth she should think about it for a moment.

"Oh, *save it?*" Elizabeth replied, smiling at her. "For someone?"

"Yes, for someone," Palmer confirmed.

"Like a sixteen-year-old Princess?" Elizabeth asked, nodding along.

"Or a Prince. I don't care if we have a son and he wants to rock a tiara one day."

"We really are changing the face of the monarchy now, aren't we?" Elizabeth laughed. "It's still so strange to me," she said as she sobered.

"What is?"

"My entire life, I never thought I'd have the things I'm about to have with you. I sometimes forget they're possible now."

"They're not just possible; they're happening, Lizzy," Palmer reminded, taking her hand and moving it into her own lap.

Palmer's phone buzzed in her pocket.

"You should get that before we take off. You always pass out pretty much right away and end up drooling on my shoulder. If only the people of St. Rais could see a picture of *that*," Elizabeth said, teasing.

"Don't you dare," Palmer replied, laughing. She pulled out her phone and stared at the text message from her old boss. "Holy crap!"

"What? Is everything okay?" Elizabeth stiffened in her seat.

"I completely forgot he was going to message me."

"What about?"

"The Pulitzers are announced in April for the previous year. So, next year, my piece about you, St. Rais, what happened, and us would be eligible."

"Okay..."

"He has close contacts on the jury. He said he doesn't want me to get ahead of myself, but he has it on good authority that I'm on a very short list."

"Meaning?" Elizabeth leaned over the armrest to get a better look at Palmer's phone.

"Meaning, he thinks I might win the Pulitzer for a distinguished example of reporting on international affairs."

"He *does*? Wait. Of course, he does. It was brilliant," Elizabeth said, smiling at her girlfriend.

"I honestly forgot about it. What does *that* say about me?"

"So, my future wife is going to be a Pulitzer award-winning writer?" Elizabeth asked.

Palmer turned to her, surprised, and said, "I don't have a ring on my finger." She winked at her.

"You will," Elizabeth replied with a nonchalant shrug of a shoulder.

Palmer pocketed her phone and said, "Victoria told me

Queens of St. Rais don't wear wedding rings. Is that true?"

"Yes, that's true," Elizabeth confirmed.

"Does that mean that as a Consort, *I* wouldn't wear one?"

"There's never been a Queen Consort to a Queen, sweetheart. I think we can make up the rules on that if we want."

Palmer nodded silently, thinking back on that text message. She didn't want to get ahead of herself. There were still a few months left in the year for journalists in that category to write amazing pieces and blow her own out of the water, but just knowing that she was in the running made her so happy. Then, she turned to see her girlfriend staring back at her with those gorgeous blue eyes. She knew it was time.

***

When they arrived at the airport in St. Rais' capital city, they did so with unexpected fanfare. People were happy their Queen was home and that Palmer was now there to stay. Palmer was happy, too. Without Elizabeth noticing, she'd made a few calls to shift their schedule around, and things were in motion by the time they got back home to Coburn.

"Hey, I was wondering," Palmer began. "Any chance you could come into the backyard with me?"

"Right now?" Elizabeth asked.

"Yes, right now." Palmer laughed. "Come on."

She tugged on Elizabeth's hand until they made their way outside to the spacious backyard with its small running fountain and greenhouse just beyond. When Palmer opened the door to the greenhouse, her heart began beating wildly, and she worried that maybe she was getting ahead of herself. She'd planned to do this in a few months. Maybe she should wait until she'd lived here for a while. Then, she could ask.

"Oh, my God!" Elizabeth cupped her hand over her mouth.

Palmer looked around and smiled. No, this was the right time and the right way to do this.

"When I left here, Palmer, there weren't this many roses in our greenhouse."

"There are one hundred and eight of them." Palmer moved around Elizabeth to where she found what she needed. She picked them up, looked down at them, and then held them out for Elizabeth. "Two roses entwined together symbolizes eternal love. The ring attached to the ribbon on them also does that, though, I think."

"Palmer…"

"The one hundred and eight red roses around this room mean I get to ask you a question." She swallowed hard. "Will you marry me, Elizabeth? I want every day with you, beautiful. And I want us to start the new chapter of our lives with you wearing this ring. I don't know if that's okay because you're a Queen and–"

Elizabeth pulled Palmer into her and kissed her, interrupting the speech she'd been planning for the past many months. It didn't matter, though; Palmer was being kissed by the only woman she ever wanted to kiss again.

"Yes," Elizabeth said when she pulled back. "And I will absolutely be wearing this ring. We've already broken all the rules anyway, right?"

Palmer noticed Elizabeth's hands were shaking as she tried to untie the ribbon around the roses to remove the ring.

"Let me," Palmer offered, and Elizabeth passed her the flowers.

"I love you," Elizabeth told her. "I have one of these for you." She pointed at the ring. "I was going to give it to you in a couple of months. I've planned a trip to the hill to camp out and watch the Northern Lights."

"I ruined your plan?" Palmer asked, feeling bad.

"I don't care. This is better." Elizabeth laughed. "This is *way* better. I get to marry you sooner."

Palmer slid the ring off the ribbon and nervously

placed it on Elizabeth's hand.

"Thomas is going to have a panic attack." Palmer laughed.

"I don't care. He can breathe into a paper bag for a minute." Elizabeth laughed again. "Palmer, you're the love of my life." She wrapped her arms around Palmer's neck. "I can't wait to marry you."

Palmer leaned in for another kiss and suggested, "I can ask if someone will bring all these roses into the house. Do you want to go back inside?"

"Yes, to our bedroom." Elizabeth kissed Palmer's cheek.

Palmer laughed and said, "Good. It's getting cold out here."

Elizabeth laughed even louder, and Palmer knew she'd never get tired of that sound.